AFLAME WITH DESIRE

Her head fell back under the insistent pull of his hand and his fingers delved into her upswept hair, scattering pins everywhere as it tumbled down her back in tangled waves of silver satin.

"I've wanted to do that for months," he confessed huskily, his lips grazing her throat just below her ear.

Laurel's heart was beating within her chest like a captive bird. She wound trembling fingers into the wavy darkness of Brandon's hair, forcing his mouth to hers as she raised up on tiptoe to offer him her parted lips. She was dizzy with delicious desire. A tingling fire danced along her flesh and through her blood, making her skin more sensitive to his touch than she could ever have imagined. His hands caressed the length of her spine, molding her more closely to him. She shivered in anticipation, helplessly arching into his touch.

By her reaction, Laurel was unconsciously encouraging him to continue, but she was too caught up in strange and glorious emotions to care whether it was right or wrong. She only knew she wanted more; more of Brandon . . . .

SATIN AND STEEL

CATHERINE HART

LEISURE BOOKS ❦ NEW YORK CITY

A LEISURE BOOK

Published by

Dorchester Publishing Co., Inc.
6 East 39th Street
New York, NY 10016

Printed in the United States of America

CHAPTER 1

B randon Prescott sat astride his horse, his steel grey eyes blazing as he viewed the cut and broken fence along the northern border of his ranch. Anger and frustration made the lines of his face hard beyond his twenty-three years. His mouth slashed a firm line above his granite jaw and his nostrils flared in pent-up rage. "How many did they get this time, Sam?" he asked the man next to him.

Saddle leather creaked as his foreman shifted to spew a stream of tobacco juice toward the ground. "Only eight head this time around."

Brandon gave a short humorless laugh. "Only eight! How fortunate can we be!" His teeth ground in frustration. "Damn it! Twenty-two this month!"

Another rider came cantering up. "Sorry, Brand," the man said sheepishly. "We followed the trail east until it joined with so many other fresh tracks that it's impossible to say where those steers are now."

Nodding at his younger brother, Brandon replied, "I expected as much, Hank! Burke seems to be a better rustler than he is a rancher. What I wouldn't give to catch him at it, though!"

"There's always those fresh brands on some of

Burke's cattle," Sam suggested, shoving his wad of tobacco further into his cheek. "That's mighty suspicious, if ya ask me."

"You that that, and I know it, but proving he changed those brands from mine to his is another matter," Brandon reminded the older man. "Hell! Those fresh brands cover the old ones so perfectly, even I can't swear which cattle were ours originally. All I'm sure of is that Burke is definitely behind this spree of cattle rustling, for reasons of his own."

"You talking about the feud?" Hank asked, eyeing his older brother skeptically.

Brandon lifted his hat and swiped impatient fingers through his coffee-brown hair. "I don't know. Maybe I am. When I was younger, I used to think Dad exaggerated quite a bit when he told us about fights with the Burkes over land and water rights and all. Dad had heard most of it from Grandad, and I figured the stories got embroidered over the years."

"Some, maybe," Sam put in, "but your Dad had his own share of trouble with Rex Burke over fences and cattle, too. Not to mention the fact that your mother chose your Dad over him."

Those grey eyes hardened into twin pieces of flint. "Yeah, well I'll bet old Rex Burke really had a laugh when his daughter had me all tied up in knots a couple of years ago and then dumped me like a hot brick! He made it a point to let me know she was only playing me for a fool." Brandon snorted in self-disgust. "She was already engaged to some fellow back East—some friend of her family's. It had been arranged years ago, but Laurel never said a word. She led me around like a pet bull with a ring through my nose for months, then she goes off without a word and the next I hear she's gone to Boston to marry someone else. God, what a prize idiot I was!"

"I hear Laurel is coming home next week," Hank piped up. At his brother's sharp look, he said, "Well, I did, Brand. Mr. Swaney told me the other day when I was in town. His wife heard it straight from Laurel's Aunt Martha."

One rather cynical eyebrow raised, and Brandon commented dryly, "I sure hope Laurel married rich, because Rex certainly is in no position to help feather the newlyweds' nest. It's no secret that he's had some heavy financial losses the last few years."

"Could be why he's rustling cattle these days," Sam deducted.

Hank's blue eyes lit up at this. "Sam's right. First his prime watering hole dried up in the drought, then his barn burned down with all his new hay in it, not to mention most of his best horses."

"That proves exactly nothing," Brandon was quick to point out. "What we need is some indisputable, solid proof; and lacking that, a way to put a stop to his rustling without it."

"Well, when you come up with something, be sure to tell poor Jim Lawson. He's been hit pretty hard lately, too, so ya don't need to think it's anything personal," Sam added.

"Other than the fact that Jim is my best friend and Rex hates both of us, no. I just wish Burke would slip up and get caught soon.." Brandon's gaze turned eastward. "And I wish Laurel Burke was *not* coming home," he added to himself.

Laurel strained to see the scenery outside the grimy, streaked train window, the effort forming a frown between her fine cocoa-brown brows.

Violet eyes squinted out from between thick, long
lashes. Just as she raised her delicate handkerchief to the windowpane, the woman next to her
said sharply, "Laurel, don't you dare ruin that
handkerchief on that filthy window! And stop
frowning. You'll have wrinkles soon enough as it
is."

With a sigh, Laurel lowered the handkerchief
and sat back, looking sheepishly at her companion. "I just wanted to see out, Aunt Martha. We're
almost home, and I haven't seen this part of the
country in two years. Besides, I'm all of eighteen,
and I think I can hold the wrinkles at bay a while
longer."

The older woman gave her a weary smile. "Oh,
to be your age again, with my whole life ahead of
me!" she sighed poignantly. For just a moment she
allowed herself to dwell on her too-short, ten-year
marriage, and the young husband she had lost to
cholera sixteen years before. In the years that followed, she'd had little time to feel sorry for herself. Her brother, Rex, had needed her and so had
baby Laurel. With no children of her own, and no
desire to marry again, Martha had gladly moved
into Rex's home and taken over the chore of raising Rex's only child.

Laurel had been two years old, a chubby-legged
toddler just out of diapers, and the only mother
she had known until then was the Mexican housekeeper Rex had hired after Laurel's mother had
died giving birth to her. Francine had been beautiful, with the same silver-blonde hair and violet
eyes she'd bequeathed to her infant daughter—the
same delicate bonestructure that made her seem
like a finely wrought piece of china. She'd seemed
too delicate for the harsh ranch life of these south-

western Texas foothills; and she had proved too frail for childbirth when the time came.

Laurel was absorbed in thoughts and memories of her own. Every clack of the train wheels was carrying her closer to Crystal City and their ranch a few miles out of town—and closer to Brandon Prescott, the man she loved, the man who had broken her heart. The two short years away from him had seemed like a century. She'd longed to see him a thousand times, to toss her pride away and beg him to love her. Now, after months in that stuffy finishing school, she would soon be home, but Brandon was beyond her reach. He belonged to Becky Willis.

Laurel had been shocked when her father had told her Brandon had been seen several times in and around Crystal City with Becky. She hadn't wanted to believe it. She wanted to chalk it up to Rex's hatred of the Prescotts.

Sure her father was exaggerating, she had wanted to discuss the matter with Brandon, but Rex was furioius that she had made a fool of herself over a two-timing member of the "enemy" clan. He had ordered her to stay away from him, and convinced her to talk to her Aunt Martha.

Martha had reluctantly confirmed what Rex had told Laurel, obviously uncomfortable about relaying this terrible news to her stricken niece. Then, as if to deliver the final blow to her confused feelings, she'd seen him with Becky. Laurel had gone to town with Martha to shop, and they'd arrived in time to see Brandon helping Becky into her buggy outside the hotel. Stunned, Laurel had watched as Brandon held Becky's hand long after she was seated. The perky brunette had smiled tenderly down at him, and something she said made Brandon's face light up in delight, and he'd laughed happily with Becky over their private joke.

Laurel's heart and dreams of marriage were shattered. She had believed Brandon's declarations of love. For months he had told Laurel how much he adored her; how they would overcome their families' objections. They had been together as much as possible; the entire town was aware of it and waiting to see how the young lovers fared. At dances, Brandon was constantly at her side; at church, he sat with her despite their fathers' mutual glares, and afterwards they would go for a Sunday drive in the buggy or on a picnic with friends. Often they were seen riding across the countryside together. Now—suddenly—it seemed it had been but an amusing game to him, and he had turned his attentions toward Becky. She would receive the silken promises from his lying lips, the adoring looks from eyes that looked like molten steel, the tender kisses and caresses when no one was looking.

Brandon did not see Laurel that fateful afternoon, or any time afterward. She went straight home, and refused to see him when he came—nor did she bother to tell him why. She left that to her father and Aunt Martha. While Rex hastened to make arrangements to send her to Boston, Laurel hid away in the house, weeping and licking her wounds like a crippled little animal. She lost weight, and the misery in her eyes was enhanced by dark circles beneath them.

She didn't think to argue with her father about attending school in the East. In truth, she cared not where she went as long as she could escape Crystal City and the heartbreak there. She did not want to see the pity on the faces of her friends, nor be around to witness Brandon's courtship of Becky. Two weeks later, she had boarded the train for Boston, having ignored all of Brandon's attempts to talk to her, refusing even to see her friends before she left. She did not need to have them carrying tales back to him about how heartbroken she was. Her hurt was too deep, and her pride too strong.

Now she sat next to Aunt Martha, heading for home at last. She was glad to have her aunt beside her, for she was nervous about seeing everyone again—especially Brandon and Becky. Crystal City was a small town, and everyone knew everything about everyone else. Laurel wondered how long Brandon and Becky had been married now, whether they had any children yet. The letters she had received from Rex and Martha had been full of other news, but no mention of Brandon at all, and Laurel had refrained from asking, afraid of reopening wounds barely begun healing. Even when Martha had met her in Houston for the last leg of the journey home, Laurel had not asked about him, though her heart ached to know and a lingering sadness haunted her lavender eyes.

Martha looked over at her niece and knew instinctively that Laurel was thinking of Brandon. She wondered how Laurel would react when she discovered how she and Rex had lied to her. Martha had not wanted to do so, but she had knuckled under to Rex's adamant arguments at the time. Wanting to part the two mismatched lovers, Rex had deliberately lied to Laurel, and Martha had confirmed those lies. Then to have Laurel stumble upon Brandon and Becky at just that confused time, innocent as it was, was enough to send the girl fleeing.

Lord knew, Martha had felt guilty enough when Laurel had left. Then Rex had spread the rumor that Laurel had gone East to marry a family friend she'd been engaged to for some time, and Martha had been forced to continue the lies. Laurel knew none of this, of course, but Martha knew she would soon enough—and so would Brandon. Each thought the other married by now, and Martha had seen how Brandon had hardened over the last couple of years. The laughing, carefree youth was gone, erased by Laurel's supposed deceit and the death of his father a few months later. He was a man now, with enormous responsibilities, a level head, wide, work-broadened shoulders, and a bitter attitude toward the Burkes.

Martha gave a tired, heartfelt sigh. The next few weeks would certainly be interesting and revealing to all concerned. She just hoped Laurel would not despise her or Rex when all was said and done.

Brandon stood braced against a cornerpost of the train depot, his stance deceptively relaxed. He knew Laurel would be on this train when it arrived. Coincidentally, so were about thirty head of cattle he'd bought, and rather than send someone else to coordinate the drive to the ranch, he'd let his curiosity get the better of him and come himself. Under the pretext of collecting his cattle, he would also see Laurel again. He wondered if she had changed in the two years since he'd last seen her. Would her husband be with her? How long would she be visiting? No one seemed to know, and Brandon had not asked. It seemed beyond hope that she would be plump or less beautiful than before, but he kept wishing she'd aged. If she was less attractive to him, perhaps he could feel fortunate to have lost her, and the old hurt would miraculously disappear after all this time. Brandon did not know why he was torturing himself by being here now. He just knew he had to see her once more, only to set the ghost of her to rest in his memory.

The actual sight of her as she stepped down from the train nearly stole his breath. By God, she was beautiful! If possible, more perfect than he had remembered. His gaze raked hungrily over her, taking in the stunning silver hair that reminded him of desert moonlight, the lavender eyes sparkling with excitement, the delicate features, and that unexpectedly sensual mouth. Brandon's guts tightened, and he forced himself not to reveal his reactions on his face as his eyes skimmed her trim figure, lingering on the full curves outlined by her traveling costume.

As if drawn by the force of his stare, her head turned; and suddenly, across the twenty feet separating them, their eyes locked. Brandon watched with bitter spite as her eyes widened and the color fled her face. His own eyes narrowed into stormy grey slits, and he thought her chin trembled slightly as she struggled to form a smile on uncooperative lips.

The impact of seeing Brandon made Laurel reel. For a few seconds, she thought she might faint, but the thought of making a spectacle of herself for all to see stiffened her spine.

Her gaze drank in his tanned features—those remarkable steely eyes, now throwing daggers her way; the long, straight nose; that stubborn cleft chin of his; the dark brown hair just showing beneath his hat. He looked older, more sure of himself, angry for some reason—and oh, so handsome and dear to her love-starved eyes.

She blinked, and the spell was broken. Her heart flew into her mouth as she watched him flip the cigarette he was smoking to the ground and grind it out with the sole of his worn boot. With deliberate ease, he pushed away from the post and started toward her. Panic made her lips tremble as she tried to muster a congenial smile.

She need not have bothered. Eyes hard as steel, lips in a cynical twist, he did not pause. With a tip of lean fingers to the brim of his hat, he grunted, " 'Lo Miss Martha; Laurel." Then he simply ambled on past them toward the rear of the train.

Even as she revelled in the low, pleasant sound of his voice once more, Laurel bristled at the obvious snub. This first encounter, brief as it was, had hurt more than she had thought. "Why is he acting so mean and hateful?" she wondered, tears gathering behind her eyelids. Blinking rapidly to disperse them, she thought righteously, "*I* am the one who has been hurt in all this. If anyone should be spiteful, it is *me*!"

She had no more time to sort things out, for she had caught sight of her father hurrying toward them. Rex Burke was of average height and build, with snapping blue eyes and plenty of grey liberally streaking his brown hair. His usually stern face was lit with a smile of welcome for his only child. His arms opened, and she rushed into them with a glad cry.

"Oh, Dad! It's so good to be home!" she told him, hugging him tightly.

"I've missed you, Muffin," he admitted readily. Then, holding her at arms length, he studied her critically. "You're all grown up. Not my little girl any longer," he decided, proud and sad at the same time.

"I'll always be your little girl," she consoled. Then, a twinkle of mischief in her eyes, she patted his stomach just above his belt where a small bulge was in evidence. "*You*, however, seem to be growing more than I am. You've put on a little weight since I've been gone. Rosa must be feeding you too well."

Rex laughed. "Is that where all my money went the last couple of years—so you could learn how to insult your old Dad? Seems to me you already knew that before you left! I had high hopes that girls' school would make a lady out of you!"

"They tried, Dad," Laurel laughed, "but I fought them every inch of the way. They couldn't squash my tomboy ways altogether up there in their fancy, crowded city. I think I've got too much Texas blood in my veins."

Martha grunted shortly. "Too much Texas dust and sun in your brain, more likely," she said tartly. Then to Rex, "Are we going to stand here and fry all day? I'm hot, I'm tired, and I'm hungry, and I'm not looking forward to that bumpy buggy ride home, so we'd best get it over with while I can still stand the trip."

"You're a grouchy old bat, Martha," Rex chided lovingly, hugging his younger sister roughly.

"I know," Martha grinned, "and your charm doesn't work on me now any better than it did before."

Laurel chuckled at them both. Maybe being home wouldn't be so bad after all. It was where she belonged, with family to love her and a feeling of belonging to her home and this land. She was through with hiding. Now she would face up to herself, Brandon, and her friends, and find out just how tough and resilient Laurel Burke was after all.

Within a few days of being home, Laurel realized without being told that her father's situation had changed quite a bit while she'd been gone. The house was still the same, with the same furniture and drapes and rugs as when she'd lived at home. They were a couple of years older, and a few pieces were showing more wear, especially the rug in her father's study. Martha and Rosa kept everything neat and clean, but nothing had been replaced.

Outside, the new barn stood out sharply against the older buildings, making one aware that the house needed a new coat of paint in comparison. Different horses stood in stalls where older, more familiar animals had resided in the old barn. The place still smelled of fresh wood and resin, and the lofts were nearly bare of the hay Rex had had to buy to see them through the winter. New saddles and equipment hung on hooks and sat on benches, still shining, mutely stating their recent purchase.

There had been obvious repairs to pens, corrals, and fences about the ranch, necessary temporary repairs meant to buy time until finances allowed better. There was a new windmill in one of the north pastures where there had been none before, and Rosa had told Laurel that the well for the ranch buildings had been dug deeper during the drought.

"So much to be replaced because of the drought and the barn fire," Martha said, shaking her head. "It's been hard on your father, but things are finally starting to even out again. Luckily, he could still pay the hands and didn't have to let anyone go. We just tightened our belts a bit and waited it out."

"Tightening belts didn't build that new barn, or buy new livestock," Laurel reminded her.

"No, but the Burke family has been around for a long time, and our name means something here. Your great-grandfather helped found Crystal City, and your grandpa and father have been very influential. Folks don't foget that just because you have a run of bad luck."

Laurel's level look demanded truth. "Did Dad have that kind of money in the bank, or did he have to borrow it?"

Martha frowned, "He borrowed it—some from the bank, and some from friends."

Laurel was exasperated. "If things were that bad, why didn't he have me come home?"

A dubious look creased Martha's worn face. "Honey, what could you have done?"

"It would have saved him the outrageous expense of keeping me in that dreadful, snobby school!" Laurel insisted. "The cost of my keep there would have nearly paid for the replacement of the barn! Not only that—he kept sending me spending money, telling me to buy myself a new dress, or hat; and all the while, he was borrowing money and scrimping on needed repairs here."

"He wanted to do it that way, Laurel, and he was adamant that you not know or feel guilty about it."

"Well, I feel plenty guilty now!" Laurel declared heatedly.

"No use crying over spilt milk," Martha advised. "Besides, everything is looking up now. There is a new crop of hay almost ready to cut, the bills are being paid each month, the weather has been cooperating, and the cattle have fared well. There are quite a number of new calves this spring, and if all goes well, there will be a lot of money from the sale of cattle this fall. This place will be back on its feet before you know it.''

''At least Dad won't have to pay my keep in Boston any longer. That should help tremendously. Why did he do it when he could least afford it, Aunt Martha?''

''He'd kill me for saying this, but I'm sure he was hoping you would find a rich, handsome husband back East, and forget—uh—forget . . .''

''Forget Brandon,'' Laurel supplied grimly. It was the first time she had mentioned his name.

Martha nodded. Then, as if eager to change the subject, she suggested, ''Why don't we go into town tomorrow and buy you some sturdier clothes and a new pair of boots? Those frilly dresses you brought home from Boston just are not serviceable for ranch life, honey.''

''Can we afford it?'' Laurel asked with a rueful grin.

''We'll manage,'' her aunt assured her.

''Good! Then I want to purchase a couple of pair of those new denim trousers I've seen some of our wranglers wearing. They'll be perfect for riding.''

''Perfectly indecent,'' Martha grumbled.

Laurel's lavender eyes sparkled. ''Then why did I find a pair exactly your size with all your other clothes out on the wash line the other day?'' Laurel challenged.

''Hmph!'' Martha mumbled, neither admitting nor denying anything.

''*Hmph*, indeed!'' Laurel gloated. ''If you can wear denim pants, so can I!''

CHAPTER 2

The very next day, Laurel and Martha made their trek into town. At Miller's Mercantile and Dry Goods Store, Laurel found the blue denim trousers she wanted, plus a couple of plaid cotton shirts to wear with them and thick white socks to wear under her boots.

While Martha was stocking up on canned goods, sugar, flour, salt, and other necessities, Laurel chatted with Jake Miller.

"You just missed seeing Mrs. Lawson," he told her. "In fact, she was askin' about you." Laurel fingered the hair ribbons, trying to remember if she had any blue ones at home in her drawer. She answered doubtfully, "Jim Lawson's mother?" She wondered if old Jake was losing his mind. Ada Lawson had died four years previously.

Jake gave her a frown that clearly said he considered her daft. "Lord, no! I'm talking about Jim's *wife*, Becky."

Laurel's head snapped up, and she threw a quick look in her aunt's direction. Martha was busy with Ethel Miller, concentrating on getting everything on her list. "I didn't know Jim had gotten married," she told Jake.

Jake chuckled. "Yeah, he and Becky Willis tied the knot a couple of years ago. They've got two youngsters already. Come to think of it, I guess they got married a few weeks after you left."

Laurel was in shock. "Jim Lawson and Becky Willis got *married*?" she echoed. She didn't know whether to laugh or cry.

Jake was already rambling on. "We all thought you and Brandon Prescott would do the same, but then you took off back East about then, and Brandon just sort of disappeared for a few months. After all this time, we figured you'd found yourself some slick Easterner and settled there. Sure didn't expect you'd be back this way. How long you staying?"

"I—uh—I'm back for good, Jake," she stammered. Then she mustered a weak grin. "You really didn't expect me to marry someone else, when I've been waiting all these years for you, did you, Jake?" she joked.

Jake chuckled, sixty years of white hair and wrinkles tickled by her reply. "Don't you let my Ethel hear you talk that way," he warned. "She'll have the hide off of both of us!"

When they left the store, Laurel took her aunt by the arm, steering her along to the bootery. "Why didn't you tell me Becky married Jim Lawson?" she hissed into Martha's ear.

"So that's what you and Jake were talking about." Martha sighed. "You couldn't keep anything quiet in this town if you put it in a jug with a stopper! I knew you'd find out soon. I told Rex you would."

"What happened between Brandon and Becky?" Laurel prompted. "Jake also said Brandon left Crystal City for a while."

Martha stopped in front of the bootery. "Yes, he did, and by the time he got back Becky and Jim were married," she related, leaving a lot of things unsaid.

"How did Brandon feel about that?" Laurel asked.

Martha was becoming upset. "I wouldn't know, Laurel," she said sharply. "I don't speak to the man. All I know is that his father died shortly afterward, and Brandon had his hands full managing their ranch. No one saw much of him in town for long stretches at a time. He kept pretty much to himself."

"Is he married?"

Martha gritted her teeth. "No."

Laurel's eyes widened as she blurted, "Lord, he must have loved that girl something fierce!"

It was Martha's turn to be surprised, as Laurel continued her train of thought. "It must have hurt him pretty badly to have Becky throw him over for his best friend. If I wasn't so hurt myself, I'd feel sorry for Brandon. I certainly know how he must have felt!"

"Yes, well, it's all water under the bridge now, girl," Martha put in hastily, extremely uncomfortable with this conversation. Before Laurel could say more, she hurried her into the shop. Lord help them all when Laurel found out that Brandon had never been interested in Becky at all. If he had been hurt, it had been Rex and Martha's doing—and inadvertently, Laurel's.

Laurel met two of her old friends in town that day and received invitations to visit their homes when she had the time. One was now married and expecting her first child. The other still lived at home with her parents. Neither mentioned Brandon, though Martha suspected they were certainly curious. They both asked if Laurel was married yet or engaged to someone back East, and both seemed surprised to hear that Laurel was home to stay.

Brandon was going crazy. Between the cattle rustling problems, the rumors that Laurel was evidently still single and home for good, his mind was in a jumble. He was irritable and grouchy—"a real bear to live with," as his brother Hank expressed it.

Brandon didn't know what to think these days. Blast it all, Rex had told him that Laurel went East to get married. Now here she was, back again; not married, supposedly not even engaged, and planning to stay. Why the devil had she left in the first place, and where had she been—doing what—all this time? What the heck was going on?

The only thing Brandon knew for sure was that she was as beautiful as ever, and just as desirable. "God, I must be crazy!" he thought to himself. "I think about her all the time, I can't sleep for wanting the deceitful witch, and all the while her father is stealing me blind!" He knew he had to see her again, and so, for the first time in months, he planned to go to church, where he was almost positive she would be on Sunday morning.

Laurel, her father, and Martha were all seated by the time Brandon arrived, Hank in tow. The Prescott brothers were late, as Hank had been slow and reluctant to be dragged along. Luck was with them, however, and against the Burkes, as the only space available was directly behind Laurel and her father.

Laurel could have died—and she thought Rex really might, as Brandon and Hank wedged past those already seated in the pew, stepping on a few toes in the process and apologizing profusely, thus drawing more attention to themselves and to Laurel than otherwise. However, to be truthful, Laurel expected the entire congregation was already as curious as they could possibly be. Gossip was the mainstay of Crystal City, and they certainly had had enough to keep their tongues oiled since Laurel's return.

The service started within minutes, and everyone quieted down for the opening prayer. Then, as the rustle began to find the first hymn in the hymnal, Brandon leaned forward to whisper loudly, "Laurel, honey, could you lend us a hymnal back here, or would you prefer I lean across your shoulder and sing along with you?"

Rex coughed to cover a curse too ready on his tongue in God's house. Without a word, Laurel slammed her hymanl into Brandon's chest, her eyes flashing lavender fire, and her teeth gritted so hard that her jaw ached, as everyone within hearing smothered chuckles.

After the hymn, the sermon began. Laurel thought surely there would be no further problems for a while. Her father looked ready to explode and she was embarrassed to the roots of her hair. What sort of game was Brandon up to? she wondered, unable to concentrate on the pastor's message. The other day, he had practically glared holes through her, and now, here he was being friendly as a puppy. If he was deliberately trying to confuse her, he was doing a superb job of it.

Something bumped Laurel's foot, and she shifted out of the way, only to have her shoe knocked off seconds later by another bump. She glanced down, astonished to see her shoe disappear under her seat. Immediately she looked back to glare at Brandon, who gave her an angelically sweet smile, and nodded as he kicked her other shoe loose while she was busy shooting visual daggers at him.

Her mouth flew open to deliver a whispered threat—and snapped shut again as her father elbowed her in the ribs. Laurel faced forward, trying in vain with one stocking-clad foot to locate her shoes beneath the seat, all the while pretending interest in the service.

Her wriggling got her aunt's attention. "Will you please sit still, Laurel?" Martha hissed. "Your father is going to have a seizure!"

"He stole my shoes!" Laurel whispered.

"He what?"

"Brandon stole my *shoes!*"

A loud "Ssh!" came from behind her, and Laurel could gladly have killed Brandon.

Laurel bit her lip and stopped fidgeting, tucking her feet beneath the pew so no one would notice her shoeless state. By this time, Martha at last understood the situation, and it struck the older woman very funny. Her silent laughter vibrated the pew, earning her a disgruntled glance from Rex, and a desperate look from Laurel.

Brandon nudged her feet again, and Laurel mistakenly assumed he was attempting to return her shoes. She wriggled one foot about, feeling nothing, then nearly leaped out of her seat, as Brandon's large, booted feet shot out from under her seat, planting themselves comfortably where her own feet should have rested. She threw him one, quick, imploring look over her shoulder, but he smiled blandly and shook his head, refusing to remove his feet so she could at least put hers together.

By the end of the service, Laurel was nearly as furious as her father. As everyone prepared to leave, Brandon again leaned forward. "Promise to meet me right after dinner down by the creek, and I'll let you have your shoes back," he whispered.

"No!" she answered.

"You are going to look awfully funny going out of here without your shoes," he warned.

"Laurel!" Rex barked. "I'd like to go home sometime today, if you'd hurry along."

"Promise," Brandon urged quietly.

"All right! I promise!" she hissed angrily. Immediately, her shoes popped out from beneath the pew, and she hurriedly wriggled into them as her father waited impatiently.

It still took quite some time to get to the door, as Laurel was stopped time and again by friends she had not seen in over two years. Brandon was long gone by the time they shook hands with the preacher, and Rex was beginning to settle down a bit with Brandon out of sight.

Rex had tried to get Laurel to stay longer at that fancy boarding school, but she had wanted to come home. He had hoped and prayed she would meet another man and marry before coming West again, or that she would have completely gotten over her infatuation with Brandon Prescott by this time. Now he faced the possibility that Laurel would discover his scheming and hate him for it. In a community this size, there was no keeping Laurel and Prescott from bumping into one another from time to time, and sooner or later the truth would come out. Loving his daughter as he did, Rex hoped it would be later—much later—or miraculously, not at all.

After dinner, Laurel donned her denim breeches and plaid shirt and casually meandered out to the barn. Consulting Lester about which horse was available for her to ride, she saddled the mare herself and trotted easily out of the ranch yard, a rifle resting in a scabbard by her knee. One of the first rules of the range was always to be prepared to defend yourself against predators.

It felt unusual riding astride after all these months, and Laurel was sure her muscles would complain tomorrow. She rode lightly in the saddle, her horsemanship readily reasserting itself, and she was familiar with the route, knowing exactly where she would find Brandon waiting for her. They had met there several times before in the past years—or was it in a different lifetime?

Brandon was already there, sitting on the ground, his back propped against a tree, his hat pulled low over his face against the glare of the sun on the water. His horse stood grazing placidly nearby. "See you made it," he drawled, tipping his hat to eye her from beneath the brim. His silver gaze widened considerably as he noted her tight denims and the shirt that clung to her pert breasts.

Laurel leaned on the pommel but made no move to dismount as yet. "I gave my word. What do you want, Brandon?" Outwardly, she was calm, even curt, but her insides felt like a quivering mass of jelly. Just meeting him alone like this made her want to stammer and blush, then wrap him in her arms and kiss the breath out of him.

Brandon answered with the first words to come to mind. "I want you, Laurel!"

His blunt statement brought her abruptly out of her daydreams. Without a word, she grabbed the slack reins, intent on heading back the way she had come. Her usually gentle lavender eyes were now as cool as a frosty mountain morning.

He was on his feet in a flash, his hand over hers on the reins before she could ride off. For a moment they stared at one another, each taking the other's measure. "But I'll settle for knowing why you ran off two years ago—why you suddenly refused to see me or talk with me," he stated.

To Laurel, one word explained it all. "Becky."

"Becky?" Brandon echoed with a confused frown. "Becky Lawson?" She was the only Becky he could recall.

Laurel nodded, swallowing the lump in her throat. She was determined to be compassionate about this. Her eyes softened to lavender pools as she gazed down at him. "I'm sorry if she hurt you, Brandon. I'm sorry about a lot of things, but maybe it all works out in the end."

"What is that supposed to mean?" he demanded.

Laurel shrugged helplessly. "I'm not sure yet myself. I'm still trying to sort things out in my own mind and understand them."

"What things don't you understand, Laurel?" His voice was velvety, his eyes mesmerizing as he awaited her answer.

"Why you are so darned changeable from day to day!" she burst out. "Why we fall in love with the people we do. Why we can't help loving the wrong persons? Why the ones we love most don't return our love. Why it hurts so badly when they don't." By the end of her list, she was crying, tears streaming down her cheeks, but she wasn't aware of them. She was caught up in memories and longings too long held at bay.

Brandon saw his opportunity and took it. Before she could decide to run off again, he pulled her out of the saddle and held her close to him. Oh, but she felt soft and small against his hard frame! So fragrant and feminine as she sobbed into his shirt.

He let her cry for a few moments, and when her tears began to slow, he held her away from him so he could see her face. "What has any of this to do with Becky Lawson?"

"Blast you, Brandon Prescott!" she wailed. "You don't have to pretend you don't know!" She beat her fists against his hard chest, but she might as well have been hitting an oak tree for all the effect her puny blows had.

Brandon glowered back at her. "You're right. I don't have to pretend! I don't have a clue in hell about what you're hinting at!" he roared.

"I am talking about you being in love with Becky, as if you didn't know!" she shouted back.

Stunned, he nearly set her loose, regaining his hold just before she slipped out of his grasp. "When was I in love with Becky?" he asked confusedly.

"Oh, for heaven's sake, Brand, don't be difficult!" she said irritably. "Two years ago, just before Becky threw you over for Jim—and just after *you'd* sworn to marry *me!*" Where before she had willingly sobbed in the shelter of his embrace, she now sought to free herself from his arms.

Brandon did not understand this explanation any better than the others she'd thrown at him. He shook her heartily, "You're crazy!" he told her flatly. "I've never been in love with Becky! Where did you get such a hare-brained idea?"

She stamped her foot in rage, catching his toe with the heel of her boot and causing him to wince, but not to loosen his hold on her. "Don't try to deny it, Brandon! I know differently. I must have been the only one in town not to notice, but I was too wrapped up in dreams of you to see what was right under my nose. Dad was the first to open my eyes, then Aunt Martha told me, too. Once I was aware of it, I saw for myself."

"Laurel, honey, you are the only woman I've ever loved,"·Brandon said softly, his eyes like soft grey clouds.

Laurel closed her own against his spellbinding gaze. "Oh, Brandon! Don't do this to me again! It hurt too much the first time! I barely survived it!" she moaned.

"Tell me something, baby," he murmured, his breath whispering over her hair, "and I want the truth. Why did you leave Crystal City?"

Laurel gulped back another sob. "I couldn't bear to see you and Becky together again."

"Again? When did you ever see us together?"

She told him about the day she had come upon them outside the mercantile, and they had looked so happy together. Brandon could not recall the incident, so trivial had it been to him. He posed another question. "Where did you go when you left here?"

"To Boston."

"Why? What did you go to Boston for?"

"I was attending a finishing school Dad enrolled me in there."

"You didn't go East to marry someone else?" he asked.

She shook her head.

"You're sure?" he pressed.

"I ought to know!" she snapped, her natural spirit reviving with her anger. "Why has everyone been asking me that? Isn't anyone glad I came home? Did you all hope I'd gone for good?"

"Rex started that choice piece of gossip on its rounds," Brandon said, a bitter glint of remembrance hardening his gaze.

Laurel digested this new information. "I suppose Dad couldn't stand to have it known that his darling daughter was jilted by a Prescott, of all people."

"Damn it, I *didn't* jilt you, Laurel!" he growled through gritted teeth.

She shrugged slightly. "Call it what you will, Brandon, it boils down to the same thing. It's ironic that Becky did the same to you a few short weeks later, when she decided she'd rather marry Jim."

Brandon sighed heavily. "What is it going to take to convince you that there was never anything between Becky and me but friendship?"

"At this late date, I don't think there is anything you *can* say, Brand. Besides, what does it matter now?"

"It matters to me," he declared. "It also matters that you thought so little of me that you would believe such lies, and not give me so much as a few minutes to defend myself against them. You readily believed the worst of me! So much for love and trust, eh, darlin'?" That cynical tone was back in his voice again, and his arms released her as if he was loath to touch her further.

Defensively, she railed at him, "If you loved me so much, why didn't you try to find me?"

"Where was I supposed to start looking, woman? No one else knew where you'd gone, either, and your father and Aunt Martha would have withstood torture rather than tell me!"

"That much I can believe!" She sniffed haughtily.

"But you don't believe that I loved you and only you," he stated wearily.

"There were other women, too, so I heard at the time," she accused. "Women you visited above the saloons in town."

Brandon rolled his eyes and cursed under his breath. "Lord, lady," he declared loudly, "I figured *one* of us ought to have some experience at lovemaking before the time came, and I'd rather it was me than you! Besides, I was visiting those rooms long before you were even out of braids, and I sure as hell was never in love with any of them!"

"Why won't you at least admit you loved Becky?" she insisted.

"I'll admit that the day you tell me you ran off to marry some fellow back East," he countered angrily.

"But I didn't!"

One dark brow raised over a glittering eye. "Precisely my reason!"

She turned away from him, grabbing for her horse's reins. "I've got to go, Brandon."

"Laurel?" His voice halted her actions momentarily. "Do you ever wonder what might have happened if you hadn't left when you did?"

With a nod of her silvery head, she said, "Yes, but it hurt too much to stay and find out."

"It hurt *me* when you left as you did, with no explanation, no good-byes, no reasons."

Tears blurred Laurel's vision as she hoisted herself into the saddle. With a catch in her voice, she questioned, "Do you suppose we will ever forgive one another someday, Brandon?"

"I don't know, Moonbeam," he said sadly, using his old pet name for her. "Love and trust are hard things to mend, once they're broken. Right now, I'm angry that you had so little faith in me then, and that you don't believe what I tell you now."

"I'm so confused, I don't know who or what to believe just now, Brandon."

His hand reached out to grasp her arm. "Well, believe this, Laurel. Regardless of all else I do or do not feel, I still want you, and I mean to have you someday."

He pulled her down until her face was close to his. His free hand reached up to cup her chin and his lips covered hers in a warm caress, full of urgent desire and masculine demand. When her lips softened and parted beneath his, signaling her surrender, unwilling though it was, his mouth deliberately enticed hers until she swore she felt her bones melting, and clutched at his broad shoulders for support. His tongue played briefly with hers, eliciting a moan of desire from her throat.

As suddenly as his lips had captured her, he released her, gently shoving her upright in the saddle. "Dream on that, lovely Laurel, until the next time," he whispered softly, studying her bemused expression.

She shook her head. "There won't be a next time, Brandon," she said sadly, tears glistening like dew in her lilac eyes.

"Yes, there will, darlin'. I'd stake my ranch on it."

As she rode away, Brandon watched, wondering suddenly why he had not questioned her about her father. Did Laurel know about Rex's cattle rustling? Did she even suspect what her father was doing? Brandon had a lot to think over and sort out since his revealing conversation with Laurel. He also had a few things to check up on before he saw her again.

CHAPTER 3

B randon had cause to reflect on these very thoughts the next day. During the night, a dozen more of his cattle were stolen, and he was raging mad. Again, there was no solid evidence that Rex Burke was behind the rustling, just a gut feeling. However, Rex was still a very influential man in the territory, and the sheriff would have laughed Brandon out of town if he had come right out and accused Burke without some very good reasons and a lot of indisputable proof.

Once more, Brandon wondered if Laurel had any knowledge of her father's activities. Had she run right home yesterday and told Rex that she had met him by the creek? Did they sit down and have a good laugh about what a fool Brandon was making of himself by telling Laurel he still cared for her, still wanted her? How much of what Laurel said could he believe? Was she just stringing him along again, as she seemed to have done two years ago—or had Rex been behind their separation then? Had Rex manipulated both of them out of spite and hatred toward the Prescotts, or was Laurel telling lies and pretending innocence?

Brandon was angry and confused. Laurel's father hadn't taken kindly to Brandon's presence at church yesterday. Burke had been mad enough to spit, and now Brandon was sure he was reaping the effects of his folly.

Sunday night had been very busy and profitable for the rustlers evidently, for later in the day, Brandon received a visit from his friend, Jim Lawson. Jim's ranch, too, had been hit the night before; ten head were missing from his herd.

"I tell you, Brandon, I don't know how much more of this I can take, financially or otherwise!" Jim complained morosely. "Becky and I have barely been making it as it is. It would make me mad enough to strangle Burke with my bare hands if I lose my ranch while he rakes in the profits.

At least Brandon wasn't totally dependent on his ranch for his income, as Jim was. His grandfather on his mother's side of the family had made a fortune during the gold rush of '49 and yet another fortune in silver in Nevada. He'd left the entire sum to Brandon, his first grandson—a beautiful mansion on Nob Hill in San Francisco, holdings in a major railroad, a lumber company in Oregon, and a bank, plus a tidy amount of ready cash gathering interest in a vault.

Hank had also come into a sizeable inheritance from Grandad Harris, but the boys had been born and raised on the ranch, and both were content to stay and work the ranch now that they were grown. Someday maybe, when they married and had families of their own, they would feel differently, but they had strong ties to this land they loved so well. They were happy with their lives, and neither felt compelled to flaunt their wealth. In fact, very few people had any idea the brothers owned more than the ranch they lived on and the livestock they raised. To the people of Crystal

City, they were what they appeared to be—two hard-working young ranchers plagued by all the problems and worries that confronted everyone else.

"I could loan you a little, Jim, just to tide you over until we catch him at it," Brandon suggested.

"Thanks for the offer, but I'll wait a while before I accept. Things might get that desperate before much longer, but I'll hold off as long as I can. I hate borrowing from anyone if I can help it."

"Don't let pride stand in the way of your family's welfare, old friend," Brandon advised. "After all, it's not as if any of this is your fault. Everyone knows how hard you work. Just let me know if there is any way I can help."

Jim grinned at him. "From all you've told me about you and Laurel, you might try marrying her. Maybe then her father would stop rustling your cattle, and you could ask him, as a family favor, to stop stealing mine, too! I'd even stand up as your best man! After all, it would hardly do for a man to rob his own daughter's husband and best friend," Jim joked.

"Well, I sure can't figure you at all," Brandon chuckled wryly. "You won't accept my money, yet you readily ask me to give up my freedom for life. Some friend you are!"

"Aw, Brandon, I can think of worse fates for you than marrying Laurel! You sure can't say she's not pretty enough for you, and you've been sweet on her for a long time."

"True, but can I trust her?" Brandon was suddenly dead serious. "After all, she's Rex Burke's daughter."

For the next few weeks, Brandon avoided

Laurel. At church on Sunday he sat on the opposite side of the church from her. In town, if forced to acknowledge her, he would tip his hat politely and go on. Whenever possible, he would duck into the nearest doorway or cross the street to avoid her. The day he inadvertently barged into the milliner's shop to keep Laurel from seeing him proved almost more embarrassment than it was worth to him. After that, he made sure which establishment he was near before deciding to escape.

Laurel realized right away that Brandon was deliberately going out of his way to avoid her, but, for the life of her, she could not understand why. The man had certainly made it clear that he desired her, yet if she came within ten feet of him, he ran like a rabbit!

"I wish he would make up his mind!" she fumed. "First he wants me, then he doesn't! The weather changes less often around here!"

Laurel had to admit her vanity was bruised by his attitude, though it certainly made her father easier to live with. It also gave Laurel time to reconsider how she felt about Brandon. "Lord knows, I love the man!" she admitted to herself, "but just having him want me is not enough. I'll never be able to accept being second best with him. If only he hadn't fallen so in love with Becky!"

Regardless of how adamantly Brandon had denied it, Laurel still believed that he had loved Jim's wife. "He's just trying to cover up a broken heart by telling me otherwise," she reasoned, "and trying to spare my feelings now that he understands why I left town so quickly."

Still, if Brandon was trying not to hurt her again, why was he so pointedly ignoring her? It made no sense whatsoever! "He just plain doesn't want to settle for me when he really wants Becky," she decided sorrowfully. "It's probably best this way. If he can never truly love me with all his heart, I don't want him anyway! I refuse to play second fiddle for the love of any man! I certainly deserve better than that out of life!"

Laurel was very busy, even without Brandon's attentions. She helped Martha with the housework, did what odd jobs she could around the ranch, and ran errands when everyone else was too busy to be bothered.

As a child, Laurel had always had the run of the ranch, within reason, and the ranch hands had tolerated her with amused resignation. Now that she was grown, everything seemed to have changed. She had gone away a child and returned a woman, and it seemed no one quite knew what to make of her.

All of a sudden, men she had known and been comfortable with all of her life, acted like strangers. The younger ones, who had seemed like cousins in years past, stammered and stuttered like schoolboys when she passed their way; or resorted to showing off in front of her. Most of them, the older men especially, were extremely respectful these days, no longer teasing with her as they had before. A couple of the more recently hired hands dared to leer at her, and were quickly set straight by the others.

"What happened to Bailey?" Laurel asked one day, catching sight of the fellow's swollen lip.

"He let his mouth overload his appetite," Lester explained cryptically. Of all the men on the ranch, old Lester was the only one who didn't treat Laurel any differently than he had before. He'd been around as long as she could remember, and he never seemed to change a bit. Laurel often thought he must have been born old; his bushy grey hair never seemed to get any thinner, his legs were permanently bowed from years in the saddle, and the lines burned into his thin, tanned face had always been there.

"Is that what happened to Curt, too?" she asked curiously.

"Somethin' like that," Lester mumbled. Then with the audacity that all his years with the Burkes had entitled him to, he added, "It would help if you didn't flit about in them tight pants of yours, like some floozy advertisin' her wares."

"Lester!" Laurel stared at him in open-mouthed amazement.

"He's right, Miss Burke." Laurel swiveled to find Ned Nolan, their ranch foreman, behind her. She hadn't heard him come up.

Ned's too-narrow eyes stared unblinkingly out at her from his beefy red face. "Snake eyes," Laurel thought to herself for the thousandth time, shivering inwardly with distaste. In the ten years that Ned had been with them, Laurel had never liked him. It was nothing he had ever done, exactly. He was unfailingly polite and deferential toward the boss's daughter, never out of line in any way she could complain about. He was a hard worker, never drunk or rowdy, and he knew every-thing there was to know about running the ranch. He knew how to control the men under him, and while not harsh or cruel in his manner, he knew how to get the most work out of them. He did what needed to be done and did it well. He was an ex-cellent foreman, but Laurel had never warmed up to him personally, and she couldn't really say why. She was always supremely uncomfortably around him.

"It must be his eyes," she thought. "They're so cold and unblinking! It makes me feel as if he could kill a man for no reason at all, and feel no remorse about it afterward."

Now, as Ned looked at her with those same eyes, he said, "Sorry if I offended you, ma'am, but it's the truth. Dressing like that just riles the men up in ways best left alone. It can only lead to trouble, and I've got enough to do without having to beat heads together or settle fights over the boss's daughter."

Laurel nodded coolly. "I'll think about it, Nolan, for the men's sake." Left unstated was the fact that she would not go out of her way to do anything for him. In the short time since she had been home, the two of them had locked horns several times. It seemed every time she wanted to do something interesting around the ranch, like ride along while the men herded cattle or watch while they branded calves, Nolan put a stop to it before she got the chance. Unfortunately, her father agreed with him. "I didn't spend all that money sending you to that fancy school to have you chasing around behind the ranch hands, making a nuisance of yourself and bothering the men when they're trying to work," Rex told her firmly. "Go bake a pie, or visit your friends, or help Martha with some kind of woman's work about the house."

Now Rex added another directive to his list. "You have a closet full of pretty dresses. Surely you have plenty to wear, without exhibiting yourself in those denim trousers!"

"I only wear them for ranch work and riding, Dad. Even Martha wears them."

"Martha doesn't look like you do in them," he pointed out bluntly. "Furthermore, since you shouldn't be puttering about in the barns, anyway, you have no further excuse for wearing them. Wear a riding skirt like other women, but I forbid you to wear those atrocious pants again."

After that, Laurel took pains not to be caught in the pants again, though she still wore them for riding at times. They gave her so much more freedom of movement, and they never snagged on bushes or rocks when she went exploring in the hills, as even her split riding skirts tended to do.

Laurel renewed acquaintance with several of her girlfriends in the next weeks. It was not as difficult as she had imagined, and gave her a feeling of belonging in the small community again.

Most of her friends had never been far away from Crystal City, and were ever so curious about her experiences in Boston.

"Was it as cold as you expected?" Mary Lou questioned.

"Worse. Much worse!" Laurel said with a shiver. "I had to go out and buy the warmest wool coat I could find. What I will ever do with the rabbit fur hat and muff I brought home, I don't know. Maybe Aunt Martha can dust the furniture with them!" she laughed.

Deborah asked curiously, "Is life in the big city really all that different?"

Laurel smiled in remembrance of her first frightened reaction to the crowds and noise. "Oh, Deb! I can't begin to tell you! There are so many people crowded into one place, and all of them going somewhere all the time. The streets are crowded with traffic; horses, carts, and even horseless carriages. The smell and noise of the new gasoline-powered carriages is awful, and scares many a horse into bolting. It's a strange sight at first."

"Imagine that!" Imogene sighed, brown eyes wide with wonder.

"I got used to it after a while, but I don't think I'll ever stop marveling at Mr. Bell's miraculous telephone."

"Oh, I wish we had those here!" Sara exclaimed. "How wonderful to be able to speak to someone across town without having to ride over or send a message!"

"Yes, I do miss the convenience," Laurel admitted. "It is amazing how soon you become accustomed to calling the department store or the grocer and ordering what you need sent over."

"What department store!" Mary Lou laughed. "Does Miller's Mercantile qualify?"

"Only if it doubles as the grocer's, too!" Imogene put in with a giggle.

"Well, at least we have the new ice cream parlor," Deborah consoled, "and bicycles to rent when we want."

"Only if you want to look like a fool!" Sara complained. "I simply can not seem to pedal and guide the thing and manage to keep my skirts from getting caught at the same time. One of these days, some poor girl is going to strangle before anyone can rescue her!"

"I wish Ben would allow me to order one of those lady's cycling outfits!" Mary Lou said. "They are so stunning, with those Turkish pants under the short skirts, and the matching jackets!"

"Ben would lock you in the closet and keep you there, Mary Lou!" Deborah warned. Mary Lou was married to Deborah's brother, and Deb knew Ben too well to imagine him letting his wife wear such

an outfit. "Just be happy with the kerosene cooking stove he got you. Mother doesn't even have one
yet!"

Mary Lou smiled. "Yes, well, Ben only bought it
so I would quit harping at him to load the kitchen
wood bin all the time. Now I'm trying to get him to
buy me an ice box for the kitchen. Guess I'd better
concentrate on that and forget about the cycling
costume."

As time went on and Brandon continued to
ignore her, Laurel saw no reason to discourage the
various young men eager for her attention. There
was not one more special to her than the others,
and Laurel had no intention of becoming serious
about any of them. She usually arranged for
herself and her escort to be part of a group of
several other couples. Weekend picnics, bicycling
sprees, and Sunday afternoon buggy rides were
pleasant ways to spend the time.

The Sunday morning that Joe Adams, Henry
Jenkins, and Caleb Oates got into a heated discussion over who was to sit beside Laurel in
church made her father chuckle with delight,
especially when he noted the expression on
Brandon Prescott's face. Laurel, too, saw the grim,
angry look Brandon tossed her way, but she
shrugged it off. After all, *he* was the one avoiding
her, and acting like a mule!

A full month after her return to Crystal City,
Laurel was in town picking up an order of groceries for the ranch. Henry Jenkins had happened
along just as she was leaving, and offered to help
Jake load her packages.

As Henry put the last sack into the back of the
wagon, Brandon walked up, a scowl darkening his
handsome features. "If you needed help, Laurel,

all you had to do was ask me," he growled.

Her mouth flew open, and her temper flared immediately. "How was I supposed to manage that, Brandon Prescott, when you have made it abundantly clear you want nothing to do with me?" she asked tartly, her eyes flashing. "I don't need your help, or anything else you have to offer!"

A dark eyebrow quirked upward over cynical steel-gray eyes. "Are you sure about that?" he questioned in an insinuatingly soft tone of voice.

"Absolutely certain," she answered him, meeting his look squarely.

"Then you won't mind if I challenge that statement, will you, Laurel, honey?" Before she could guess his intentions, Brandon wrapped her in his arms and planted his lips firmly upon hers. Every muscle in her body stiffened in objection to this sudden public display which she certainly had not anticipated. Her palms pushed against his rock-hard chest, but Brandon merely pulled her closer in retaliation.

His lips were warm and enticing, and doing marvelous things to her. Too soon, she forgot to fight him, her body melting against his, her lips parting slightly to admit the sweet thrust of his tongue. Flames of desire raced through her, and she felt the rapid beat of his heart beneath her open palm, signaling his own desire. Giddily, she returned his kiss, her own lips and tongue meeting his greedily.

Just before he released her, his lips left hers to wander across her cheek to her ear. "You do need me, Laurel, whether you admit it or not," he whispered. Then he quickly released her. Weak-kneed, she stumbled without his support. As quickly as he had appeared, he now walked away from her, outwardly unaffected, as if it was common practice for him to stop women on the street and kiss them senseless.

Shock held her silent for only a moment. Then she shouted after him, "Brandon Prescott, you drive me *crazy!* You can't just grab me and kiss me like that, before God and everybody, and then walk away!" If she could have seen the triumphant smile on Brandon's face, she would have been angrier still, but he just kept right on walking.

"What was all that about?" Henry muttered. "I didn't know you and Prescott were still seeing one another."

"We're not!" Laurel snapped, confusing the fellow further.

"That's not what it looked like from here," Jake Miller taunted from the doorway, his plump wife chuckling at his side.

"Laurel, dear, that man just put his brand on you, plain as day," Ethel added cheerfully.

Unconsciously, Laurel's fingers flew to her lips, her lavender eyes misty as they followed Brandon's retreat. Ethel was right. Brandon had indeed left his mark on her—but deep in her heart, and years before.

A few days later, Deborah Werling had a birthday, inviting all her friends to an afternoon lawn party. Deb, wanting it to be as sophisticated an affair as Crystal City had experienced in years, asked Laurel to help her organize it. Happily, Mrs. Werling loved flowers, and her back yard was filled with blossoms of every imaginable size and color. The women arranged tables and benches around the flower-bedecked yard. Mrs. Werling's best china and crystal glistened, and there was an abundance of food. Knowing the hard-working young men invited would not be satisfied with tea cookies, there were platters of sliced ham, beef, and chicken, and bowls of potato salad, baked beans, and cole slaw. A huge cake and an enormous crock of home-made ice cream rested on another table next to two large bowls of punch and pots of black coffee.

Because she was helping to oversee the preparations, Laurel had stayed overnight with Deborah the night before. With everything arranged, the two girls dashed off to Deb's room to dress for the party.

Deb's mother had sewn a new dress for her birthday, patterning it after the fanciest day dress they could find in the Sears catalog. The rose colored gown, trimmed with pink lace on the bodice and skirt, was every bit as beautiful as the one Laurel had bought in Boston and was wearing today.

The girls fussed over one another's hair, and when they were done, each paused to admire the other. Laurel wore a light blue dress, the sleeves entirely fashioned of intricate lace, shoulders to wrists. Matching lace covered the high-necked bodice and accented the skirt and the edge of the decorative overcape across her shoulders. A wide ribbon made Laurel's waist seem small enough to be spanned by a man's hands. The color brought out the violet highlights in her lilac eyes. Her shining hair was pulled to the nape of her neck in a sleek, intricately braided loop, thanks to Deb's nimble fingers, with delicate kiss curls near her ears.

"I wish I had hair as beautiful as yours, Laurel, instead of this drab brown mop of mine," Deborah complained wistfully.

"Your hair is not drab, Deb. It is thick and shining, and very pretty. You can't imagine the number of times I've wishes I had your coloring."

"For heaven's sakes, why?" Deb was amazed.

"I feel so pale and washed-out sometimes next to other girls! I love being outdoors, but I have to be so careful not to burn or freckle. Then, too, in certain light, my hair looks white, as if I were eighty years old instead of eighteen!"

"I doubt any man in his right mind ever mistook you for an old lady!" Deb giggled.

Laurel laughed with her. "Not yet, anyway," she admitted.

"Speaking of men," Deb said slyly, "I heard about Brandon's performance in front of the mercantile the other day."

Laurel groaned. "I suppose the entire town has heard by now."

"Priscilla Vaughn is having fits," Deb said hesitantly. "You know she's sweet on Brandon, don't you?"

Laurel's eyes widened speculatively. "No, is she?"

Deb laughed and rolled her eyes expressively. "Lands! If that girl thought it would make him take notice, she would walk down Main Street buck naked at noon!"

Laurel couldn't help grinning. "I hope she never gets that desperate!"

Deb shrugged, "We'll see. At any rate, both she and Brandon will be here today, and I thought you should be forewarned. Priscilla can be such a cat when she wants."

Laurel was soon glad of Deb's warning. The moment Priscilla saw her, she glared daggers at Laurel. When Brandon arrived, matters naturally got worse. Priscilla glued herself immediately to his side, simpering and cooing up at him, and batting her lashes in the most painfully obvious display of affection. Laurel actually felt sorry for her for a while, but Brandon seemed pleased by Priscilla's attentions. In fact, after a brief greeting to Laurel, he totally ignored her in favor of Priscilla's blatant admiration.

More confused than ever, Laurel determined to stop trying to figure out how Brandon would behave from day to day, or what he might do. The man had her totally baffled. Since there was nothing she could do about it, Laurel set about enjoying herself with her other friends. Henry finally worked up enough nerve to take up a place at her side, where Caleb and Joe were already dancing attendance on her.

Just when she had succeeded in pushing Brandon to the back of her mind, congratulating herself on her success, Laurel felt an arm steal about her waist from behind. Before he spoke, she knew him by his touch, and the tingling excitement that shot through her at his nearness. His breath feathered the curls at her ear as he said softly, "I thought I proved the other day whose woman you are, sweetheart."

He sounded so smug that she was instantly furious with him. Whirling about, she glared up at him. "Will you stop this insanity, Brandon!" she hissed. "You can't ignore me for weeks on end, then calmly walk up and act as if you own me!"

He grinned at her easily. "Settle your feathers, Laurel. People are starting to stare."

"*Ooh!*" She stamped her foot in irritation.

His arm looped about her waist again, and he tugged gently. "Come and eat something with me."

"No!" she sulked, her lower lip pouting slightly. "Go eat with Priscilla."

"I want to eat with you, Moonbeam," he cajoled. Then he gave her a look filled with mock menace. "If you refuse, I'll pick you up and carry you off over my shoulder. That will certainly get everyone's attention."

"You wouldn't dare!"

"Wouldn't I?" He certainly looked as if he might.

"All right, you devil! But this is absolutely the last time I'll allow you to manipulate me!" she warned.

They filled their plates and found an empty bench. As they sat chatting and watching their friends, much of Laurel's anger dissolved. It was so good to be near him, to hear his deep voice ringing pleasantly in her ears. It was like old times, when they had talked so easily and been so comfortable with one another, sure of each other and their love.

Brandon's hand found hers, and he simply held it within the warmth of his. A deep feeling of contentment washed over her.

They were sitting quietly hand in hand when Priscilla fluttered up. "I wondered where you'd gotten off to, Brandon," she simpered. "Here—I brought you some ice cream." Priscilla pushed the plate toward him, in the process "accidentally" sliding the entire contents of the plate into Laurel's lap.

Laurel let out a startled shriek and leaped up, shaking the melting mess from her skirts. Glowering at Priscilla, Brandon offered Laurel his handkerchief, trying to help her rescue her ruined gown.

"Priscilla, you are a vindictive little witch!" he growled.

"It's all right, Brandon, really," Laurel soothed, aware of the attention they were drawing.

"No, it's not! Come on, Laurel, I'm taking you home." He headed her toward the gate.

"Truly, Brandon. There's no need," she pleaded, knowing how fast gossip could travel to her father's ears. It simply would not do for the two of them to leave together.

"Shut up, love," he said softly, a tender, protective look glinting in the depths of his eyes.

CHAPTER 4

After Brandon had taken her home from Deborah's party, Laurel expected to see more of him, but Brandon was having problems at the ranch. The rustlers had struck again, destroying a lengthy section of fencing, which needed to be repaired immediately. To add to his troubles, not only had they stolen several of his steers, but other cattle had wandered out of the break in the fence and had to be rounded up, which took time and manpower to accomplish.

The Fourth of July was upon them before they knew it. All Crystal City geared up for the traditional summer celebration, complete with picnic, games, exhibits, booths, rodeo, and barn dance.

The festivities started in earnest around noon, and Laurel rode into town in the buckboard with her father and Aunt Martha. A lunch basket for two was riding securely under the seat of the wagon, filled with cold fried chicken, potato salad, deviled eggs, fresh fruit, cheese, and apple crumb pie. The lucky fellow who outbid all others would share this succulent feast with her. The baskets were to be numbered, and supposedly no one would know ahead of time which lady a particular basket came from, but each year word would leak out, and the men would bid highest on the lunch baskets of their fairest, finest favorites. Still and all, it was great fun, and often some young gourmet would totally ignore the basket of some beautiful young lady in favor of the culinary delights hidden away in one of the older women's baskets. Martha's basket always had a great number of bids and brought in a good deal of money, for she was a marvelous cook.

When Laurel turned her basket over to the officials, she tried to make certain that no one would find out which basket was hers, but her efforts were all in vain. When her number came up, Joe, Henry, and Caleb immediately set up clamorous bidding. The price had risen to two and a half dollars, when Brandon Prescott suddenly raised the bid to five dollars even. This was the first Laurel was aware he was present in the crowd. The bidding continued, and when it reached ten dollars, an exorbitant sum, Brandon claimed his lunch and Laurel as his dining partner, while Rex glowered at them both.

As they spread their basket beneath a shade tree, Laurel asked curiously, "How did you know that was my basket, Brandon?"

"I didn't," he admitted with a sparkling flash of white teeth, "until your three gallant musketeers began bidding so earnestly for it. Why? Did you think I had cheated, and bribed someone to tell me?"

"It crossed my mind," she admitted, almost ashamed of herself for thinking it of him.

His grin widened. "It crossed *my* mind, too, but it was totally unnecessary, when your avid admirers gave the game away."

"Then you admit you *would* have cheated if you'd had to," Laurel persisted.

"Absolutely!" he readily agreed. "It would have

been worth it to have lunch with you, even if you turn out to be the world's worst cook."

"Why, Brandon, when I've heard nothing from you since Deb's party? You know, you treat me very shabbily, then expect me to forgive and forget and come running whenever you snap your fingers." She was quite put out with him, even while she rejoiced at seeing him again.

"Laurel, I'm sorry. I honestly was not deliberately ignoring you. I was busy," Brandon told her.

"Doing what?" she asked.

"Rounding up steers and repairing broken fence." As he gave her this information, he watched closely for her reaction.

Her eyes searched his face just as avidly, revealing only her fervent wish to believe him. "You were truly busy?" she asked shyly, her face open to his scrutiny. "You weren't just avoiding me again?"

If she had any knowledge of his problems, she was concealing it well. Brandon wanted desperately to believe Laurel was ignorant of Rex's nefarious doings. "I swear, I was honestly busy at the ranch," he vowed.

When she rewarded his answer with a sweet smile, he found himself saying, "Will you go with me as my partner to the barn dance this evening?"

Laurel hesitated only long enough to wonder briefly what her father would say, and how angry he would be; then she accepted Brandon's invitation regardless of the consequences. "I'd love to, Brandon."

Laurel spent the rest of the day with Brandon, and when she wasn't actually with him, she watched him as he participated in various events of the rodeo. It was a day of fun and laughter, filled with activities, delicious food and drink,

shared joy with friends—and dreams of the
evening to come.

"Are you sure you are up to all this cavorting
around?" Laurel teased later that night, looking
dreamily into Brandon's eyes. "That bull threw
you pretty hard."

Brandon sucked in his breath at the adoration
glowing in her face, his arms tightening about her
as they danced. "Sweet Laurel, I could dance with
you like this all night, especially if you promise to
keep looking at me like you are now."

Laurel blushed prettily at his words. "That's
sweet, Brandon, but if you are hurting, we can rest
a while."

"I plan on it later, but right now I'm enjoying
holding my Moonbeam in my arms and seeing her
so happy. You *are* happy, aren't you, Laurel?"

She nodded shyly, and rested her head in the
hollow of his shoulder, sighing contentedly. It was
a magical evening, and sheer heaven to be held in
his arms this way. All their differences seemed to
have melted away.

Her contentment was marred slightly to find
Becky and Jim Lawson at the dance. Awkward
greetings were exchanged. Thankfully, Brandon
had not suggested they sit together, sensing
Laurel's discomfort. Later, he would straighten
out all her misconceptions, but for now Brandon
wanted Laurel to himself.

A while later, Rex and Martha came to collect
her. They were ready to go back to the ranch, and
Rex was none too happy that Laurel was spending
so much time in Brandon's company.

"Come along, Laurel," he said gruffly, "We're
going home now."

Laurel jerked out of her dreamy state with a

start. She darted a quick look between her father and Brandon, obviously torn.

Brandon's hold tightened on her waist. "I'll see Laurel home safely, Rex," he said smoothly. "Later."

"I think not." Rex's hard blue eyes bored into Brandon. His hand reached out for Laurel's arm, but she backed away, seeking the shelter of Brandon's embrace.

"No, Dad," Laurel corrected softly but determinedly. "I'm staying for a while longer."

"You don't know what you are doing, Daughter," Rex warned. "You should know better by now than to trust a Prescott."

Laurel stood her ground. "I'm a big girl now, Dad, old enough to make my own decisions."

"Very well," Rex said coldly. "We'll discuss this at home later. The matter is not closed!" He stalked away, his back stiff with anger. Martha threw Laurel a sympathetic look, then hurried off in her brother's wake.

Laurel hated having to choose sides, and began to shake in reaction to the confrontation. Brandon felt her trembling and led her gently to a chair. Kneeling next to her, he stroked her hair tenderly, his eyes glowing like twin stars as he gazed into her face. "Thank you, Laurel. I really wanted you to stay with me."

She nodded. "It is what I want, too, Brandon."

They were alone for the first time in a quiet corner of the barn. "Marry me, Laurel," Brandon blurted suddenly.

Laurel's huge lilac eyes grew even larger as she stared into his serious face. For a moment she was tempted to accept, but then she caught a glimpse of Becky on the dance floor, and her heart gave a lurch of pain and regret. She shook her head sorrowfully. "No, Brandon, I can't." She closed her eyes to shut out his mesmerizing gaze, and two fat tears slid out from beneath her lashes, rolling silently down her cheeks.

His fingers tenderly brushed them away. "Why not?" he whispered.

As she spoke, her voice cracked on a sob. "I just can't, Brandon!" It was the one thing she wanted more than life itself, but she could not marry a man who still yearned for another woman. She looked at him pleadingly, wanting so badly to throw herself into his arms and hold him tightly for all eternity.

The cleft in his chin was more defined as his jaw hardened stubbornly. "I don't give up so easily, Laurel," he warned. "I'll ask again and again until you say yes."

It was her turn to ask, "Why?"

"Because I want you," he answered simply, "and you want me. We could be so good together, Moonbeam."

She smiled shakily. If only he had said he loved her! "It is a lovely, tempting dream, Brandon, but dreams fade in the bright reality of sunlight. You are forgetting all the problems in our path."

He sighed heavily, drawing her to her feet. "Then dance with me, and just for tonight we'll forget the problems and enjoy this time together."

She went gladly into his arms, willing to pretend and dream for just a few hours, like Cinderella at the ball.

Rex cornered her at the breakfast table the next morning. "I'm very disappointed in you, Laurel," he began sternly, his face a hard mask of parental disapproval. "I would have thought you'd learned your lesson with Prescott two years ago."

Laurel continued buttering her muffin, maintaining a sullen silence.

"I want your word that you will stop seeing him," her father insisted.

"No, Dad," Laurel answered quietly. "I shall see anyone I wish to see, anytime I want."

"Listen here, Missy!" Rex exploded. "You still live under my roof and eat my food, and if I say you are not to see him, that is how it will be!"

Laurel slammed her butter knife on the table. "That state of affairs can be remedied any time at all!" she shouted back, her face as determined as his. "I don't have to stay here if you begrudge me food and shelter! If you no longer wish to provide for me, just say so, but don't make it a condition hanging on my obedience!"

"Then you intend to disregard my orders and continue to make a fool of yourself over that—that rake? I remember, even if you don't, how brokenhearted you were over his philandering!"

"I haven't forgotten for a moment," she assured him heatedly. "Neither have I forgotten how eager you were to send me off to Boston in such an all-fired hurry!"

"You went willingly enough, girl."

"That may have been a major mistake," she admitted. "If I had stayed and faced Brandon then, perhaps things would have turned out differently."

"It was for your own good," he persisted. "The Prescotts have meant nothing but trouble to the Burke family for years!"

"Is that why you sent me away so hurriedly, then told everyone I had gone East to get married?" she threw back angrily, her eyes flashing violet lightning. "Was it really out of compassion for me, or was it merely that you couldn't bear the thought of your only child falling in love with a Prescott?"

"Who told you that?" he demanded.

"Never mind who told me! It's the truth, isn't it?" she cried.

"I *don't* want to see you hurt, Laurel. You mean the world to me." Rex felt defeated by her righteous anger. "Prescott will only break your heart in the end."

"That is my decision to make and my risk," she pointed out.

Rex ran a hand distractedly through his greying hair. "I should lock you in your room until you come to your senses," he threatened weakly.

"You could try it, but you would have to let me out sooner or later," Laurel said.

Rex heaved a sigh. "Are you going to see him again?" he asked more quietly.

"I don't know yet, Dad," she answered. "Perhaps." After a moment she added sadly, "I probably shall, but I'm not sure it will amount to anything between us. However, I need to make my own decisions, right or wrong, and deal with the consequences myself."

Rex looked at her sadly. "Where did my little girl disappear to, Laurel?"

Tears glistened in her eyes as she went over to him and hugged him. "She grew up, Dad."

He nodded wearily, but rallied for one parting decree. "I'll never stand for your marrying him, Laurel. I hope you realize that."

The old anguish tore at her heart. "Yes, I know that, Dad. I know."

For the next few weeks, Laurel and Brandon continued to see one another whenever time allowed. Much of the time, Brandon was busy at his ranch, especially since the rustling was still a continuing problem. Many times he had to bite his tongue to keep from telling Laurel what he thought of her father, or ask her if she was aware of what Rex was up to, but he could see she was still torn between the two men in her life, so he kept still.

They kept things nice and easy at first, sitting together at church, and riding together afterward. They attended gatherings at friends' homes, went to the ice cream parlor, or enjoyed an occasional dinner at the hotel dining room or cafe. The one thing Brandon refused to do was go cycling.

"Laurel, I'd look and feel like a trained bear on one of those spindly things! If I want to make a spectacle of myself, I can think of better ways, with less risk to my knees and elbows!"

One Sunday after church, toward the middle of August, Brandon and Laurel were riding in the buggy. All of a sudden it dawned on her that they were headed toward Jim Lawson's ranch.

Feeling unsure of herself, she asked, "Brandon, shouldn't we start back soon? It's almost time for dinner."

"We're having dinner with Jim and Becky this afternoon, Laurel," he told her, glancing quickly in her direction.

Laurel gasped in dismay. "Brandon, no! How could you!"

"Damn it all, Laurel! You are going to see once and for all that you have been mistaken about Becky and me! I thought if you could see Jim and Becky with their children, you would see how happy they are together. Once you get to know her, I'm sure you will like her."

"Oh, God, Brandon!" she wailed. "I don't doubt they are happy, and I don't need to know Becky to prove anything to myself. It's your feelings for Becky that I can't do anything about—that makes me feel so miserable!"

"Then watch and observe, Laurel, honey," he instructed. "You will see that I am not the least bit uncomfortable around them. You won't catch me giving Becky any lustful looks behind Jim's back, because I don't desire her—I never did. I like her; I admire her; but I do *not* love her. It makes me glad to see what Jim and Becky share, and I hope one day you and I can have the same loving relationship. We could, you know, if you would only take off the blinders and see what is right before your eyes!'"

Out of respect for Jim Lawson, and because she was a guest in their home, Laurel did her best to be friendly and polite. Still, the atmosphere was noticably strained, with sudden lapses in conversation. Several times, Jim or Brandon would start to discuss the cattle rustling, then stop in mid-sentence, remembering that Laurel's father was the culprit. This knowledge also made Becky more reserved in her manner toward Laurel than she might have been otherwise.

The Lawson children saved the day from being a total disaster. The older child was fifteen months old, a sandy-haired boy who bore a distinctive resemblance to Jim. Their baby daughter was just three months, a darling little doll with curly, dark hair. Despite her uncertain feelings about Becky, Laurel was immediately taken with the bright-eyed cheerful children.

"They are so adorable!" she said sincerely. "You must be very proud."

"We are," Becky agreed, smiling tenderly at her husband. "Jim will talk your ears off, given half a chance, bragging about them."

After dinner, when the men went outside for a bit, Laurel offered to help clear the table. In an effort to fill in the awkward silence, she again mentioned the babies. "You certainly must have your hands full, with two children so young," she commented.

Becky nodded. "They are cute, but they certainly are a handful, especially since Tad has learned to walk. To be truthful, I never planned to have another child so soon after Tad was born, but Nature had other ideas, I guess. At least this time I can nurse Emily, and Doc Jameson says I probably won't have to worry about adding to the family as long as the baby is nursing."

"At least they will grow up close," Laurel pointed out. "I always wanted a brother or sister."

Becky chuckled. "Well, Hank is a bit old, I guess. Still, he'll be a brother to you when you and Brandon get married."

Laurel almost dropped the plate she was drying. The look on her face must have revealed her shock, for Becky continued hastily, "Maybe I'm speaking out of turn, Laurel, but Brandon needs a good woman. He's been alone too long. He is a good man—kind, hard-working, considerate—and his looks aren't bad either," she added with a wink. "If I hadn't tumbled head over heels for Jim, I might have set my cap for Brandon myself. He certainly will make a handsome groom!"

By singing Brandon's praises, Becky had unknowingly confirmed Laurel's suspicions. Becky must have been attracted to Brandon for a time before falling in love with Jim; just long enough for Brandon to lose his heart to her hopelessly. That familiar cloud of depression settled more firmly about Laurel's shoulders. Laurel wanted to dislike the perky brunette, but it was nearly impossible. Reason told her it was not Becky's fault she'd fallen for Jim instead of Brandon. In fact, Becky seemed oblivious to Brandon's feelings for her, so perhaps Brandon had never had the opportunity to tell her before Jim had come onto the scene. How could you hate someone for something they knew nothing about, especially someone as vivacious and lovely as Becky, so abundantly proud of her husband and small family?

Through the waning days of summer, Brandon continued to court Laurel in his sporadic, crazy way. With the fall round-up coming up, he spent what time he could spare with her, but he was often preoccupied and moody when they met. Still, he squired her about when he could, sent her candy and flowers on several occasions, and repeated his offer of marriage.

They argued again and again over the subject, Brandon always insisting that he did not love Becky. Laurel eventually ceased to mention the other woman, claiming instead that her father would never forgive her.

Brandon did not like this excuse any better than her first. "For God's sake, Laurel, you are a grown woman!" he ranted. "When are you going to take your father off that pedestal you've erected for him and realize what kind of man he really is?"

Laurel bristled. "Would you care to explain that remark?" she challenged icily.

One large hand on each of her arms, he shook her roughly. "Don't you ever take your head out of the clouds long enough to see what's going on right under your nose?" he demanded. "Are you that blind to the man's faults, or is it merely that you don't care? Anything Daddy does is fine and just, no matter who else it hurts?"

"What *are* you raving about?" Laurel was thoroughly confused and distressed.

Brandon clamped his jaws tightly shut, before he said more than he should. "Never mind, Laurel," he groaned disgustedly. "Just go home to your dear Daddy and forget I said anything."

Though it was not quite as it once had been before the homesteaders and railroads had invaded the West, the fall round-up was still a busy, bustling time for all the ranchers. It meant hours of hard, back-breaking work, rounding up the cattle, separating the marketable steers, and branding those that had been missed heretofore. The cattle had to be brought down from their summer pastures, and the strays located and added to the herd. The cattle were at last driven to stockyards in town, or holding pens along the railroad line, to be loaded on boxcars and shipped to market in the larger cities.

Though not as long and drawn out, the cattle drives were just as hot, dusty, and tiring as before, and there was still the constant discomfort of bad weather, long hours in the saddle, and breathing more trail dust than air for days on end. Added to that, there was the flighty temperament of the beasts to contend with. The animals were prone to straggle and wander unless constantly prodded and watched, and the least little thing could set off a monumental stampede.

Before Brandon and Laurel had a chance to settle anything between them, Brandon found himself knee-deep in the tremendous task of leading the fall round-up. He, Jim Lawson, and another of their neighbors were joining their herds this year and driving them to town together, thus combining their manpower. This took priority over seeing Laurel for the time being. In fact, as the long, aching days of back-breaking work wore on, Brandon had little time to think of Laurel or to try to solve their problems. At night, lying in his bedroll and looking up at the star-filled sky, his thoughts would turn to her at last, but his bone-weary body would soon urge him to sleep before he could do more than wonder how she was and if she missed him. And always, there was the nagging doubt as to how much she actually knew about Rex's activities.

Laurel didn't realize how used to seeing Brandon she had become until he was no longer there. She missed him terribly, but she understood how busy he was. It was busy at home, too, with their own round-up in progress. The ranch was a bustle of activity for days beforehand, and then suddenly unearthly quiet with most of the men gone.

The women were busy themselves. Though the men had the chuckwagon along to provide their meals each day, a supply wagon would be sent out from the ranch every few days with added supplies. Martha and Laurel took turns overseeing the loading of foodstuffs for the men. In the meantime, they fixed large kettles of soups, fresh pies, cakes, and bread to send along on the next wagon.

Toward the end of the third week, the weather changed. The hot, dry days of endless blue skies and sunshine soon turned muggy and sultry. The hazy, humid atmosphere foretold a gathering storm, and meanwhile it sapped the energy of every living thing within its reach. If Laurel had felt listless before because of Brandon's continued absence, she was now limp as well from the still, moisture-laden air that seemed to suffocate with its moist heat.

Feeling the perspiration drip between her shoulder blades beneath her damp dress, Laurel wondered how much worse the men felt, working so hard outdoors, without a breath of a breeze and very little shade. Still, once the storm broke at last, with all its pent-up fury, neither man nor beast would find decent shelter, and it would be much worse than now. Her thoughts turned even more often to Brandon, and she hoped he was faring well.

CHAPTER 5

A low rumble of distant thunder resounded through the foothills, and high lightning flashed eerily from atop the mountains to the west of their camp. The air was deathly still; not a breath of a breeze.

Brandon and the men with him watched the skies with worried, expectant eyes. "The calm before the storm," one fellow murmured, and the others nodded in agreement. It had been building for days, and within a few hours, all hell would undoubtedly break loose from the sullen heavens.

The cattle were restless, sensing the impending storm. More men than usual had to be stationed around the uneasy herd, in the hope of averting a stampede if the thunder and lightning sent the fidgety cattle off.

"Think it will go around?" Jim asked hopefully, though his intuition told him differently.

"I doubt it," Brandon growled irritably. "Not with the luck we've been having lately."

"Well, I guess I'd better get out there and do my share at settling this nervous bunch of critters down. Times like this, I wish cattle weren't so dumb and flighty," Jim grumbled.

"Gonna sing lullabies to them, Jim?" Hank

teased, as he, too, prepared to ride out to the far fringes of the herd.

Jim laughed. "I'd better not, if what Becky tells me about my singing is true! Cattle may be dumb, but they're not deaf!"

Brandon chuckled dryly at Jim's joking. "I'll be out to relieve you in a couple of hours," he told his friend.

"Yeah," Jim answered. "Meanwhile, you'd better try to grab some sleep while you can. It's gonna be a long night, buddy."

Brandon did try to nap, but he was as tightly strung as the cattle. Finally he gave up, going to the campfire to pour a cup of the hot, strong coffee ever ready there, carefully avoiding looking into the flames that would destroy his night vision.

He'd just finished the bitter brew when the first fat drops of rain fell, hissing on the hot stones surrounding the fire. With no more warning than that, it was as if a dam had suddenly burst, and within seconds, everything and everyone was drenched.

Those men still in camp hurriedly ran for cover, hastily dragging waterproof ponchos over their heads and pulling their hats low over their faces. As lightning lit up the countryside, followed by a loud blast of thunder, the cattle gave a collective low of alarm and shifted as a unit. Brandon cursed under his breath.

The rain came down in torrents, creating a thick liquid curtain; the dark, cloud-filled night was lit only by the increasingly recurrent bursts of jagged white light from the heavens. The men didn't need to see to know how fractious the herd was becoming. Between loud crashes of thunder, they could hear the cattle milling about nervously.

Knowing where his duty lay without needing to be told, each man hurriedly saddled his horse and mounted up, grimly joining his companions already guarding the herd.

Thunder roared overhead and rain poured from the brim of his hat as Brandon made his way around to where Hank and Jim were stationed, only the flashes of lightning and his horse's natural sure-footedness to guide him over the rough ground. So far, the herd was still under control; with a whole lot of luck, maybe they could keep it that way.

Then, between flashes of lightning, when the valley was cloaked in inky darkness, Brandon caught a flash of light off to his left, near ground level, and a second later, a sharp retort. Instantly alert, he recognized it as gunfire, and ducked instinctively as a bullet whizzed past his head. As if this was a signal to others waiting nearby, several other gunshots were heard amidst the heavy rumbling of thunder. With a bellow of heightened alarm, the herd lurched, the cattle trying to go several ways at once. As a new volley of shots erupted, the steers overcame their indecision, and surged forward with one accord.

It was too dark to see much of anything but the mass of cattle on the move. In the blinding rain, it was impossible to tell friend from foe, and too risky to try to take aim at any dark figure on horseback, but one thing was for sure—the rustlers had decided to make their move against the chaos of the storm, and there was very little that could be done to stop them now.

The herd was gaining momentum with every passing second, and the cowboys' main priority was to try to head off a full-scale stampede. Those men too far away to be aware of the rustlers' presence knew only that the herd was taking flight and had to be stopped. As well trained cow ponies went into action, horses and riders trying to restore order and keep the panicked herd from breaking up, several horsemen rode full out to outdistance the lead steers and try to turn them back.

After many frantic minutes and much effort, they finally succeeded. The befuddled cattle loped slowly to a confused halt, the rest following suit, and partial order was restored—for the moment, at least. However, no one could afford to let down his guard just yet, as a new outbreak could occur with the least provocation.

As soon as the herd began to settle, Brandon barked out orders to those men closest to him. Within minutes, a group of wranglers was following him in pursuit of the rustlers. Brandon had seen a small section of the herd break away from the main body, but his primary concern had been to save the rest. Now he and a few of his men were after those steers that had been deliberately cut out by the rustlers in the chaos of the moment. Under cover of the storm and near-stampede, the thieves had made off with a goodly number of cattle at one stroke.

Brandon was more than angry—he was furious! With rain streaming down his face, and the storm raging about him, he pursued the dark mass of cattle and riders well ahead of him. There was little hope of catching them now, in the black of night, but he was determined to try.

Encumbered by the cattle they were stealing, the rustlers made slower progress than Brandon and his men, and several of the thieves dropped back to give cover fire for their comrades in crime.

Shots rang out from both sides as the cowboys slowly gained ground.

It was an impossible task to dodge bullets and chase after the marauders in the pitch-black night, and Brandon had to settle for concentrating on the small band of rustlers nearest him. But in the darkness, the thieves disbanded, melting into the night one by one.

Slowing his horse to a trot, Brandon stared into the darkness ahead and cursed. With the rain battering down on him, he could not even hear the hoof beats of retreating thieves' horses. "Damn!" he muttered in frustration, then nearly lurched from the saddle as his horse sidestepped suddenly. "What the devil?" he said in surprise. Then his bleary gaze picked out the inert form almost beneath his horse's hoof.

Brandon's fellow riders gathered quickly around the fallen rustler. One of them dismounted, rolling the unresisting body onto its back. "He's dead, boss," the man proclaimed after a brief search for a pulse.

"That figures," Brandon replied curtly. "We finally get one of them, and he's beyond telling us anything." Pivoting his horse, he headed back for camp. "Bring him back with you. At least we can try to identify him, if nothing else."

More bad news met Brandon upon his return to camp, startling and distressing as nothing else could have been on this disaster-filled night. Hank met him as he rode in, his face creased in worry. "Brandon," he choked out, grabbing for the reins, "Jim's been hurt. We've got him in the chuck wagon, but he needs a doctor real bad."

Brandon leaped out of the saddle, heading for the wagon at a lope. "Can he be moved?" he demanded.

"No, he's too bad off. One of the men is riding for the doctor now, but I don't think he'll make it back in time for it to matter." Misery coated Hank's words, making them thick in his throat.

Hank wasn't exaggerating. Brandon saw at first glance that Jim was fading fast. His friend's face was grey with pain even beneath the coating of mud, and a steady stream of blood trickled from his nose and one side of his mouth. Jim's thick blonde hair was matted with blood, where a steer's hoof had struck. He lay unmoving, battered and broken, his breathing labored and laced with deep moans of agony.

"He wasn't just trampled," Sam explained from his position near Jim's head. "He's been shot!"

Brandon crawled to Jim's side, gently taking his friend's hand, his own face a mask of anguish. "God, Jim," he groaned helplessly.

Jim opened his eyes, and his lips worked spasmodically as he tried to speak. The only word Brandon could make out was "Becky."

Brandon nodded, tears misting his vision. "Don't worry, Jim. I'll make sure she and the babies are taken care of," he promised huskily. He wanted to tell his friend to save his strength—that the doctor would be here soon; but Jim knew he was dying, and there was no sense lying to him.

Jim tried to thank him but choked on the words, his hand tightening on Brandon's as a spasm racked his broken body. His grip eased, his pain-filled features started to relax, and Brandon knew Jim was gone.

"I'll get the man who did this, Jim," he vowed grimly, his last promise as his friend's spirit slipped away. "I'll make them pay!" On a thick sob of anger and sorrow, he added, "I swear it!"

* * *

When Brandon rode up to the Burke ranch the next morning with several of his men, Laurel was delighted to see him. But no sooner had she answered his imperious pounding on the door, than he shoved her roughly aside as he strode into the house.

"Where is your father?" he demanded angrily, his face set in hard, uncompromising lines. Never had she seen him so angry.

"He's out on the range," she answered with a confused frown. "We're in the middle of the cattle drive, same as you are."

Brandon's eyes were like glittering swords of vengeance. "Where are they camped?" he barked, no hint of tenderness in his voice or gaze.

"Why?" she asked hesitantly.

Brandon lost what little control he had. Grabbing her roughly by the arms, he shook her until her teeth rattled. "Where is he?" he roared.

"N-near the n-north f-fork of the creek," she stammered, her eyes wide, frightened circles in her pale face.

He released her with such force that she stumbled up against the wall. "Wh-what do you want with him? Brandon, what is wrong?" she exclaimed. She had never seen him like this, and it frightened her. He was like a madman!

Brandon glared down at her, his teeth bared in a grimace of fierce hatred. "Jim Lawson was killed last night!" he snarled.

Laurel gave a sharp gasp of dismay, her lavender eyes wide with dismay. "Oh, Brandon!" she cried. No wonder he was so upset. "Dad will be so sorry—he always thought so highly of Jim."

Brandon spun on his heel, headed for his horse. "Tell that to someone else, Laurel—maybe

Becky!" he snapped. "Maybe she will believe you, but I don't!"

He bounded off the porch, Laurel hard on his heels. "Wait! Brandon, please! I don't understand! What has Jim's death got to do with my father?"

Glancing back at her disgustedly from atop his horse, he grated out, "Have your father explain it, Laurel. He's the one you worship. His word is gospel to you, isn't it?"

Her silvery hair flying about her shoulders, she shook her head in confused dismay. "No," she denied quickly, "and I still don't understand."

She was speaking to the wind, for Brandon and his men were already riding away. "Oh, Brandon!" she moaned softly. "What is going on?"

Brandon rode briskly into Burke's camp, his men right behind him. "Burke!" he bellowed, sighting his quarry within seconds.

Rex Burke shaded his eyes from the glare of the sun, watching as Brandon approached him. "What is the meaning of this, Prescott?" he demanded harshly.

Brandon motioned to one of his men, who rode up to Rex and dumped a death-stiffened body at his feet. "I believe this is your man," Brandon growled.

Rex glanced at the dead man. "He's not one of mine. I've never seen this man before. What made you think he was?" His blue eyes met Brandon's, matching the anger he saw there.

"Let's cut the crap, Burke," Brandon snarled. "You and I both know you are responsible for all the rustling that's been going on around here!"

"Rustling!" Rex bellowed. "How dare you come onto my ranch and accuse me of cattle rustling!" His face was mottled with rage. "You are as insane as your old man, but even *he* was smart enough not to accuse a man without some sort of proof to back up his words!"

Black fury made Brandon forbidding to behold. "I'll get the proof, Burke. Rest assured of that! And I'll prove that your men killed Jim Lawson last night, too!"

Rex's eyes narrowed dangerously. "Get off my land, Prescott! And don't let me catch you around my daughter again! You're a crazy man, with your wild talk of rustling and killing!"

"My sanity has nothing to do with Jim being dead—shot in the back in the dark of night by a sniveling coward!" Brandon snarled. "And it wasn't my imagination that sent his wife into hysterics when we delivered his cold body into her arms this morning!" His eyes narrowed into steel shards of pure hatred, his nostrils distended as he glared down at Burke. "I hope your conscience eats holes in your gut, thinking of Becky and those two fatherless babes you robbed, Burke," he ground out through gritted teeth. "Someday soon, I'll see you pay for all your crimes! You'll have just enough time to squirm and beg for mercy before they hang you. I'll make sure of it!"

Burke glared back, not intimidated in the least. "Get off my land before I throw you off!" he roared. "And stay away from Laurel!" he warned, as Brandon swung his horse about.

Brandon gave an ugly laugh. "Why?" he asked contemptuously. "Are you afraid she might confess your crimes to me in the throes of passion, Burke? Or doesn't the poor girl know about your secret nighttime forays? Maybe I can enlighten her the next time I'm whispering sweet nothings in her ear. What would she think of her dear Daddy then, I wonder?"

Burke paled noticeably. "You lay a hand on my

daughter, and I'll kill you, Prescott!" he threatened.

"How do you know I haven't already taken all she has to offer?" Brandon jeered. "Think about that the next time you're stealing my cattle. You just might be robbing your future son-in-law!" With that, he rode off, leaving Rex sputtering and cursing behind him.

By the time Rex arrived home, Laurel and Martha were as nervous as could be. The minute he entered the house, Laurel was asking questions. "Dad, is everything all right? Did Brandon find you? He said Jim Lawson is dead. Why would he want to talk to you about that? What is going on? What are you doing home?"

Rex poured himself a stiff drink and lowered himself wearily into a chair. "I'm home because I wanted to talk to you, Laurel," he said gruffly, his blue eyes full of questions as he scrutinized her severely.

Frowning, Laurel said, "What about?"

Her father's brows came together in an ominous manner. "About Prescott, what else?" he snapped sharply. Without further preamble, he blurted, "Have you gone to bed with him, girl?"

With a shocked gasp of outrage, Laurel stared at her father in stunned amazement. "What a thing to ask me!" she exclaimed, as Martha stood staring at both of them.

"*Rex!* I don't believe what I just heard!" Martha declared in shocked surprise. "Whatever gave you such an idea?"

Rex surveyed Laurel's stunned face. "Have you?" he asked again, just as sternly. "Your would-be lover insinuated as much."

Tears swam in Laurel's eyes, making them

glitter as brightly as amethysts, "I don't believe you!" she cried. "Brandon would never say such a thing!"

Rex exploded in a burst of angry words. "Well, he did just that today, as well as other things just as insane! He even had the gall to accuse me of Jim Lawson's death!"

Martha gasped in alarm, her face suddenly pale. "How? Why?" she stammered.

"Because he thought the rustler they caught worked for me."

"Did he?" Laurel asked cautiously, still smarting under her father's unjust accustation.

"No!" Rex answered curtly. "I never saw the man before."

"Why would he kill Jim Lawson and then say he worked for us?" Martha asked, confused.

"The man was dead, Martha, so he wasn't saying much," Rex grunted. "I suppose we'll hear more later, but from what Prescott said, Lawson was shot in the back."

Both women drew in sharp gasps of dismay. "No wonder Brandon was so upset!" Now Laurel could better understand Brandon's actions this morning. His best friend had been shot in the most despicable manner without even a chance to defend himself. Poor Becky, left with two small children and a ranch to run! How awful for her!

The anger blazed in Rex's blue eyes again. "You needn't be concerned over Prescott any longer, Laurel," he directed firmly. "I forbid you to ever see him again!"

Laurel bristled immediately. "We have been through all this before."

"That was before he accused me of everything from murder to rustling!" Rex roared.

"He was angry and upset over Jim's death,"

Laurel said, "and rightly so. What kind of man would he be to take his friend's murder lightly?"

"He is a lying, cheating, conniving weasel, like all the rest of his clan," Rex bellowed, "and I want you to stay away from him or I'll send you back to that school in Boston!"

"Not this time you won't," Laurel promised grimly, her lavender eyes alight with stubborn determination.

When Rex discovered that Laurel was determined to attend Jim Lawson's funeral, he locked her in her room. It took very little time for Laurel in her denim pants to toss a dress, hat, and shoes in a pillowcase and climb onto the porch roof outside her second-story window. Then she shimmied down a porch pillar, crept around the house through the bushes, and when the coast was clear, dashed for the barn. After putting a side-saddle on her horse, she changed into the clothes she'd brought and stealthily rode away.

The preacher had just begun the graveside services when she edged into the group of mourners to stand next to Deborah Werling.

"I wondered if you were coming," Deb whispered. "I waited at the house as long as I could."

"I had a bit of a problem with Dad, but I'll explain later," Laurel murmured back. She glanced around surreptitiously through her lowered lashes until she located Brandon.

He was standing next to Becky, his arm about her shaking shoulders, supporting the young widow as she sobbed out her grief. His face was a weary mask of misery, his eyes like dull grey clouds reflecting his sorrow. Once, during the service, he looked up to see Laurel watching him.

His jaw hardened in anger, his eyes boring hotly into hers; then he turned away, ignoring her.

Laurel cringed. He was evidently still angry with her, though she had done nothing to deserve his wrath. She watched with sad, longing-filled eyes as he helped Becky greet their friends. Then he put her and the babies in the buggy and drove off in the direction of the Lawson ranch, never giving Laurel a second glance.

"He treats her like fragile glass," Laurel noted with aching misery, wondering fleetingly—and, she knew, unworthily—if Brandon had been granted a second opportunity to woo his true love.

This thought came to her more than once in the following days. Brandon was making himself scarce again. At first Laurel waited patiently, for she knew he had gone back to help with the cattle drive. Once it was over, however, Brandon still did not come around, and Laurel discovered he was spending much time at the Lawson place.

As much as it hurt her, this time Laurel did not run away. Even when Brandon escorted Becky to town and to church on Sunday morning, behaving like a protective husband, Laurel held her head up with a brave if wobbly smile.

Most of her friends were unaware of how hurt she really was by Brandon's behavior, but Deb saw through her. "I'm sorry, Laurel," Deb told her sincerely.

Laurel shrugged. "What are *you* sorry for, Deb? You have nothing to do with Brandon's attitude."

"No, but I wish I could do something to help. I hate to see you so miserable."

"Does it show that much?" Laurel sighed. "I had hoped I was doing a good job of covering it up."

Deborah smiled gently. "For the most part, you

are, Laurel, but I can see it because I know you so
well.''

Rex and Martha were not deceived, either.
Martha took pains to be especially kind and understanding with her niece, for she saw the deep
sorrow in Laurel's lavender eyes, and often heard
her sobbing long into the night.

Rex·could not help being glad for this turn of
events. He took every opportunity to point out to
Laurel what a blind fool she had been, gloating
over Brandon's open attitude toward Becky
Lawson and repeating to Laurel every morsel of
gossip that came his way.

''I heard Prescott repaired that rickety fence
along the front of the Lawson property,'' he would
say pointedly. Or, ''Prescott has been three days
now painting the barn for the new widow.''

Laurel had to grit her teeth to keep from
screaming at him, and the blistering looks she
threw his way should have fried him to a crisp.

One bright October afternoon, Laurel was in
town visiting with Deborah. The two young
women had gone shopping, and were walking
toward the ice cream parlor with their purchases
when Deborah suddenly recalled some blue
thread she was supposed to buy for her mother.

''I'll just run into the mercantile for a second,''
Deborah said.

Laurel held up her hand for mercy. ''Oh, no,
Deb! I refuse to go back into that store and be
interrogated by that nosy Ethel again! I'll wait for
you right here, but please do hurry! My feet are
about to drop off, and I am dying of thirst!''

Deborah hurried off, and Laurel stood in front
of the clock shop next to the mercantile. Laurel
had only been waiting a couple of minutes when

two drunken cowboys reeled out of the saloon a few doors down and stumbled in her direction. Holding her breath, she eyed them warily, trying to decide whether to stay where she was and hope they did not notice her, or to hurry off in search of Deborah. Before she could make a move, the taller man looked straight at her. Nudging his partner, he squinted at her, then both ambled toward her grinning like idiots.

"Oh, Lordy!" Laurel muttered, wishing she'd taken flight. Turning on her heel, she started off down the street.

"Hey, girlie!" came a slurred voice behind her. "Don't run off!"

Making the mistake of glancing behind her, Laurel nearly tripped on the hem of her dress, and her packages flew out of her arms. The next minute, the two sodden cowboys were upon her. Stepping cautiously over her packages, Laurel backed away from them, her heart hammering in her throat as two pairs of glazed eyes leered at her.

"Where ya goin' in such a hurry, purty gal?" one of them asked. Alcoholic fumes blasted Laurel in the face as he spoke.

The other, taller man, reached out to try and grab her arm, and Laurel shrieked, "Don't touch me!"

Drunk as they were, both men laughed uproariously at this. "Hear that, Jess? The little lady wants *me!*" said the shorter one.

"Doesn't neither!" Jess denied. "Who'd want you? Why, I've seen *mules* better lookin' than you, Charlie!"

Laurel had retreated as far as she could, and as her back came up against a wall, she looked about frantically for a way to escape. Two other women, looking nearly as scared as Laurel felt, were staring in dismay, but no one else was nearby.

"What say we go somewhere for a drink, honey?" the fellow called Charlie suggested. "Then you can decide which of us you'd rather get to know better."

"Yeah," Jess agreed hazily. "We'll show you a real good time . . ."

"Just be on your way, and leave me alone!" Laurel demanded loudly, hoping her stern tone would run them off.

Jess glared at her through bloodshot eyes. "Who do you think you are, a queen or somethin'?" He reached out again, grabbing at her hat and missing. "This your crown?" he sneered, as Laurel screamed and cringed away from him.

"Aw, don't get ugly, Jess," Charlie pleaded. "You'll ruin all our fun, and this little filly is the purtiest thing I've seen in a long time."

"The filly is mine," came a deep, familiar voice. Behind the men, Laurel saw Brandon standing tall and sturdy, a dangerous gleam in his narrowed steel-grey eyes. "She belongs to me."

The tall man, Jess, glowered drunkenly at Brandon. "You can have her back when we're done with her," he challenged belligerently and managed one step toward Brandon before Brandon's first smashed into his face, followed by a blow to his midriff that doubled him over. A final punch sent him sprawling on his back in the street, unconscious.

Charlie, seeing his friend fall so easily, decided to try his luck elsewhere and stumbled as fast as he could in the opposite direction.

Laurel was weak with relief. Leaning against the wall to keep from falling down, she heaved a sigh. "Thank you, Brandon," she whispered gratefully.

"I don't know where you came from so quickly, but I'm so glad to see you I could cry!"

Two large hands planted themselves on either side of her head, and his tight-lipped face loomed over hers, his eyes blazing down at her. "What the hell are you doing wandering the streets alone?" he demanded furiously.

Blinking up at him in surprise, Laurel stammered. "I—I wasn't alone."

"You could have fooled me," he snapped.

"Deborah and I were shopping. She had to go back for something, and I was waiting for her. Honestly, Brandon, she's only been gone a few minutes," she explained.

"Long enough for you to get yourself into trouble. Tell me something, Laurel. What would you have done if I hadn't come along just now?"

"I don't know," she admitted, swallowing hard. "Run, or screamed, or something."

Brandon's mouth twisted into a cynical smile. "It was your scream that brought me running, honey."

"I'm glad," she said, looking up at him with her heart in her lovely lavender eyes.

"So am I," he admitted finally. With a deep sigh, he shook his head. "Lovely, lovely Laurel, what *am* I going to do about you?" he asked softly.

"What do you *want* to do about me, Brandon?" she whispered, her eyes searching and finding the tenderness she sought in his face.

His hands came close, to cradle her face in his rough palms. "I want to hold you, and love you, and never let you go," he answered, his lips only a breath away from hers. "I want to kiss you until you melt into my arms like warm honey." His lips claimed hers in a searing demonstration of his wishes, as Deborah and several other passersby watched in delighted amusement.

"If they aren't fighting privately, they're loving publicly," Deborah thought in wry amusement. "I wonder when they'll give in and reverse the procedure!"

CHAPTER 6

A week had passed since the episode in town, after which Brandon had escorted her home. Since then, Laurel had seen Brandon nearly every day, but he had also been a regular visitor at the Lawson ranch. Brandon had told her he was helping Becky around the ranch, and Laurel did not press the issue, though she wondered about it. Today, the two of them were alone, riding on his ranch, and Laurel had him to herself.

"How is Becky?" she asked hesitantly.

"She'll make it," Brandon answered, "but she has her hands full trying to learn how to manage the place for herself. I'm going to talk to a man tomorrow, and if he sounds like he will work out, I may have found her a decent foreman to help run things."

Laurel simply nodded, not knowing what else to say. Guiding her horse alongside his, she rode in silence for a while. Finally Laurel said, "Will you tell Becky for me how sorry I am about Jim?"

Brandon shot her a quick, assessing look. "You can tell her yourself at the harvest festival Saturday," he commented. "I told her we would meet her there."

Laurel looked away from him, her long lashes hiding the hurt and confusion in her eyes.

"Laurel, look at me," Brandon said. When she did not respond, he reached out for her reins, drawing both horses to a halt. Vaulting from his mount, he pulled her down to stand beside him.

As she still refused to meet his look, he tipped her jaw up with his fingers, frowning as he caught sight of the tears shimmering in her soft lilac eyes. "Laurel, honey, don't cry," he said softly, kissing each eyelid with infinite tenderness.

With a frustrated sigh, he asked, "Is it too much to ask that you be Becky's friend? She's going through a rough time right now, and she needs all the help and friendship she can get."

"Oh, Brandon! You make me sound so selfish! I don't know what to do! Truly, I feel sorry for Becky, losing Jim that way, but . . ."

Laurel did not know how to make him understand that she was afraid of losing him to Becky again—that she did not want her father to be right—that she feared she would end up nursing the same broken heart she had barely salvaged before.

"But what?" he urged.

"Aren't you spending an awful lot of time with her?" Laurel blurted out. "Everyone is wondering what is going on, Brandon."

His eyes widened at her distressed tone of voice. "Laurel Burke! You're jealous!" he exclaimed.

"I am not!" she snapped defensively.

"You are!"

"All right, I am!" she confessed heatedly, "but I think I have a right to be."

Brandon laughed down at her. "You may have a right, but you have no reason." His face sobered in remembrance of Jim's death. "I promised Jim that I would take care of Becky and the children. There is no way I will break that promise I gave to my dying friend, Laurel."

Looking up at him with sorrowful eyes, she answered softly, "I wouldn't want you to, Brandon —but are you sure you aren't using that as a convenient excuse to see Becky and be near her? Are you just fooling yourself, and me, when you're really in love with Becky—just waiting for her to recover from Jim's death and decide she wants you, too?"

He looked down at her with a steady, solemn gaze. "Laurel, my little silver Moonbeam, when are you going to believe me? It's *you* I love; you I want."

With his arms tightly about her, he pressed her body against the lean length of him. Through their clothing, she could feel the proof of his desire burning between them. "Can't you feel how much I need you?" he whispered into her hair.

Her head fell back under the insistent pull of his hand, as his fingers delved into her upswept hair, scattering pins everywhere as it tumbled down her back in tangled waves of silver satin.

"I've wanted to do that for months," he confessed huskily, his lips grazing her throat just below her ear.

Laurel's heart was beating within her chest like a captive bird. She wound trembling fingers into the wavy darkness of Brandon's hair, forcing his mouth to hers as she raised up on tiptoe to offer him her parted lips.

Warm, firm lips plied hers with skilled precision, testing, moistening, sucking at hers. His tongue traced the contours of her tingling mouth, then delved inside for a taste of honey. Tentatively, her tongue teased his, and his low groan of desire enhanced her pleasure. Laurel was dizzy with delicious desire. A tingling fire danced along her flesh and through her blood, making her skin more sensitive to his touch than she could ever have imagined. His hands caressed the length of her spine, molding her more closely to him. When his palm came about to cradle one breast, she shivered in anticipation, helplessly arching into his touch.

By her reaction, Laurel was unconsciously encouraging him to continue, but she was too caught up in strange and glorious emotions to care whether it was right or wrong. She only knew she wanted more; more of Brandon. Through the thin covering of her blouse, the brush of his thumb across her enlarged nipple was like a shock wave, and she gasped as she felt a jolt of white hot lightning flash through her, leaving a liquid heat in her loins and an empty yearning in her belly.

"Brandon, oh, Brandon," she moaned against his lips, and her words were a plea that he could not resist. When he lifted her into his arms, carrying her to a shaded spot away from the horses, Laurel did not resist. Even as he laid her on the ground, she clung to him, showering his neck and face with quick, hot kisses.

For just a moment, Brandon paused, sanity reasserting itself. He knew he should call a halt while he still could. But a tiny voice seemed to whisper in his ear, suggesting that Laurel would have to marry him after this, and Brandon, too, was lost. He had wanted her too badly for too long. He had to make her his by foul means or fair. As his lips touched hers once more, he surrendered to the sweet temptation of her yielding innocence.

His lips took on an insistent mastery of hers, making her blood sing in her veins; his hands caressed her body, until they could not resist touching her skin. With unsteady fingers, he unbuttoned her blouse, and held the warmth of her bared breasts in his hands.

As if beyond her control, Laurel's hands reached out to tug at his shirt front, baring his furred chest to her touch. With a sense of awe, she ran her fingers through the mat of dark hair, the soft curls tickling her palms deliciously.

His lips slipped from hers, to nibble a path along her neck to her ear where his tongue traced the delicate shell, making her shiver in delight. "Oh, Brandon, what are you doing to me?" she sighed in wonder.

Tracing a path of tingling kisses along the sensitive hollow of her shoulder and along her collarbone, he murmured fervently, "Laurel—honey— let me love you, dearest. Let me taste your sweetness . . ."

She was beyond answering, as his warm mouth captured a tender breast, his teeth gently grazing the nipple, his tongue laving it. Half mad with the pleasure coursing through her, she clung to him, her head spinning dizzily, her body turned to flame. Her hands roamed his broad, bare back, then came up to hold his head to her breast, loath to give up the forbidden delight his touch was creating within her.

He lay half over her, his leg thrown across hers, his arousal branding into her thigh where her riding skirt had bunched up to reveal long, shapely legs. His hand caressed in long, smooth strokes the sensitive silk of her inner thigh, his thumb tracing hot patterns on her skin there. Laurel had never been so mesmerized by pleasure.

It was not until she felt his fingers loosening the waistband of her skirt that she stiffened in resistance. "No, Brandon," she murmured, her lips moving against the warm skin of his shoulder. "We mustn't . . ."

Groaning with the force of his own passion, he whispered, "Yes, Laurel. Please! Let me show you how wonderful love can be." His mouth left her breast to cover her quivering lips, stilling her protests, as his hands quickly removed her skirt and undergarments. Somehow he even managed to remove her boots, his enchanting mouth creating havoc as he showered kisses across her quivering belly.

With eyes as hot and bright as quicksilver, he surveyed her nude, perfectly-formed body. "You are so beautiful, my love," he said reverently. As his hypnotic gaze met hers, Laurel could not resist. Neither could she move to cover herself or keep from watching him as he rose to dispose of his own clothing.

When he again lowered himself to her side, his hot flesh seemed to sear into hers. With shaking hands, she explored the warm, vibrant contours of his body, so different from hers, yet so enticing and beautifully formed to complement her own. Trembling with awakened curiosity and quickening desire, she touched her mouth lightly to the salty skin of his neck, his shoulder, his muscled chest, her tongue flicking out to shyly taste the texture and flavor of his male body.

Brandon's eyes closed, his hands tangling in the silver-blonde waves of her hair, as he bit back a groan. "Yes, love," he whispered huskily. "Touch me—feel what you are doing to me."

A heady feeling of her own feminine power came over her as she felt his heart race beneath her lips, his muscles tremble at her untaught touch. In her turn, she quivered beneath him, her breath caught in her throat as his lips and hands brought her body to life as it had never been before—as she had never dreamed it could be. His hot, moist mouth was everywhere—on her lips, her shoulders; capturing each aching breast in turn; skittering down the soft, sensitive flesh of her stomach, making her muscles tighten in alarm and desire; burning into her very soul.

Once again, she stiffened in alarm as his seeking hand slid up her thigh, finding and cupping her femininity, tenderly caressing where no man had touched before. Resistance melted under his touch as new waves of passion drowned her senses, urging her to arch into his hand and the wondrous rapture engulfing her. Small, strangled moans escaped her throat, and she was awash in a wild new world of sensation. A burning heat flamed through her, making her ache for him, melting her body into his, creating a hollow yearning only he could assuage.

His fingers teased and tantalized until she was mindless in her need of him, and when he slid over her, his hard masculinity prodding for entrance into her moist body, she willed him to take her, to make her totally his.

As her flesh gave way to his, she had a moment of panic. Gentle as he was, there was no way to ease the sudden hurt as her maidenhood gave way to his insistence.

"Easy, love," Brandon soothed, his lips capturing her gasp of pain and surprise. "Relax, honey, and the pain will soon be pleasure again, I promise." With soothing caresses and words of love, he enticed her to relax in his embrace, holding back until he felt her begin to respond to him once more.

With easy, measured strokes, he began to move within her, his silver gaze capturing her wide violet eyes, watching as her fear turned to wonder, until her lashes fluttered down to feather softly against her flushed cheeks.

She felt filled with him—body, heart, and soul. Just when she was sure she could hold no more joy within her, a new yearning, strong and urgent, began to spiral through her. Clutching at his shoulders, her fingers dug into his muscled back; her hips undulated to the demanding rhythm in her blood, moving to match his. Under his tutelage, and with the guidance of his hands beneath her hips, she surrendered to the primitive urgency building within her. Tighter and tighter, it bound her within its grasp, her breath coming in short gasps as she strove for some unknown, beckoning summit just beyond her grasp. Then, suddenly, she was there, her world exploding in spectacular wonder about her, as her body shattered in spasms of rapture, her glad cries of ecstasy joined by Brandon's, as he joined her in a magnificent splendor that was theirs alone.

Spent and breathless, Laurel could only marvel at the wonders she had just experienced. A sense of awe held her spellbound, her body utterly and bonelessly relaxed beneath Brandon's.

"Sweet, sweet Laurel," Brandon sighed, as she shyly brushed the damp, brown hair from his forehead. Raising his head, he gazed deeply into her eyes, silver and lavender meeting in a soft loving look. "You are everything I've always dreamed you would be—my magical moonbeam, my silver-haired angel."

A slight frown etched his brow as he studied her face. "You're not sorry you gave yourself to me, are you?" he asked.

"Oh, Brandon," she sighed, her face aglow with her love for him. "How could I regret sharing such glory? I never dreamed being a woman brought such wonder and beauty with it!"

"*My* woman," Brandon corrected gently but firmly. "You are mine now, Laurel, and I'll never let you go. Say you'll marry me, love."

"Yes, yes," she whispered softly, her lips reaching for his. "I love you so much, my darling." Her hands cradled his head and he kissed her again, passionately, thoroughly.

Though she had agreed to marry him, Laurel still wanted to wait a while longer. "We have to give my father time to adjust to the idea, and I would rather break it to him in stages than shock him with it all at once. You know he's going to have a royal fit!"

Brandon wanted to roar in frustration. "Laurel, I've waited more than two and a half years as it is! Rex hated the idea then and he'll hate it now. In fact, he'll always object to me simply because my name is Prescott. If you are waiting for the two of us to miraculously become friends, you are dreaming. It will never happen. He despises me, and I feel the same about him. I wish to God you were anyone's daughter but his!"

Hurt by his attitude, Laurel was nonetheless determined. "I have to at least try to make him understand, Brandon. He is my father; he has loved and cared for me all these years, and I love him. I don't want to hurt him if I can help it. He'll feel so betrayed and deserted!"

"Damn it, Laurel!" Brandon exploded angrily, his eyes blazing into hers. "You act like he is a god! The man has lied to you and decieved you, yet you feel you must appease him!"

Laurel stood her ground. "He raised me, and he deserves my respect," she said evenly. "I can't just break his heart and walk away."

"How long?" Brandon demanded stonily. "How long before you tell him?"

"Soon, Brandon. I promise." Laurel gazed up at him with soft lavender eyes, and he felt his anger dissipating.

"It had better be," he said gruffly, pulling her hard against him, his lips claiming hers hungrily. "I can't wait forever."

Martha was worried and very much concerned. Laurel had been seeing Brandon Prescott steadily for several weeks now. He had escorted her to the harvest festival, confusing everyone by inviting Becky Lawson and her children as well and carrying young Tad on his shoulders when the child got tired. Laurel had worn a look of quiet acceptance on her face that day, but had refused to talk to Martha about it later.

In fact, Laurel rarely confided in her aunt at all these days, and Martha suspected she knew the reason why, though she prayed she was wrong. A luminous inner glow radiated from Laurel lately. Her eyes sparkled like gems, her smile was wondrous, as if she had discovered the secrets of the universe—as if she had a lover.

Martha saw the signs, and sighed in despair. Rex was in a perpetually black mood, constantly blustering at his daughter for being a fool as she continued to accept Brandon's invitations. Each time Brandon came to take Laurel out, Rex nearly exploded. Though Laurel had tried several times to talk reasonably with her father about the situation, Rex always cut her off, refusing to discuss the matter and stamping angrily out of the room.

To confound matters, while Brandon seemed to be courting Laurel, he also spent a great deal of time with Becky Lawson. Martha could see the hurt and confusion in Laurel's face at times, and she longed to comfort the girl. If Laurel knew the full extent of the deception Martha and Rex had practiced years before, perhaps she would not be so miserable now, for Martha could see how much in love Laurel was. Her heart ached for her niece, and her conscience was a heavy burden on her these days.

As the days and weeks sped by, Laurel was having no more success with her father than ever. While he could not prevent her seeing Brandon, since Laurel had inherited the Burke stubbornness, he resented the fact and did nothing to hide his annoyance from her. At every opportunity, he pointed out how often Brandon was seen at the Lawsons', even suggesting that Brandon must be forcing the young widow to pay for the repairs made there.

Laurel did her best to convince her father that Brandon was not the ogre Rex considered him to be and to try to get him to soften in his attitude toward Brandon. When she suggested she and Brandon might marry, Rex flew into a rage that shook the rafters and lasted for days, threatening disinheritance, incarceration in a convent, and anything else he could think of. With a sinking heart, Laurel despaired of ever getting Rex to accept Brandon, let alone condone their marriage. Caught between the two men she loved most in the world, she did not know what to do next.

In the midst of it all, Laurel worried that Brandon would get tired of waiting and propose to Becky after all. Try as she might, she could not quite convince herself that Brandon did not care for the lovely widow, and she could sense Brandon's impatience as time dragged on, with

Laurel still hesitant to set a date for the wedding.

Brandon was indeed beginning to doubt that Laurel would ever defy her father and marry him, though he could not doubt the strength of the passion they had shared. Each time he saw her, his body burned for hers, remembering their afternoon of love. It was with great effort that he maintained a proper public demeanor as he escorted her to church socials, parties, and neighboring barbecues. Always in the back of his mind he was recalling the satin textures of her skin, the fire of her nude form in his arms, her cries of ecstasy.

The waiting was telling on Laurel, too, so it was not too hard for Brandon to convince her to meet him secretly. Before long, they were meeting regularly, neither able to stay away from the other for long. Innocent afternoon rides on her mare turned into long, lazy hours in Brandon's arms. Picnics with friends often found the two of them wandering off for a while by themselves. More and more, they intentionally left gatherings early, giving themselves time to make love and still get Laurel home at an acceptable hour.

One afternoon, after getting caught in a rainstorm, they took shelter in a line shack where they shed their wet clothing and lay skin to skin on the narrow, lumpy bunk while Brandon made luxurious, beautiful love to her. With her rapturous sighs in his ears, and her silken limbs entangled with his, he took his fill of her. Laurel was sure they had never before reached such glorious heights. Afterward, for a time, she was content to lie warm and sleepy in his arms.

"It is nice to have time to spend with you for a change, instead of having to worry about the hour or who might discover us," she commented lazily.

"No one will expect me back until the rain lets up."

"It could always be like this, if we were married. Laurel, I'm tired of hiding our love, of ducking around corners for a quick kiss." His frown reflected his discontent.

Laurel put a tentative hand on the muscles of his arm. "Dad has to give in sooner or later," she soothed.

Brandon's eyes suddenly speared hers, anger and impatience making them glitter like diamonds. "What if it's *later*, Laurel? Have you give any thought to the consequences of our hidden trysts? What if you're already carrying my child? Have you thought of that?"

Her huge amethyst eyes and pale face told him she hadn't. "Think about it, Laurel," he advised harshly. "Think good and hard before you let your father ruin our lives—and the life of our son or daughter!"

The fact that Burke still persisted in rustling his cattle made Brandon's temper flare even further. At least Becky's cattle were no longer a target, if that was any consolation. Maybe the man had a spark of conscience in him. It would take a hard, cold man to have a woman's husband killed and then continue to steal from the poor widow. Brandon never told Becky how much of his own money went into running the ranch, and luckily, she never asked about such things. Brandon considered it part of his promise to Jim, and heaven knew, he'd never miss the money. He could afford to help out until Becky decided to remarry.

Having her monthly flow on schedule, Laurel

was at least relieved of one worry for the time being. However, there was plenty else to keep her mind in turmoil; Brandon's persistant demand for marriage, their continued secret affair, Rex's adamant rejection of Brandon, Becky's constant need of Brandon's aid. Added to his, Aunt Martha was giving her some extremely speculative looks these days, as if she knew what was going on behind Rex's back.

"I think Aunt Martha suspects about us, Brandon," she told him apprehensively. "When I went home after the storm, she noticed the rumpled state of my clothes, and my straggling hair. I got the impression she was implying much more than she said, and she didn't believe that getting caught in the rain caused all that damage."

"She'd have to be blind not to have noticed something by now," he told her. "I'm surprised your father hasn't realized it yet."

Laurel's face crumpled in distress. "He's too caught up in his anger and hatred to notice how anyone else feels. Oh, Brandon! I love you so much, but I feel so *torn* right now!"

Not giving him the chance to respond with his usual demands, she threw herself into his arms, her lips seeking his with a demand of her own. "Hold me, Brandon. Love me, please!"

Delighted by her open, fervent passion, Brandon shelved his ready arguments in favor of making sweet love. His lips found hers, hot and hungry, and demanding every ounce of sweetness from her. She gave willingly, her lips clinging to his, and parting to admit the seeking thrust of his tongue. Understanding his need to dominate her at this time when she was stubbornly making him accede to her wishes for more time before marriage, she readily surrendered to him now. Here, in the strength of his arms, she felt strangely weak, powered only by his wishes and commands, wishing only to give back to him the pleasure she received. His firm, warm lips, his long lean fingers put heaven at her doorstep. She had only to return his heated caresses and demanding kisses to cross the threshold into rapture's realm. This she did gladly, falling under the spell of his deep, velvety voice whispering words of love for her alone, engulfed by the fires he lit within her—flames only he could ignite or extinguish. As he took her, she gazed into his blazing, mesmerizing eyes and knew she was eternally his.

But Brandon also had other, more devious thoughts racing through his mind as he held her afterward. When Laurel had told him she was not with child, he had been both relieved and disappointed. If she conceived, she would have to marry him with no more delay, or he would have to find another way to convince her, for he was fast running out of patience. He wanted to claim her openly and proudly as his wife, and Rex be damned! November was just around the corner, and Brandon had already spent six months since Laurel's return to Crystal City trying to make her his. Partial success—the claim of her passionate body—was not enough for him. He wanted it all; her love, her loyalty, her full commitment.

Now Brandon and Laurel splashed and swam in the cool water of the creek, a pleasant, if chilly, way to wash and revive after their steamy lovemaking. Bright, moonlight-colored strands of hair floated out behind her, catching stray rays of sun through the trees. Her lavender eyes were soft with satisfaction and love and Brandon thought he had never seen her so lovely as now, her pale skin shining wet, her face aglow with laughter.

So entranced were they with one another that they failed to hear the riders approach. Not until Laurel glanced up to see six onyx pairs of eyes staring from lean bronze faces was their idyllic interlude destroyed with a jolt. Her strangled, frantic scream alerted Brandon to the intruders, and after one quick look at Laurel's terrified face, he spun to face them.

Relief and caution mixed as Brandon recognized the men. Warily, he noted their extreme interest in Laurel, though he was not surprised by it. Showing no alarm, Brandon said quietly, "Laurel, stay down in the water and be still. Everything is alright. You don't need to be frightened."

His voice soothed her somewhat, but Laurel was shaking as she did as he commanded, her wide, frightened gaze never leaving the six men at the water's edge.

Regardless of his nudity, Brandon strode from the water, steadily approaching their visitors. If he was nervous, it did not show.

With much surprise, Laurel heard him speak quietly in greeting. "Hello, Red Feather. I was wondering when you would come by."

The Indian eyed him solemnly. "Greetings, Prescott. Your brother told us we would find you here. He said you would tell us which of the cattle will be ours to take."

"You may select any six you want from the herd in the south pasture. Just latch the gate when you leave."

Red Feather's eyes flickered to the girl in the water. "Would you consider a trade for the woman with the winter hair?"

At Laurel's muffled shriek, Brandon nearly smiled, but managed to keep a straight face as he shook his head. "No, Red Feather. She is mine to keep. Besides, she would not please you. While she is lovely to look upon, she is stubborn and willful, and her cooking is terrible." Brandon struggled to keep his lips from twitching, feeling Laurel's rising anger from where he stood.

"Then why not exchange her for a better one?" the Indian suggested.

"I think in time she will make a decent wife, and provide me with strong sons. And since I already have a cook at the ranch, I need not eat what she prepares."

The Indian gave a philosophical shrug and accepted Brandon's explanation. "If you change your mind, let me know. If not, we will be back next year."

Brandon watched as the Indians rode away. Finally, he turned to meet Laurel's furious glare.

"How *dare* you say those things about me, Brandon!" she demanded.

"Would you rather I traded you to them?" he asked with a devilish glint in his eyes and a grin to match. "It's not too late to catch them."

"*No!*" she shrieked in renewed alarm, cringing back into the water.

He threw his dark head back, laughing heartily. "Laurel, honey, I was just trying to dampen their interest in you. You needn't be so offended." He offered her his hand. "Come on out of the water now. Your lips are turning blue."

"Is it safe?" She darted a quick, anxious look about her.

"Of course. They are after their cattle, and they've probably lost all interest in you by now."

Wounded vanity flared anew, but she suppressed it. "Who are they? What are they doing off the reservation?"

"They've come every year for as long as I can

remember—they or their relatives," Brandon explained, as he dried and warmed her with his shirt. "Dad told me it's easier to give them a few cattle each year to see them through the winter than to have them sneaking about stealing them at will."

"I've never heard of such a thing!" she countered in amazement.

With Rex for a father, Brandon was not surprised. "It's an easy compromise, and it promotes good will. At any rate, I feel better knowing their women and children are fed."

Laurel's heart swelled with pride in him. He was such a good, decent man! Something he'd said to Red Feather came back to her.

"Do you really think I'll give you strong sons?" she asked shyly, looking up at him through her lashes.

Brandon grinned. "You'd better, or I just might reconsider and trade you off to Red Feather after all," he threatened, gathering her slim form into his strong arms.

Laurel's arms went readily about his neck, her fingers delving into his thick hair. "No you wouldn't," she whispered, tugging his head down to hers.

"No, I wouldn't," he agreed, his breath warming her lips, his teeth teasing at the edges of her lush mouth. "Not in a million years!"

CHAPTER 7

A few days later, Brandon came by to take Laurel to dinner in town. As Laurel was not quite ready when he arrived, she was thankful that Rex had left earlier, saying something about a business meeting in Crystal City.

When she finally joined Brandon in the parlor, her beauty nearly stole his breath, sending a raw yearning coursing through him. Her purple dress, trimmed in lavender lace on the bodice, sleeves, and skirt, accented her sparkling amethyst eyes to perfection, making Brandon feel he could drown in their depths. Her shining, silver-blonde hair was swept softly away from her face, gently framing it, and caught up at the crown in a loose knot of curls. She looked totally feminine, all satin and lace, soft and shining and vulnerable, striking Brandon with a fierce need to possess and protect her, to put his strength between her and the world so that nothing would ever harm her.

As Brandon's heated gaze was silently complimenting her, Laurel, too, was busy appreciating Brandon's appearance. He wore brown pants and jacket, the color nearly matching his sun-streaked brown hair. A snowy white shirt was visible above a gold and brown brocade vest, a string tie carefully secured with a gold clasp. His wavy hair, usually so unruly, was brushed into submission, except for one untamed lock in front which insisted upon falling across his broad forehead just above his brilliant eyes.

Martha voiced their thoughts aloud when she sighed in admiration, "My, my! Aren't you a handsome couple this evening!" Even though she suspected they were already lovers, and knew her brother's adamant hatred of the Prescott's, Martha could not help but admire the way they looked together. It was plain to see they loved one another desperately, and Martha could not find it in her heart to condemn them. She found herself warming to Brandon more and more, if only because she was sure he loved Laurel, and Laurel was the person most dear to her heart.

She prayed they would find a way to work things out, even if Rex were to be hurt in the process. Martha loved her brother, but there were times she wished she could shake some sense into his thick skull. It was time to bury long-held prejudices and lay aside suspicion and hatred. Carried to this extreme, stubbornness became blindness, protectiveness smothered those you loved most, and your own vindictiveness ate at your soul. If Rex were to keep his daughter's love and respect, he was going to have to soften his attitude soon, or he risked losing her altogether.

Brandon took Laurel to the finest dining room in the best hotel Crystal City had to offer. Though they had been here before, tonight seemed special for some reason. The crystal shone brightly and china and silver reflected the dim candlelight of the single candle in the center of the small, intimate table. In their secluded corner, the room seemed completely private, only low murmurings to be heard from the other tables. There was an aura of romance enveloping them, heightened by their sense of intimacy, the flickering candlelight, and the single red rose Laurel found beside her plate.

Gently touching the delicate petals of the crimson rosebud, Laurel's gaze locked with his. "Oh, Brandon, it is so beautiful, and so perfect."

"Not nearly as beautiful as you, love," he responded softly. "If I could have gotten some mountain laurel, I think it would have been more appropriate to your nature. I've always thought your name fit you so perfectly—a mountain flower, so delicate and deceptively fragile, growing wild, its fragrant white flowers kissed with sunlight, caressed by gentle rains and soft breezes."

His tender words and the love shining from his eyes made her love him all the more, if it were possible to do so. The meal consisted of steak, fluffy rice, tender green beans with baby mushrooms, and stewed tomatoes, with Laurel's favorite lemon pudding for dessert. Brandon had ordered wine with their meal, and her glass was never empty, though she was careful not to drink too much. There was no need, for she was drunk on her love for him, on the romantic aura surrounding them, on the sight and sound of him alone.

Once the table was cleared, they sat talking quietly, gazing ardently at one another over the rims of their wineglasses, letting their love and longing grow and build. When the moment was right, Brandon drew a small box from his pocket, holding it out to her as he opened the lid. Inside, on a bed of blue velvet, lay a ring—one beautiful perfect, lustrous pearl surrounded by tiny amethysts.

At her stunned look, he took her hand, sliding the ring on the third finger of her left hand. "Your engagement ring, Laurel," he said softly. "I would have given it to you sooner, but I had to order it specially. Do you like it?"

Her eyes shining as brightly as the stones in the ring, her hand clasped his tightly. "I adore it," she said breathlessly. "Oh, Brandon, I love you so!"

"Then tell me when you will marry me," he urged, his silver gaze scanning her delicate features, willing the answer he sought. "Let's set a date and announce it."

Small white teeth nibbled nervously at her lower lip as she frowned slightly. "Please, Brandon," she pleaded. "Not just yet. Give me just a little longer to bring Dad around. Let him get used to the fact of our engagement for a while."

A short, humorless laugh barked from his throat. "And how long will that take? Another six months? How about a little concern for ourselves once in a while? Either you are going to be my wife, or you are not! Which is it?"

"I want to marry you, Brandon," she sighed. "I've always wanted that, but I want my father's blessing, too, if possible."

"And if it's not possible?" Brandon's voice was edged with impatience.

"Then I'll marry you regardless," Laurel conceded softly, her eyes begging him to under-stand.

Running a hand through his hair in frustration, Brandon answered wearily, "Just don't take too much longer, Laurel. My patience is wearing thin. I can't stand this in-between state of waiting much longer, especially when it is so unnecessary and fruitless. Your father is never going to consent, and we both know it. The longer you put me off, the more I'm beginning to believe you really don't want to marry me, and if that's the case, there are plenty of women who would be more than glad to trade places with you. They wouldn't hesitate to accept my proposal.''

A wounded look clouded her eyes, and if Brandon had not been so hurt himself, he would have berated himself for putting it there. As it was, he was at the point of trying anything to get Laurel to commit herself. If she doubted her hold on him, perhaps she would stop hesitating.

Sitting across from him, the weight of her engagement ring so new on her finger, Laurel was again assailed with uncertainty. Was he talking about Becky? How long could she afford to wait, trying in vain to convince her stubborn father, and all the while risking the loss of Brandon's love? Laurel knew she must do something soon, even if Rex never spoke to her again, even if he threw her out and refused to ever see her. She had lost Brandon once—she could not bear to lose him again.

Time was running out! Laurel could sense it, and it sent a sick panic through her. It was this terrified despair that finally prompted Martha to talk to her.

Entering Laurel's bedroom just as the girl was about to retire to another long night of worry and fretful dreams, Martha sat on the edge of the bed. A sad, resigned look on her face, she patted the space next to her. "Sit with me, Laurel," she urged quietly.

When Laurel complied, she took the young woman's hand in hers, gazing down at the engagement ring that had rested proudly there for the last week. "You love him awfully, don't you, dear?" Martha asked at last, raising her head to look into Laurel's flushed face.

"Yes, I do, Aunt Martha," Laurel admitted without hesitation. "I love him more than I've ever thought possible—with my whole heart. I just wish Dad could accept it."

Martha shook her head. "If that's what you are waiting for, you'll have a long wait, and if my guess is right, Brandon is already impatient. Am I right?"

Laurel nodded, a frown knitting her brow, worry darkening her eyes to violet. "Brandon wants us to marry soon, and I am afraid I'll lose him if I wait much longer. Oh, Aunt Martha! I don't want to hurt Dad, but I couldn't bear to lose Brandon a second time! What should I do?"

Martha gave a troubled sigh. "Honey, you never lost him the first time," she murmured at last. At Laurel's questioning look, she steeled herself and went on. "Your father lied to you, Laurel, and I backed him up on those lies."

"No," Laurel said, shaking her head in confusion. "No. I saw Brandon and Becky together myself."

"Oh, Laurel." Martha pulled the girl into her arms, holding Laurel to her as if she were still a child. "That was just a stroke of fate that day, and with Rex's suggestion fresh in your mind—and mine—you were ready to believe the worst. Brandon never was interested in Becky other than as a friend."

"But then why did he leave Crystal City just before Becky and Jim got married?"

"You've got your facts wrong. Brandon left

town after Rex told him you had gone East to
marry the son of an old family friend, an engagement arranged some years ago. Brandon left,
thinking you had been deliberately deceiving him
all along—that you had been playing with him,
practicing your wiles on him in preparation for
your husband. I think it devastated him, and when
he returned, he was a different man—harder,
colder, keeping to himself a lot more, as if the joy
was gone out of him."

Laurel listened in stunned disbelief. She didn't
know what to think, and words tumbled off her
tongue. "Then Brandon *did* love me! He thought I
had played him for a fool, just as I thought the
same of him?" Her eyes begged Martha for confir-
mation.

Martha nodded sadly. "Your father hated the
idea of you and Brandon together. He detested the
Prescotts so much that he lied to both of you, and
convinced me to do the same."

Pain-filled lavender eyes condemned her, as
Laurel accused, "You sent me away! You packed
my clothes and put me on that train! Both of you!"
She pulled out of Martha's embrace to sit stiffly
erect, resentment straightening her spine.

"I know," Martha sighed. "Your father thought
it was best for you, and I went along with him. I
am as much to blame as he is. I'm so sorry, Laurel.
You've always been like my own child, and I'd
never deliberately hurt you. Please believe that
what I did, I did to protect you, as your father did.
You are his only child, and he adores you."

"Yet you sent me away, knowing my heart was
breaking—not caring that Brandon was hurting,
too!" Laurel cried, tears steaming down her face.
"How could you! How *could* you?"

"Dearest, I can only apologize for all the pain we caused you, and ask that you try to find it in your heart to forgive us."

"Why are you telling me all this now?"

Tears dampened Martha's cheeks, too, and her lips quivered as she answered, "I have come to see that what your father and I did was a mistake. It was wrong, Laurel. You and Brandon belong together, for neither of you are happy apart. Your uncle and I once shared the kind of love you and Brandon have, and it was glorious. I cannot deny you the same joy. Rex is blind to this, and I can see nothing that will change his attitude. Don't wait for his blessing, Laurel. Don't hurt yourself and Brandon further by trying to spare your father. It is not worth the price you would have to pay."

Laurel's face was stiff with righteous anger and hurt. "I have already paid with two and a half years of my life, as has Brandon. All that time wasted! All the heartache and tears! All caused by one man's vindictiveness!"

"Laurel, your father loves you," Martha repeated. "So do I. Rex did what he thought was best for you at the time. Please try to understand that, honey. He was trying to spare you the heartaches and unhappiness he was afraid you would find with Brandon."

"He is still trying to keep Brandon and me apart, Aunt Martha! How can Dad be so stubborn and self-righteous, so angry and petulant, when *he* is the one who has been deceitful and dishonest with me all along? If *you* can see that Brandon and I belong together, why can't Dad accept it? Oh, why does it have to be this way?" she wailed. "Right now, this minute, I want to hate both of you!"

"Please don't feel that way, baby!" Martha begged, holding out her arms to the distraught girl. "I know we deserve it, but please don't hate us."

Laurel fell into her aunt's arms, weeping uncontrollably now. "I can't hate you, Aunt Martha," she choked, "or Dad either. I'm hurt, and I am angry, and I am confused—and I don't really know how long it will take me to forgive you for this, but I don't hate you. You are all the family I've got, and I have loved you too long for that, but Lord knows, it will be a long time before this wound heals, especially considering Dad's obnoxious behavior."

"He still thinks he is right, honey," Martha explained tearfully. "Your Dad feels he knows what is best for you, and Brandon is not it!"

Laurel's chin came up stubbornly. "Then it is up to me to change his mind for him and prove him wrong." The light of challenge glimmered in her lilac eyes.

"Then you are going to marry Brandon?" Martha asked.

"I've meant to all along," Laurel replied, "but now I mean to set Dad straight on a few things first. It is time he learned that his little Laurel is a woman, with a mind and will of her own, not a child to be manipulated by his whims!"

Martha's eyes widened in sudden understanding, and she shook her head negatively. "If you think you are going to force his approval, you'd better think again, dearest. You will only succeed in making him even more angry and set in his course."

Martha was right. When Laurel stormed up to

her father the next day, castigating him for his deceit, the feathers flew. Their angry words and Rex's shouts of rage were heard throughout the house, and halfway to the barn.

"I am going to marry Brandon, so you'd best get used to the idea!" Laurel declared toward the end.

"You'll be no daughter of mine if you do!" he countered angrily.

"How you can say you love me, and act this way, I do not know!" Laurel shrieked. "What kind of father denies his only daughter her happiness?"

"Happiness!" he roared. "Prescott will make you so miserable, you'll gladly come crawling home, your head hung low! He only wants to best a Burke! You're a challenge to him that's all! Once he has you, he'll break your heart, girl! You'll be no more than a broken toy that ceases to interest him!"

"You're wrong, Dad," Laurel said heatedly. "Brandon loves me. If all he wanted was to demean me, he had his chance weeks ago, when we first became lovers."

"You *what*?" Rex exploded, his face red with rage. "I'll kill him!"

"Why? He didn't take anything I didn't willingly give," she told him, then added slyly, "are you sure, under the circumstances, you shouldn't make certain Brandon marries me as soon as possible?"

Rex was angry almost beyond speech. "How could you give yourself to that man? I ought to— I mean to—damn it all!" he blustered, his hands clenched into tight fists, one of which he pounded heavily on the table.

Laurel rose, pushing away her untouched breakfast. "Think about it, Dad," she advised curtly. "I won't stop seeing him, and even you must see that marriage is prudent under the circumstances. Chances are, I could even now be carrying his child. Brandon and I *will* marry. I only wish I had your blessing."

"No. *Never!*" Rex declared adamantly.

Laurel sighed and shook her head. "I love you, Dad. I hope, once you've had time to think about it, you will reconsider."

She left him then to think about all she had said, hoping it would have some effect on him. "I'll give him a few days to mull things over, then I'll approach him again," she decided. "Surely he must admit how impossible it would be for me to marry anyone else now! Certainly he will see how wise it would be for him to give in gracefully and accept the inevitable!"

Like a shadow, the dark shape blended into others in the night. Silently, the man raised the bedroom window, slipping unnoticed and unheard into the house. Stealthily, he went from drawer to drawer, removing items and stuffing them in the saddlebags he carried, doing the same in the small, cedar-lined closet. As a floor board creaked beneath his careful tread, he muffled a curse, throwing a quick glance at the sleeping figure on the bed, then continued his looting. Several items he laid aside, and when he was done, he crept toward the bed.

A heavy hand clamped heavily over her mouth prevented Laurel from screaming as she jerked awake. Heart thudding like a drum in her chest, she stared fearfully at the dark shape of the intruder looming over her.

"Ssh, Laurel! It's all right! It's only me!"

Hushed as it was, Laurel recognized his deep voice. Confusion and anger warred in her as she mumbled against his hand, trying to push it away.

"Quiet, girl! Promise you won't scream the house down, and I'll remove my hand."

Laurel nodded, and the instant his hand was gone, she hissed loudly, "For God's sake, Brandon! What are you doing here? You scared twenty years off my life!"

He chuckled softly. "Luckily, with hair your color, no one will ever know!" he taunted. As she started to sputter again, he covered her lips with his, effectively silencing her. The warm demand of his lips on hers, the surprise of finding him here, and her sleep-befuddled state all served to set her senses spinning. Her lips moved pliantly beneath his, accepting and responding immediately.

For the moment, Brandon reveled in the taste and feel of her, forgetting his purpose in waking her. Still warm and flushed from sleep, the aroma of her lilac-scented body and freshly washed hair drifted up to him, and he felt he could gladly drown in her sweetness.

Prying his lips from hers, he whispered, "You smell delicious, but we don't have time for this now."

Reminded of the hour and place, Laurel asked again, "Why are you here?"

Still leaning over her, he sought her features in the darkened room. "I'm leaving for Mexico tonight."

A stifled gasp of dismay escaped her. "You came to say goodbye?" she croaked.

"No, love, I came to take you with me." As he felt her stiffen, he hastened to explain. "Come away with me, Laurel! We'll get married in

Mexico, and then, after I've concluded my business there, we'll have a honeymoon. How does San Francisco sound?"

"Wait!" she interrupted, sitting up and brushing the hair from her face. "Why are you going to Mexico? How long will you be gone?"

He hadn't expected her to agree immediately. Still, her lack of enthusiasm stung. His jaw hardened in agitation. "I'm buying cattle from a friend. How long I am gone depends on you, Laurel."

"I don't understand."

"I've told you I would not wait much longer, honey. Your time is up; my patience is depleted." He paused, making his ultimatum even more dire as he said, "Either you come with me and marry me, or we part now—forever. The choice is yours." He heard her sudden painful intake of breath.

"Brandon, please! Martha confessed to me how she and Dad lied to separate us. I've confronted Dad with his deception, and I truly believe he is near to conceding. Give him a few more days, darling—a week at most—and if he does not see reason by then, we will arrange the wedding anyway."

She felt, more than saw him shake his head. "No, Laurel," he said firmly, his own heart breaking. "Now or never. If I walk away from you tonight, we are through. No more courting, no more kisses, no more sweet loving—nothing."

"Brandon, don't do this!" Her voice was thick with tears. "Please don't throw our love away!"

"Darlin,' as I said, the choice is your. I've packed a saddlebag with some of your belongings I thought you would need. The horses are waiting in the copse, and time is fleeing." He rose from the bed. "Are you coming with me, Laurel?"

"Oh, God!" she cried quietly, her heart aching in her chest. "Brandon, you are not being fair—to me or Dad! Think what you are asking of me!"

Brandon sighed wearily. "I've thought of nothing else for weeks, Laurel, and if anyone is being treated unfairly, I think it is me. I have done everything I can think of, and I've waited longer, with more patience, then you could realistically expect of me. I'm at the end of my rope." When she failed to respond, he started toward the open window. "I'm sorry, Laurel, but I guess this is goodbye, honey." His words were weighted with sorrow.'

He had one leg over the sill when she flew from the bed, hurtling herself toward him. "*Wait!* Oh, please, Brandon, wait!" Throwing her arms about his neck, she sobbed. "I'll go with you! I'll go! Just give me time to dress!"

A deep sign of relief made his chest rise and fall against her. "I've laid your clothes on the chair," he directed. "Hurry."

Her mind in turmoil, Laurel hastened to don the denim trousers, shirt, and boots he'd chosen for the long ride. As she dressed, she wondered to herself what her decision might have been if she had not learned of her father's deceit. It seemed fated that Aunt Martha had chosen now to reveal the truth, thus making it easier for Laurel to flee with Brandon tonight. Aware of Rex's lies, Laurel's conscience was clear, but she hoped her father would one day understand and accept what she was doing. Disappointed as she was in him, resentful of his interference and the hurt he had caused her, Laurel still loved him and wanted peace between herself and the two most important men in her life.

As Brandon helped her climb out the window, Laurel took one last look around the room she'd grown up in. It would never be hers again; yet even as the thought saddened her, she rejoiced in the choice she was making, the love and adventures she and Brandon would share.

"Regrets already?" Brandon murmured in her ear.

"Never, my love; no regrets," she assured him with shining eyes. "I love you, Brandon, and my place is with you, now and always."

As they rode silently away, Laurel did not look back again. Instead, she turned her thoughts ahead to the joys awaiting her as Brandon's wife, and she urged her horse into a trot, eager to begin their life together.

CHAPTER 8

They rode steadily south toward the border,
urging the horses on as fast as they dared in
the dark over unfamiliar terrain. Stopping only
when necessary—once when Laurel needed a coat
to ward off the night chill, and a few times to rest
the horses—they had put a good seven hours ride
between themselves and Crystal City by dawn.
They were well into the foothills when Brandon
finally decided they could stop for awhile.

Laurel heaved a heartfelt sigh of relief as she
slid from the saddle. "Is it really necessary to
hurry so, Brandon?" she asked wearily.

He knew he had pushed her hard on little sleep.
"Sorry, Laurel, but I don't want to chance your
father catching up to us this soon. He'd just as
soon shoot me as look at me."

Laurel sank to her knees on the bedroll Brandon
spread out for her. "I should have left a note for
him and Aunt Martha so they wouldn't worry."
She looked up at him accusingly. "If you had given
me time to think straight, I could have."

'If I had given you more time, you would have
found fifty reasons not to come with me." He
grumbled with a dark frown. "This way, if we are
lucky, you won't be missed until later this

morning. By the time anyone begins to panic, Hank will have spread the word that you and I have eloped. Rex will be mad as a hornet, but we will have enough of a lead that it will be impossible for him to catch up."

"I still regret having to do things this way," Laurel said. "As much as I love you and want to be your wife, I know this will only anger Dad more."

"He'll have to accept it once we're married, Laurel. There won't be anything he can do about it, then." He arranged his bedroll next to hers.

"You'd better get some rest while you can," he suggested more gently. "We can only stop a couple of hours here if we hope to make the border today."

Slanting a look at him through lowered lashes, she said, "Are you afraid Dad will drag me home again if he catches us?"

"Only after he holds an old-fashiond lynching," Brandon drawled, "and I'm partial to breathing at regular intervals!"

It was dark when they passed through Eagle Pass and crossed into Mexico. Bone-weary and saddlesore, Laurel nearly burst into tears when Brandon refused to stop and get rooms at a hotel for the night.

"But, Brandon," she argued, "I am ready to drop! What difference can a few hours in a decent bed make? If anyone *is* following us, they have to rest, too!"

"Obviously you do not put the same faith in your father's reaction as I, or you would know he will ride his horse until it drops in order to find you before you marry me. If we stayed in Eagle Pass, you would be easily recognized, my lovely bride-to-be, and Rex would know he was on the right trail. As it is, I'm hoping to avoid drawing attention to ourselves—unless you've been dropping a trail of bread crumbs for him to follow."

Tired as she was, his reference to the fairy tale of Hansel and Gretel made her giggle. "Just protect me from any wicked witches, and don't start treating me like your sister, and I promise to try to stay in the saddle, awake or not."

"Honey, the day I start thinking of you as a sister will be the day I have not one drop of red blood left in my veins!" he promised.

It must have been around midnight when they finally stopped for the night.

"We'll camp here until morning," he told her.

Gazing about her at the moonlit mountains looming over them, Laurel shivered in the cool night air. "Are you sure we won't freeze by morning?"

Brandon approached her from behind, wrapping his arms about her waist, his warm breath fanning the hair near her ear. "I'll keep you warm, my lovely Laurel."

She shivered again, but not from the cold this time, and a smile as old as Eve curved her lips.

True to his word, Brandon kept her warm, and even managed to make her forget her aching muscles for a short time. Snuggled down next to him, her head pillowed on his broad shoulder, Laurel sighed blissfully. "Look at the stars, Brandon. They are so bright and clear tonight. I look at them, and I immediately think of your eyes, all silvery and mysterious."

She felt his chuckle vibrate the shoulder

beneath her head. "You're starstruck, darlin'."

"No, I'm just in love with the most devastating man I know." Laurel raised her head to nibble at his collarbone. "You even taste good," she murmured in a voice made sultry by rising passion.

His hands came up to tangle in her hair, loosening it so that it fell in a silver curtain about their faces. "Will I never get enough of you, Laurel?" he groaned. Then his lips captured hers in a searing kiss that set her pulse pounding and her body aching against his once more.

Sunlight pierced her eyelids long before Laurel was ready to face the day. With a groan, she rolled over, trying to find one spot on her tormented body that did not ache. Just as she realized that the warm length of Brandon's body, which had kept her own toasty through the night, was no longer next to hers, the tantalizing aroma of freshly brewed coffee wafted past her nostrils. Prying one eyelid barely open, she saw Brandon's laughing face. He sat on his haunches before her, waving a cupful of the brew beneath her nose, his eyes sparkling with devilment.

"Awake, my beauty, and face the morn. The birds await your stirring before they dare to sing."

Laurel moaned, torn between laughter and despair. "Ugh! How *can* you wax so poetic this early in the day, Brandon! It is absolutely unlawful!"

"Are you always so grumpy in the morning, love?" he teased. "If so, perhaps I'd better reconsider my offer of marriage."

"Help me up from this bed of rock, swear to shoot that bony creature you dare to call a horse,

and I promise my mood will improve," she
retorted.

Brandon laughed. "Up, woman! How dare you
lie abed while I slave over your breakfast!" He
offered her a hand to help her stand, pulling her
into his arms as she found her feet. Several long,
leisurely kisses later, he swatted her on her
bottom and pointed her in the direction of a small,
sparkling stream. "Go wash and wake up. You
have a long ride ahead of you today on that bony
mare you've come to adore so much!"

"Music to my ears!" she muttered, adding,
"which must be the only part of my body left
unbruised!" His warm laughter followed her as
she stumbled toward the stream.

They were riding west now, crossing the mountains in northeastern Mexico, heading toward the
town of Chihuahua. It was there Brandon's friend
lived, the one from whom he was purchasing more
cattle. For two days they wound their way through
mountain passes, over crests, and across valleys,
coming at last to flat land and a small, Mexican
village.

Prior to entering the village, Brandon made
Laurel put on her jacket. "I know it's hot, sweetheart, but it's also prudent. Now, tuck all your
hair up under your hat, keep your eyes lowered
and the brim pulled down—and for heaven's sake,
hunch over!"

"Why the disguise, Brandon? I doubt Daddy will
think to look for us in this tiny, dirty little town.
He probably doesn't even know this place exits."

"I know that, but this is pretty rough territory
around here. Places like this draw all manner of
desperados and bandits hiding out from the law.

It's safer all around for everyone to think you are a boy."

"Then I assume we are not going to be married here," she said, making a wry face. "It really wouldn't look right for you to marry a boy, would it?" She finished tucking her hair into her hat.

"We'll be married when we reach Chihuahua," he told her. "Besides, I doubt this town has seen a priest in a long time."

"Do they at least have a room to rent? I'd sell my soul to sleep in a real bed!"

"We'll see what they have available, but believe me, it won't be anything fancy, and you'll be lucky if you're not sharing it with bedbugs and lice."

Laurel made a face and shivered at the thought.

They rode down the dusty, drab main street, pulling up before the solitary general store. Hitching their horses to the rail, they started into the store, but Brandon stopped her with an arm slung over her shoulder. "L.B., old pal," he muttered, "no one is going to believe for ten seconds that you're a boy if you swing your behind like that when you walk. Take bigger steps, lad, and if you must sway from side to side, try to swagger instead."

"Swagger?" she repeated. "Oh! You mean sort of strut, the way you do?"

Brandon narrowed his eyes at her, trying to decide if Laurel was sincerely innocent in her comment, or teasing him again. Unable to decipher her bland expression, he gave her the benefit of the doubt. "Sort of," he grunted. "Also, don't speak unless necessary, and if you must, then try to lower your voice a bit. You sound too much like a girl."

"Thank you, mister," she growled huskily, then

ruined the effect with a gamine grin. "Should I also learn to roll and smoke cigarettes, or would chewin' and spittin' be more my style?"

Brandon rolled his eyes to the sky and sighed heavily. "Come on, Shorty!" he said, shoving her ahead of him. "Let's load up on supplies and get out of here before you come up with any more wise ideas!"

As luck would have it, there was no hotel in town, and the only rooms for rent were above the cantina. After casting a wary eye at the disreputable clientele, Brandon decided they might be wise to move on, and Laurel heartily agreed. They ate a hot, fairly decent meal, and made a hasty retreat.

Laurel did not draw a full breath until they were two miles down the road. "You certainly didn't exaggerate, Brandon," she finally conceded. "I've never before seen an entire town where soap and razors have apparently been banned!"

"I'll refrain from saying 'I told you so,' " he returned magnanimously.

"And I readily bow to your superior knowledge of such seamy and disgusting places. Neither will I bother to ask how you came to be so familiar with this sordid side of life. I really don't think I would care to know."

He nodded and smiled benignly. "Ignorance is bliss," he agreed, and left it at that.

Just before dark, they crossed a small river, and Brandon told her they would camp here for the night. "If you want a bath, this will be your last opportunity for a few days. Come morning we will be headed into the desert. We'll give ourselves and the horses a good rest here."

Laurel took his advice, though she did pause to

wonder what difference it made to wash her hair and clean up now, when a few hours in the desert would surely undo all her efforts. Her sole reward was feeling fresh and feminine for this one night, and it did feel wonderful!

They bedded down early in preparation for the hard ride ahead. It was in the wee hours of the morning when they were abruptly awakened by the whinny of Laurel's mare. No sooner were they alerted than three intruders stepped into the small clearing.

By the sharp moonlight, Laurel made out the bulky shapes of three men, their guns glinting as they brandished them. As she let out a gasp of alarm, Brandon made a desperate grab for his rifle.

Too late! Fire flashed from the muzzle of one of the bandit's guns. The report sounded in her ears, and Laurel screamed as she saw Brandon draw back hastily. It was several seconds before she was assured he was not hit.

The three desperados advanced a few steps, their leader grinning and shaking his head at them. Thickly accented English revealed his Mexican lineage, as he said, "*Por favor,* do not try that again, *señor,* unless you wish to die." His teeth gleamed wickedly beneath his flowing mustache. His companions laughed with him over some private joke, and Laurel was sure they meant to kill them anyway.

As their gaze turned to her, Laurel thought she would die with fright. Heart pounding madly in her throat, lips trembling violently, a frightened whimper escaped her. Paralysis seemed to have attacked her weakened limbs, and all she could do was quake beneath the blanket. As she stared with wide violet eyes, the men seemed to leer and loom closer, lust boldly imprinted on their dark faces.

The leader took another step closer, and Laurel's fright-induced paralysis vanished as quickly as it had come. Without conscious thought, she leaped from the bedroll. Clad only in one of Brandon's shirts which served as her night dress, she scrambled on hands and knees the few feet to Brandon's gunbelt. In a flash of jerky, uncoordinated movements, she was on her feet, the pistol in her shaking hands.

As she faced their attackers, she noted their wary amusement. Here she stood, one small frightened girl against three armed men, who still had their weapons leveled on her and Brandon. Half-crouched, she faced them, the Colt held in both tembling hands.

"What you theenk you gonna do weeth that gun, *señorita?*" the lead bandit taunted. "One wrong move, and your man, he dies."

He made a step forward, and Laurel shrieked, "Stop! Stay where you are!"

The man did as she said, but held out his hand toward her. "Geeve me the gun, or we keel your man now." To reinforce his threat, he cocked his pistol, training it directly on Brandon.

With a defeated sob, Laurel stepped forward to hand the grinning *bandido* her gun. As she did so, the pistol slipped from her sweat-slickened hands. Reflexively, both she and the man grabbed for the Colt. Laurel's hand closed clumsily about the grip, her fumbling finger somehow finding the trigger and tightening over it.

The explosion was deafening. Suddenly everything was happening at once, making swift impressions on Laurel's stunned mind. Brandon snatched up his rifle, firing unerringly at one of the other bandits. The leader had dropped his own weapon while trying to catch Laurel's, and before he could retrieve it, Brandon dropped him with a second shot. The third man was on his knees in the dirt clutching his chest, where Laurel's errant shot had torn a hole. As she watched with disbelieving eyes, he toppled onto his face, lifeless.

Shock held her frozen for timeless moments. Just minutes before, three menacing strangers had threatened their lives. Now all three lay dead in the dust! Her frantic sob echoed in the night, and the pistol slipped from her numb fingers. Tears blurred her vision as a terrible trembling buckled her knees. Then, mercifully, all went black . . .

Laurel floated upward through the wispy gray mist. As consciousness returned, she heard Brandon's gentle murmurings and felt the cool dampness of a wet cloth touched to her face. Ever so slowly, her eyelids fluttered open, and reality reasserted itself.

Brandon leaned over her, gently wiping the tears from her cheeks, smoothing the damp, silvery hair from her forehead. "Laurel," he crooned. "Wake up, darling."

Memory crashed in on her and Laurel launched herself into Brandon's arms, clinging and crying as she recalled their narrow escape.

"It's all right, honey. It's over. All over. You're safe now," he assured her. Hugging her tightly to him, he said, "Never will I forget how brave you were, Laurel, standing up to those men the way you did. I felt so helpless, and you saved both of us!"

"I wasn't brave, Brandon," she hiccupped, leaning back to gaze up into his beloved face. "I just didn't want to die before I had the chance to live with you as your wife."

"Regardless of your reasoning, I am thankful and proud." He kissed her long and hard. Both were aware of how close they had come to losing one another. When finally they pulled apart, Brandon said, "Let's break camp and get out of here. The sun will be rising in a couple of hours anyway, and I doubt either of us could sleep again tonight."

Laurel nodded vigorously, a shiver running up her backbone. "Are they all dead?" she whispered.

"Yes."

"I'm glad." Her voice quavered on the words. "I'm glad you killed them."

Brandon eyed her curiously, one dark eyebrow quirking upward. He debated the wisdom of reminding her that she had shot one of them. Knowing the revulsion she would surely feel if she remembered killing the man, he said only, "So am I, Moonbeam." Later, she might recall more clearly what had happened in those frantic last moments. It would be easier to deal with it then.

The day was hot and dry and miserable beyond belief. An hour after sunrise, Laurel felt baked, roasted, basted in perspiration, and thoroughly wilted. Time seemed to crawl minute by agonizing minute, the pace made slower by the fact that they dared not push their horses, for to be stranded afoot in the desert always meant certain death. One thing in their favor was that they now had spare mounts—those ridden by their attckers—so when one set of horses tired, they could switch to the fresher animals.

Around noon, they stopped to rest during the hottest hours of the day, when no sensible creature dared to overtax itself beneath the broiling sun. By stretching blankets over some tall cactus, Brandon created makeshift shelters—the only available shade in the entire desert, Laurel was sure.

It helped only slightly to be sheltered from the glaring rays, but it was better than nothing. Even with her hat pulled low over her face, Laurel could feel her skin becoming sunburnt. She could almost hear the freckles popping out across her nose. She'd tucked her long hair under her hat to keep it off of her neck and back, and still she felt as if her brains were cooking inside her skull. Her head ached from squinting against the waving glare of the sun on white-baked sands. It was a relief to lie back and close her eyes against the brightness.

As the sun slanted downward toward the western horizon, they rode on, Laurel blindly following Brandon's lead through the desolate, arid land. When the sun eventually set, a sudden chill replaced the intense heat, making Laurel's teeth chatter as she struggled into her buckskin coat. The abrupt change in temperature surprised her, though she had often heard others tell of it.

Another thing that amazed her after a miserable day of riding through bright, endless heat was the startling beauty of the desert at sunset. It was as if an artist had gone berserk with his pallet and brush, painting the sky and landscape first with gold, then every shade of pink and red imaginable, and finally velvet blues and deep, majestic purple. The stars appeared in the dark night sky, so close and brilliant that she felt she need only reach out her hand to collect a palm full of stardust. They glistened like diamonds on a velvet cloth, shining and glorious.

In the clear, sparkling sky, it was the moon that reigned in the end, shedding its soft illumination like a blessing across the desert, transforming it into a thing of ethereal beauty. Like a gentle mist, it performed a special magic, changing the land from gold to silver, the dry scrub and cacti to charmed sentinels of the night. The moonlight danced lightly over everything in sight, sprinkling enchantment, turning the world into a mystical fairyland such as Laurel had never beheld.

"It's so unbelievably beautiful!" she breathed, stunned. Slowly, she spun about in a circle, her arms held out as if to collect the magic surrounding them. "I feel as if this is unreal—a dreamworld —and if I blink it will disappear!"

"Is that why you are whispering?" Brandon asked, his own voice hushed.

Laurel nodded, her eyes finding his and glowing brightly. "It is wonderful, Brandon."

"So are you." His hand gestured to the beauty about them. "I wanted you to see this, Laurel—to experience the magic of the moonlit desert. Here, there's a celestial quality to the light, a beauty like no other." His fingers touched the loose strands of her hair. "The first time I saw it, I was reminded of you, with your gentle beauty, your shimmering silver-white hair drifting about your angel's face." His voice caressed her as he drew her slowly into his arms, nuzzling his face in her hair. "You are my desert moonlight, Laurel—my own satin moonbeam."

Laurel melted in his arms, bewitched by his loving words, the night, and Brandon. Slowly, gently, his lips touched hers as lightly as a butterfly's wings. The moon had cast a spell, and they were caught up in its enchantment.

Laurel's lips quivered beneath his, warm and soft, and she felt light and boneless as his arms gathered her close to him. Then she was lost in his kiss, in the timeless sorcery of his touch. Scarcely did it register on her bedazzled mind when Brandon undressed her and lowered her to the blanket. How he managed to dispose of his own clothing without releasing her lips from his, she knew not. She was adrift in a world of sensual wonder. The night air had lost its chill, replaced by the warmth of Brandon's body over hers—his breath on her skin, his hot lips caressing her breasts, his hands stroking her body. With reverent tenderness, he made love to her—slowly, deliciously—while she trembled in his arms, totally alive, her every sense attuned to his, her body tingling with desire.

Slowly, surely, he carried her with him to the stars, showing her the wonders of the universe. When at length their passion peaked, they were afloat in a mystical world of moonlight and mist, drifting hazily amidst the clouds where only the two of them could go, and nothing else existed . . .

Laurel removed her hat and wiped the sweat from her forehead with her sleeve. Perspiration had long since plastered her blouse to her back, and itchy trickles ran in a river along her spine and between her breasts. With a sigh she made a coil of her long, thick braid of hair and stuffed it back under the hat once more. Tendrils clung damply to her neck and cheeks.

"It's nearly impossible, in this heat, to

remember that it is November. I keep thinking summer has returned with a vengeance."

"By this time tomorrow, we'll be on greener ranges again," Brandon assured her. "In fact, by tonight you should be able to see foothills outlining the western horizon."

A few miles further, they stopped to rest. Brandon unsaddled the horses and set up a shelter while Laurel rummaged through their supplies for lunch. Wrinkling her nose in distaste, she pulled out strips of jerky, dry biscuits, three shriveling apples, and a can of beans.

Noting her sour look, Brandon laughed. "Tomorrow we'll be able to have a hot, cooked meal," he promised.

With a disgruntled look, Laurel said, "I have news for you Brandon. The beans have baked in the can, and the apples have literally roasted in the saddlebag. This *is* a hot meal. Even the water has boiled in the canteens!"

After eating, Laurel lay back listlessly in the shade of the canopy Brandon had fashioned. The relentless heat of the day was fast sapping her energy. Soon her lids grew heavy and she slept.

Laurel moaned and shifted restlessly, trying in vain to throw off the visions of her nightmare. Tossing her head back and forth, she could not dislodge the menacing shadows.

It was dark—so very dark. A horse whinnied and stamped, and her spine grew rigid in expectation. Shadows moved in the darkness, barely discernable in the night, until three forms separated from the others and took the shape of men. Teeth flashed in the faint moonlight. Words of warning and crude laughter made shudders of fear creep along her flesh. Evil faces leered menacingly. Intense, disabling fear held her motionless, and a part of her fear was the knowledge that Brandon's life was also in danger, and he was as helpless as she.

Suddenly there was a pistol in her hands, and she was facing one of their grinning attackers. The gun slipped from her cold, trembling fingers, and when she caught it, the explosion was unexpected, the flash and sound startling. A second report sounded nearby, and then a third. The man closest to her lay at her feet, blood flowing from a gaping hole in his head. A few feet away, a second man fell to his knees, clutching his hands to his chest. Streams of crimson gushed from between his fingers, staining his shirt and falling in steady drops to wet the ground. With a final, agonized groan, he fell forward onto his face.

Laurel's stunned gaze fell to the still smoking gun in her trembling hands. With sudden clarity, she realized she had killed this man. The barrel of the Colt was still aimed at where he had stood, her finger still on the trigger. The enormity of her deed overwhelmed her; and a scream strangled in her throat. More cries welled up behind the first, and tears streamed down her face. Laurel screamed and screamed, unable to stop, unable to forgive herself for having killed another person.

Through her hysteria, she felt strong hands on her arms, shaking her. Gradually, with the insistance of Brandon's voice repeatedly calling her name, night became day; and when she at last opened her eyes, the bright sunlight nearly blinded her.

A swift, startled glance told her where she was, and Laurel collapsed with a sigh against Brandon's supporting chest. It had been a dream!

Only a dream recalling the events of the previous night! Her galloping heart finally eased its thumping, and Laurel swallowed hard to rid her mouth of the taste of fear and revulsion.

Still, the awful knowledge remained with her. "I've killed a man, Brandon," she whispered, and felt his arms tighten in answer to her need for comfort. "I've never hurt another human being before—and I *killed* him!"

"Don't condemn yourself for it, Laurel. They would have felt no remorse at having killed us, believe me! Besides, it was an accident that your finger found the trigger." Brandon's broad hand gently but firmly caressed the muscles of her tense back.

"That doesn't help much just now. It can't erase the fact that I killed another human being."

"I know, and I also know what you are going through at this moment. You have taken a life; necessary or not, it's not pleasant to face. But you must accept it, Laurel. In time, the episode will fade, and God willing, you will never have to harm anyone again. Just remember, you did it because you had to. You defended yourself, and me. If you hadn't, we both might be dead now."

A shudder rocked her slim frame. "I suppose, if I'm truthful with myself, I'd have to say I'd do it again. That alone makes me guilty and ashamed."

"Don't be, love. Fear, and the will to live, make us all do things we never dreamed we would. All the guilt and remorse you're feeling is natural and normal, but to save your life you'd probably do the same again." His hands came about to frame her face and raise it to his unwavering gaze. His silver eyes held truth and understanding as he said, "Self-preservation is one of the strongest instincts in the world. Love is another—and that is why we are so blessed. Please don't suffer over something you could not help and cannot change—and never doubt how much I love you, Laurel. Without you to light it for me, the world would be a dull and ugly place."

As Brandon had said, the next afternoon brought them into the higher, greener ranges of north-central Mexico and the following evening saw them camped along the Rio Conchas. Recalling what had happened the last time they were camped beside a river, Laurel was apprehensive, jumping at the slightest sound. Positive she would not sleep at all well, she was relieved to hear that, with luck, they would reach Chihuahua and their destination by the next night. After a week in the wilds, she would welcome civilization with a glad cry and open arms. And most important of all, she would become Brandon's wife at long last.

CHAPTER 9

The Corona ranch lay north and east of the town of Chihuahua. On previous visits, Brandon had stayed with the family, but this time there was Laurel to consider. Brandon was almost certain they would extend the same courtesy to his fiancee, but he was not sure how they would feel about an unwed woman travelling all this distance alone with a man, and he did not want to put Laurel in an embarrassing situation. If the atmosphere was cordial, they would stay. If not, they would find lodgings in Chichuahua while they arranged their marriage and he conducted his business transactions.

They reached the ranch house just before dark. The day's work done, the family was relaxing in the *sala* before dinner. When the servant announced their arrival, Miguel Corona came out to greet them. "*Como esta*, Brandon? It is good to see you again." His warm smile and ready handshake were evidence that he and Brandon were friends as well as business associates.

As the men greeted one another, Laurel took the opportunity to study their host. Miguel was younger than she had expected, perhaps only a few years older than Brandon, and very handsome. A couple of inches shorter than Brandon, he was slender and dark, with snapping black eyes, and a long, slim nose above a smiling mustached mouth.

Brandon explained her presence to his friend. "Since leaving home, this is our first opportunity to marry," he concluded. "We will be wed while we are in Chihuahua, as soon as we can find an official to perform the ceremony."

Miguel frowned, and for a moment Brandon thought he might disapprove of their actions. But shaking his head, Miguel said, "Surely you do not intend to insult me by staying in town, *amigo.* You and your *novia* will stay here. My mother and sisters will be delighted to help arrange your wedding!"

At this, Laurel stepped forward. "Señor Corona, we would not want to impose. A brief ceremony is all we require to make us man and wife."

"Nonsense!" The single, sharp word was spoken by an older woman in black now approaching them. Her dark eyes assessed Laurel at a glance, narrowing slightly at the dusty denims tightly outlining her legs. Her expression softened as she noted the weariness of Laurel's stance, the exhaustion of her young face. "You are only wed once, and it should be done correctly, and with great celebration. However, we can discuss the details later."

She turned to Miguel. "I am shocked that you would fail to see how tired our guests are, Miguel. You make them stand here while the señorita is ready to drop!"

Laurel was surprised to see Miguel, a grown man, look suddenly sheepish. "*Perdoneme, por favor.* My mother is right, as usual. Welcome to our home. Come, we will see to your comfort *immediatamente.*"

Again Señora Corona took charge. "You, Miguel, may see to Brandon's accommodations. I shall see to the señorita's needs myself." With that, she took Laurel's arm and led her into the house.

Stunned into silent obedience, and too tired to argue if she had wanted to, Laurel let herself be led along a wide hallway, only half listening as Señora Corona chattered on. "This hallway leads out onto a courtyard. Directly off of it, you will find the main *sala* and the dining room. The kitchens are to the back of the house." As in many Spanish homes, the patio was the center, with the house forming a circle about it.

Señora Corona took a turn to the right at the end of the hall. "This section of the house serves as residence for the children and unmarried señoritas." Her direct look added emphasis to her next words. "Your room will be here until after you and Señor Brandon are wed."

"*Gracias*, Señora," Laurel managed to mutter, feeling a flush of embarrassment stain her cheeks.

With quiet efficiency, Señora Corona ordered a bath for her, at the same time eliciting an abbreviated version of Laurel's circumstances. "So, Señorita Burke! You have come all this way to marry your *novio* at last, and escape your father's disapproval. Am I correct?"

Laurel nodded. "My father would never approve, no matter how long we waited. Brandon finally got tired of waiting." With a sigh, she added, "I hate deceiving my father, but he left us no choice. Perhaps once we are married, he will learn to accept it."

"Perhaps." Turning to more urgent matters, Señora Corona asked, "Do you have a dress to wear, Señorita?"

Laurel shook her head. "We were traveling light, and Brandon thought trousers would be best for such hard riding. I shall have to go to town and purchase more appropriate clothing."

"Men!" Señora Corona gave an exasperated sigh. "So impatient and impetuous!" For the first time, she smiled at Laurel, a twinkle in her dark eyes. "And so *romantico, si?* Never mind. We will find a dress for you."

While she would have liked nothing better than to crawl into bed after her bath and sleep for a week, Laurel allowed herself to be fussed over. Inez, Miguel's younger sister, came to her rescue with a lovely peach gown and slippers. Luckily, the vivacious brunette was very nearly the same size. "Fortunate for you," Inez said with a mischievous giggle. "My older sister, Dolores, is sweet, but after three children, she is also wide here . . ." Inez spread her hands out from her hips, and out from her breasts, expressively, "and here, Latin women have constantly to guard against becoming plump, though our men rarely complain. Still, when Ramon and I are wed, I do not want that to happen to me. I want always to be the woman he fell in love with."

Looking at the beautiful young woman, Laurel could not envision her any other way. Petite, thoroughly feminine, with even features and flawless olive skin, Inez was lovely. With a slightly sultry mouth and enormous brown eyes with glinting golden highlights, Inez would certainly catch many a man's eye.

Since she was an only child, with no real family to call her own except for Rex and her Aunt Martha, Laurel was in for a treat. The Corona family was overflowing with relatives. Miguel's mother, Señora Marguerita, widowed five years ago, ran the household now; but her husband's mother, Abuela Juanita, still lived with them. Marguerita came from a family of ten children, and Miguel's father was the oldest of eight. Hence, there were over thirty aunts and uncles and scores of cousins, some working on the hacienda, and some living nearby. Still others lived further away, coming for visits and holidays.

Miguel, as Marguerita and Julio's eldest son, officially headed the hacienda, but he received help and advice from his uncles and cousins. Though there were disagreements, for the most part there was harmony. On a ranch of this size, there was plenty of work for everyone, and eventually everyone found his or her particular niche.

For the first couple of days, Laurel was overwhelmed. She counted herself lucky to recognize Miguel's sisters, Inez and Dolores, and his two younger brothers. People were coming and going constantly. The continual activity made her head swim.

Amidst all this organized confusion, Laurel was taken in hand. Señora Marguerita was adamant that she be allowed to direct Laurel's wedding plans. With Inez and Dolores backing her decisions, Laurel was outnumbered.

The idea of having a magistrate perform the rites was immediately overruled. Marguerita insisted on a priest to bless the union. "Padre Bernardo will be happy to do it, and his *iglesia*, his church, is very pleasant. So peaceful and pretty— not too big or too small, but always with a feeling of God in residence."

Even Brandon was helpless to stop the family's plans. Miguel hustled him off to town to be measured for a new suit, and Laurel went with the women to find an appropriate wedding gown. The engaged couple set up an appointment to talk to Father Bernardo and almost before they knew it, the date was set.

"Brandon, I feel so—so manipulated!" Laurel complained. "I know I sound ungrateful, but everything is being arranged around me, while I stand in a daze, helpless to stop it."

Brandon laughed. "I know the feeling! But Laurel, you must understand and forgive them if they are overzealous. These people celebrate life with such zest! They love weddings and christenings—any event that gives them cause to celebrate. Besides, wouldn't you have been disappointed to have been married in a judge's chambers with no flowers or candles or friends to witness our vows?"

"You make me ashamed of myself," she admitted. "I guess I'm just a little nervous."

"And you think I'm not?" Brandon cocked an amused eyebrow at her. "Sweetheart, I am about to forfeit my long-prized bachelorhood; to take on the responsibilities of a wife and future family."

"Thinking of backing out?" she teased.

"Not on your life!" Gathering her into his strong arms, Brandon kissed her long and hard, days of enforced celibacy adding fervor to his kiss.

A loud cough and accompanying giggles caused them to break off the embrace. Both Laurel and Brandon looked up to see Señora Marguerita frowning at them and tapping her foot impatiently. Behind her, Inez stood with her hand over her mouth, eyes twinkling with glee. "The groom will please refrain from such behavior until after the wedding," Marguerita suggested sternly.

"Yes, ma'am," Brandon said meekly, sending Laurel into giggles of her own.

Dolores, having been through all of this herself, understood Laurel's confusion. "Mother does tend to take over," she confessed, "but she means well, and she is superb at organizing this sort of thing. She loves it! I hope you don't mind too much. We are all so fond of Brandon. We just want to see you have a proper wedding, one you can look back on with joy in years to come."

With Dolores to intervene, Laurel managed to have some small say in the organization. Her flair for clothing held her in good stead, and she found the perfect gown—an ivory satin covered in yards of candlelight lace, with a matching lace mantilla. Laurel declined the high Spanish combs, preferring to drape the mantilla over her hair in a simpler style. For her bouquet, she would carry a small arrangement of snow-white lilies and trailing violets atop a Bible. Doña Juanita was lending her an old, ornately filigreed cross on a silver chain to carry with the Bible, and Brandon had gone to a jeweler in Chihuahua and purchased a delicate amethyst necklace and earrings for her.

They were to be married in the early afternoon, providing them ample time to return to the hacienda before dark. The Corona family had planned a grand fiesta afterward, the celebration to go on into the wee hours of the night.

Laurel barely slept the night before her wedding. Her stomach was a knot of convulsive nerves, her hands icy to the point of being numb. A hot bath in fragrant oils soothed her somewhat, but her brain seemed to have vacated her head. Try as she might, she could not concentrate on all the thoughts that flooded her head, bombarding her from all sides. At last, mere hours before dawn, exhaustion took its toll, and she slept fitfully.

Brandon was spared a similar agony. Miguel and his many male relatives decided to help him celebrate his final night of freedom. Tequila and rum flowed freely, with much joking and back-slapping. At about the same time Laurel finally slept, Brandon fell into a liquor-induced oblivion of his own. Hours later, and only due to Tío Fernando's sure fire hangover cure, Brandon managed to dress for his wedding.

Without Marguerita's aid and that of several other women, Laurel would never have managed to get ready in time. Efficient as always, the señora delegated duties right and left. Laurel watched in mute amazement as a skillful cousin arranged her silver-blonde tresses in a coronet of braids on top of her head, leaving a few tendrils to curl gently about her face and nape to soften the effect. When the mantilla was draped over her head, Marguerita produced two perfect lavender orchids to fasten the veil to her hair.

"Perfecto!" she declared, pinching Laurel's cheeks to bring some color to her pale face.

Somehow, they all managed to pile into the waiting carriages and buggies for the short ride into town. Miguel had been ordered to keep Brandon well away from Laurel's carriage so he would not see his bride before the proper time.

There was a problem at the church when they arrived, however. Miguel, in his role of best man, was doing his best to set matters straight. It seemed Father Bernardo was nowhere to be found.

"What do you mean, Father Bernardo is not here?" Marguerita screeched, beside herself. "The church is decorated, and the bridal party is here!

Where is he?"

"I'm sorry, *Madre.*" Miguel shrugged helplessly.
"I don't know. There is a new priest here I have
never seen before—a Father Pedro." Miguel
gestured to a tall, broad-shouldered man in
priest's garb standing next to Brandon, obviously
discussing the dilemma with the other men. "He
says Father Bernardo left early this morning on an
emergency call. In his hurry, Father Bernardo did
not say where he was going or how long he might
be gone. Also, he did not mention the wedding to
Father Pedro."

Overwrought, her nerves stretched to the breaking point, Laurel suddenly burst into tears. For
years her father had conspired to keep her from
marrying Brandon, and even now, miles from
home, and with all the arrangements made, they
still had to wait. Maybe their wedding was not
meant to be! She sobbed quietly, her hands over
her face, her slender shoulders shaking. She did
not respond to Marguerita's assurances that "All
will be well, Laurel. Do no cry so," or Inez's
sympathetic murmurings. Even when Brandon
approached her, gathering her tenderly into his
embrace, his lips brushing the tears from her
cheeks, she could not be soothed.

"Take me home, Brandon. Please take me
home," she sobbed. Neither of them were sure
whether she wanted to return to the Corona
hacienda or to Texas.

The sudden clapping of Marguerita's hands
startled them. "What a bunch of stupid cattle we
all are!" the woman explained. "We have a priest
here! Father Pedro can marry you!"

All eyes turned expectantly to the young priest,
who looked stunned and suddenly unsure of

himself. "Truly, I cannot!" he said hurriedly. "You must wait for Father Bernardo!"

Inez leveled her devastating gaze at the man. "*Por favor,* please, Padre," she implored. "Surely you are qualified to perform the ceremony."

"*Si,* yes," he agreed hesitantly, "but I am new to the priesthood, and I have never performed a marriage before . . ." His voice trailed off apologetically.

Used to having her every command obeyed, Marguerita was firm. "There is a first time for everything, Padre," she informed him briskly. "You may as well start with this couple as any other."

"But . . ."

"No more excuses," Marguerita said. "We will understand if you fumble and falter a bit, will we not?"

Everyone was in agreement. Laurel raised tearful lavender eyes in a silent plea, and the priest wavered. "If you will give me a few minutes to prepare, I will do my best," he said at last.

Though halting in places, as the young priest stumbled through the various phrases of the rite, Brandon and Laurel were at long last declared man and wife. A collective sigh of relief and congratulations echoed through the church.

"Well, Mrs. Prescott, we finally managed it, nervous priest, trials and all." Brandon's eyes blazed with unvoiced emotion as he gazed down at her tenderly. Then his dark head bent to hers, as he claimed his first kiss as her husband.

Laurel was deliriously happy. A radiant smile lighted her face throughout the carriage ride back to the hacienda. At her husband's side, she clutched his arm with trembling, possessive fingers, and gazed raptly at the shining gold band resting on the third finger of her left hand. Inset in the band were several small amethysts which matched the stones of her engagement ring. It was not the rings, however, that held her attention, but what they signified. She was Mrs. Brandon Prescott at last; her dreams were finally realized. It seemed almost a miracle—a wonderful, unbelievable, fantastic miracle! How strange to hope and dream and plan for years, yearning toward this time, and suddenly in a matter of a few bright, shining minutes, have it all come true!

"It *is* true, isn't it Brandon? This *is* real?" Her shy words voiced the need to have him reinforce the reality.

"As real as our love, my darling," he assured her with a quick kiss. "And don't think you are going to get out of the part about obeying me just because it was recited in Spanish. I happen to know you understood every word perfectly." His silver eyes teased her.

Laurel sighed in mock dismay. "That is what I get for being raised with a Mexican housekeeper! I should have known better!"

"Too late now," Brandon said with a laugh. Then he sobered, his gaze intense and possessive. "You are mine now, Laurel! All mine!"

She met his look with one of her own, lavender eyes alight with love. "I'm glad," she said softly. "I want to belong to you forever."

The wedding fiesta was lively and gay, with music and dancing, and plates piled to overflowing with mouth-watering foods of all kinds. The meal was delicious, the wine delectable. Even the children were allowed to partake of limited amounts under strict adult supervision until the hour when they were shepherded off to their beds.

Then the celebration truly began. Laurel and Brandon danced first with one another. After that, Laurel rarely saw her husband, as she was whirled around the patio by partner after partner. Whenever she did manage to spot him in the crowd, he was similarly engaged. At first unsure of the strange and sometimes intricate dance steps, a few glasses of wine and much good-natured encouragement soon relaxed Laurel enough to enjoy the dancing immensely. The gallant, profuse flattery of these Spanish gentlemen had her smiling continually, their flowery compliments on her beauty making her blush with shy pleasure.

Much, much later, her feet practically numb, she begged off more dancing, wending her way toward a small table where she was sure she'd seen Brandon seated. She pulled up short, taken slightly aback as she saw him, an attractive dark-haired woman seated close to him. Laurel vaguely recalled having been introduced to her. She was one of Inez's many cousins, Carmen or Carmelita something-or-other. She was leaning toward him, blatantly offering Brandon a provocative view of her breasts as she did so. Her long, pointed nails curved into the cloth of his jacket as she gazed at him seductively.

Laurel's temper ignited immediately, her good humor evaporating in a hot mist. How dare this woman make eyes at her husband! With firm determination, Laurel strode forward. Planting herself in the remaining chair, Laurel cleared her throat loudly, distracting Brandon's attention from the brunette.

"Hello there," she simpered, her fingers tapping the tabletop in annoyance. "Remember me?"

Brandon smiled at her lovingly, not in the least

aware of her mood. "Hello, sweetheart. Having a good time?"

"So far," she replied.

"Have you met Carmen?"

"I seem to recall our being introduced." Laurel's tone was decidedly cool, seeing that Carmen had yet to remove her hand from Brandon's sleeve.

Correctly interpreting Laurel's expression, Carmen said, "Yes, I have met your so sweet little bride, Brandon." Her sultry voice literally dripped syrup, her deceptive smile oozing venom. "How young and untaught she is! Such a baby yet! Who would have thought such an innocent would have led you to the altar?"

"Who indeed?" Laurel said, her own smile forced and tight. Absently she fingered the knife lying on the cheese tray.

Brandon was beginning to notice the tension in the air. "Carmen has been telling me of her travels. She just came back from a trip to Spain, and she may be visiting in San Francisco soon."

"Perhaps I shall come to call on you while you are there," Carmen suggested slyly, her fingers lightly caressing Brandon's arm.

"I wouldn't count on it, Carmen," Laurel advised, her eyes narrowing in a warning Carmen chose to ignore.

"Why ever not, dear child?" Carmen's amused gaze swung to Brandon's face, expecting his instant approval of her suggestion. Her dark eyes suddenly widened at the cold feel of steel, and she looked down to see the small cheese knife quivering between her outstretched fingers, its point now imbedded in the table top. With a startled cry, she pulled back her hand, abandoning her grip on

Brandon's sleeve with amazing speed. Her stunned gaze flew to meet Laurel's.

"As I was saying, Carmen dear," Laurel said slowly and distinctly, her look calm and challenging, "I do not think it would be wise of you to visit us anytime in the near future. In fact, it could prove hazardous, if you take my meaning." With precise movements, Laurel reached over to extract the knife from the table. Sitting back, she studiously ran her finger back and forth across the blade.

Brandon looked on in amusement as Carmen attempted a wavering smile. "Well, on second thought, I *am* expected to visit relatives in Los Angeles for a while . . ." She excused herself and departed hastily.

Brandon stared at his new bride with a mixture of awe and delight. "Laurel, I am amazed at you! Somehow, I've never pictured you as the jealous type."

"I am a lot of things, Brandon, most of which you have yet to discover. Maybe, after sixty or seventy years, you'll get to know them all." Now that Carmen had retired in defeat, Laurel's sense of humor was returning, and with it a growing yearning to be alone with her husband. Her violet eyes were now sending him definite messages.

"Shall I start discovering those hidden assets soon, my love?" he asked suggestively, his husky voice grating pleasantly in her ear.

"Please yourself, darling." Her tongue slipped out to tease provocatively between her teeth, sending his already heated blood surging.

"Oh, I shall, sweetheart. And I promise that neither of us will be disappointed." Together they slipped quietly away to the room they would share for the duration of their stay.

When they reached their quarters, Brandon surprised Laurel by giving her a few moments to herself, saying he would be in after smoking a final cigarette. Upon entering the room, Laurel suspected Brandon had planned this all along, for there was champagne chilling in ice, the sheets had been turned down, and her filmy new negligee was laid out at the foot of the bed. A single red rose rested on her pillowcase, mute testimony of Brandon's wish to make her wedding night special in every way.

It was silly to be nervous now, after having been intimate with Brandon for months, but Laurel's hands shook with eager anticipation as she took off her bridal gown and slipped into the sheer blue peignoir. It flowed over her body like a lover's touch, floating about her as she walked, then clinging to suggest barely hidden curves to tease and tempt the beholder. Dabbing a wickedly sensuous perfume in strategic spots, she sat down before the mirror to brush her hair.

It was thus that Brandon found her when he entered the room, and the sight of her, so sensually clad and beautifully flushed made him wish he could freeze time forever at that moment. That this bewitching vision was truly his at last was almost too good to be true; the feeling was so fragile and new that he feared to speak lest it be only an illusion, to be shattered at the first word.

She sat before him, her glorious hair cascading like a silver waterfall down her back. Their eyes met in the mirror, hers bright and shy as fresh violets, his wide with love and wonder and shining like sunstruck swords. As he watched, her lips parted, revealing small white teeth, her voice caressing the syllables as she breathed only his name.

"Brandon."

As if held in a spell, he crossed to her. His hands reached out to stroke her silver tresses, gathering handsful and feeling the satiny strands slide through his fingers and tickle his palms like a whisper. Baring her shoulder, he placed a kiss in the tingling hollow, his eyes holding hers in the mirror, and watching them deepen to a darker shade as his lips burned a trail of fire up her slender neck to her ear. Warm, sure hands slid down her arms, slipping to curve enticingly about her breasts; holding them, warming and weighing them in his palms. As his fingers slid across her nipples, causing them to tighten and bud out at his touch, her eyelids fluttered shut, closing out the images reflected in the glass. Her emotions already whirling, she moaned, a small sound of desire, pure and simple, that told him all he needed to know.

With Laurel's eager hands to aid him, Brandon quickly divested himself of his attire. Then Laurel's filmy blue gown, worn for such a brief time, joined his clothing on the floor. Breast to breast, flesh against yearning flesh, they embraced; Brandon's mouth claiming hers in a timeless exploration as he held her in his arms. Her limbs already weak, Laurel thought surely she would collapse with delicious delight as his lips and hands began to wander to other sensitive areas of her body. Chills danced along her spine following the path of his fingers even as her breasts, so sensitive from contact with his chest hair, quivered at his touch. When his mouth closed over one nipple, his tongue teasing the tip, his teeth gently tugging as he suckled, she cried out.

Reaching out to steady herself, her seeking hands clutched at his shoulders as he lowered himself to his knees. His hot lips left her breast to claim the soft, ticklish flesh of her stomach. Laurel sucked in her breath sharply as his tongue circled her navel, then delved into it, sending sharp darts of desire to her toes and back again.

Brandon's hands were on her hips, steadying her as his lips swept downward. His mouth charted a damp path through golden curls, sidetracking briefly to nip lightly along her inner thighs before claiming the moist target they sought most. As her knees nearly buckled beneath her, Laurel's hands clutched at his head, her fingers delving into Brandon's crisp dark hair. Pleasure so sharp and sweet it was almost painful shot though her.

"Brandon! Oh, Brandon, *please!*" She was not sure at this point whether she was begging him to stop or to continue with this divine torture. Lips parted, head thrown back, her entire body was straining and quivering, then jolted as if by lightning as he took her over the edge.

Still in the throes of passion, spasms still quaking through her, Laurel cried out with the force of her pleasure as Brandon stood and entered her. Together they fell upon the bed. Wrapping her legs about his lean hips, Laurel held him tightly to her, her movements matching his as he led them both to higher plateaus of passion. Now her hands were free to explore the muscled planes of his arms and back, the smooth mounds of his buttocks, and she revelled in the feel and texture of his hard flesh against hers.

Their rapture rose higher and higher until she

felt a surge rippling, growing as if a gigantic wave washed over her, drowning her in ecstasy and drawing Brandon into its sparkling center with her where they spun in its magnificent vortex together.

Adrift on clouds of sated passion, Laurel settled happily into his embrace, her head on his shoulder, his arm possessively about her waist. "You are the most wonderful man in the world, my darling," she sighed.

"Not *just* a man any longer, my love," he reminded her. "From this day forward, I am your husband; and you are my beautiful bride, my own lovely wife."

Laurel smiled, her lips curving against his throat. "You are my husband, my man, my lover—always. We are going to have such a marvelous life together, Brandon. Nothing will ever destroy the love I have for you."

His lips feathered the damp tendrils of hair at her temple as he kissed her. "Promise?"

"On my very life."

Was it the solemnity of her answer, Brandon wondered, or merely a chance breeze from the open window that caused a shiver to dance over his skin?

CHAPTER 10

On impulse, Brandon decided to take Laurel to Mexico City for a brief honeymoon. Telling the Corona family they would return in a week's time, they boarded the southbound train, leaving friends and business matters behind.

For Laurel it was idyllic, a perfect moment out of space and time, heaven on earth created just for the two of them. Brandon was gallant and charming, and though she had thought it impossible, Laurel found herself falling more deeply in love with him every day.

A good deal of their time was creatively spent in their hotel suite, but Brandon insisted on showing her the city, too. "It is rich in the history and passion of the Mexican people, and it would be a shame not to see it. After all, it may be years before we have the opportunity again."

They saw all the sights. First there was the beautiful *Paseo de la Reforma*, the three mile flower-bedecked boulevard from Chapultepec Park to Zócalo Square in the center of the city. Wide and tree shaded, it was lined by some of the most magnificent buildings and monuments, old and new, to be found anywhere. In Zócalo Square alone they spent many hours touring the palaces, museum, and cathedral.

As Brandon had said, the city was rich in its own heritage. The National Palace occupied the site of Hernán Cortés' own home, begun in 1692, and now housed several government offices, as well as the National Museum. Above the central portal hung the Mexican Liberty Bell rung in 1810 to rally the people in their struggle for freedom from Spain.

The cathedral was ornate and enormous, probably the largest in all of North America and certainly the oldest, built in 1525 on the ruins of a great Aztec temple to the god of war. It was truly breathtaking, and Laurel could well imagine former Mexican emperors being crowned with elaborate ceremony within its walls.

They toured the shops and vendors' stalls with enthusiasm, buying mementos of their stay. They ate in elegant restaurants and enchanting open-air cafes. One evening they attended an opera in the Palace of Fine Arts, and Brandon pointed out President Diáz in his private box. The next day they took a drive through Chapultepec Park past Chapultepec Castle, now Diáz's official residence and formerly the home of the executed emperor Maximilian and his poor insane wife, Carlota.

Most of their tours Laurel truly enjoyed, loving the architecture and unique aura surrounding this old city. One particular place, however, sent shivers up her spine and goose flesh peppering her skin. It was the area below the School of Medicine, original headquarters of the Holy Office of the Inquisition. Here, cells of the unfortunate victims could still be viewed along with the dreaded instruments of their horrible torture.

Lips trembling, eyes wide with amazed horror, Laurel clutched at Brandon's arm. "Take me out of here!" Her voice was almost frantic in her desire to escape, her face pale and drawn.

Once outside in the bright sunlight, it was several minutes before her breathing regulated and her color returned to normal, and Brandon was very concerned and apologetic. "Honey, I'm so sorry! I never dreamed this place would affect you this way, or I would never have suggested seeing it."

It seemed the dark, musty odor of that torture chamber would never leave her nostrils, and Laurel gulped the fresh air gratefully, trying to rid herself of the panic that had gripped her. "I don't know what came over me down there," she confessed weakly. "It was as if the spirits of all those pain-wracked victims were still lingering in the gloom, crying out unbearable agony, shrieking and screaming for an end of their torture." A long shiver convulsed her. "I've never felt so hopelessly sad! That place should be destroyed, banished from existence."

"I think it has been preserved deliberately, Laurel," Brandon said quietly, "and perhaps with good reason. It is there to remind us of those very atrocities, lest we forget what the past has tried to teach us and allow history to repeat its darkest moments."

To cheer her, Brandon took her to an exclusive supper club that evening, where they watched several flamenco dancers perform. Impressed by the impossibly rapid click of heels and the beautifully suggestive movements of the dance, Laurel was soon captivated by the music, completely forgetting her disturbing mood of the afternoon. So entranced was she by the dancers that she barely tasted the delicious meal.

"If I'd known you were going to seduce the young dancer, I would have requested a table further from the stage." Brandon's voice near her ear jerked her back from her fascination.

For a moment, she nearly thought he was serious. Then she caught the glow of mischief in his eyes. A flush brightened her cheeks as she swept him a shy glance through her lashes. "I'd rather seduce *you*, Brandon," she whispered.

"No sooner said than done!" Motioning for the check, Brandon helped her to her feet. "Let's go."

A knowing smile curved her lips, as he led her out of the restaurant. "Why are we suddenly in such a hurry?" she teased.

Brandon gave her a wicked wink and helped her into the waiting carriage. "The sooner we reach the hotel, my love, the more time you will have to ply me with your wiles. I must confess, my curiosity is aroused. You see, I've never before been seduced by my own wife, and I can hardly wait to see how you'll go about it!"

"Slowly," she said, her tongue sneaking out to moisten her lips, as her eyes promised him delights untold. "Slowly, thoroughly, and absolutely!"

Barely a quarter of an hour later, she proved to him exactly what she had meant.

The next day, they visited the fabulous floating gardens south of the city. Laurel was immediately entranced by the floating fantasyland of flowers and gaily decorated boats. With a picnic lunch in hand, they hired a flat-bottomed canoe, elaborately decorated with a shaded arch made up completely of flowers. In addition to the boatman, who piloted the craft through the intricate winding canals, there was also a guitarist who played soft lovesongs as they drifted along.

It was a day to remember and treasure all their lives. They laughed and cuddled, gazing dreamily at their surroundings and one another. Seated on cushions in the boat, Laurel snuggled serenely in Brandon's embrace. Whether it was the scent of the multicolored blossoms, the wine, or merely pure happiness, Laurel was floating on clouds of bliss. Like some mythical pampered princess, she had everything she had ever wanted in the palm of her hand. It was an intoxicating feeling.

Brandon was at his most charming. As the guitarist strummed and sang, he whispered the translation of the lyrics into Laurel's ear, his warm breath sending tingles down her spine and along her flesh. His glinting eyes sparkled with love and promises as he fed her tidbits of cheese and fruit, then proceeded to lick the sticky juice from her lips. When she reciprocated, he cleansed her hands by running his tongue sensuously across her palms, then took each fingertip by turn into his mouth, gently sucking and teasing until Laurel was mindless with desire. She saw her own needs echoed in his face and mirrored in his silvery gaze, and she wondered that her thundering pulse could not be heard by both the boatman and the musician.

"Brandon, you've got to stop this," she choked out, all the while silently hoping he never would. The yearning in her wide violet eyes belied her plea.

"Why?" His eyes never left her flushed face as he laved her palm with his caressing tongue.

"Because it's . . . we're . . . it's not private here!" she stammered.

With a wicked chuckle, he sipped at her fingers before answering, relishing the quiver that ran through her and the pulse beating madly at her throat and wrist. "Anticipation is half the enjoyment, my love," he told her. "It makes the reward all the sweeter, the loving that much more intense."

"It's sheer *torture!*" Laurel felt as though she were melting inch by steaming inch into the cushions.

Brandon's eyes were steel lances spearing her. "Do you want me, Moonbeam?" he asked huskily.

"I'm weak with wanting you." She could barely speak for the hammering of her heart.

"Are you on fire for me?" he persisted.

Her eyes were liquid pools, her lips trembling just inches from his. "Consumed in flames," she confessed shakily.

A smug, satisfied look joined the passion smoldering in his eyes, making Laurel frown in sudden suspicion. "Are you trying to pay me back for last night, by any chance?"

He smiled. "Repay you for what, sweetheart? For blatantly seducing me in a public place?"

"You are being deliberately hateful, Brandon Prescott! You had no complaints when we reached the hotel!" The thought of how boldly she had acted the previous evening made her blush.

"And neither will you," he promised, gathering her close in his arms, his lips feathering light kisses over her face. "It will always be this way with us, my lovely Laurel. You have only to look at me, and I go up in flames. I have only to touch you to ignite your hidden fires. We were created for one another as surely as the sun was meant to light the day!"

A pleased, mischievous smile touched her lips. "Then may I suggest that, before we set this boat on fire, we find our way back to our hotel and smolder in private?"

* * *

On Sunday afternoon, with what was surely half the population of Mexico City, Laurel and Brandon attended a bullfight in the *plaza de toros*. As he led her to their seats on the shaded side of the arena, Brandon teased her about her reluctance. "Cheer up, Laurel," he said. "This has been Mexico's national pastime from generation to generation. It's a tradition. No visit to Mexico would be complete without it."

"Horse feathers!" she grumbled irritably, failing to share his enthusiasm over a sport she was sure she was going to detest.

He laughed good-naturedly. "Actually, it would more appropriately be *bull* feathers, I think."

She found her seat and hit him lightly on the shoulder with her parasol in response. "I fail to see how anyone can enjoy such a dangerous, bloodthirsty sport!"

Brandon groaned in mock dismay. "Don't tell me you're going to be one of those silly females who feels sorry for an angry thousand-pound bull?"

"Don't be dense, my dear," she said, wrinkling her pert nose at him. "My concern is for the fool who risks life and limb facing such an unpredictable animal on foot. God alone knows what makes men do such irrational things!"

"It's a demonstration of skill and bravery—man against beast, brain against brawn," Brandon attempted to explain.

"Are you positive it's not just a demonstration of vanity and stupidity?" she countered.

With the annoyed and superior look one might bestow on a stubborn child, he said, "Why don't you reserve judgment until after you've seen for yourself?"

With a shrug, Laurel settled herself on the hard seat and prepared to do just that.

The pageantry of the opening ceremony was indeed alluring, with the band playing and three matadors presenting themselves to the officials. Laurel thought the matadors' suits of light very beautiful. Each wore a different color, but all had skin-tight breeches with silk panels and short jackets embroidered with sequins and shimmering metallic thread. They walked tall and proud, backs straight and heads up, brave warriors ready to battle the foe. If they had any doubts or fears, it did not show.

Then with a blare of trumpets, the gates were opened and the first bull roared into the arena. For a moment he paused until he caught sight of the yellow and magenta cape teasing at him from the matador's hands. Like a huge black cannon-ball, he charged.

As cheers sounded in her ears, Laurel dared to open one eye to see the matador challenging the beast again. Once more the animal charged, and once again Laurel squeezed her eyes shut, her jaws tightly clenched. When she chanced a peek through fluttering lashes, she caught a blur of the thundering black beast and the flash of the cape as it whirled about the matador's head. A trembling sigh of relief escaped her stiff lips.

The crowd roared its approval of the matador's expertise on the next pass, and finally, intrigued in spite of herself, Laurel watched the action through the lattice of her fingers over her eyes.

The vibration of Brandon's shoulder against hers drew her attention from the ring. He was chuckling, regarding her with great amusement. Sheepishly, she lowered her hands, and Brandon took one cool hand into the warmth of his.

"Honey, I think you'll see better if you don't cover your eyes!"

With grim determination, she faced forward, forcing herself to view the action. How the matador could be so calm in the face of such danger was bewildering, even though she knew that the man had trained and fought for many years. The more she watched, the more amazed she was at his confidence and grace. She could see that each movement was calculated to produce a certain result, each motion precisely planned to test the bull and learn his reaction, to manipulate the beast to a desired position.

The *picadores* came on next, mounted on horses protected by thick padding. With their lances, they pricked the bull. Confused, Laurel questioned Brandon about this. "Why are they doing that?"

"To slow the bull down to a point where the matador can better control his movements. But a good matador will not allow so many *pics* that the animal is badly weakened."

Laurel watched as, between placement of the *pics*, all three matadors took turns working the bull with their capes. Next came the planting of the bright *banderillas*, the barbed sticks placed into the bull's shoulders, which discouraged the bull from raising his head. Many a matador had been gored by a bull who lifted his head at a completely unexpected moment.

Laurel watched the final act of her first bullfight with a mixture of fear and anticipation. Exchanging the long cape for the shorter red *muleta*, the matador then requested permission of the authorities to kill the bull, then dedicated his bull to a lovely woman seated in a reserved box. As she stood to receive his proffered hat, Laurel saw that she was obviously expecting a child.

"His wife," she heard someone say, and wondered how the woman could bear to watch her husband face death in the bullring, especially now with his child growing within her. What if he was gored, or killed? But maybe waiting at home was harder on her than being here and knowing what was happening. Silently Laurel offered a prayer for the man's safety, and a sigh of thankfulness that her own husband was not in such a perilous profession.

With flair and remarkable skill, the matador enticed the bull closer and closer to his body, his expertise and daring drawing gasps and excited shouts from the onlookers. So close did the animal pass, that the blood from his wounds stained the gold cloth of the matador's suit of lights. When the time came, he killed the bull with one perfect thrust of his sword and was awarded two ears and the tail.

"This is truly remarkable, Laurel," Brandon said, "to witness such a feat at your first bullfight. A matador has to be superb, and the bull brave and good, for the judges to award both ears and the tail. You are fortunate to have seen such a superb performance."

As the day wore on, each of the three matadors fought two bulls for a total of six contests. The second matador was good, but he did not have the flair of the first. The third was just beginning his career, and though enthusiastic, his style was rough.

In his second event, the first matador drew a cowardly bull. The audience and the matador were equally displeased, and with a minimum of passes, the matador dispatched the bull as soon as possible.

Laurel was beginning to enjoy herself. Little by little she became caught up in the excitement of the bullfight. Soon she was cheering and clapping and shouting along with everyone else.

The fifth bull was a dangerous devil with an uneven set of horns, one of which spiked out from the right side of his broad head at a precarious angle.

The crowd recognized the danger of the situation, and tension gripped them, pulling them to the edges of their seats in morbid fascination as man and beast challenged one another. The matador was careful to avoid the irregular horn, not pulling the bull in as closely as he would have otherwise. Even at that, he had to backstep hastily on the last pass.

The *pics* were badly placed, for the *picadores* had problems, too. The bull pinned one horse and rider to the barrier before the others lured him away. Only the padding saved them injury. The *banderilleros* hastily planted their barbed sticks and retreated to safety.

His *muleta* and sword in hand, the matador faced the bull for the final few cautiously executed passes. The animal did not follow the red cloth, preferring to break his charges, changing directions at will. The crowd held its collective breath, and an unearthly quiet permeated the arena.

Signaling his intent to go in for the kill, the matador positioned the bull, sword ready. It happened so suddenly! One moment the man stood arched on his toes, his body curved to avoid that evil horn, sword raised. The next brought disaster as the bull changed stride, tossing his

head up and out, impaling the matador's thigh.
The man was raised high, suspended in midair,
dangling helplessly. Then he was thrown to the
ground with a great heave of the beast's black
head. Automatically, his arms came up to shield
his head. Amidst shrieks and screams of the crowd
gone crazy, the other matadors and *banderilleros*
rushed to his aid. While some lured the bull away
from the fallen man and kept him at bay, others
carried the barely conscious man out of the ring.

As they passed by a white-faced, stunned Laurel,
she saw the long, wicked gash in his leg. Bleeding
profusely, his thigh was ripped practically from
knee to groin. She sat stiffly, sick at heart and
physically shaken as the more experienced
matador stepped in and finished the kill.

By the time the last matador had fought his final
bull, some of the shock had passed. It amazed
Laurel that this young man had witnessed a fellow
matador being gored, yet faced his own bull with
vigor and determination. He was awarded both
ears for his efforts.

Before the audience could disperse, one of the
officials called for attention and announced that
the injured matador would live to fight another
day.

CHAPTER 11

The morning they were to leave Mexico City and return to the Corona Ranch, Brandon rose early. He had an unpleasant chore to accomplish and wanted to get it done before his ever-curious young wife woke. So engrossed was he in his distasteful task, that he never heard Laurel tiptoe quietly across the carpeted floor toward him. Not until she leaned over him, intent on a surprise morning kiss, was he aware of her presence.

Startled, Brandon jerked back, scattering his papers off the desk top and at the same time causing Laurel to overbalance. Both she and the papers tumbled to the floor. Before he could react, Laurel was retrieving his work.

Laughing at her clumsiness, Laurel gathered the papers from around her. "What are you slaving away at so early this morning?" As she spoke, she glanced at one letter, her interest caught as she realized it was addressed to her father. If not for Brandon's instant attempt to grab the missive from her hands, Laurel would have assumed the letter to be a simple announcement of their marriage. However, certain words seemed to leap off the pages, causing her to draw back, withholding them from Brandon's grasp. A frown creased her brow as her eyes widened, hardly able to believe what she was reading.

"Oh, my God!" Her hands trembled as she quickly scanned the message. It read:

Burke,

This is to inform you that Laurel and I were married on November the eighteenth, in church and before witnesses. Let me assure you, annulment is out of the question. She is now, and will remain, my wife. As such, she has vowed to obey me, as I have vowed to protect her. At the moment I feel I must protect her from you. She will go where I go and stay where I stay.

That brings me to my second reason for writing. You realize, of course, that I hold you responsible for Jim Lawson's death, and consequently, Becky Lawson's loss. I warned you to stop rustling, but evidently you feel you are above the law. I must admit, you've been very careful to avoid being caught redhanded. My own losses are not an issue here, but the others you have harmed and stolen from are another thing.

Now I must insist that you cease your thieving immediately, for I possess what you hold most dear to your heart. If you ever hope to see your dear daughter again, there are certain conditions to be met. You must stop your cattle rustling. You must also reimburse Becky Lawson for all property stolen from her ranch. It is the least you can do after robbing her of her husband and her children of their loving father. I don't care how you go about it, what excuses you give to anyone, or what hardship it causes you. Just do it! Hank will keep me informed of your activities, and the consequences will rest on your head if you do not comply.

You may write to me (at a later date) in San Francisco when you have completed the repayment, not only to Becky but to all the others from whom you have pilfered, myself excluded. The time table I leave to you, since I am in no hurry to return to Crystal City at present. When—and if—I return with Laurel is up to you. The sooner you make restitution, the sooner you will be reunited with your only child.

Also, speaking of children, I will do my utmost to try to provide you with a grandchild as soon as possible, a duty I will perform with great pleasure. Whether or not you ever see your grandchild depends on your compliance with my demands.

My kindest regards and best wishes for the happiest of holidays to Martha. You may contact me in San Francisco in a few weeks, after Laurel and I conclude an extended honeymoon.

Your Son-in-Law,
Brandon Prescott

The pages fluttered from her nerveless fingers. Betrayed! A hollow numbness spread through her, chilling her very soul. *Betrayed!*

Too stunned for tears, she raised huge, hurt eyes to the face of the man she loved above all else in the world—the man she had always loved—the man she had believed in and trusted . . . until now. Oh, she still loved him. That was something over which she had no control. But now the trust had been broken, and mixed with that helpless love was hurt and rage.

She did not cry or rave or scream at him. Laurel simply sat and stared at this stranger who was her husband as the light slowly died in the enormous lavender eyes. Then she turned away from him, loathing the sight of this man she had thought she knew so well, this betrayer who had so soon abandoned her precious gift of love, leaving her with only the shimmering shards of broken dreams.

Rising, Laurel walked silently from the room, ignoring Brandon when he rose and called her name. With quiet deliberation, she began packing her suitcase, carefully folding each garment to avoid wrinkling. From the corner of her eye she saw Brandon come to the doorway. She did not care. She felt dead inside, bereft. Any emotions she felt were trapped in ice, frozen somewhere deep within her. With a tiny part of her mind she was grateful for this eerie calm that held her in its grasp, for it held the hurt at bay—that unbearable heartache she knew would kill her if she had to deal with it now.

One solitary action betrayed to Brandon how deeply she had been wounded. The flower doll he had bought for her the day they had visited the floating gardens sat on the dresser. When she came to it, she stood holding it for a long time, tenderly stroking the colored petals as she gazed down at it. Then, without a word, she turned and dumped it into the waste basket and walked away without a backward glance.

The train ride to Chihuahua was for the most part a silent one. Laurel sat quietly staring out the dirty window, though she saw nothing of what they passed. Several times Brandon tried to talk to her, but she ignored him.

He was helpless to know how to deal with her. God knew he'd never meant to hurt her. He loved her desperately! He needed to reach her, to reason with her, to try to explain his action without upsetting her further. He was not sure how he would handle it if she were to suddenly fly into a rage or start to cry hysterically, but he had to try to make her understand.

When he reached for her hand, she flinched involuntarily and tried to pull her hand away. When he refused to release it, she gave up, letting her fingers lie limply in his grasp, her drawn face turned away from his gaze. Her reaction made him frown in concern. Did she hate him so much now that his touch was abhorrent to her? Lord, what a miserable situation! And he had no one to blame but himself—and Rex!

"Laurel, I never meant you to see that letter," he said softly.

She shot him a look that said she was well aware of that fact, then turned away again.

"Have I made you hate me?" Brandon studied what he could see of her face, praying her answer would not be "yes."

Her lips quivered, but at last she answered. "I don't know. Perhaps. At this point, I am not sure what I feel."

Pain lanced through him at her words. Had he killed her love for him, or was her heart just so bruised that it would take time and love to heal it again?

There was another question pounding in his brain, demanding an answer. "Are you afraid of me, Laurel?" He felt her stiffen, and watched miserably as she plucked nervously at the folds of her skirt with her free hand.

"Should I be?" she whispered so quietly that he barely caught her words.

Swallowing hard, he said, "No, love. I know I've hurt you terribly, but I never intended to do so.

Certainly I would never deliberately harm you in any way."

A long silence followed his words. At last she asked hesitantly, "What about the threats in that letter to Dad? What did you mean about consequences?"

He thought a moment, trying to recall the wording of his letter to Burke. "I only meant to imply that I would keep you from seeing him, Laurel, or contacting him in any way until he repays what he has stolen. In no way do I want you to think I would do you physical harm. You should know that. You are my wife and . . ."

"Is that why you married me, Brandon? To get back at Dad for the awful things you accuse him of?" Her voice was strained, her face white with tension.

Taken aback, he could merely stare at her in shocked disbelief. Where had that idea come from? Had he destroyed her faith in him so completely? Angry at himself and at Laurel for thinking such a thing, he shot back, "Is that what you think, Laurel?"

When she failed to answer immediately, his temper rose further, and with it deeply buried doubts of his own. "And why did *you* finally marry *me*, Laurel, after putting me off for so long? Was it out of love, or because you feared I might catch your father at his nefarious deeds? Did you know about his cattle rustling all along? Did you marry me to protect him, thinking I would not pursue the matter once he became my father-in-law?"

Turning stricken features to him, she said quietly but emphatically, "No! Brandon, you can not truly think that of me!"

Glacial steel-grey eyes stared back intently. "I don't want to, but it makes a certain amount of sense."

"About as much sense as my father rustling cattle!" she retorted sharply, hurt and anger making her words sting. "You'll never make me believe that, Brandon. Not in a million years! My father may be many things, but he is not a thief, nor is he a murderer. If you didn't resent him so, you would see that! Your hatred has made you blind to all but your need for revenge, and is turning you into a monster!"

"On the other hand, maybe your love for your father is making you blind to the truth, Laurel. That is, if you truly had no knowledge of his activities."

Unshed tears made her eyes glisten and threatened to choke her. "I thought I knew you, Brandon. Now I wonder if I ever truly knew you at all. Just now I don't like you very much. I resent your accusations more than I can say." After a short pause, she said softly, regretfully, "It might be better, after all, if we were to go our separate ways. I'm not sure I want to stay married to a man who has so little respect for my father and for me."

Brandon's heart almost stopped beating. Then, just as suddenly, his blood started pounding fiercely through his veins. "No! You'll never leave me, Laurel! I won't let you! Love me, hate me, resent me all you will, but you are mine, and nothing on this earth will ever change that!"

It was a much subdued couple of newlyweds that arrived at Miguel's ranch. More than one pair of eyebrows rose in curiosity; but then, brides and grooms had been known to squabble through the ages, only to make up as suddenly.

Miguel tried to tease Brandon out of his morose

mood. "Trouble in paradise already?" He grinned. "You two certainly didn't waste any time!"

"It's more serious, I'm afraid. I'm not sure I didn't ruin things permanently, and that scares the hell out of me. If there were any way to make it up to her, I'd break my neck doing it."

"An apology?" Miguel suggested.

"The only kind of apology Laurel would accept right now would be for me to back down completely and let her father continue to raid the countryside. My conscience would never allow me to do that. I have to be able to live with myself."

"Well, you are going to have to find a way to live with Laurel, too, and in some semblance of harmony, or you will both be miserable."

"Time, *amigo*," Brandon sighed, patting his friend on the shoulder. "Time—and maybe a miracle."

Thinking it might be better to give Laurel time to come to terms with her feelings, Brandon did not pressure her. For the next few days, he made himself scarce. When they were together, he was pleasant and considerate. Each night as he lay beside her in bed, it took supreme effort not to take her in his arms and make love to her. His body ached for hers, but her cold attitude held him back, making him give her time. He was determined not to give her further reason to detest him.

Laurel was smarting not only from the shock of Brandon's letter and his newly voiced distrust of her, but from his avoidance of her these days. Where before he could scarcely keep his hands off her, he rarely touched her now. Her mind was in turmoil. Why didn't he want to make love to her? As angry as she was with him, as hurt and disillusioned, she still desired him. Her body craved his with a passion that amazed her.

Not only could she not control her body's longing for him, she could not convince her crazy heart not to care. As hard as she tried, she could not hate him. It was too soon to forgive him, yet she could not keep from loving him. Her love was as strong as ever, like some incurable disease she could not recover from.

"A fool, that's what I am!" she railed at herself. "A stupid, weak, absolute fool!"

Because he was not sure she wouldn't try to leave him, Brandon gave orders that Laurel was not to go riding or to leave the ranch without being accompanied by someone else. The first time she tried to take a horse from the stable for an early morning ride alone, the stable boy politely refused to allow it. Laurel's usually even temper went up in flames. With fire in her eyes, she stomped off in search of Brandon.

She found him with Miguel, looking over some of the cattle he had selected. Marching directly up to him, she faced him angrily. "Brandon, what is the meaning of your giving orders that I am not to ride? I demand to be given my horse immediately!"

An abrupt silence followed her words, as every ranch hand within earshot waited to see how Brandon would react to being spoken to in such a manner by a mere woman. Knowing the others were watching, Brandon had no recourse but to be firm with her.

"You will get nowhere making demands, Laurel. My order stands. You are not to ride by yourself. If you wish to ride, find someone willing to escort you."

Mad enough to spit, she settled for stamping her

foot at him. "I have been riding alone since I was twelve, and I do not need an escort now!"

"Then you won't ride at all," he said.

"*Why?*"

"Because I said so."

"That's not a reason!"

"It is now."

Fists planted on her hips, she glared up at him. "Blast you, Brandon!"

He grinned down at her. "You look as fierce as a mad banty hen," he taunted.

Jutting her chin at him stubbornly, she gave him a frosty smile. "Is that so? Well, just remember, roosters aren't nearly so cocky without their tail feathers, and someday someone is going to pluck yours!"

His hearty laughter followed her as she went off to ask Inez to accompany her on her morning ride. She needed it now more than ever, for if she didn't do something physical to release some of her tension, she was sure she would explode!

Later that afternoon, Laurel had just stepped from the bathtub and was reaching for a towel, when the door to their room opened. Laurel froze, mesmerized by the look of pure longing on Brandon's face as his heated gaze traveled the length of her naked body.

Neither spoke as Brandon quietly closed the door and flipped the lock, never taking his eyes from her. The late afternoon sunlight bathed her in golden droplets. Her skin seemed to shimmer, the water running in rivulets down her sleek body, tracing lines his hands longed to follow. The creamy globes of her breasts rose and fell with her agitated breathing, the rosy tips puckered invitingly. In that moment, he thought her the most exotic, seductive creature he'd ever beheld.

He stepped forward, and the spell was broken. Hastily, Laurel retrieved the towel, shielding herself with it.

"Don't," Brandon rasped, closing the space between them. Gently he pried the towel from her grasp, tossing it to the floor. With a touch bordering on reverence, he ran his fingertips along her flesh, creating fiery shivers in their wake. "You're so perfect; so beautiful!"

A shuddering sigh escaped her parted lips. "Brandon . . ." His hands circled her waist, pulling her hips close against him, letting her feel his desire. Hot lips trailed flaming kisses over one bare shoulder, then stopped to savor the feel of the pulse pounding at the base of her throat.

As though with a will of their own, her fingers found the buttons of his shirt, freeing his broad chest to her caress. Slender fingers wound through the thick mat of brown hair, finding and fondling the flat nubs hidden there.

He aided her efforts, shrugging out of his shirt. Then she was in the tight embrace of his arms again, her breasts crushed against his hard chest, her nipples rubbing and tingling in the soft hair that teased them as he moved against her. "I've never wanted anything the way I want you," he murmured.

With a groan, his lips claimed hers; staking, possessing, devouring. Hungrily she answered his desire, lips parting to accept and savor the fierce thrust of his tongue. Warm, work-roughened hands caressed her hips, her back. She melted willingly against him, barely noticing the hard belt buckle pressing into her stomach. His hips ground against hers, his lips dominating hers with sweet demand. His fingers delved into her upswept hair, flinging pins everywhere as he loosened it to let it tumble in shining silver waves down her bare back. Then his fingers were combing through it, the thick strands sensuously imprisoning his hands as though eager for his touch.

Head spinning in breathless delight, Laurel moaned her desire against his lips. Pulling away from her, Brandon bent to lift her into his arms. "Let me love you, sweetheart," he implored, covering her face with urgent kisses as he carried her to the bed.

When he lay her on the coverlet, she answered him by reaching for the clasp of his belt buckle. Quickly he slipped out of his clothes and joined her on the bed. Hot hands and lips covered her, claimed her as she was claiming him with eager, trembling touches. She held him in her arms, loving the feel of him, his scent, the warmth of his skin beneath her fingertips. Loving hands reached out for him, seeking and stroking, making him groan aloud for want of her.

With practiced ease, he brought her to the brink of desire, making her quiver and writhe beneath his touch, creating a desperate hunger within her that only his body joined with hers could appease. "It's been so long—so long! Oh, Brandon! Please! Love me now!"

He came into her with the hunger of a starving man at a banquet, with all the pent-up longing in his soul. It was wild and wanton and wonderful. Passion flared between them like a flaming whirlwind, catching them up in its twirling tempest, tossing them about in its raging wonder. The time for tenderness was past as their bodies surged together, seeking, demanding the ultimate satisfaction. His hands were caught in her hair, his hot breath panting in her ear, his teeth nipping at the flesh of her neck and shoulder. Slender fingers dug into his muscled shoulders and then, as ecstasy swept over her, slipped to score his back with long, clutching nails. Sharp cries of rapture mingled in the afternoon air, and then all was still as they clung breathlessly to one another, letting the final gusts of ecstasy brush over them, carrying them into a valley of gentle breezes and soft sighs.

"I've missed you, honey," Brandon whispered into her tangled hair.

Tears misted her lavender eyes, turning them to dewy lilac. Tenderly she stroked his shoulders, running her fingers into his thick hair to hold him close to her. "I've missed you, too, darling. I thought I'd die for wanting you, and I thought you didn't desire me any longer . . ." Her words choked off as tears clogged her throat.

"There will never come a day I do not want you, Laurel. Through all my bull-headedness, your stubbornness, and all the problems that come along, I will always need you. You are as necessary to me as air to breathe, as sweet as rain after a long drought."

The moisture of her tears wet his cheek, and he raised his head to kiss her lashes. "I love you, sweetheart."

"I love you, too, Brandon. There are so many things left unsettled between us; things that stand between us like a shaky ledge, and it scares the wits out of me! Still, I love you with every fiber of my being. I don't want our differences to tear us apart, to wear away at our love until it ceases to be."

"We'll work it out, dearest," he promised. "Our love is strong enough to stand any test."

"I hope so. Dear God, I hope so!" whispered Laurel.

Though they were back on speaking terms and no longer overtly angry with one another, neither felt completely comfortable in the following days. Their relationship had sustained its first major shock and both Brandon and Laurel were still shaken and slightly wary. Even as they lay in one another's arms, they felt the unspoken strain. Even as they admitted their love, they held back a bit as if uncertain what to do or which direction to take next. The wound had started to mend, but total healing would take time and care. Little by little they had to learn to trust each other again.

If they were awkward with one another, it was not for lack of trying. Gradually, as the days passed, they began to respond more naturally, to relax, to laugh and tease and smile more spontaneously.

It was during this tentative time that Brandon came bounding up to the house one day, excitedly calling for Laurel.

"For heaven's sake, what is it? Is something wrong?" Laurel's heart was in her throat, fearful that something dreadful had happened.

"Come out into the courtyard and see for yourself. I promise you'll be delighted." Grabbing her arm, he nearly dragged her outdoors, as excited as a small boy.

Beside herself with curiosity, Laurel nearly ran to keep up with him. She had never seen Brandon this way and could not wait to see what had caused this strange behavior in her husband.

Pulling her to a halt in front of Miguel, Brandon simply said, "Look."

There sat Miguel, holding in his lap what appeared to be a small baby fox, except that it was not the usual reddish color. Instead, its fur was a remarkable pale silver. It was very young, perhaps six to eight weeks old—barely weaned. It sat shivering nervously in Miguel's grasp, its shining amber eyes wide with fright.

Laurel was immediately enthralled with the tiny bundle of fur. "Oh, it's adorable, Brandon! Where did it come from?" She knelt down to stroke it, and Miguel gratefully released it into her care.

"Miguel and I were riding along when suddenly my horse shied for no reason I could see. I stopped to look around, and I spotted the little fellow. He was all alone, apparently either abandoned by the mother fox, or lost during the change from one den to another."

Miguel picked up the tale. "We looked for the den, but could not find it. Now knowing what else to do, we decided to bring it back with us. It is unusual for fox kits to be born so late in the season. By fall, the kits are usually half grown and able to fend for themselves when their families split up. This one probably would not survive long on his own."

"From the size of him, he would have been buzzard bait soon," Brandon agreed. "I thought his mother wouldn't mind too much if you adopted him."

Laurel's face lit up as she gazed at Brandon in delight. "Truly?" she asked. "I can keep him?"

"If you want him." If Brandon had known

Laurel was going to be so excited and smile at him so lovingly, he'd have tried to find the entire litter for her.

"But when we leave for San Francisco . . .?"

"We'll take him with us. Fox kits make good pets. They can be trained almost like a dog, and they have very friendly dispositions."

Laurel looked down at the silver fur ball in her lap. "He's so small, but isn't he a marvelous color? I've never seen a fox with these shadings before."

"It is rare," Miguel put in, "but once in a while you will see a black or silver fox. His fur almost perfectly matches your hair, you know. That, I think, is why Brandon decided you must have him."

"Miguel is right, Laurel. I took one look at this little mite and thought of you."

Laurel smiled and shook her head. "You are both wrong. His coloring is the exact shade of Brandon's eyes when he is particularly pleased about something."

Brandon looked dubious, but Miguel studied his friend a moment and nodded. "I agree. He matches both of you. You will make good foster parents." They all laughed.

"What will you name him?" Brandon wanted to know.

"He is so tiny, I think I'll call him Tyke."

"Tyke Prescott," Brandon mused. "That has a nice ring to it, don't you think?" This set the three of them laughing once again.

Tyke was then and there adopted into the Prescott clan. Laurel took him under her wing, and soon the little silver fox was following her about like a trained pup. The best thing about Tyke was that his timely appearance had succeeded in further healing the breach between Laurel and Brandon. It seemed to Brandon that he had been granted a miracle in the form of a small bundle of silver fur.

CHAPTER 12

Laurel was fast becoming homesick. Because they were in Mexico, they had missed celebrating the traditional American Thanksgiving holiday. Now the Christmas season was beginning, and Laurel was heartsick at not sharing the festivities with her father and Aunt Martha. She had been away at school for the last two Christmases, and had looked forward to being home with friends and family this year.

Brandon refused to budge on this issue, though the two of them had several hearty disagreements about it. With the ghost of their first fight still lingering in the air, they were reluctant to get into another full-fledged argument, and so far they had limited themselves to bickering and a few lively discussions.

The Corona family insisted they would be delighted to have Laurel and Brandon stay for the holidays. With this offer, plus the fact that Brandon was not yet ready to go to San Francisco, it was decided they would spend Christmas at Miguel's ranch. As Brandon pointed out, it made more sense to spend the holidays in Mexico with friends than in San Francisco with strangers. Besides, it would give Laurel the chance to experience firsthand the Mexican way of celebrating the nativity, which was quite different from festivities in the States.

In Mexico, as Laurel found out, the holidays began on Advent Sunday, the first Sunday of December, though the Christmas season truly came alive in mid-December. From December sixteenth to Christmas Eve, the people re-enacted what they called the *posada,* or "lodging." Each night a group of people would dress as travelers from the time of Christ's birth. One would be selected to play Joseph, another to portray Mary. From house to house they would go in search of lodging for the expectant mother. At length they would come to the house where someone would represent the innkeeper. Here they would plead for a room, only to be told that none was available. The two would beg the innkeeper to find space, chanting their rehearsed requests in unison, and the innkeeper would finally reply that the couple could lodge in his stable.

Then he would open the door, and the travelers would enter to share food and drink with the benevolent innkeeper and his family. There would be carols sung and cheer exchanged. For the children, there were games and candy, often in the form of a *piñata* to be broken. Each *piñata* was unique, some in the shape of stars or camels, stables, donkeys, or whatever the talented creator had fashioned. All were brightly decorated and designed with love and care. With squeals of delight, the blindfolded children took turns swatting at the swaying *piñata* with a stick. When a skillful youngster finally succeeded in breaking the gaily decorated clay container, all would scramble for the candy that fell from it.

On several evenings, Brandon and Laurel went into Chihuahua with the Corona family to participate in a *posada* at a friend's or relative's home. In each house they found a beautiful representation of the nativity stable handed down from generation to generation. Whether of wood or finest china, simple or elaborate, large or small, the nativity scene held a place of honor in the home. Each scene contained figures of Joseph and Mary, along with shepherds, cattle, donkeys, and sheep. And all contained an empty manger, waiting for the Christ child's arrival on Christmas.

In Chihuahua they found street parades, vendors selling candy and cookies for the holidays, and groups of other people on their way to *posadas*. In varied areas, they would encounter entire sections of streets blocked off where *piñatas* were set up outdoors for neighboring children, or where parades had stopped to perform for the watching crowds.

Laurel was enchanted. "It is so charming—so warm and friendly! It's as if these people are inviting the world to help celebrate the Birth! Work and worry are pushed aside to make way for joyous celebration!"

Brandon agreed. "The people are warm and honest in their beliefs and festivities. They work hard, they pray hard, and they celebrate with zest."

Laurel enjoyed the Mexican Christmas, though she did miss certain elements of the Christmases she was used to. As she said to Inez and Marguerita, "It is so unusual not to see Christmas trees with piles of gaily wrapped gifts under their fragrant bows. When I was in Boston, we would form groups and go carolling house to house in the snow. Once we rented a sleigh, with ribbons and bells tied to the horses, and went riding through the countryside. It was great fun!"

Inez shivered. "Brrr! That sounds cold!"

"It was, but we bundled up in scarves and robes and huddled together, so we really didn't mind."

Marguerita helped explain another difference. "To us, the celebration of Christmas is a religious experience more than anything else. We have no St. Nicholas—here, the three kings who brought gifts to the Christ Child are believed to deliver gifts to good Mexican boys and girls. On the Eve of Epiphany, the twelfth day of Christmas, the children set their shoes out of the windowsills or around the fireplace for the kings to fill with toys and candy. On the morning of January sixth, if they have been good, they awake to find their gifts. Of course, they always find their shoes filled, regardless," she added with a shake of her head and a kindly smile.

Right in the middle of all the Christmas festivities came All Fool's Day on December twenty-eighth. This was confusing to Laurel, as she had always thought it fell on the first of April. With a shrug, Brandon said, "Things are different here. When in Rome . . ."

From the idea that it was foolish to lend anything of value to someone else and expect it to be returned, there had arisen a quaint custom among the Mexican people. It was said that on All Fools' Day, all items borrowed need not be returned to the foolish lender. Therefore it became a game to get another person to lend you something on this day, usually an item of little value that the lender would never expect to see again, or feel its loss.

Lighthearted fun ensued, with much bartering and a lot of laughter. Nonsense items such as stockings, spoons, string, combs and clothespins were loaned and borrowed over and over again. Cigars, tobacco, hairpins, ribbons, hats and gloves changed hands several times. Even pencils and paper, hair brushes and kitchen utensils joined the list.

By day's end, everyone sat down to take stock and compare their loot. Laurel had lost six ribbons, eleven hairpins, a pair of gloves, one stocking, and two scented sachets. She had gained a sash, three spoons and a fork, a pan lid, a hair-brush, twelve clothespins and a bottle of cologne. Brandon had fared better, having loaned only ten cigarettes, three cigars, a necktie, and a hat; he now possessed a different hat, a borrowed shirt, a pair of used work gloves, three pouches of chewing tobacco and a ball of string. Everyone went to bed that night feeling contented, happy, and a little bit richer—if only in laughter and friendship.

Each year, one member of the family was chosen for the honor of dressing the Christ Child figure and placing it in the manger on Christmas Eve. This year, Laurel was granted the honor.

"The clothing for the babe was made by my great-grandmother years ago," Inez explained. "The doll is even older, and is very precious to us. Every figure of the nativity has a special story behind it, and something new is added every year. It is a family tradition we all love."

"In many families, the one chosen to dress the Christ Child is responsible for providing the clothing for it, buying or making the outfit. Since we treasure the clothing we have and prefer to dress Him in those, you need do nothing but perform the ceremony," Dolores added.

"Is there nothing else I can provide? Some gift for the nativity?" Laurel asked, intrigued by the custom and honored to be allowed to clothe the precious babe.

Marguerita, realizing Laurel's sincere desire to be a part of the activities and sensing the girl's grief at being away from her family during the holidays, suggested quietly, "Last year, little Carmelita accidentally knocked over a candle and nearly set fire to the manger scene. It was a near disaster, saved only by Dolores's quick actions. However, the baby's shawl, the blanket in which we wrapped Him, had the fringe badly singed. I've been thinking we should provide Him with a new one."

"Let me get it," Laurel pleaded. "Please! I cannot make it in such a short time, but I promise to find one that will be worthy of Him."

She searched Chihuahua for the finest baby shawl she could find, at last discovering what she wanted in a tiny shop selling hand woven goods. The moment she saw it, Laurel knew this was the one she must have. The material was woven of the finest pure white lamb's wool and delicately crocheted in an intricate lacy pattern. Thick fringe bordered it all around. To touch it was like grasping a cloud.

She had spent what little money she had on the shawl, so Laurel resorted to trickery in order to provide Brandon with Christmas gifts. Mexican custom or not, she was determined he should have presents to unwrap on Christmas morning and again on the sixth of January. Several times Laurel asked Brandon for shopping money, a good portion of which she managed to squirrel away for his gifts.

To add to her savings, she enlisted Miguel's aid. Miguel brought several of his friends together for an "innocent little poker game" and managed to fleece Brandon without his becoming suspicious, and the proceeds were immediately added to Laurel's hoard.

With Miguel's guidance, she found a tradesman who dealt in the most beautifully hand-tooled leather goods Laurel had ever seen, and Laurel purchased a magnificent saddle and bridle. Each had tooled designs of mountain scenes in the leather and elaborate silver trimmings. They were very expensive, but Laurel knew there were no others exactly like them, and the workmanship was worth every cent.

She also bought Brandon a beautifully tooled belt, and in another shop found a silver belt buckle in the shape of a horseshoe to go with it. These smaller items she tucked away in her bureau, while Miguel hid the saddle and bridle for her.

Brandon was busy doing some shopping of his own, with much the same thoughts of Christmas as Laurel. He was not insensitive to her longings to be home, and was determined she would have gifts to open on Christmas. He, too, chose hand-tooled leather goods. Finding a pair of remarkably crafted riding boots in her size, he purchased these and a beautiful handbag as well. Discovering a bright multicolored shawl in a marvelous Indian pattern, he added this to his cache. Then, in a silversmith's shop, he finished his shopping.

On Christmas Eve Laurel dressed the Christ Child figure with all the reverence the ceremony required, and He was gently laid in his manger bed at last. Various members of the vast Corona family arrived in groups all through the evening. Though they did not exchange gifts, each guest brought something—candy, a loaf of sweet bread, a dish to add to the already delectable dinner. All day, delicious aromas had wafted through the house from the kitchen, making Laurel's mouth water in anticipation of the holiday meal.

As was the custom, however, dinner would wait until they returned from church services in town. This was the first time Laurel and Brandon had attended church in Chihuahua since their wedding, and Laurel looked forward to the service, though neither Padre Bernardo nor Padre Pedro would be there. For reasons no one could explain, Padre Bernardo had not been seen since his abrupt disappearance over a month ago, and Padre Pedro had suddenly departed a few days after the wedding. The entire parish was befuddled. They had requested a new priest, and one had recently arrived, but neither he nor the Church knew what had happened to either of the others. In fact, the bishop insisted he had never heard of Padre Pedro, and swore he had not sent him. It was all very confusing, but at least they had a new priest now to officiate at the holiday services and tend to the people's religious needs.

The service was beautiful and moving, and Laurel came away feeling content and at peace, though still homesick. The ride back to the ranch beneath star-studded skies was peaceful and lovely, with everyone quietly contemplating his or her blessings and the true meaning of this night. The meal awaiting them was every bit as delicious as anticipated, if a bit chaotic with all the people and noise accompanying it.

Laurel and Brandon at last made their way back to their room and tumbled into bed, Laurel was pleasantly exhausted. Snuggling her head on the pillow of Brandon's shoulder, she was asleep almost before she could wish him a groggy "Merry Christmas."

After their late night, they slept until a sinfully

late hour Christmas morning. Coming awake, they
made slow, delicious love, luxuriating in the feel
of one another, their whispered words of love, the
lazy caresses and unhurried kisses.

When they were at last washed and dressed,
Brandon presented Laurel with her gifts. Unwrapping the largest first, Laurel discovered the
leather handbag, hand-tooled with cactus
blossoms. Inside, Laurel found a large sum of
money. "Brandon! For heaven's sake! The purse is
beautiful, but what am I to do with all this money,
darling?"

"Ever since I whisked you away with scarcely
more than the clothes on your back, I've felt
guilty. I want you to buy yourself anything you
need—dresses, underwear, nightgowns, skirts,
blouses, scarves—anything you want."

Laurel smiled up at him. "I've managed to pick
up enough to get by on in Chihuahua, and you
bought me several dresses while we were in
Mexico City."

Brandon shook his head and smiled back.
"Beautiful brides deserve beautiful things. Spend
it on anything your heart desires, my love."

The smaller gift rattled when she shook it.
Eagerly she tore off the wrapping and lifted the
lid. A gasp escaped her parted lips, and her fingers
trembled as she touched the shining pendant. It
was finely wrought silver, delicately fashioned
and inlaid with turquoise in the shape of a pair of
lovebirds. The pendant hung on a slim silver
chain. A matching bracelet and dangling earrings
lay alongside. Completing the set was a small,
delicate ring of the same design.

Overcome with emotion, Laurel could not speak.
Eyes brimming with unshed tears of joy, she flung
herself into Brandon's arms, holding him tightly

and showering his face with kisses.

Nearly strangled, he laughed at her reaction. "I take it you like them," he chuckled.

"I love them!" she exclaimed. "They are perfect, and beautiful, and I'll adore them always. Thank you!"

He helped her put them on, and stood back to admire them and her. "You're right, honey. They *are* perfect and beautiful—just like you, my love."

"Now," Laurel said, grabbing hold of his arm and excitedly tugging him toward the door, "we must go to the stable to find *your* gifts. Miguel hid them for me so you wouldn't suspect!"

Intrigued, he followed her lead. There, crowning a bale of hay where Miguel had promised to leave them, were the magnificent saddle and bridle.

Brandon was stunned. He stroked the supple leather and studied the silver inlay and embossed scenes. "This is the most fantastic gift anyone has ever given me. They are marvelous!"

Then his brow puckered as a new thought assailed him. "This must have cost a fortune! How did you ever pay for it?"

"I have my ways," Laurel teased. "Don't you know you are not supposed to look a gift horse in the mouth? Or in these case, a gift *saddle* for said horse?"

Instead of returning her smile, his frown deepened, his steel-grey eyes becoming sharp and piercing. "Where *did* you get the money, Laurel?" he demanded ominously. "Have you been in touch with your father? Did you write to him and ask for funds?"

Astonishment and anger made her sputter in indignant fury. "Just how was I supposed to manage such a miraculous feat with you dogging my every step?" she screeched. "I go nowhere on or off this ranch without an escort at my elbow, watching my every move!''

Brandon was not to be put off. "I know how that inventive little mind of yours works, love. It wouldn't be too hard for you to find a way to slip a letter out if you were desperate enough. You might even have talked someone into sending it for you."

"Well, I didn't!" she declared angrily, overcome with the desire to beat him over the head with something—*anything*—as long as it was heavy enough to bash his thick skull. "And I'll thank you not to refer to my mind as 'little'! Most of the time, I display more sense than you do—like now, for instance!"

"Then where did you get the money for an expensive gift like this?" he insisted. "I demand an explanation!"

"I ought to let you wonder about it now till next Christmas!" Her own lavender eyes were narrowed with searing intensity. "If curiosity killed the cat, perhaps it would do the same for you! Lord knows you deserve it!"

"Don't push me, Laurel," he warned on a growl.

"You are a *beast!* A hateful steel-hearted, mule-headed *beast!*" Her anger voiced, the hurt she felt at his unexpected reaction was now making her chin wobble precariously as she tried desperately to hold the tears at bay. She turned to stalk away from him, but his hand on her arm halted her. "We'll stand here all day if that's how long it takes, but you are going to tell me."

"All right!" she shouted, "but you are going to feel like the fool you are! Miguel and the others arranged for you to lose at poker and passed their winnings on to me. You were set up deliberately, so that I might have enough money to buy your

Christmas gifts without having to ask you for it directly!" Her answer surprised him into loosening his hold, and she jerked away from him. "Now, are you satisfied?" she choked.

His face was a mask of surprise and misery. "Laurel, I'm so sorry! I just couldn't think of any other explanation for the amount you must have spent."

"I used my 'inventive little mind,' Brandon," she said caustically. "You really don't give me enough credit for intelligence. I can't say I'm awfully surprised, but it hurts to realize how little you really think of me!"

He sighed remorsefully. "I adore you, Laurel. Truly I do! You must believe how terrible I feel about accusing you unjustly. Can you ever forgive me? I've been so unfair to you, when I should have been grateful for such a wonderful gift."

Sorrow made her eyes wide, shimmering pools in her face. "When are you going to realize that I love you, Brandon? You hold my heart in your hands, and that is the most precious gift I could ever give to anyone. Yet you insist on trying to destroy that love. Your suspicions are eating away at it daily."

"I know," he admitted. "I am trying, honey. Please believe that." He approached her slowly, as if fearful she would turn from him. His arms reached out, and he breathed a sign of profound relief when she walked into his embrace, to be held tightly to him. "I love you, Laurel."

"Are you sure?" she asked quietly, her head nestled against his hard chest. "Or did you just want me for so long that you *think* you love me?"

"My love for you is the one thing in this world I *am* sure of, sweetheart. It makes me crazy and jealous and suspicious as hell sometimes; it even makes me strike out at you when you least deserve it, but I do love you so very much!''

Her heart was in her eyes as she gazed longingly up at him. ''With all my soul, I want to believe that, Brandon. I *need* to believe it.''

A week later they welcomed the New Year of 1906 at a party given by the Coronas. With all the festivity, music, dancing, and liberally laced punch, Laurel was tipsy long before the clock struck twelve. Brandon first became aware of it when she started giggling at every little thing. Her beautiful face was flushed a rosy pink and her tinkling laughter rang out freely.

Brandon eyed her with amusement as they danced.

''You, my sweet, are definitely intoxicated,'' he laughed.

''Thank you,'' she murmured, leaning into him. Then she giggled. ''Imagine that! I'm 'toxicating!''

For a moment, he frowned, and finally followed her line of thinking. ''You are indeed intoxicating, Laurel, but I was referring to your inebriated state. You are quite tipsy.''

Leaning back to glare at him indignantly, she declared, ''I am not!'' Then she promptly tripped, and had to clutch at his arms for support. ''Don't you think it's hot in here? It's making me dizzy.''

''The wine and punch made you dizzy,'' he corrected. ''Would you like something to eat? It might help.''

She shook her bright head, loose waves of silver flying about her shoulders. ''I think I need some air.''

He found her a secluded seat on the veranda overlooking the rear courtyard. ''Sit right here and breathe deeply. I'll get you a plate of food and be right back."

"Don't forget the punch," she called after him. As he walked away, shaking his head, he heard her humming to herself. If he had realized how potent the innocent-tasting punch was, he would have limited Laurel's intake several glasses ago. Too late now! All Brandon could do was get her to eat something to help absorb some of the alcohol.

Intent on filling a plate for her from the buffet tables, it was several seconds before he realized what he was hearing above the music and continual din of voices. "Oh, good grief!" Brandon nearly dropped the half-filled plate. From the darkened veranda where he had left Laurel, came the sounds of a woman singing *Skip To My Lou* in a soft Texas drawl.

Before he could push his way out of line and head in her direction, the singer switched to a spritely rendition of *Oh! Susanna,* slightly off-key and noticably slurred so that the words became "Oh, Shoe-zhanna."

By now, several other people had taken notice, and heads were turning curiously in the direction of the veranda. With a muttered oath, Brandon fought his way through the crowd, his progress slowed by the many people in his path and the plate full of food in his hand. Just as he neared the doorway, Laurel began a rousing chorus of *Buffalo Gals* that made him wince.

With a speed and dexterity that amazed even himself, Brandon hurriedly closed the veranda doors behind him, and turned to confront Laurel. There she sat, slouched in her chair, her shoes kicked off and bare feet tapping in time to her singing. Her arms dangled at her sides, and her eyes were closed as her head rocked back and forth against the chair cushion in accompaniment to her unsteady rhythm.

Quickly Brandon set the plate down and rushed to clasp his palm over Laurel's mouth. Muffled curses reached his ears as her singing abruptly ceased. "Hush, Laurel! For heaven's sake, do be quiet!"

When she was quiet, he hesitantly removed his hand, ready to slap it back again if she resumed her noise. "Where did you learn to curse like that?" he chastised.

"From you," came the immediate, cheerful reply.

His brow creased as he frowned at her. "I doubt that. At any rate, you should be ashamed of yourself for such unladylike behavior."

Tilting her head, she studied him through her fuzzy vision. "You don't like my singing!" she pouted, her lower lip thrust out petulantly.

"Heaven help us!" he groaned. "What am I going to do with you? You are stinking drunk!"

"Correcshun! I am shlightly spiffled." She blinked, trying to bring him into focus.

Brandon retrieved the plate and set it before her. "You'd better eat some of this."

A ghastly green cast came over her face, and she gulped and pushed the plate away. "I don't think thatsh a good idea, Brand . . . I really don't."

"Oh, boy! You're worse off than I'd guessed. We'd better get you to bed. Can you walk?" He was thankful that they could reach their room by crossing the open courtyard and did not have to re-enter the crowded house.

Laurel stood and teetered precariously on her feet. "Whoops!" she shrieked, falling heavily against him as he caught her weaving figure. This set her to giggling uproariously.

"Oh, hell!" Sweeping her into his arms, he marched swiftly across the cobblestone courtyard, hoping no one was watching the spectacle she was making of them both.

It took him several minutes of batting away her playful hands and contending with her overly relaxed body to remove her clothing. The tussle seemed to exhaust her, and she curled into a sleepy ball on the bed. With a last giggle and a huge yawn, she fell immediately to sleep.

Brandon drew the covers over her. Bending to kiss her forehead, he whispered, "Oh, honey, are you going to regret this in the morning!"

She did, indeed. Laurel spent the entire next day alternately holding either her head or her stomach. She could not remember ever being so sick. It hurt even to blink! Every movement brought a moan of agony from her, and God forbid anyone make any undue noise. In Laurel's present state, a mosquito sounded like a buzz saw. "If I live through this, I swear I'll never drink again!" she vowed.

Knowing what misery she was enduring, Brandon was appropriately sympathetic. "How much of that evil punch did you consume?" he asked.

"Several cupsful, I'm afraid. It tasted wonderful, and I was so thirsty! I never dreamed it was as lethal as all that! All I tasted was the fruit."

"From now on, do yourself—and me—a favor and stick to the stuff they serve the children," he advised. "It will save both of us a lot of trouble and embarrassment." He then regaled her with the tale of her antics the previous evening.

Laurel cringed against the pillow. "I'll never be able to face anyone again!" she wailed.

"Yes, you will. It could have been worse, I suppose. At least none of them know how loudly you snore when you're dead drunk!" he chuckled.

Laurel groaned and pulled the covers over her head.

CHAPTER 13

Laurel's bout with her first hangover lasted for two days until she finally began to feel human again. Even then she wasn't completely back to normal. For some reason the queasiness stayed with her, especially in the mornings. The very sight or smell of certain foods sent her stomach into instant rebellion.

"How long does it take to get over this?" she complained to Brandon.

He was concerned. "Most people only feel bad for a couple of days at the very most. Either you are particularly sensitive to alcohol, or there's something else wrong. If this keeps up, you must see a doctor."

The thought of seeing a strange doctor who didn't know her and didn't even speak her language was not welcome. When the nausea persisted, she managed to hide it from Brandon. Since she felt fine otherwise, and it did not get any worse, she reasoned there could not be anything seriously wrong.

Laurel puttered about the house, helping Abuela Juanita and Marguerita prepare for Epiphany on January sixth, and making candies and goodies for the children's gifts the night before. She shopped for small gifts for family members; hair combs, perfumes and sachets for the ladies, tobacco, pipes and money clips for the men. Brandon agreed they should give some small token of appreciation and friendship in return for the warm hospitality they had received.

She also helped Inez make hundreds of decisions about decorations, clothing, and food in preparation for her upcoming engagement party the middle of January. The ordinarily calm and cheerful Inez was a nervous wreck these days. Just when a color scheme or menu had finally been agreed upon she would suddenly change her mind. At other times, she could not seem to concentrate long enough to make a decision at all. While the other women took care of the necessary arrangements, Laurel did her best to keep Inez occupied.

Unlike their tumultuous Christmas, Epiphany was a calm and joyous day. Laurel arose to find her shoes replaced by the beautiful boots Brandon had bought for her. Folded and tucked inside was the warm, colorful shawl. She was delighted with both. Brandon was likewise pleased with his belt and silver buckle and donned them immediately. From the Corona family they received various small gifts of friendship.

Laurel's stomach upset was now accompanied by recurring heartburn, which she attributed to the spicy Mexican food. It was an added annoyance, but too insignificant in her thinking to warrant a trip to the doctor, so she said nothing of it to Brandon.

Her main concern right now was trying to convince Brandon to go home. Not even when she had been away in Boston had she been so awfully homesick. Then she had left with her father's blessing, and on good terms with both Rex and

Martha. There had been long, chatty letters from her aunt and short notes and gifts from her father, and she felt their love and understanding across the miles that separated them. Now there was nothing but silence, and Laurel dreaded to think how hurt and disappointed they must be with her —especially her father. She wanted with all her heart to go home, to explain, to gain their understanding and forgiveness.

Laurel tried to explain all this to Brandon, to make him see how important it was to her, but it was like talking to a wall—only this wall yelled back and argued and ranted. He refused to listen, or even try to understand. Firm in his stubborn stance, he would not be moved by her heartfelt pleas. They fought and argued regularly about it, only to make up soon thereafter and clash again a short time later. It was becoming a hateful habit, one which both Laurel and Brandon despised. Neither enjoyed their heated disagreements, but neither would give in. Laurel continued to try to change Brandon's mind, and he kept digging his heels in deeper, flatly refusing to listen.

Much to everyone's relief, Inez and Ramon's engagement fiesta was finally upon them. The house looked lovely, the food was prepared, and after the first guests arrived, Inez was once more smiling and congenial, radiantly beautiful beside her handsome *novio*, all her nervous fidgeting forgotten.

The fiesta was definitely a success, with so many guests that Laurel was amazed they all fit into the house. The array of gifts the couple received was magnificent, both in quantity and selection, and Laurel was glad she had found the pair of antique silver candlesticks she and Brandon had decided upon.

That night, Laurel limited herself to lemonade and one small glass of wine with dinner. Perhaps it was because she was completely sober that the conversation she accidently overheard had such a stunning impact on her. She was standing near a group of women when her attention was suddenly arrested by their words. Edging nearer, Laurel listened closely. The ladies were discussing the symptoms of their various pregnancies, and the complaints they listed were remarkably similar to those Laurel had been experiencing. They even mentioned some that Laurel had not considered significant enough to take note of at the time, but now she felt sure they were all related to one common cause.

Besides the nausea and heartburn, she had occasionally found herself suddenly dizzy. This she had attributed to the fact that her nausea often kept her from eating properly. Anyone could get dizzy on an empty stomach! Later she would make up for it by a spree of eating once her stomach had settled. Then there was a lethargic feeling she'd had lately, times when she felt drained of energy and so sleepy. Again, she had felt this was due to the emotional strain of her arguments with Brandon, as her sudden changes of mood from cheer to anger, laughter to tears— or so she had thought. The tenderness of her breasts she had ignored, and it had never dawned on her that she had twice missed her monthly flow, a fact she now realized as she made a quick mental tabulation.

Laurel was shocked at her own stupidity. How dense she was not to have connected all these

small, annoying problems! It made perfect sense,
but it was also new and confusing and brought
with it a whole new set of problems.

Disturbed by her sudden discovery, Laurel
slipped quietly away to the privacy of her room.
She needed time to herself to digest what she had
learned, to decide how she felt about all of it and
what to do next. Many conflicting feelings and
thoughts were bombarding her at once, tumbling
about in her head in a confused jumble.

On the one hand, she was delirious with joy that
she was to bear Brandon's child. Just thinking
about holding their child in her arms made her
glow with happiness and anticipation. Boy or girl,
it would be a beautiful baby, a part of both of
them, created in love. They would raise it with
loving care, watching it grow and learn and
discover new things each day. They would have to
start considering names for the baby. Had
Brandon ever thought about what he would name
his first son or daughter?

Laurel's smile slowly fade. How *did* Brandon
feel about children? Would he be pleased by her
announcement? Should she tell him immediately,
or wait a while? How should she break the news to
him? How would he react?

Laurel chewed anxiously on her thumbnail,
unconscious of her nervous gesture. She wished
she had Aunt Martha with her now to advise her.
This thought sent tears brimming to her eyes as
renewed waves of homesickness assailed her. "Oh,
how I yearn to go home!" she thought helplessly.
"I want to see Dad again and tell him about the
baby. Angry or thrilled, ranting or speechless with
joy, I want to share this time with him and Aunt
Martha. This child might bring Dad and Brandon
to an understanding. The baby could be a common

ground on which to build a foundation of mutual respect between the two men I care about most. If only they could learn to talk sensibly with one another, they might even like one another.

Under the present circumstances, it seemed a miraculous thing to wish for. Dejectedly, Laurel recalled the conditions and consequences outlined in Brandon's letter to her father. Especially, she remembered what he had said about providing Rex with his first grandchild, and making sure he never saw the child. Had Brandon intended for her to conceive his child only to get revenge against Rex?

Doubts began to assail her mind. Could Brandon's love for her be just an elaborate sham, a part of his overall scheme to hurt her father? Could the man she loved actually be so cold-hearted, so vengeful? Oh, she knew he desired her. That was quite evident. Laurel had to admit that her mirror reflected a very attractive image of youth and loveliness. Brandon could have no complaints with her looks. But did he truly love her as he claimed? If he did, how could he continue to hurt her by accusing her father of such awful deeds and keeping her apart from the family she loved?

It was all so confusing! Laurel had no one to confide in, to turn to for advice; no one to counsel her in her time of need. Her head was swimming with half-formed ideas and overwhelming worries.

Exhaustion, both emotional and physical, was taking its toll and sought release in the form of hot tears. Flinging herself face down upon the bed, Laurel gave vent to her heartbreak, pouring out her torment in a torrent of weeping.

This was how Brandon found her when he

entered their room a little while later. Her body was heaving with uncontrollable sobs that shook both her and the bed.

"Laurel, what is it?" he exclaimed, rushing to her side. She stiffened as he pulled her into his arms and turned her tear-stained face to his. "What's wrong?"

Still crying, she nearly shrieked at him. "I want to go home, Brandon! I need to go home! *Now!*"

His concern immediately changed to exasperation. "You know the answer to that! We've been over that at least forty times in the last month! I am not going to change my mind. We'll go to San Francisco soon, but I will not take you home until your father complies with my requests."

"*Demands,* Brandon! The term is 'demands'—or less politely put, blackmail!"

His jaw hardened. "That is a pretty strong accusation, don't you think?"

"So is murder!" she fired back. "And cattle rustling, which you claim my own father is guilty of!"

Rising from the bed, Brandon towered over her. "You'll defend him to the end, won't you, love?" he sneered, "yet you readily condemn me. What will it take, I wonder, to win that fierce loyalty for myself?"

"Take me home!"

"No!"

"Yes! I *need* to go home, especially now!"

"Why especially now?"

"Because . . ." she hesitated, knowing she could not tell him about the baby now, not while they were tearing away at one another.

"Go on." He glared at her and waited for her answer.

"Go to hell, Brandon!" she shouted in frustration. "You don't care about anything but your blasted revenge! I should have listened to Dad all along! It would have saved me a lot of misery!"

Boiling with anger, he loomed closer, teeth bared into a snarl. "I ought to thrash you for that!"

Reacting instinctively to his threat, Laurel shrank from him, her anger forgotten in a wave of fear at the anger on his face.

The look of fright in her eyes drew him up short. Her face had suddenly lost all its color, and her eyes were huge dark circles against her pale skin.

With a snort of self-disgust, Brandon turned away from her. "Damn it, Laurel, don't look at me like that! I'd never hurt you!"

She was crying again. "But you are! We're both hurting each other! We fight constantly these days!"

"It might help if you'd grow up!" he countered. "You're not Daddy's little girl any longer. You're my wife, and it's high time you started acting like it!" He headed for the door, jerking it open.

"Where are you going?"

"I don't know. Out. I'll be back when we've both had time to calm down. Maybe then we can make some sense of this mess we've made of our lives!"

Brandon was gone a long time. Laurel wept until the tears would no longer flow. Then, her face stiff and swollen from crying, she considered their problem. Clearly, Brandon was disgusted with her. They could not go on like this. They were both miserable, and the situation was getting worse day by day. And now she was going to have a child. If Brandon had his way, she would bear it far from home, lonely and heartsick. Laurel could see no way to change his mind.

As she paced the room, Laurel's thoughts flew. Perhaps there *was* a way to resolve the conflict! If she were to run away, to go back home, Brandon would surely follow! If he really loved her, he would come after her and then he and Rex would have to settle things between them. Then they could all settle down to normal lives. She would be near her family, Brandon could resume running his ranch, and they could await the birth of their child in peace. They would be happy again, she was positive of it!

Laurel quickly packed a bag and hid it under the bed. She could not leave now and chance Brandon catching her right away—besides, she had to see him again before she left. She could not go carrying with her the image of his angry face. It might be a long time before she saw him again, if ever. The dreadful thought occured to her that he might not care enough to follow her. If so, this might be their last night together.

Her heart lodged in her throat. What if he didn't come after her? Loving him as she did, it nearly killed her to think of this. More than ever, she was determined to have this one last night; a memory to cherish always. She would hold him and love him and pray he loved her enough to follow her back to Texas.

When Brandon at last returned, Laurel was waiting for him in the darkened room. Knowing her face was a fright from crying, she did not want him to see her. Quietly he undressed and slipped into bed beside her, assuming she was asleep.

Gently she reached out and touched his shoulder. "Brandon, I'm sorry. I said some awful things, and I apologize." She did not want to leave with harsh words between them.

"I said some pretty hateful things myself. Let's just try to forget it, Laurel."

"I hate fighting with you, darling. It breaks my heart to see what we are doing to one another. I love you so terribly!" Her voice broke on the last word, and she buried her face in his shoulder.

With an anguished groan, he turned to her, taking her in his arms. "Oh, Laurel, I love you, too, so very much! This has got to stop, for both our sakes!"

His words only reinforced her decision to leave. It was the only resolution she could see. Turning her face up to his, she sought his mouth with trembling lips. "Love me, Brandon. Please, please love me!" Her words were a prayer from the heart, a plea not only for his physical love now, but for his heartfelt love always.

Their lovemaking that night held a special poignancy. Brandon felt he was about to lose her somehow. With tender words and sweet caresses he loved her, and she gave back to him the full measure of her love. "You are like stroking satin," he whispered. "Your bright hair, your sleek skin, your soft curves. I love the feel of you against my lips."

Those lips were everywhere, exciting and caressing her, worshipping her feminine form that contrasted so perfectly with his own. Beneath her stroking hands, she felt his tempered strength, the firm skin and rippling muscles that shifted beneath her touch like steel sheathed in velvet. She gloried in the sensual excitement of caressing him, of running her hands over his hard, warm body that gave her such intense pleasure.

His body merged with hers, and they were one. Their passion rose, heating them, forging them into one entity as the final ecstasy burst upon them. Satin and steel blended and flowed as one molten mass of quivering splendor.

CHAPTER 14

Laurel stood in the doorway and took one last longing-filled look at Brandon's sleeping form. His face was softened in slumber, a wave of brown hair falling boyishly across his forehead. To leave him like this was the hardest thing she had ever done. Head bowed in despair and eyes clouded with threatening tears, she stepped from the room and softly shut the door behind her.

Making her way quietly toward the kitchen, Laurel managed to pilfer water and food for her flight. Just as stealthily, she made her way through the dark stable, saddled her horse and secured her blanket and saddlebags behind. As she was leading the mare out of the stableyard, she tripped over something soft. It gave a small yelp, and in the dim starlight she made out the fuzzy silver shape of her pet silver fox cub.

"Oh, Tyke!" she breathed. "You scared me witless!" She hoped what little noise they made had not awakened anyone, after all the care she had taken so far. Bending down to pat his head, she told the fox, "You can't go with me, boy. I'm sorry. You have to stay here with Brandon." Before she changed her mind, she mounted her horse and urged the mare into a brisk trot.

Traveling at night in rough, unfamiliar terrain

was risky, but Laurel headed east and let the mare have her head, trusting the horse to keep her footing. Equally risky was the fact that she was a woman riding alone. She'd taken the precaution of tucking her long hair under her hat and donning her denims and a loose shirt. With her rifle at her knee, she felt safe enough for the time being. Still, she hoped she did not encounter many other people on her way.

A few miles away from the ranch, she noticed a small silver blur that seemed to be keeping pace with her. Almost at once she realized what it was. Tyke had followed her! With a sigh of exasperation, she slowed enough for the fox to catch up.

"Okay, Tyke," she relented, looking down at him. "You can come with me as long as you don't slow me down." In truth, she was glad of his company, for it would be a long, lonely ride to Texas.

Brandon woke later than usual, perhaps because Laurel was not wriggling next to him and tossing restlessly about in their bed. At first, her absence did not alarm him. He knew her penchant for early morning rides, and assumed she had persuaded Inez to go out with her. When neither Inez nor Laurel appeared at breakfast, it only seemed to reinforce his presumption.

It wasn't until midway through the morning that he became suspicious. Dressed in a frilly gown, Inez came from the house and asked one of the ranch hands to get the buggy ready. She and Marguerita wished to go in to town to shop. Overhearing her request, Brandon greeted her and asked, "Is Laurel going with you?"

"I don't think so. I haven't seen her to ask her," Inez replied with a smile.

Brandon was instantly alerted. "What do you mean, you haven't seen her? Didn't you two go riding together this morning?"

"No. In fact, I was so tired from the fiesta that I just awoke a little while ago. Why do you ask?"

Brandon did not waste time in answering. He was off and running toward the stable. As he suspected, her horse was missing. "Did anyone see my wife take her horse out?" he asked the stable boy. "Did anyone go with her?'"

"No, *señor*, not that I know," the lad replied. "The horse was gone from its stall when I came to the stables earlier this morning."

On his way to their room, Brandon asked others he met if anyone had seen Laurel. No one had. Once there, a quick look about confirmed his fears. Some of her things were missing, along with one of the saddlebags, a rifle, and a canteen. Tyke was nowhere about. Laurel was gone!

"Damn you, Laurel!" Brandon's agonized cry tore from his constricted throat. Pain such as he had felt only once before, when she had left Crystal City without a word of farewell, ripped through him. "Damn you for running out on me again!"

What a fool he had been to let himself fall in love with her! He should have known better than to trust his heart to that deceitful witch a second time. She had left him once before. Now, nearly three years later, she was up to her old tricks. What a prize idiot he was! He should have learned his lesson the first time around.

Searing anger set his blood pounding in his head. "Not this time, woman!" he declared through clenched teeth. "You won't get away so easily this time! If I have to chase you to hell and back again, I'll find you and drag you back, see if I don't! You belong to me now, like it or not, and you'll stay with me if I have to chain you to my side!"

With the lead she had, it took Brandon three days to catch up to Laurel. It hadn't been hard to guess in which direction she was headed. Even if he hadn't known, her trail was easy enough to follow. There weren't too many riders accompanied by fox cubs, and with no rain, it was easy to distinguish Tyke's paw tracks in the dust alongside the mare's hoofprints. He'd hoped to catch her sooner, but she was too stubborn to stop and rest for long. "Hell, she must be sleeping in the saddle!" he thought furiously. "She sure must want to escape me in the worst way!"

Finally on the third day, Laurel was forced to slow down. She had pushed herself as hard as she could, and had long since reached her limits. If she kept on at this pace, her horse would never survive the hard desert trek ahead of them. Besides, as nearly as she could tell, she was not being followed. Still, she hoped with all her heart that Brandon was somewhere behind her—not close enough to catch her before she reached Crystal City, but following.

Had she realized how close he actually was, and how furious, she would have pressed on, regardless. With every mile, his anger grew, and as her trail became fresher, he pushed his horse hard in an effort to overtake her.

The sun was setting in the foothills behind them when he finally caught sight of her. She was crossing an open stretch of flatland, and he knew she would soon spot him behind her. The first time she turned around to check her backtrail, she would see him, and the chase would be on, but Brandon knew he held the advantage here. His stallion was much more powerful than her little mare. In a race across open land, she didn't stand a chance. A grim smile of triumph creased his face as he urged his horse into a gallop.

Laurel was not aware of his approach until she heard the pounding of hooves behind her. Swinging swiftly about in the saddle, surprise and wariness evident on her tired face, she cast a quick look at the rider. He was close enough that she had no trouble recognizing Brandon, or the look of angry determination on his face. Dread coursed through her, mixed with a quickening fear of what he might do when he caught her. Knowing she stood no chance of outrunning him, she nevertheless spurred her mount into a headlong gallop. The faithful mare obeyed her command and ran full-out for a quarter of a mile, but the effort was too great for the weary horse, and though she'd given it a gallant try, she could not outdistance the long-legged stallion.

Fearful of being unseated, Laurel did not look back again. There was no need. She could hear horse and rider gaining on her. Just as she caught sight of the stallion racing alongside, Laurel was jerked from her saddle. For several yards, she dangled helplessly, caught about the waist and held firmly in the grasp of Brandon's arm until he at last brought his horse to a jarring halt. Abruptly, he released her, and she tumbled to the ground.

Brandon was out of the saddle and looming over her before she could stand. She sat quaking at his feet, looking up into a face black with rage, waiting for the full force of his anger to strike her.

She did not wait long. "You conniving, back-stabbing little witch! Horsewhipping is too good for you! On the other hand, a good beating might do wonders. It just might pound a little sense into you!"

His hand shot out, and she backed away, scooting on her bottom, but she was not fast enough. His big hand clamped about her wrist, and he jerked her to her feet before him.

"No, Brandon! No!" Frantically, she tried to pull loose, but his fingers were like steel biting into her flesh, nearly crushing the fine bones of her wrist. When she tried to resist, he stopped her attempts by simply applying pressure and twisting her arm, effectively quelling her small rebellion.

She faced him warily, tension in every line of her body. He was stiff with restrained fury, and for a long moment they stared at one another.

"*Why*, Laurel? Twice you have run from me; once to Boston and now. Does it give you some sort of thrill to dupe me into falling for your sweet lies, and then disappearing once you have me convinced? Does it amuse you to see me make a fool of myself over you, to hear my declarations of love, when all along you're planning your escape?" His eyes blazed down at her, his mouth twisted in a derisive sneer. "Well, think again, Laurel, because it's not going to work this time."

"It's not like that, Brandon! You don't understand!"

"Don't bother with lies. I'm not buying them anymore!" he snarled. "Just get it through your head that you are not going anywhere without me. When you married me, you entered into a binding commitment. If you're having regrets, that's too damn bad, because I'm holding you to your vows. You'll just have to learn to live with it, and believe me, you'll have plenty of time to adjust—a lifetime. I'll never let you get away from me again!"

The pressure on her wrist increased and Laurel winced. "You're hurting me!"

Brandon scowled. "I'm considering turning you over my knee and whaling the daylights out of you, just for the sheer satisfaction of it!"

Luminous lavender eyes stared up at him, a hint of fear making them appear even larger than usual. "You wouldn't, Brandon. You can't!" she whimpered.

He was too angry to heed her plea. "Oh, I can't, huh?" Both her arms held in his relentless grip, he shook her like a rag doll. "What's it going to take to get through to you? I can do anything I please with you! You're mine, signed and sealed!"

With almost every word, he gave her a hard shake, sending her hat sailing and her silver hair flying about her shoulders. Frightened, her head snapping back and forth and her teeth clattering, she sputtered, "Brandon! For God's sake, I'm *pregnant!*"

He froze. "What?" he hissed, staring down at her white face. "What did you say?"

It was a moment before she could catch her breath and speak again. "I'm expecting our child."

With a frustrated roar, he released her. Hands clenched into fists at his sides, he said, "How *could* you?"

Startled, she blinked in confusion. Finally, she said quietly, "I would say that was evident, Brandon. You were there, and you had as much to do with it as I."

She could hear his teeth grinding from where she stood. "Blast it! That's not what I meant, and you know it! I was referring to your headlong flight, alone, across lands filled with hazards and danger! How dare you risk our child's life for your own selfish satisfaction?" Had he not clenched his fists at his sides he would have shaken her again. "You're as irresponsible as a child yourself! Haven't you any sense at all?"

Nervously chewing her lip, Laurel wondered if he would continue to succeed in controlling himself. "I was desperate," she said softly.

"Desperate!" he snapped. "Desperate to do what? Run home to Daddy and cry on his shoulder? Or would you have shared a laugh at my expense? Perhaps desperate to keep me from learning about your condition? Is that why you ran and didn't bother to tell me about the baby— so you could present Rex with a grandchild without the complication of a son-in-law? How long did you intend to keep the news from me? Forever? Until the child was six? Twelve? Twenty?" His voice rose with his renewed anger. "Damn you, Laurel! You are more devious and spiteful than I would ever have given you credit for!"

"If you would only listen! That was never my intention! I was only trying to help solve matters between us—between you and Dad. I thought if I could go home, if you and Dad were forced to talk face-to-face, this thing could be settled once and for all."

"Pretty sure of yourself weren't you?" he grated. "Awfully certain I would follow you, but I put a snag in your plans by overtaking you too soon. Bad luck, sweetheart!" His smile was nasty.

Tears glistened in her eyes. "Do you think that it didn't break my heart to leave you? I wasn't positive you would follow, but I hoped and prayed you would. Yes, I wish I'd made it home before you caught up with me! It was the only solution I could imagine. I want a normal, loving relationship, Brandon! Is that too much to ask? I want to go back to Crystal City, to live contentedly there with you, to have my family near me and all of us living in peace and understanding!" She was crying openly now, the tears rolling unchecked down her cheeks.

Unmoved by her tears or her impassioned declaration, he said, "Well, you're going to have to settle for San Francisco, because that is where I am taking you. We'll return to Chihuahua, pack our belongings, and say a proper farewell to our hosts. Then we will travel by train to San Francisco, and you can be sure you will never leave my sight the entire time. I am going to keep a very close eye on you from now on, even if I have to resort to hiring someone to guard you when I am otherwise occupied."

"I will not be treated like a prisoner!" she cried.

"You will be treated as you deserve, and as I decide best," he informed her coldly.

They started back the next day after a strained and uncomfortable night. Brandon was too angry and Laurel too distressed to utter more than the bare minimum of words. They rode silently and sullenly, each engrossed in his own troubled thoughts.

All through the day, clouds were gathering. By late afternoon they were boiling masses in the dark, threatening sky. The wind had risen and was now howling across the land. As the weather worsened, it was evident they were in for a bad thunderstorm and Brandon decided they had better seek shelter.

"There is an old abandoned mission not far from here, if I recall correctly. We'll hole up there!" he yelled over the wail of the wind. Motioning for her to follow, he led the way.

By the time they located the mission, the storm had broken. They arrived soaked to the skin and shivering, but before they could attend to themselves, they had to take care of the horses. Leading the animals into the dilapidated building, they stabled them in a corner. When the horses were tended to, they could at least turn their attentions to their own needs.

"You rummage through the saddlebags for some food," Brandon instructed. "I'll see if I can find something to fuel a fire, and maybe a container of some sort to catch water in."

He found nothing useful in the main room, but located a small anteroom that looked as if it warranted exploration. In the gloom of the storm, he could barely see in the small, windowless room, but he thought he spotted a chair in the corner and a small table he could break up for firewood. He had barely reached the chair when Tyke, who had followed at his heels, started yelping excitedly.

"What's the matter, boy?" Brandon asked. No sooner were the words out of his mouth than a flash of movement caught his eye. The ominous warning rattle came too late. With deadly accuracy, the snake struck, sinking its lethal fangs deeply into Brandon's thigh. Brandon let out a startled cry of pain and surprise. Instinct, more than anything, led him to grab immediately at his leg, catching the snake behind the head just as it was withdrawing its fangs to strike again. With an oath, he threw the rattlesnake from him as hard as he could. It bounced off the near wall and landed on the floor, momentarily stunned, and Brandon had suffucient time to draw his gun and shoot. The blast of his Colt was deafening in the small room, but his aim was good. The snake was dead. Brandon's leg was already paining him, and he knew he was in trouble. The random thought flashed through his mind that his luck was running bad lately. First Laurel, and now this!

The sound of the gunshot brought Laurel running. "What . . . ?" The question died on her lips as she saw Brandon clutching his leg, and the dead snake on the floor nearby, its head blown off. "Brandon!"

Turning his head to look at her, Brandon said gruffly, "Don't get hysterical on me, Laurel. I need your help."

Gathering her wits, Laurel swallowed her panic. "Let's get you into the other room so we can get a look at that leg." She helped him hobble into the main room. "Did he get you more than once?"

"No, just once on the thigh. Hell! It was so stupid of me! I should have been more careful. Tyke even tried to warn me."

"Shall I rip the pant leg, or do you want to try to take them off? They're wet anyway, and should be dried."

"Just rip them for now. I didn't bring a spare pair when I came racing after you. With my luck, someone will show up here, and I'll be caught with my britches down!" he joked weakly.

Laurel wasn't laughing. She was too busy castigating herself. It was all her fault they were out here in the middle of nowhere with no help for miles around.

Using Brandon's knife, she slit the pant leg and gingerly examined the wound. Already it was turning red and swollen, with ugly purple bruises about the two puncture wounds.

"How does it look?" he asked, twisting about to see for himself.

"Not good." This was no time for trying to sweeten the vinegar. "Let me have your belt. We need to keep the poison from spreading." She looped the belt about his thigh and pulled it tight, cutting off the flow of blood. "Just lie back and keep this tight, Brandon. I'm going to have to get a fire started so I can see what I'm doing." She headed for the anteroom again.

"Laurel! Don't go in there! There may be more rattlers."

"I need that table and chair for wood," she told him. "I'll be careful."

Tyke went in with her, and she retrieved the furniture without incident, shaking all the while. She also found a couple of planks leaning against a wall and a small unbroken wooden bowl.

Brandon was right where she had left him, and from the looks of him, not feeling very well. As fast as possible, she got a fire going, then sterilized the knife blade by running it through the flames.

Brandon watched, knowing she was preparing to lance the wound and let the poison drain. Bracing himself on his elbows, teeth clenched against the pain, he watched as she made small slits across the punctures. As she applied pressure, trying to squeeze the venom and blood from his leg so it would drain, he let out a low moan and a sharp hiss of agony. Otherwise, he gave no indication of the pain he was suffering.

"This isn't working, Brandon." Setting aside the knife, she repositioned herself and lowered her mouth to the wound.

"Laurel! No! You can't!" He tried to push her head away. "Think of the baby. It's too big a risk!

One small open scratch in your mouth—one tiny drop of venom . . ."

"Brandon, I've got to. There is no other way. Please, darling! It's because of me that you are in this predicament. Let me help you."

Once more she lowered her head, her lips closing tightly about first one puncture wound and then the other, sucking out as much of the venom as she could and spitting it out onto the earthen floor. Time and again she fought the urge to swallow, held back the reflexive gagging, as she worked over his leg. Finally, she had pulled as much poison from his wound as possible. The rest was up to nature and Brandon—and God.

Washing the bowl as best she could, she heated some water from the canteen and washed his thigh, using strips of her shirt tail to bind it. She set the bowl out in the rain to collect more water. Arranging their blankets and other belongings, she made him as comfortable as possible. Then she sat back to watch and wait.

Brandon slipped into a fitful sleep. Soon he was feverish. As he unconsciously fought the poison in his system, his color rose and his breathing became more shallow. He tossed about restlessly, and several times Laurel had to lay her full weight upon him to keep him still. He began to mumble in delirium; strange, disjointed phrases, distorted references to Jim and Rex and Laurel. Once he cried out in his sleep, calling her name and reaching for her. When she bathed his forehead and soothed him with comforting words, he looked up at her with fever-glazed eyes that she knew did not truly see her.

It was a long, sleepless night for Laurel. Repeatedly, she cooled his brow with the wet cloth and cleansed his wound, checking for tell-tale streaks of red along his thigh that thankfully did not appear. Finally, near dawn, his fever broke and he slept deeply and naturally. He would live.

Throughout her vigil, Laurel had a lot of time to think. A few hours ago, she had been fleeing him. Now that he was so helpless, she could easily slip away. Once she was sure he would recover, she could escape and head once again for Texas. By the time he was well enough to travel, she would be far ahead of him.

These thoughts did occur to her, but she quickly rejected them. The near-fatal disaster had shown her anew how much she loved this man. He could be unyielding and hateful at times, untrusting and stubborn and resentful, but she loved him more than life. She would stay with him. She would go to San Francisco with him and bear their child. Beyond his safety, her one prayer was that somehow, someday, she could prove to him how wrong he was about her father. She needed to convince him fully of her love and gain his in return, as well as his faith and trust, which she knew she had nearly destroyed by her flight.

When he awoke, lucid at last, Brandon was surprised to find Laurel by his side. "I thought you'd have left," he murmured.

Her eyes, so dark with lack of rest, held his in a solemn gaze. "No, Brandon. I couldn't do that to you—to us. I love you too much. I'd never leave you helpless."

"I won't be helpless long, you know. We're still going to San Francisco. I haven't changed my mind about that."

"I suspected as much."

"You still have time to run. I couldn't very well follow you now."

Laurel shook her head. "If I thought it would change your attitude about Dad, and give our lives some peace and normality, I'd be sorely tempted. But I can see now that I was wrong."

"About what—your father?" Brandon asked warily.

"No. Wrong to run away. I still believe in my father's innocence. Nothing you can say will change how I feel about him; about what kind of man I know in my heart he is."

"Then we're bound to argue about it again and again," he warned, "because I am positive he is guilty."

Laurel shrugged and gave him a weary smile. "I'm sure we will, Brandon, but not until you are well."

"Not one to take advantage of a man while he's down, huh?" he teased weakly.

"That's right, darlin'," she said cockily. "If it's worth fighting over, we'll at least do it right!"

CHAPTER 15

Nothing, not even her two years in Boston, had prepared Laurel for San Francisco. The train pulled into the Southern Pacific Railroad station at midday, at the very height of the city's business day. The steep streets were teeming with vehicles of every sort; horses, buggies, automobiles, cable and trolley cars. New concrete and brick buildings towered as much as eighteen stories toward the sky, vying for space between neighboring wooden structures. Sidewalks were crowded with people, some hurrying about on lunch breaks, others on errands, shopping, or simply enjoying the city. San Francisco was wide awake and bustling with the clatter of traffic, crowds, and the clang of cable car bells.

As their hired carriage transported them through the streets, Laurel was fascinated, her head turning this way and that, trying to see everything at once. She was also a bit intimidated by the commotion, and sheer size of the city. As she gaped and gawked about, her hand clutched tightly at Brandon's arm, seeking assurance and security. "My goodness!" she exclaimed breathlessly time and again.

Brandon was more than a little amused by her reaction. "Honey, if you don't stop twisting your head around like that, you'll have a stiff neck for a week! Those buildings aren't going anywhere. They'll still be here after we've settled into our house. You'll have plenty of time later to explore to your heart's content."

Laurel laughed with him, too excited to be abashed. Then another unusual sight caught her eye. "Oh, my! Look at that!"

Following her pointing finger, Brandon nodded. "Those are Chinamen. There are a great many of them in San Francisco. Not far from here there's an area of the city called Chinatown where most of them live. It's a thriving community, with its own business section, residential area, and even its own bawdy district."

"Is it true that many San Franciscans have Chinese servants?"

"Yes," Brandon said. "They are hard-working people and make reliable help. However, Chinatown has its own codes and vices, and no respectable white person in his right mind would risk entering Chinatown after dark."

"Is it really so disreputable?" asked Laurel, wide-eyed.

"It is that *dangerous*," Brandon corrected. "I want your promise, here and now, that you will never wander into Chinatown, no matter how curious you might be. Too many men and women and children have mysteriously disappeared in those narrow, twisting streets, never to be seen again."

Laurel's lavender eyes were wide with horror. "Killed?" she asked.

"Or worse," Brandon answered solemnly.

"What could be worse than that?"

Laurel was sorry she had asked when Brandon explained. "*Worse* to find yourself drugged on opium, helpless in the clutches of the evil men who deal in the drug. Worse is a child or woman kidnapped and forced into service as a prostitute or 'pretty boy' of some would-be Chinese potentate; or forced to sell your favors in one of the multitude of bawdy houses and filthy cribs that line those dark lanes to anyone who has the price."

Laurel had heard more than enough. Embarrassed by his blunt words, color rushed to her cheeks, and she found it impossible to meet his gaze. Her head turned away, she begged, "Brandon, please! I find this talk offensive!"

He laughed shortly, without humor. "You'd find it a damned sight more offensive to actually be in such a situation. I want your word that you will never go near Chinatown without me. If you are truly curious, I will take you on a short tour one day, and we will have a Chinees meal and you may shop for souvenirs, but you are not to go alone or with anyone else."

She gave him her word, shuddering in disgust as she did so. "I'll only go when you take me," she promised. "Even then, I don't think I want to spend too much time there, and only in broad daylight."

"I didn't mean to give you the impression that all Chinese are evil, Laurel. There are many honest and good people among them, but they are a race apart, with their own ideas, religions, and values. Not too many of them care overmuch for white Americans, either. Their ways and ours differ too greatly for there to be much common ground between us, and the white man has exploited the Chinese shamefully.

"You'll find a lot of contradictions in San Francisco. It is a city unique unto itself, unlike any other on earth. In time, once you become accustomed to the noise and bustle, I'm sure you will come to like it.''

There were more surprised in store for Laurel. Brandon had told her his grandfather had built a house on Nob Hill which had been bequeathed to Brandon upon the elderly gentleman's death. Imagining a modest home in a pleasant neighborhood, Laurel was unprepared for the sight that met her gaze.

The crest of Nob Hill was crowned with more magnificent mansions than Laurel had ever dreamed existed. The wealthy gold, silver, and railroad kings of a bygone era had spared no expense in erecting these monuments to high society and rich living. Set like jewels on large lots, some were grand, stately homes, subtle statements of wealth, comfort, and immense power. Others were so ornate and outrageously fashioned as to be ostentatious displays of wealth, gaudy and almost offensive.

Brandon pointed out some of the homes to her. There was the Stanford mansion, now the headquarters and offices of Stanford University. Across the way was the Hopkins house, now the Hopkins Art Institute. Another mansion sat regally empty, formerly the home of a railroad magnate, Charles Crocker.

Laurel stared at the hand-wrought bronze fence surrounding the forty-two-room mansion of James Flood. According to Brandon, Flood had made his fortune in silver, and had paid the grand sum of sixty thousand dollars for the fence alone! Such extravagance was beyond Laurel's comprehension.

And then there was the nearly erected Fairmont Hotel in all its regal splendor. Immense, its walls were constructed of marble, with terraces and pillars abounding. The property, once owned by another silver millionaire, James Fair, now belonged to his daughter. Tessie had a modern, beautiful home of her own in the Western Addition. Having more wealth than she could possibly spend in six lifetimes, she was indulging a favorite whim by building the hotel, which she hoped would prove to be the grandest hotel in San Francisco. Downtown, the famed Palace Hotel had long held that distinction, but Tessie was about to put the Palace's reign to an end.

A short distance from the Fairmont, their carriage turned onto a tree-shaded lane, passing first beneath a wide stone arch at the head of the drive. Lush, well-tended lawns were gentle on the eye and beds of fragrant flowers dotted the rolling green at intervals, with ornate birdbaths and small marble statues to delight the viewer.

"What a lovely park, Brandon!" Laurel exclaimed delightedly. "Is your home near here? I would love to be within walking distance of this place."

Brandon exploded in mirth and Laurel was at a loss to understand his laughter until, with some effort, he composed himself and explained. "Laurel, you are looking at our front lawn. This is our property, and I assure you, you can play in it to your heart's content."

Laurel's lips formed a mute "O" as she stared at him. Before she could formulate a reply, the carriage emerged from the trees and pulled to a stop before an imposing mansion. Laurel's hand flew to her throat as she gazed in wonder at what was to be her home.

Constructed of dark wood and light-colored stone, it towered four stories tall with turrets at the four corners. It resembled a miniature castle. The long, narrow windows were grouped together to provide the owner an unobstructed view of the city below. Near the apex of the steepled roof, a magnificent stained-glass window looked down upon the cobbled walk and the hedges fronting the house. A small porte cochere provided a protected approach to the wide double doors in any weather.

Laurel blinked in amazement. As Brandon assisted her out of the carriage, a giggle escaped. With a toss of her head, she eyed him skeptically, humor sparkling in her eyes. "What? No draw-bridge? I'm disappointed!"

He roared with laughter. "You are priceless, Laurel! Simply priceless!"

The inside of the house was equally spectacular. A wide entry hall ran the length of the house, front to back, exiting onto the rear veranda which over-looked a huge, rambling garden and more rolling lawn. At one side of the hall was a broad staircase to the upper floors. Several large rooms opened up on either side of the corridor. The front parlor, dining room and kitchen took up one half; a spacious library, private study, and sunny rear parlor the other. Upstairs were bedroom suites, each with its own bath and sitting room. On the third floor were more bedrooms, a sewing room, and an entire wall of closets for clothes and linens. The fourth floor consisted of the attic and servant's quarters, and the basement held a bountiful pantry and wine cellar.

To the rear of the house, past the gardens and to one side, was an enormous carriage house. Right in the center of the garden, to Laurel's delight, stood a lattice-enclosed gazebo, and under the rose arbor hung a swing. Scattered about the lawn were huge shade trees, interspersed with palms, a

grape arbor, and fruit trees. More statuary graced
the garden and rear lawn.

The furnishings of the house were tasteful and
obviously very expensive, though the decor varied
from room to room, as if Grandad Harris got
easily bored with one period or color scheme.
Laurel noted several paintings she felt instinctively were very old and valuable. The draperies
were of brocade, velvet, silk or satin, depending on
the room. Several rooms were thickly carpeted,
while others had decorative throw rugs scattered
over highly polished hardwood floors.

"This is all very impressive, Brandon." Laurel
hesitated, then added, "It's also quite a surprise."

He heard the note of accusation in her voice.
Brandon had never let it be known to Laurel, or
anyone else in Crystal City for that matter, that he
possessed such wealth. "You're angry that I never
told you," he surmised.

Laurel bit her lip, her eyes searching his. "I
think I'm more hurt than anything, that you felt
you had to hide this from me. Did you think I
would want to marry you for your money if I had
known?"

"Actually, it wasn't so much a matter of hiding
my wealth as not flaunting it, Laurel. I didn't need
to impress anyone, and I certainly didn't want to
lord it over anyone or set myself apart from my
friends and neighbors. I'm a rancher, plain and
simple. All this," he gestured to the house, "is just
an added benefit, bequeathed to me by Grandad
Harris—an insurance policy of sorts against hard
times."

"Some insurance policy!" Laurel retorted.
"You're altogether too modest, Brandon!" On
second thought, she asked, "Is there anything else

I should know about that you have neglected to tell me? Any more little surprises?"

Brandon had the grace to look sheepish. "A few inconsequential things," he admitted.

"Such as?"

"Such as holdings in various areas—a bank, a railroad, a lumber company in Oregon, and a fair amount of ready cash." Brandon shrugged helplessly at Laurel's stunned expression. "Grandad believed in diversification. He thought it unwise to put all his eggs in one basket."

Laurel tried to assimilate all Brandon had told her, but her brain was simply too overwhelmed to cooperate. With a shake of her head, she gave up trying to understand it all. "A fine, wise fellow was Grandad Harris," she said with a shaky smile.

Brandon laughed with delight and relief. "I'm glad to see you're taking all this so well, Laurel!" he teased.

Her eyes twinkled up at his with suppressed laughter. "Just lead me to my featherbed and my satin-covered down comforter. I feel the need to swoon in decadent elegance!"

The next few days Laurel spent settling into the house and accustoming herself to being surrounded by servants. It was a new experience for her, and took some time getting used to. There was Kramer, the butler; Gertrude, the cook; Hanna, the housekeeper; Millie, the upstairs maid who also served as Laurel's personal maid; Wanda, the downstairs maid; Ching, the gardener, whose son helped keep the grounds; a coachman and a stableboy; and Thomas, the chauffeur. Laurel had trouble keeping their duties and stations straight, let alone their various names. In the end, she con-

ferred mainly with Hanna, and left her to delegate
the household chores. Millie was the only other
servant Laurel had close personal contact with,
for it was her duty to run Laurel's bath, lay out her
clothes, turn down the bed, and do whatever else
her young mistress required. It was all very
confusing at first, but it was also very nice. As her
pregnancy advanced, Laurel quickly became
accustomed to being pampered.

Laurel was enthralled with all the modern con-
veniences available in San Francisco as well as in
her new home. How lovely it would be if Crystal
City had all these marvelous innovations available! She had only to pick up the telephone to
make an appointment with the hairdresser or
order something from one of the downtown shops.
Outside, gas lamps lighted the drive and gardens,
while indoors one had only to touch a button or
flip a switch, and the electric lights chased away
the gloom from the dark corners of any room.
There were even lights in the closets.

The bathrooms delighted Laurel. Each had taps
for hot and cold running water. It was the same
with the kitchen sink, and there was a gas refrig-
erator rather than the familiar icebox in the
sparkling, modern kitchen. Next to the piano in
the parlor was a new Victrola, an invention to
which Laurel was especially partial. A few years
previously, Brandon had had central heating
intalled with heat registers throughout the house;
for winters in San Francisco, though not usually
terribly cold, could be miserably damp and chilly.
This February was proving wet and cool for the
most part.

One of the first things Brandon insisted upon as
soon as they were settled in was that Laurel see a
doctor. Though she resisted the idea, assuring him

she felt fine, Brandon was adamant. "I want to be certain everything is as it should be. Humor me, sweetheart. I need to be sure both you and the baby are healthy. Also, there might be some special things you should be eating or doing—or not, in your condition."

Laurel finally gave in, and discovered Dr. Davis to be pleasant and informative. After reassuring Brandon that Laurel and the baby were progressing normally, he also gave her some basic instructions. Of course, she was to get proper meals and plenty of rest, and make sure she drank enough milk. He advised her to drink no more than one glass of wine at supper, and to avoid emotional upset if possible. Naturally, she could expect to be more emotional than usual as were many expectant mothers. A few dry crackers or biscuits would help alleviate her morning nausea, and avoidance of spicy foods would ease the heartburn.

She was to get plenty of fresh air and moderate exercise, but was not to ride horseback until several months after the child's arrival. According to his calculations, the baby was due in mid to late August. Laurel was to see Dr. Davis regularly until then and to contact him immediately if any problems arose.

Rather more pleasant for Laurel was meeting some of her neighbors and friends and acquaintances of Brandon's. As soon as word got about that the Prescotts were in residence, everyone was eager to meet Brandon's bride and to include the couple in social activities.

Most of the people Laurel met were extremely nice. She especially liked James Fair's daughter, Tessie, she of the Fairmont Hotel. The woman was friendly and warm, an outgoing individual. Muriel

Cook, the daughter of another neighbor, was another story entirely. Her flaming red hair and tall, lithe figure did nothing to make Laurel like her any better. The woman was devastatingly beautiful and she knew it. Young, gorgeous, and outrageously rich, she was also unmarried and *very* available, a fact she went out of her way to impress upon Brandon. With imperious disdain, she looked down her nose at Laurel, both literally and figuratively. She had the temerity to criticize Texas, Laurel's distinctive drawl, her taste in clothing, even the color of her hair.

"Dear girl," she shrilled, "it must be dreadfully hard to find a hairdresser capable of producing that pale blonde shade accurately twice in a row. If you have difficulty, call me. Perhaps, as a special favor, Alphonse will give you an appointment."

Laurel bristled immediately, aware that all twenty people in the crowded room had heard Miss Cook's catty comment. Determined to stay calm, she summoned every bit of control she could muster, and answered smoothly, "Unlike yours perhaps, Muriel, the color of my hair is quite natural. I know you meant no offense, though. You must have had an extremely trying day, dear. Did someone happen to hide your sandbox, or did they neglect to fill your saucer with milk?" Amidst snickers and smiles from others and a hateful glare from Muriel, Laurel turned on her heel and regally walked away. She heard someone call out quite distinctly, "Meow!" and couldn't keep from smiling.

For the most part, Laurel liked Brandon's other friends and the acquaintances she met through Tessie. Soon she was accepting invitations to teas and luncheons and shopping expeditions with the other women. As long as Thomas drove her about in the motor-car and delivered her home at a reasonable hour, Brandon did not object, but would not allow her out of the house on her own. Laurel wondered if this was because he did not trust her fully, or merely because he was concerned about her going out into a strange city alone. Regardless, she was enjoying herself immensely.

Laurel loved the stores the city had to offer. There was everything from the smallest specialty shop to the vastness of the famed Emporium. A visit to the Emporium was like a trip to a vast fairyland, a shopping extravaganza. It was considered the world's largest and most complete department store, with goods imported from all over the globe.

In addition to her shopping sprees with the other women, Brandon too took her around to many of the stores. With a nonchalance that amazed her, he approved her selections and paid enormous sums as she added to her wardrobe. Laurel had never seen this side of Brandon before. (Of course, she'd never realized he was so incredibly wealthy, either.)

Here in San Francisco, socializing with the elite, she needed many more outfits, especially formal attire. It took her breath away to see the price Brandon paid for one evening gown alone. Then, in an extravagant gesture that almost sent her straight into a swoon, he bought her a sable coat.

As she stroked the luxurious fur, Laurel whispered in awe, "Brandon, this is much too expensive!" But even as she spoke, she hugged the collar closer about her throat.

He smiled. "Call it a birthday present, if it makes you feel better."

"You know perfectly well my birthday isn't until the first of May." Her words were muffled as she snuggled her nose deeply into the fur.

"Ah, the month of emeralds! I knew we were forgetting something." From there he took her immediately to the jeweler's, where he lavished her with pretties—rings, bracelets, earrings, necklaces, even a tiara.

"Brandon, I'll never wear all this! Truly, it's not necessary," she protested weakly.

Brandon ignored her protest. "Your beauty needs no jewels to enhance it, I grant you. However,I will not have others think I am too stingy to provide my wife with the proper adornment, and I will not have you feeling dowdy next to the other women."

Laurel was soon to find that Brandon was correct in this. At parties and theatres she saw women bedecked from head to toe in sparkling jewels. Often the display was positively gaudy, especially with the newly rich who tended to flaunt their newfound wealth. It was not uncommon to see a woman wearing two or three diamond bracelets, a necklace, a tiara, several rings, brooches, earrings, even jeweled clips on her shoes and in her hair, all at once. Laurel's innate good taste combined with Brandon's knowledge of society's ways, prevented her from such ostentation. When they went out, Laurel was always tastefully arrayed, her jewels only enchancing her already sparkling beauty.

In order to acquaint Laurel with the city, Brandon often took her sightseeing. Each day they would do something different, and each day was for Laurel a special holiday to treasure.

To satisfy her curiosity, Brandon even took her

to Chinatown. Together they wandered the twisting streets, dodging children and vendors alike, investigating intriguing shops along the way. In one shop, Laurel bought a delicious herbal tea, and in another, a delicate hand-painted fan. They stopped in a little restaurant for a mouth-watering lunch of delicately seasoned chicken with rice and vegetables.

On their way back they passed an interesting shop, and Brandon stopped to look at a brass figurine of a stallion. It was there that Laurel found the most sensually beautiful silk garment she had ever seen, a long, slim sheath designed to cling to a woman's curves, outlining her body even as it hid and enticed. Of vibrant turquoise shot through with shining silver threads, it had short cap sleeves and a stand-up collar with a low-cut vee opening that ended suggestively between the breasts. The skirt was so narrow that long slits had been left on both sides in order for the wearer to walk, slits that ran well above the knee and revealed tantalizing glimpses of thigh.

Laurel was mad for it, even though her pregnancy would not allow her to wear it for long. "If I buy you this dress," Brandon said huskily, already envisioning how she would look in it, "you must promise you will wear it only for me. It's much too alluring for public display."

Laurel laughed. "Afraid I'll start a stampede, Brandon?"

"As a matter of fact, yes—a stampede of every red-blooded man in San Francisco straight for our door." Brandon shot her an amused look. "Think what damage that would do to our lawn!"

She demurely gave him her promise and received the dress. Later, in the privacy of their bedroom, Brandon reaped the rewards of his generosity in the arms of his beautiful, passionate wife.

Rain, fog, or sunshine, Laurel and Brandon did not let the weather keep them from indulging themselves in the sights and sounds of the City by the Bay. Most evenings they ate out, until Gertrude began to wonder why they bothered to keep her on as a cook. Brandon was as delighted to show Laurel the wonders of San Francisco as she was to discover them. The theatres were fabulous, the restaurants divine.

One day Brandon invited her to go with him to a boxing match at the Pavillion. It was an experience she would not easily forget. She sat in mute distress as the opponents proceeded to pound the daylights out of each other. Never would she understand the attraction boxing seemed to hold for the male species! The haze of cigar smoke did nothing to hide the damage the boxers were suffering; the only thing it did was make Laurel slightly nauseated and give her a headache. She winced as blows connected, blood spurted, and faces swelled. Heartily glad when the contest was finally over, she suggested the next time Brandon wanted to go, he go with someone else.

Their days were full, their nights long and loving. The only thing that marred Laurel's contentment was that she had heard no word from her father in response to Brandon's letter. Brandon had checked the mail when they arrived, receiving only a letter from his brother. According to Hank, all was well at the ranch. Rex was fit to be tied over Laurel's marriage, but had made no mention to anyone of Brandon's letter as far as Hank knew.

Also, Rex had not begun making restitution to Becky Lawson or the others, unless he was doing it secretly and Hank had not heard of it.

Rex needed time to think things over, Laurel, decided. When he had calmed down, they would hear from him.

CHAPTER 16

The Mechanic's Pavillion was also the scene of the annual Mardi Gras Costume Ball. It was a festive occasion, and one everyone looked forward to attending. While not averse to a party, Brandon was not thrilled with costume affairs. For days, he and Laurel argued over what to wear. No matter how many ideas she came up with, he found some fault.

"What about Cleopatra and Mark Antony?" she suggested.

"Too overworked," he said. "Besides, you'll never get me into a skirt!"

Marie Antoinette and King Louis was also too common, and he balked when she suggested Guinevere and Lancelot. "If you think I'll put on a pair of tights, you are crazy!"

Clowns, bears, elves, animals or fairy tale and nursery rhyme characters were far beneath him. "I'll not make a fool of myself before hundreds of people, Laurel, not even for you. And don't suggest a devil either," he warned with a dark look. "Horns, tail and pitchfork are definitely out." It was a shame, for she thought his attitude suited the part perfectly just now.

At last she threw up her hands in frustration.

"All right, you stubborn cowboy! Go as your mean, ornery self!"

His head swiveled about, and his eyes lit up in amused satisfaction. "You're right, Laurel! By heaven, I think you've hit on something! I'll go as a cowboy!"

She looked at him as if he had lost his mind. "And what am I supposed to be dressed as—an Indian?" Pulling at a lock of her pale hair, she waved it at him.

"You can go as a pioneer woman, poke bonnet and all."

Laurel wrinkled her nose in disgust. "Not on your life! I'll not spend the entire evening looking dowdy, homespun, and fat, and feeling even more miserable than I look!"

"Well, then come up with another of your brilliant schemes," he challenged. "It was your idea that we dress to match one another."

For several minutes she contemplated the problem. Brandon could almost hear the wheels spinning in her head. "I have it!" she declared suddenly, a wicked light dancing in her lavender eyes.

Brandon groaned audibly. "Why do I feel I'm going to regret this?" he muttered half to himself.

"It's perfect! I'll go as a dance-hall girl!"

Brandon nearly choked on his cigarillo smoke, and Laurel pounded him enthusiastically on the back. When he could speak, he said, "Honey, don't you think that's a bit out of line, especially in your condition?"

But Laurel was not to be dissuaded. She was already assembling her costume in her mind. 'I'll need a bright, gaudy dress with lots of frills and a full, flounced skirt—maybe even a few sequins on it . . ."

"Not too short," he warned, but he wasn't sure she heard him as she rambled on. "And not too revealing," he added for good measure.

"A low neckline, maybe off the shoulder, and a feather for my hair, and net stockings and high heeled shoes!"

"How do you know how a dance hall girl dresses?" he asked suspiciously.

She gave him a look of exasperation. "I'm not stupid, Brandon, nor blind! I've seen some of those women around Crystal City, and what I haven't actually seen, I've heard the ranch hands talk about."

Brandon gave in, though not without reluctance. "Don't forget your fancy garter, Miss Know-It-All!"

In the end, Laurel made a very fetching dance-hall girl indeed, with her hair caught back to one side and a tinted ostrich plume waving saucily about her head. Around her neck she wore a satin ribbon to match her dress, which was full skirted and low bodiced, of pink and black striped satin, with rows of ruffles accenting the neckline and hem. Just above the knee of her black net stockings, a pert garter could be glimpsed once in a while in tantalizing flashes as she moved.

With her carefully accented lips and rouge-blushed cheeks, she was a very tempting morsel, and Brandon was hard put to keep his jealousy under control, or his hands off her as she clung to his arm. When the clock struck midnight, the cowboy made off with his woman, and they brought their "flirtation" to a very satisfying conclusion in their own bed.

* * *

Valentine's Day lent its own special sentimentality to the young lovers. Laurel planned an intimate, candlelight dinner for two, and Gertrude finally found her moment to shine in the kitchen.

When Laurel appeared before Brandon early that evening in a sleek apricot satin peignor guaranteed to raise any living man's blood pressure, she smiled at the delight and appreciation on his face. His eyes gleamed like polished swords as his heated gaze traveled her body. Her perfume teased his senses when she drifted closer to wrap her arms around his neck and offer her lips for his kiss.

When they eventually parted, he noted for the first time the carefully set table, complete with fresh flowers and lit candles. "What is all this?"

Her lavender eyes sparkled. "A private, intimate evening for just the two of us."

Brandon laughed and shook his head. "If I'd known, I wouldn't have made a reservation at the St. Francis."

"If you had known, it wouldn't have been a surprise." She gazed up at him beguilingly, and Brandon was immediately lost. "Call and cancel the reservation, Brandon," she whispered suggestively. He didn't need to be asked twice.

The dinner was delicious, proving Gertrude well worth her wages. The wine and Laurel were going straight to Brandon's head. After the meal, she led him into the darkened parlor, where she had drawn the drapes and had Kramer light a fire in the fireplace. There she handed him a small, gift-wrapped box and a frilly, Valentine's card.

Laurel had gotten him a beautiful diamond stickpin, with his initial carved in gold. He loved it.

"Unfortunately," she said, wrinkling her nose at him, "you'll be getting the bill from the jeweler soon."

"I don't mind," he assured her with a laugh and a long kiss. "I have a gift for you, too, darling," he told her. "I didn't forget. I just thought it best to wait."

He left the room and returned a few moments later carrying a ribbon-bedecked cage covered with a cloth. When she had read the sentimental card, he set the cage on a stand and whisked off the cover.

Out from beneath the bars of the carrying cage stared two brilliant turquoise blue eyes in a seal brown feline face. Wariness held the slim, streamlined brown and cream body rigid. It was only a kitten, but it exuded such an aura of indignant arrogance that Laurel had to laugh. "What is it, Brandon? I've never seen a cat like this one."

"It's a Siamese. Do you like her?"

Laurel turned back to take a better look. The little kitten's face, ears, paws, and the tip of her tail were brown, with varied streaks across the cream colored chest and back. And those eyes were positively hypnotizing! "Yes, she's adorable! Thank you, sweetheart." She leaned forward to bestow a kiss on Brandon's cheek.

"Do you think she'll get along with Tyke, though?" Laurel worried. "She's awfully small!"

"Small but mighty!" Brandon chuckled. "That feisty little feline has a temper and claws to go with it, believe me, just like you. She'll hold her own."

"She does look sassy," Laurel agreed.

"Is that what you're going to call her? It certainly fits!"

"Sassy it is then. Heavens, Brandon! Our family is growing by leaps and bounds!"

His eyes laughed down at her. "Shall I take her back, then?"

"Oh, no you don't, Brand! She's mine now."

Sassy and Tyke were not destined to become fast friends. In fact, they hardly tolerated being in the same room together. Tyke, bless his foxy soul, tried his best at first to make friends, but every time he poked his inquisitive nose in her direction, Sassy tried to scratch it. She hissed and clawed and spit at him like a miniature demon. There was only so much a fellow could tolerate, after all, and Tyke soon became as belligerent as Sassy, yelping and barking whenever he caught sight of the kitten.

Life around those two was anything but peaceful, and Brandon soon came to regret bringing the creature home, especially since it had developed a distinct antipathy to him. Whenever he came near, Sassy would hiss, and the hair on her back would stand straight up, and her tail would bristle. At first he could not understand her behavior. The kitten had adored Laurel from the start. Finally it dawned on him—the blasted cat was jealous! Sassy wanted Laurel's attention all to herself, with no interferences from anyone or anything.

"Well, I'll be hanged! How do you like that! And I innocently brought the little beast right into our midst, not suspecting her truly vile nature!"

"Oh, Brandon! Don't be so melodramatic!" Laurel laughed. "It's not so terrible. In time she'll learn to tolerate you, I'm sure."

"I'm *not* sure, but I suppose I can put up with it. Just make sure she's not around when we make love. Everytime I kiss you, Sassy's back goes up and she bares those sharp little claws. I don't need the skin ripped off my back by a jealous cat. You manage enough of that on your own!"

Laurel's face turned bright pink.

"Brandon! You are absolutely shameless!"

"Funny—that's exactly what I was going to say about you," he retorted with a wicked grin. "Come upstairs with me, sweetheart, and let's be shameless together!"

With a helpless laugh, she let him lead her to their bed.

In all the excitement, Laural was able to forget their problems for a short time, but they all came rushing back when Brandon received a letter from Rex at last.

He was not at home when the letter arrived. Kramer placed it on Brandon's desk in the study along with his other mail. Only Laurel's deeply-rooted sense of integrity kept her from opening it, though her fingers literally itched to rip open the envelope and read her father's reply. The suspense was nearly unbearable, and she was torn—half wanting to know what her father had written, half almost afraid of what she would learn.

The moment Brandon stepped through the door and saw the tense expression on Laurel's face, he knew something was wrong. He stood quietly, waiting for her to tell him what it was.

"You have a letter from Dad," she murmured, her eyes closing briefly, as if in pain.

Brandon felt suddenly cold. He watched her face intently. "What did he say?"

She shook her head, her hands fluttering nervously. "I—I don't know. It was addressed to you, and I didn't open it. It's on your desk."

With a brief nod, he went into his study and closed the door behind him. For a long moment he simply held the letter in his hand, staring at it. Then, with a sigh, he opened it. He read slowly, absorbing the tone of the letter as well as the words. The contents were no great surprise; it was what he had expected. When he finished reading, he sat quietly on the edge of his desk, contemplating the letter and what to tell Laurel. At last he went to face her.

"Hank was right. Your father is as mad as a hornet."

"What did he say? Has he disowned me completely?" Her lips trembled as she awaited Brandon's reply.

He smiled gently and shook his head. "It's not quite that bad, Laurel. Let's just say we'll have to do without his blessing. He doesn't blame you for any of this. It's me he detests."

He sensed the relief flooding through her. "What else does he say? May I read the letter?"

"I'd really rather you didn't. He uses some pretty strong words." As she continued to stare up at him with agonized eyes, he continued, "Rex still denies having anything to do with the rustling, if that is what you want to know, and refuses to repay the other ranchers and Becky."

"That doesn't surprise me. You can't expect a man to admit to a crime he didn't commit, or to make restitution for something he did not do!" she cried hotly.

"That remains to be seen. Also, he has ordered me to bring you home immediately, and threatens to draw and quarter me if I harm so much as a hair on your head."

Laurel almost smiled at this, for it sounded exactly like what her father would say in one of his dark rages. But her face sobered immediately, and she turned soulful eyes to Brandon's. "What now?''

A deep, resigned breath escaped his throat. ''More of the same, Laurel. We stay here; I write another letter to your father, spelling out my terms; we wait to see what he will do next.''

She turned her face from him. ''How long can we go on like this?'' she moaned.

''Forever, if necessary!'' He walked to her side, taking her chin in his hand and forcing her to look at him. ''If he were any man but your father, and if I could prove his guilt in a court of law, I'd see him hang for what he has done. I know I seem harsh to you, but my best friend died because of him, and under the circumstances I think I've been more than fair. My demands are not out of line. They are extremely lenient compared to the man's crimes. The only reason I've been patient is because of you.''

She shook her head in vehement denial. ''No, Brandon. The only reason you haven't extracted a deeper revenge is that you have no proof to back your claims; and the reason you have no proof is because my father is innocent!''

They were back to their original stand-off, both of them stubbornly insistent, neither willing to give ground. Their difference of opinion hung in the air like a pall, and it was several days before they could throw off this dark shadow that hovered over them like a cloud. Only their abiding love allowed them to regain something of their former happiness, and only by a determined effort from each of them. When Brandon awoke many nights to find Laurel sobbing quietly into her pillow, there was no need to ask what was wrong. Too proud and stubborn to admit he might be wrong, he simply drew her into his arms and held her tightly until she slept.

* * *

While Laurel could still fit into her wedding
dress, Brandon suggested they have a photograph
taken. So pleased was he with the result that he
commissioned an artist to paint a portrait based
on the print.

Laurel barely managed to squeeze into the
dress, telling Brandon it was a good thing his idea
had not come any later. Already she had found it
necessary to have many of her clothes altered.
Now comfort and modesty demanded she put
away most of her newly acquired wardrobe and
shop for looser garments. Her burgeoning breasts
and gently rounded tummy would not be
restrained any longer; her condition was now
obvioius to all.

Laurel took comfort in the fact that her dressmaker had designed lovely, elegant clothing that
minimized her growing bulk. At least she need not
look frumpy while she awaited her child's birth.
Laurel might feel fat and ungainly, but she needn't
be unfashionable.

Laurel was also glad that nowadays expectant
mothers were not expected to seclude themselves
once their condition became apparent. Thank
heavens those days were long past! What a bore it
must have been to sit home and watch everyone
else have all the fun!

March brought a few changes with its brisk,
awakening winds. There was a premonition of
spring in the air, and flowers began to bloom.
Laurel's nausea seemed to suddenly take flight on
a benevolent breeze, replaced by a strange, overpowering craving for avocados. She could not
seem to get enough of them.

"This is crazy!" Brandon claimed, torn between
amusement and astonishment at the quantities

she consumed. "I've heard of women craving many strange things when they were expecting, but avocados? Honey, if you don't slow down on these things, we are going to have the only child in history to be born *green!*"

"I can't help it," she mumbled around yet another slice dripping with lemon juice. "Besides, I'm sure we'll love it, no matter what color the baby is."

Brandon was openly thrilled about the baby. He loved seeing Laurel's body expand as his child grew within her. Constantly, he assured Laurel that he adored the changes in her and never considered her fat or ugly. In fact, impending motherhood lent a special glow to her cheeks, an added lustre to her skin. In his eyes, she was more beautiful each day.

Brandon looked forward to the child's birth with eager anticipation, helping Laurel to shop for baby clothes and nursery furniture. Together they discussed and planned for their future son or daughter. They spent many interesting and sometimes hilarious hours compiling a list of possible names, poring over them, weeding out and narrowing down to their favored choices.

"No, Harry is definitely out," Laurel stated emphatically. "The other children would tease him—hairy Harry, and all that."

George, Tom, Alan, Robert, Roger, Jonathan, Josh, Wade, Nathan, and Luke were too common to suit. Neither did Brandon want his son named after himself or anyone else in particular. "If we named him Sam or Henry, my foreman and brother wouldn't be fit to live around."

Christopher Prescott seemed too much a mouthful. Laurel suggested Wesley. "You know,

Brandon, I never knew your middle name was Wesley until we were married," she mused.

"And I never knew yours was Allison," he countered.

"Don't remind me! I've always hated that name. I just hope our child appreciates all our efforts to give it a decent name." She reviewed her list again. "What about Gardner?"

"And have him puttering around tending posies all day? Forget it!"

They considered Derek and Frazer, Shane, Jason, Quentin and Rothe. Finally, at long last, they settled on Matthew Jared Prescott.

"I like it," Laurel said. "It has a nice, solid sound to it."

"I agree. Not only that, the initials don't spell anything funny like SAP or MOP, or some such thing. I never realized before how careful you have to be about initials."

"I never realized it would be such hard work to find a name we both agree upon," Laurel added.

They went through the same procedure selecting a girl's name. Mary, Susan, Ann, Beth, and Ruth were far too often used, as were Christine and Jennifer. Brandon despised names like Felicity, Melody, Mercy, Fidelity, and Prudence. "It puts too much pressure on a child to live up to a name like that. If we called our daughter Charity, she'd probably grow up to be a miser just to spite us!"

Laurel laughed. "And if we named her Patience, she wouldn't have any; Harmony would probably be a grouch! I agree with you—those names are definitely out."

Brandon also discounted Rachel as a possibility. "I had a Great Aunt Rachel who was an absolute witch! It might be a lovely name, but I'd always associate it with her."

They considered Amber, Brenna, Eileen, Amanda, Elene and Garnet, but somehow they always came back to Amanda. In the end, they chose Amanda Garnet Prescott, should their first-born be a baby daughter.

"Dr. Davis, is it harmful for an expectant mother to eat so much of one food?" Brandon asked on Laurel's next visit to the doctor. He'd told the man of Laurel's craving for avocados.

The doctor leaned back in his chair and chuckled. "Your wife couldn't possibly eat enough avocados to harm herself or the child. I have a theory that whatever the mother craves may contain something the body has been lacking all along, at least in some cases. Just be thankful she doesn't want sauerkraut with marmalade on top!" Brandon cringed at the thought.

Brandon also consulted the physician about a trip to the Sutro Baths. "I'd been thinking of taking Laurel there, but I wanted to check with you first."

"That would be a fine idea," the doctor agreed readily. "I've been there myself, and the warm mineral waters are marvelous. With back-aches and various other complaints so common among pregnant women, it should be a wonderful way for Laurel to relax and relieve strain."

"When should we discontinue—physical relations?" Brandon asked hesitantly.

To his relief, the doctor smiled and said, "You needn't worry about that just yet. But you should abstain the final three months, or whenever it becomes uncomfortable for your wife." This was welcome news to Brandon, for although he would do nothing to harm Laurel or their child, he was not looking forward to the time when their love-making must cease.

With Dr. Davis's blessing, Brandon took Laurel to the famed Sutro Baths the following week. The enormous, palatial structure sat high above the rocks overlooking the Pacific Ocean. The estate looked as if it had been removed in one piece from a setting in ancient Greece and set down in San Francisco. Surrounding the multi-terraced marvel were fabulous gardens, with the most beautiful collection of statuary to be found anywhere in the United States. In addition to the indoor public baths, it also housed a magnificent museum.

In the past, men and women had always bathed separately, but now there were a few smaller bathing areas where married couples could bathe together. It was one of these that Brandon secured for himself and Laurel.

Laurel had never felt water so silky, so mar-velously warm and caressing. She could almost feel her skin soaking up its velvety softness. The bath was wonderfully relaxing, and strangely revitalizing at the same time. She let her entire body relax, limb by limb, muscle by muscle, until she was afloat on a cloud of tranquillity, her mind as serene as the rest of her.

When they were done, her skin had taken on even more of a healthy, natural glow. Pleasantly tired, she leaned back in the carriage, content to let Brandon's arm support her. Drifting off to sleep, she did not stir when Brandon carried her into their house and tucked her gently into bed.

The end of winter heralded a new round of dinners and parties. Laurel met everyone from San Francisco's controversial mayor to the most illustrious citizenry of the great city.

The third week of March brought two significant events, one immediately following the other.
First, there arrived another letter from her father.
Apparently Rex was giving in to Brandon's
demands in order to see his daughter again and his
first grandchild. While he agreed to replace the
cattle his neighbors had lost to the rustlers, he
still adamantly denied having had anything to do
with the thefts. He made it quite clear that he was
making the gesture only out of concern for Laurel,
not from any sense of guilt.

While Brandon would have liked a full
confession in the bargain, he contented himself
with Rex's offer. Because it would only have upset
Laurel further, something he was loath to do in
her delicate condition, he relented on this point. In
high spirits, he wrote to Rex, reiterating that only
when every rancher was reimbursed would he
bring Laurel back to Crystal City. Rex was to let
him know when the debt was paid. Brandon was in
the mood to celebrate and this coordinated perfectly with his birthday. He couldn't have asked
for a better present than the capitulation of his
stubborn father-in-law.

Happy and secure in the hope that she would
soon be back in Crystal City, Laurel was also in
high spirits, and she arranged an elaborate birthday celebration for Brandon, inviting all their
friends. It was to be a supper party, and Laurel
spared no effort to make it a memorable occasion.

The celebration was a great success. Everyone
had a good time, and Brandon especially was
pleased with the gift Laurel had chosen for him.
Knowing how much he had admired the bronze
stallion in the Chinatown shop, she'd sent Thomas

there to purchase it. Brandon was touched and delighted.

Later, after everyone had left, Laurel led him upstairs. There she undressed him and seduced him slowly and deliberately, using every sensual wile he'd taught her (and some she had invented). Brandon's birthday celebration was complete.

CHAPTER 17

As excited as Laurel was about expecting her first child, the changes in her body dismayed her. In no time at all, it seemed, she had no waistline whatsoever. She felt she was beginning to resemble a plump pear with breasts.

It bothered Laurel that as her pregnancy advanced and her body expanded, she might no longer be desirable to Brandon, but he did his best to convince her otherwise, going out of his way to be loving and attentive.

One day he arranged a delightful surprise for her, one designed to make her feel attractive and very much desired. In the early evening he took her to the Cliff House, a fabulous—and somewhat notorious—restaurant on the northwest side of San Francisco.

Upon entering, they were led upstairs to a private dining room. It was unlike any dining area she'd ever seen in the other restaurants they had frequented. There was one table only, bedecked in the finest linen, with candles and crystal wine goblets, fine china and silver and a lovely centerpiece of pink roses and carnations.

"Are we the only people dining in this room?" she asked, surprised.

Brandon smiled. "Does the seclusion bother you?"

"No, it just seems odd, that's all. Are all the rooms like this?" She gazed about her in wonder. Before the fireplace was a thick rug, with several large pillows scattered upon it. A small table stood beside a wide backless divan. Candlelight cast a seductive glow over everything, especially since the soft light was reflected in the many mirrors placed about the room. A sensual scent wafted through the air.

"There is a public dining area on the first floor," Brandon said in answer to Laurel's question. "The rest of the rooms are for private entertainment, like this one."

"This place has a distinctively seductive atmosphere," said Laurel.

"That's what makes the Cliff House so exceptional." Brandon gave her a long, wicked look. "It's said that many a lovely lady has lost her virtue here between the entree and the dessert."

His suggestive leer made her laugh. "What about the waiters? Surely they must be distracting to even the most ardent lovers."

"Oh, the waiters here are most discreet. After serving the meal, they quietly disappear, and never enter a room without knocking first and receiving permission to do so."

Their table was set next to a wide bay window overlooking the cliffs below. The view was spectacular. A movement below caught Laurel's eye. Taking a closer look, she gasped in delight. "There are *creatures* down there on the rocks!"

Brandon nodded. "Sea lions. It's a favorite spot for them, and when the management realized how entertaining it was for guests to watch them, they started feeding them so that the seals would keep coming back.''

"They're adorable! Oh, look! There is a baby seal! Isn't he darling!" Laurel cooed. She was enchanted as Brandon had hoped she would be. While they awaited their meal, they watched the seals cavort among the rocks and slip and slide into the sea. Playful creatures that they were, they put on quite a show.

Just as Brandon had predicted, a waiter served the meal, poured wine, and swiftly departed. As they ate, they watched the sun slide in a glorious blaze of color into the sea. They were enveloped in a silken twilight and in the dim glow of the room in which they sat.

Their meal finished, Brandon led Laurel to the low divan, handing her another glass of wine. At her questioning look, he said, "I don't think, just this once, a second glass of wine will do any harm."

While her hands were occupied with the wine glass, his were busy elsewhere. Ever so slowly, he pulled the pins from her upswept hair, letting it tumble in silver splendor down her back and over her shoulders. His fingers trailed through it, savoring the heavy satiny texture, the exotic feel of it. "Laurel, my love," he murmured, "you are so beautiful it almost hurts to look at you."

Bemused, she stared back at him, her gaze ensnared by the sensual light in his smoky grey eyes, like glints of steel on velvet. His fingers made short work of the multitude of buttons on her dress and pulled down her bodice baring her shoulders. With a harsh gasp, he pressed his lips to her ivory skin. Leisurely he explored each exposed inch of flesh from her shoulders to her delicate ears, making her shiver in delightful anticipation.

With deliberate care, he took her wine glass and placed it on the stand. Then, with practiced ease, he removed all but her garters and stockings. Easing her into a reclining position, he knelt beside the divan.

"Brandon, are you sure no one will come?" she whispered, then gasped as his lips nuzzled the soft skin of her throat, his hands caressing her swollen breasts.

"No one will," he assured her quietly. "Relax. Let me love you." His kisses drugged her into silence, his hands teasing at her breasts until she was mindless with desire. Fire flashed through her at his every touch, searing, burning, making her moan in passionate need. When his lips enclosed a nipple, drawing it into his hot mouth, she cried out. Adoring hands stroked her rounded belly where their child grew, then dipped lower to find the moist treasure between her thighs.

Laurel arched into his caress, her arms coming up to reach for him. "Brandon, darling! Come to me." Mounting desire lent a sulty tone to her voice that only increased his passion.

"Later," he rasped. "There's no need to rush." His lips traveled over her body in tantalizing kisses and hot little nips that sent her senses spinning. She was his to command as his hands were replaced by his eager mouth. Slowly he stripped her stocking from her, every movement a sensual caress; and all the while, his wicked tongue was sending darts of lightning throughout her yearning body. As love-spasms claimed her, she softly cried out his name again and again.

While she was still caught up in that delirious

delight, he slipped out of his own clothing and lay down beside her. Their lips met and clung in mutual desire, tongues touching and twisting in an erotic mating dance of their own.

Now her hands were as inquisitive as his. As he fanned the embers of her still-simmering passion, she built his into a consuming flame that threatened to send him over the edge of sanity.

His restraint at an end, he entered her, their sighs mingling. Then he was lost in her; in the velvet and satin sweetness that was her essence. She clung to him with trembling arms. A sharp sob escaped her as he took her with him on a flying trip to the stars, where the world exploded around and within them in shattering glory.

"You are my heaven and my earth, Laurel," he whispered. "Without you, my whole world would cease to exist."

She laughed softly, triumphantly, still tingling in the aftermath of their lovemaking. "Brandon, you never cease to amaze me! Tough or tender, sweet or arrogant, I love you. You are an ever-changing enigma. Just when I think I finally know you, you surprise me again—like tonight. Imagine —seals, sunsets, and seduction! Whatever will you think of next?"

His eyes laughed down into hers. "I'll think of something eventually."

"And I will love it." Her features softened into more serious lines. "I adore you, my darling. Without you, I would be incomplete; only half a person with half a heart."

Try as she might, Laurel could not seem to control her vacillating emotions. One moment she was happy to the point of giddiness, the next overcome by a storm of weeping. She felt well enough, but she was so short-tempered and irritable. Brandon tried to be understanding, but sometimes she strained his patience to the limit. Inevitably, they got on one another's nerves, and petty squabbles were frequent occurrences. The short-lived squalls were soon forgotten—until the next one arrived out of nowhere and without warning. Both Laurel and Brandon longed for the time when things would be peaceful again.

Laurel was now over halfway through her term. While misshappen and ungainly, she glowed with a special healthy vitality.

On their way to the theatre one evening, Laurel suddenly sat straight up in the carriage seat, a stunned, perplexed look on her face. Seconds later, one hand on her side and the other tugging frantically at Brandon's sleeve, she exclaimed, "Stop the carriage!"

Startled, Brandon could only stare at her. "What? Why?"

"Just have Thomas pull over. *Please!*"

Alarmed, Brandon issued the order. When the carriage had stopped at the curb, he asked again, "What is it? Aren't you feeling well, honey?"

Laurel flashed him an impatient glare. "Do hush, won't you?"

Shaking his head in total bafflement, he frowned at her. Laurel did not notice; her attention seemed directed elsewhere, her body tense, as if listening or waiting for something. One hand lay flat against her side, the other now over her protruding stomach.

Suddenly her entire face lit up, and a beautiful smile curved her lips. "There!" she cried excitedly, grabbing for Brandon's hand. As she laid his palm against her belly, her eyes shone into his. "Wait," she whispered, as if to speak aloud would frighten something timid nearby.

After what seemed an interminable time, he felt it—a small fluttering movement against his palm, as if a butterfly's wings had lightly brushed it. His eyes widened in awe, his gaze flying to where his hand lay. Again he waited, uncertain what to expect, and again he felt the slight movement, barely discernable; then once more a bit stronger, shifting beneath his fingers.

His eyes, full of wonder, met Laurel's again, and she saw the glint of tears in their steel-grey depths. For a long moment they gazed at each other, speechless. Finally he whispered, "Oh, Laurel! Oh, sweet love! Was that our child I felt? Was he truly moving in there?"

Nodding, she gulped back her own happy tears. "Isn't it wonderful? Oh, Brandon! Suddenly it's all so much more real! Our baby is moving within me, and I can hardly comprehend the miracle of it!" She burst into joyous tears.

Pulling her into his embrace, he held her tightly but tenderly.

By mutual consent, they changed their plans. Tonight was a special time to be treasured alone— just the two of them, like children with a cherished secret. They went home, and attended the theater the next evening instead.

Dr. Davis was pleased with the way Laurel's pregnancy was progressing, but when Brandon asked if it would be safe to take Laurel sailing, the good doctor was hesitant. The seas must be calm, and the day should be warm to prevent Laurel from becoming chilled. April weather could be so unpredictable; there was no sense in chancing an accident of any kind.

Having lived for most of her life in Texas, Laurel had never before been sailing. The craft Brandon borrowed from his friend not only had sails but also a gasoline powered engine in case the winds failed to cooperate, which made Laurel feel much safer. Though she had learned to swim as a child, she was not sure how well she would fare at her present weight and bulk. Brandon invited two other couples to join them. The yacht would accommodate all of them comfortably with room to spare. A captain and crew of three manned the craft, freeing the passengers to enjoy the cruise at their leisure.

The day Brandon chose dawned bright and clear, promising a balmy spring day. The breeze, while brisk enough to disperse an earlier pre-dawn fog and fill the sails, was warm and welcoming. They rose and set sail early in the day, determined to enjoy every moment of this beautiful day.

Laurel proved to be a fair sailor. The bay was calm enough that she did not experience any queasiness. She soon had her sea legs, and did not feel any more awkward than usual. She enjoyed the slight rocking motion, the breeze, and the water. It was great fun to sit and watch the shoreline as the yacht skimmed over the water, its sails billowing. There was something soothing about sailing that appealed to her.

The owner of the yacht provided lunch as well. One of the crew brought it from the galley and served them at tables on deck. While much too elaborate a meal to be termed a picnic, it was a unique experience to eat on deck, and they all enjoyed themselves immensely. Laurel also enjoyed the company of their pleasant companions. John was quiet; Patrick had a

marvelous sense of humor that kept them all
entertained. The women Jane and Nola, were both
vivacious and talkative. The six of them had no
trouble finding things to talk about. They laughed
and joked, and eventually began a lively game of
cards, the girls against the men. The losers would
treat the others to dinner that evening.

But dinner was unexpectedly postponed.
Around four o'clock, as they were headed back to
port, the wind suddenly died down. This in itself
presented no problem, for the crew immediately
put the gasoline engine to use. Their troubles
began when a dense fog began to roll in, blanket-
ing everything in a thick, impenetrable blanket of
white. It all happened so quickly. Land, so easily
seen just minutes before, was hidden from sight.
An eerie silence enveloped them, as if they were
suddenly swathed in cotton.

Caught unaware, even the crew was concerned,
and for good reason. Unless they wanted to chance
running aground, they had to stop the engines. As
the captain explained, it was too easy to become
disoriented and lose all sense of direction to risk
continuing. The silence was even more oppressive
as the yacht rocked slowly on the waves, with
neither sails nor engine to power it. The anchor
was dropped, but it did little to keep the yacht
from drifting with the current. Unless a breeze
sprang up again to clear away the fog, they were
helplessly marooned in the middle of the bay. Only
the men's calm demeanor kept the women from
panicking, though the men were none too easy
about their predicament, either.

Brandon noticed that Laurel's clothes were
becoming damp from the mist. Recalling the
doctor's admonitions, he immediately suggested
they adjourn to a salon below deck, leaving the

ship's crew to stand watch. Snug in the salon, with lamps shedding a welcome glow about them, the six friends settled down to wait. It was a long, nerve-racking night. Around nine o'clock, when it became apparent that the fog was not going to lift in time to get them home before midnight, the three women searched the cupboards in the galley and managed to concoct a sufficient meal with what they found. The men carried servings to the anxious crew. Later, coffee and hot cocoa made the rounds.

Near midnight, Laurel was sagging with fatigue. Deciding that staying awake would not help matters, the three couples dispersed to various sleeping areas and bedded down. With a tired, worried sigh, Laurel snuggled under the blankets, aligning her body with Brandon's for warmth and comfort. All through the night, they shifted restlessly. They slept little, and that lightly, concerned with their precarious situation and the effect this harrowing experience might be having on Laurel and the baby.

The fog had still not lifted when the couples reconvened in the salon early the next morning. None had slept particularly well, and the dark shadows beneath Laurel's lavender eyes told their own tale. They breakfasted on coffee and toast. Conversation was desultory at best, as no one felt prone to idle chit-chat.

Sometime later, as each sat wrapped in his own thoughts, the sounds of the yacht's engines coming to life jolted them into alertness. Seconds later, a crewman descended with the welcome news that the fog had finally lifted enough to return to port.

The elation brought on by this good news was nothing compared to the joy of feeling firm land beneath their feet again. Relief flooded through Laurel, making her knees shaky and her legs unsteady beneath her. As quickly as possible, Brandon bundled her into the carriage and rushed her home. The frantic housekeeper joined Brandon in hustling Laurel off to bed. Too weary to argue, Laurel obliged readily. After a warm lunch of soup and tea, she drifted off to sleep. For a long while, Brandon sat in a chair by the bedside, gazing at her serene face. With profound gratitude, he gave thanks to God for their safety. He didn't know what he would do if anything happened to Laurel. . . .

A few days later, Laurel had completely pushed the frightful episode from her mind. The weather was still mild, and she begged Brandon to take her to Golden Gate Park for a picnic. Glad of her high spirits, he was more than willing to indulge her in this small request. They packed a lunch and drove out in the early afternoon. They spent a delightful few hours relaxing on the grass, sunning and enjoying the sights and sounds of early spring. Flowers were blooming in a riot of colors, the bees busily humming from blossom to blossom while birds twittered in the trees above.

Just as Brandon had fully relaxed, he opened drowsy eyes to see Laurel gazing thoughtfully out at the vast Pacific Ocean. Feeling his eyes on her, she said, "I'm so thankful we were caught in the bay, instead of out there when we were hit so suddenly by the fog. Who knows how far we might have drifted before the fog lifted? We may have been lost for days."

Brandon sat up, taking her chin in his hand and turning her face toward him. "This is too pretty a day for such solemn thoughts!" He nudged her lips with the tips of his fingers. "Let's see a smile on those pretty lips!"

She gave him a half-hearted smile, but he would have none of that. Before she knew what he was doing, Brandon had her flat on her back and was tickling her. Unbearably ticklish, she laughed helplessly. "Oh, Brandon!" she shrieked. "Stop! Please stop!"

He eyed her devilishly. "Do you give up?" he asked.

"Give up what?" she responded breathlessly.

He looked down into her lovely, laughing face. "Your heart," he said, his tone serious.

"You hold it in your hands." Her own words echoed his.

"Your soul."

"It's yours."

"Your love."

"Always."

"Your mind."

Her eyes twinkled up at his. "Well, I don't know . . . I'll have to think about that," she teased.

His fingertips prodded her ribs, sending her into fresh peals of laughter.

"All right! All right! I've thought it over," she cried. "If it means so much to you, you can have it. But I reserve the right to borrow it now and then for my own use. You wouldn't want to be married to a witless wife, would you?"

"You could never be witless, my love. You are beautiful, and sweet, and smart, and precious to me beyond belief."

They exchanged a look filled with love and dawning desire. "You know, Laurel," he told her, "you have a bad habit of flirting with me in public places."

"Then take me somewhere more private," she

suggested with a seductive little smile, ''and have your wicked way with me.''

He nearly winded the horse in order to do just that.

CHAPTER 18

B randon sat alone at his desk, slowly reading again the letter he had just received from Miguel Corona. It was cold and rainy outside, creating a gloom in the study that matched his mood. The mild weather had departed, and disaster had struck almost simultaneously. His big hands shook with helpless anger, and a desolate feeling settled in the pit of his stomach as he read:

Brandon,

I hate to be the bearer of bad tidings; but there is something you must know immediately. We finally found out what happened to Padre Bernardo, and it is terrible news. His body or what remains of it, was discovered in the old well behind the church. He had been shot and dumped down the well. We can only hope he died quickly and did not suffer.

After investigation, it was found that Padre Pedro was not a priest at all. He is wanted by the Mexican officials for many crimes, and was on the run from them when he came to Chihuahua, looking for a safe place to hide out. Most likely, he murdered Padre Bernardo the very morning of your wedding. When we showed up unexpectedly, he had to

271

do something so we would not suspect.

Pedro (I cannot again call him Padre) posed as a priest. You must know that your marriage is not valid. What a shock, after all this time has passed! I am sure you can imagine how terrible we all feel about discovering this. Please convey to Laurel, also, our sorrow.

Marguerita and Inez are very upset, especially knowing that Laurel is carrying your child. Madre says you must marry Laurel as soon as possible or they may never forgive you.

I am sorry to have to write this, but such a situation cannot be left uncorrected. Please let us know what happens, as I feel responsible.

Miguel

Brandon sat back with a scowl, rubbing a hand distractedly over his furrowed brow. It was incredible! How could he possibly explain all this to Laurel without sending her into hysterics? He cringed to think what her reaction would be. Certainly she would not take the news calmly, and her condition required peace and serenity for the sake of their child.

Their child! Dear God! He had to arrange a new marriage immediately. The baby must be born legitimate. Brandon could just imagine the fine rage Rex Burke would be in if his first grandchild was born out of wedlock! On the other hand, if Rex even suspected their marriage was not legal, he'd probably storm to San Francisco and drag Laurel home with him, pregnant or not, and there would be nothing Brandon could do about it.

The child was due in a few months. How could he tell her they were not married at all?

Brandon's anger temperarily over-rode his

concern. If it hadn't been for Rex, they could have been married in Crystal City, by their own minister. And damn that Pedro character anyway! What freak twist of fate had led him to Chihuahua at that exact time? And why had he, in his guise as a priest, gone so far as to pretend to marry them? No wonder the man had been so nervous, stumbling through the ceremony! Had they all not been so upset, they might have suspected something was drastically wrong. Brandon blamed himself for not realizing it.

With conscious effort, Brandon stifled his anger. There was no time to dwell on recriminations. What he had to do now was concentrate on how to correct the error, and as quickly and secretly as possible. If it wasn't absolutely necessary to inform Laurel, he wouldn't even tell *her*, but he could not think of any way to avoid it—or was there? His mind was in such turmoil that he could not think straight.

A grim frown creased his forehead as he carefully tucked the unwelcome letter into a desk drawer out of sight and closed it. If only it was as easy to make their problems disappear! But "out of sight, out of mind" was far from the case here. Hearing Laurel's voice in the hallway outside the study door, Brandon rose and went to greet her, trying to compose his worried features, lest she suspect something before he was ready to tell her.

All afternoon, something about Brandon's behavior kept puzzling Laurel. It was nothing she could pinpoint exactly, but something was not quite right. He was more quiet than usual, almost moody. Several times she'd had to repeat what she'd just said, for his mind seemed to be miles away. When she'd asked him what was wrong, he'd first glared at her, then politely said it was nothing he cared to discuss.

He seemed edgy. Twice now the telephone had rung, and Brandon had rushed to answer it. When Tessie stopped by for a chat, he had beaten Kramer to the door. Who was he expecting, and why was he acting so strangely?

Every now and then Laurel would glance up, to catch him looking at her with an expression on his face that she could not fathom. When he caught her eye, he would smile, and for a while everything would be normal again. In fact, he was as sweet and considerate as usual, and if not for those flashes of nervousness and intense absorption in his own thoughts, she wouldn't have noticed anything out of the ordinary.

With a shrug, Laurel dismissed it from her mind. Perhaps it had something to do with business. Meanwhile, she had to get ready for the evening ahead. They were going to the Grand Opera House, where the great Enrico Caruso was singing tonight. Laurel was looking forward to a grand evening. Afterward, they would come back up Nob Hill, where they would dine in splendor at the Fairmont Hotel. Actually, the Fairmont was not entirely completed yet, but Tessie was throwing an opening celebration for a few of her friends, and Caruso's San Francisco debut seemed just the proper occasion. Everyone would be gorgeously attired, and eager to meet their friends for champagne and dinner after the opera.

Laurel dressed with particular care. Her dressmaker had outdone herself, ingeniously cutting and draping the fabric to disguise Laurel's thickening figure. The lush royal blue brocade set off the silver splendor of her hair. She had selected opal earrings and matching necklace, and opalencrused combs sparkled in her upswept coiffure. Her lavender eyes shone with excitement, and she decided she really looked quite beautiful.

Brandon told her as much when he saw her. "You are absolutely radiant—like a magnificent moonbeam in a velvet-dark night!"

He, too, looked quite dashing in his tuxedo and ruffled, snow-white shirt. They were an outstanding couple, even among the dazzling array of beautifully bedecked socialites attending the Grand Opera House that evening.

There were probably more jewels on display this night in this one theatre, Laurel thought, than existed in all of Texas, and also more exposed bosom. It seemed that the more expensive the theatre tickets, the lower the decolletage of the ladies, and there was much creamy flesh visible between necklace and neckline for Caruso's gala opening performance.

The Opera House was crowded to overflowing. Even people who had never attended an opera before and never would again, had come to hear the famed tenor. Madame Olive Fremstad was singing the title role of Carmen opposite Caruso as Don Jose, but it was Caruso who enthralled the spellbound audience. Despite his short, stout stature, his magnificent voice rang out to thrill and totally captivate all who heard him.

Though opera was not usually her favorite entertainment, Laurel found herself just as spellbound as everyone else—or perhaps not quite everyone. She vaguely realized that Brandon seemed distracted. While he appeared attentive enough, there was a disturbing tension emanating from him. He managed to applaud at the appropriate times, but his full attention was not on the opera.

When the curtain lowered for the final time after many curtain calls and a standing ovation, they made their way to their carriage and on to the Fairmont. Gaiety ruled for the evening. The food was plentiful and marvelous, and champagne flowing in abundance. Music and dancing and laughter knew no end. It was a magical ending for a wonderful night, as far as Laurel was concerned.

Brandon had pulled himself out of his doldrums and was once more the attentive husband. The rain had stopped earlier in the day, and though the air was still quite muggy, Brandon waltzed with Laurel on the terrace, whirling her about until she clung to him giddily. When her laughing face turned up to his, he kissed her with a desperation that both surprised and frightened her a little. There was a new and alarming element in that kiss—almost as if it hinted at farewell.

Laurel shook her head to dispel the uneasy feeling. "My, how romantic you are tonight," she whispered breathlessly, "kissing me here on the terrace where anyone might see."

"Ah, but I have been enchanted by you, my mystical moonlight lady! Who knows when you'll decide to disappear like mist through my fingers. I must take my opportunities when I find them." His teasing words held a touch of sadness and sent a chill running up her spine, and she shivered in his warm embrace.

Her hands came up to clasp his face between them, and she stared deeply into his mysterious glinting eyes. "What a strange mood you've been in all day, Brandon! Is something wrong?"

He smiled his charming smile, his teeth flashing, "You're imagining things, sweetheart. It probably comes with your condition—like heartburn and dizziness."

She frowned doubtfully. "Perhaps."

Only one other thing dampened Laurel's enjoyment of the evening. Muriel Cook was intent on captivating Brandon with her wiles, and it seemed to Laurel as the evening wore on that Brandon was much more attentive to the redhead than was actually necessary. Even Tessie raised a well-bred eyebrow at Muriel's obvious display and Brandon's imprudent interest. Several more curious looks were cast about when Brandon led the lovely heiress onto the dance floor. Muriel managed to drape herself over Brandon throughout the waltz, and he returned to Laurel reeking of the other woman's potent perfume.

Laurel held her tongue, not wanting to create a public display, but she was quietly fuming inside, and very hurt by his actions. Would he say this, too, was her imagination? Perhaps she was making more of the incident than was warranted, but then he needn't be so appreciative of Muriel's obvious charms!

The festive celebration was still in full swing when Brandon and Laurel departed around midnight. Just as they were leaving, Muriel floated up to Brandon, whispered something into his ear, and planted a sumptuous kiss on his lips. Her vibrant lip rouge clung to his mouth, and with a giggle and a sly look at Laurel, she said, "Oh, my! I've left my mark on you now, Brandon!"

As Laurel's eyes shot lavender flames, Tessie grabbed Muriel's arm and tugged her unceremoniously out of reach. "You're making a spectacle of yourself, Muriel!" their hostess hissed. "I think it's high time you went home before you cause more trouble than even *you* know how to handle!"

Rather than cause Tessie more embarrassment,

Laurel murmured a brief goodbye, as did Brandon, and made a hasty exit. Brandon was surreptitiously wiping Muriel's lip rouge from his mouth as he handed her into the carriage.

It was a short, silent ride from the Fairmont to the house, but the moment their front door closed behind them, Laurel rounded on him with all her pent-up fury. "How *could* you humiliate me that way Brandon? Not to mention the embarrassment to poor Tess!"

He glared back at her irritably. "Is it my fault Muriel had too much champagne and became—er—amorous?"

"Muriel doesn't need champagne as an excuse!" Laurel retorted indignantly. "She's like a cat on the prowl most of the time, and she sniffs around *you* as if you're the most fascinating tomcat in the neighborhood. It's disgusting!"

"I didn't ask for her attention, Laurel, and I did nothing to encourage her."

"A few of us viewed it a bit differently, Brandon, especially when you asked her to dance. The woman clung to you tighter than ivy on a wall, and you did nothing to discourage her. In fact, you seemed to be enjoying her company immensely."

Brandon sighed. "I didn't want to cause a scene, and Muriel seemed unsteady on her feet."

"That's a pretty flimsy excuse, if you ask me! Besides, you *did* ask her to dance with you."

"I danced with Tess, too, and Jane, and you didn't get your feathers ruffled."

"They are friends."

"So is Muriel."

"Ha!" Laurel gave a derisive laugh. "Calling Muriel a friend is like calling the Devil's daughter an angel! She's a conniving female who's been

trying to get her claws into you from the first. If you can't see that, Brandon, you're blind!"

"She is a neighbor. To ask her to dance is not a crime, it's being polite."

"And then there's that kiss she gave you just as we were leaving," Laurel added heatedly. "Maybe things are different here in San Francisco, but back in Crystal City she'd be asking for a split lip, if not worse."

Brandon threw up his hands in exasperation. "Good God, Laurel! The woman was tipsy as hell! She probably didn't even know what she was doing!"

"And pigs fly, too!"

"Let's just forget it, Laurel. I'm not in the mood for an argument right now. I have a lot on my mind."

"Such as?" Laurel's rigid stance told him she would not let him off so easily. When he glared at her silently, she suggested, "Why not start by telling me what Muriel whispered in your ear?"

Not an eyelash flickered at her inquiry. "I don't recall," he said quietly.

"How convenient!"

Now Brandon was becoming angry. "I'm not going to stand here and defend myself over something as silly as this!" He threw his jacket over a chair and loosened his tie. "Go on to bed, Laurel. It's late, and I'm tired."

But Laurel stubbornly stood her ground. "Then let's discuss how soon we're going to return to Crystal City," she insisted.

"Oh, hell!" Brandon exploded. "You really *are* ripe for an argument tonight, aren't you?" His steel-grey gaze shot sparks at her.

"Dad has agreed to your terms. He's already

begun to repay the ranchers who lost cattle to the rustlers. What more do you want, Brandon? You can't expect the man to confess to a crime he didn't commit! He's said he would find out who was really responsible.''

"And you believe him!" Brandon snorted in disgust and turned away from her.

"Yes, I do! I want to go home, Brandon. I want to have my baby at home!"

He kept his back to her, grinding his teeth in frustration. He could not take her home until they were legally married again; and he could not tell her about Miguel's letter until he had a chance to arrange a new wedding. "If we went home now," he told her, "Rex would undoubtedly renege on his agreement. He'd feel no need to continue once you were back in Crystal City."

Tired, miserable, and angry, Laurel lost her temper entirely. "You're a hateful, stubborn jackass, Brandon Prescott!" she screamed. "I'm sick of begging and pleading—of doing everything your way. I'm going home to Crystal City to have my baby if I have to walk every step of the way. I'll go with or without you, but I *will* go!"

"No, you will not!" He spun about, flinging out his arm to reach for her. He didn't realize how closely behind him she stood. The back of his hand connected heavily with her cheek, stunning them both as she staggered with the sharp blow. She cried out in surprise and pain. Again he reached, this time to steady her, in an agony of instant regret. "Oh, God, Laurel! I'm sorry! I didn't mean to hit you!"

Her hand flew to her smarting cheek, her huge shocked eyes filling fast with tears. "You beast! You horrid, hateful *beast!*" She backed away from him, then raced for the stairs.

Brandon ran after her, calling, "Please, Laurel! It was an accident! You know I'd never strike you intentionally, no matter how angry I become!"

Laurel tripped on the hem of her skirt, nearly losing her footing. Brandon bounded up the stairs to catch her as she teetered precariously. "You little idiot!" he growled. "Are you trying to kill yourself and our child? You know better than to run in your condition, especially on the stairs!" He held her tightly to him, fear making his words more fierce than he'd intended.

Laurel struggled in his embrace, hitting at him with balled fists. Tears streamed down her face as she sobbed hysterically, "Take your hands off me! Don't you dare touch me!"

Disregarding her struggles, he lifted her into his arms and carried her the rest of the way to their room. Laying her on the bed, he headed for the bathroom for a cold cloth for her face. Her cheek was red and beginning to swell. He felt like a monster for having hit her, however unintentionally.

When he returned, she lay sobbing into the pillow, her face turned away from him. As he tried to turn her about to tend to her face, she screeched, "Get away from me! Leave me alone! Haven't you done enough?"

"Laurel, I never meant to hit you. It was an accident. You must believe that." He tried desperately to explain, but she was too upset for his apology to mean much now. Again he attempted to press the cloth to her face.

She jerked it from his hand, flinging it across the room. "Don't touch me! I don't want you near me!"

"Laurel . . ." His voice was a desperate plea as he stared down at her with agonized eyes.

She buried her face in the pillow, shaking with sobs. "Get out! You are a brutal swine!"

Brandon rose and reluctantly walked to the door. Looking back, he sighed heavily. "I'll leave you alone for awhile, but you must try to calm down. I'm sorry, Laurel."

"Go!" she choked out. "You reek of Muriel's perfume!"

She heard the click as the door shut behind him, and his heavy tread on the stairs. For a long while she sobbed heartbrokenly, until she cried herself to sleep at last.

Brandon stared morosely into the swirling amber liquor in his glass. He'd lost track of how many drinks he'd had, but the whiskey bottle at his side was two-thirds empty, and it had been full when he'd started. God, what a disastrous day this had been from beginning to end! First the letter from Miguel, the worry all day, the episode with Muriel, then the argument with Laurel.

Would Laurel ever understand that he had not hit her intentionally? As angry as he had been, he'd never meant to do that.

Taking another drink, Brandon longed for the oblivion that eluded him. What a mess his life was in! With Laurel so angry with him, how could he tell her they were not legally married? In her present mood, she would be beyond hysterics— she'd probably shoot him! At the very least, she would most likely leave him, and he would have no legal right to stop her if she did.

He had to think of a way to correct this drastic situation. But how? Surely there was no way, other than a second ceremony, to legalize their union. His mind raced in frantic circles, his thoughts chasing each other around in his aching head. Maybe if he consulted someone else about the problem, someone familiar with the law, he could find a way out of this dilemma, a way that would not set Laurel screeching again and wanting his hide nailed to the nearest barn door. After all, none of this was actually his fault.

He ran a weary hand through his hair in tired frustration. Suddenly he stopped and sat straight in his chair. "I'll call Judge Henry!" he thought. Rising, he headed for the telephone in the front hall, intent on calling his grandfather's old lawyer, completely disregarding the fact that it was now nearly two o'clock in the morning. "Good old Judge Henry J. Henry! Why didn't I think of him sooner?"

The line rang several times before a groggy voice answered on the other end. "Judge Henry's residence."

"Judge Henry, please. Brandon Prescott calling."

"I'm sorry, Mr. Prescott, but the judge is not at home just now. Would you care to leave a message?"

"Where is he? I need to talk with him immediately." Now that he had thought of it, Brandon was frantic to speak with the judge.

"If it is an emergency, you can most likely catch him at his club. This is his poker night with his friends, and the game usually goes on until two or three in the morning," the voice advised sleepily.

"Thank you." Brandon started to hang up, then remembered to ask the address of the private men's club.

In record time, Brandon saddled a horse and raced downtown to find Judge Henry. Perhaps he was grasping at straws, but to a drowning man, any help was welcome, and Brandon felt as if he were about to go under for the third and final time.

Upstairs, Laurel awoke to hear Brandon's voice in the downstairs hall, but her weary mind could not make out his words. The jangle of the telephone as he hung up and the slamming of the door barely registered at the time. She groaned sleepily, her tear-swollen lids refusing to lift. She drifted back to sleep as Brandon's horse thundered down the drive beneath their bedroom window.

CHAPTER 19

At shortly after two in the morning, Judge Henry was a bit fuzzy around the edges when Brandon found him. The card game was just breaking up, and the judge had imbibed freely this evening, so neither he nor Brandon were in prime condition for deciding major issues. However, the two of them settled down over yet another round of drinks to discuss the problem.

Judge Henry was seventy-one years old, going on twelve and a half. Disregarding his creaking bones, the spry old gentleman flatly refused to grow old. His piercing blue eyes were as sharp as his mind and his wit, and with his neatly trimmed beard and mustache, he still cut quite a handsome figure with the ladies.

"Son, you do have a problem on your hands," he told Brandon, after listening to the bizarre tale. Henry had met Laurel at several dinners they had attended, and he sympathized with their plight. "That sweet little wife of yours isn't going to take kindly to such news, especially not with a child on the way."

"Which is precisely why I wish there was some way to get around telling her at all, but I suppose that's wishful thinking." Brandon added drearily.

"Honesty is always the best policy." Henry

nodded wisely, then chuckled, his blue eyes twinkling. "Unless you can come up with a better one."

"Got any ideas, Judge?"

"You could ply her with champagne until she wouldn't know what she was doing, and wouldn't remember the ceremony afterward."

"That would be possible, if Laurel wasn't pregnant. I can't chance it now. Too bad, really, since she gets tipsy so easily."

Henry sighed into his drink. "Then you can't slip anything into her milk, either. Drat! Well, you can't do anything until you get a marriage license. At least I can help you with that. No one will question my request for a special license. We'll take care of it as soon as the courthouse opens this morning."

"If it was Halloween, we could arrange a real ceremony under the guise of a fake wedding, and we might get away with it." Brandon was really grasping at straws, and flimsy ones at that, but the alcohol was hitting him hard now. Even the ridiculous sounded feasible in his befuddled state.

Obviously Judge Henry was having similar problems, for the suggestion seemed sensible to him. "You might still have a costume ball."

Brandon considered it, then shook his head. "No, Laurel wouldn't do it, as big as she is now. She'd want to dress as something else—a pumpkin, maybe, so she could disguise her shape. It'd never work."

This struck Henry funny, and he laughed uproariously. "Say, does she talk in her sleep? I could sneak into your bedroom some night and perform the ceremony. If you prompted her to the right responses, it would be done before you knew it, with none the wiser."

"The way my luck has been running lately, she'd wake up halfway through and I'd have more to explain than I do now," Brandon predicted glumly. "Thanks, but no thanks. We'll have to think of something else."

Both sat silently nursing their drinks for some moments, lost in thought. Brandon jumped in surprise as the judge whacked the table with his hand. "I have it!" Henry exclaimed. "Tell her you've lost your marriage license and need a new one for legal purposes!"

"Wouldn't she wonder why I didn't send to Mexico for a copy? Even in Chihuahua, they keep records."

Henry gave a shrug. "Tell her you're in too much of a hurry to clear things up before the baby arrives and it would take too long. She won't suspect anything's amiss, especially when I tell her we have to go through the motions of a new ceremony merely as a formality. Would she doubt the word of a judge?"

Brandon was turning the idea over in his alcohol-fogged brain. "It might work. It just might work! But she'll think I'm an idiot for losing the license."

"The lesser ot two evils, if you take my meaning," the judge advised.

"True. I just hope she hasn't seen our license lately. It's in the same safe where she keeps her valuable jewelry, and Laurel goes into it frequently."

"A wise husband never lets his wife into his safe. Gives 'em too much power. Remember that from now on, boy." Henry pointed a wavering finger at Brandon. "If worse comes to worst, you could fake a robbery, or set the room on fire. Just make sure that license comes up missing!"

"I can't set fire to the house, or fake a robbery. A thief would take her jewels and leave our marriage certificate, and a fire probably wouldn't do more than singe the edges of the papers inside the safe."

"Oh! Yes." Henry shook his head as if to clear it. "Then you'll have to have lost it somehow." His eyes again took on a special sparkle as a new idea occurred to him. "Just as added insurance, why don't I tell her that California state law requires all legal documents to be written in English in order to be considered legitimate? She'll take my word, surely; especially when I point out that this must be done to assure that the child is your legal heir."

"You are a genius, Judge Henry!" Brandon raised his glass in tribute to the older man. "I salute you! You may have just saved my life—not to mention my marriage."

The two comrades in deceit settled down to serious consideration of the finer points of their plot. Neither noticed that it was now nearly five o'clock in the morning, and outside the eastern sky was already welcoming the dawn.

As the hall clock struck four, Laurel stirred restlessly, rolling over onto her bruised cheek. The throbbing pain brought her awake, and she lay for a moment letting her weary brain bring back the events of the previous hours. A sob-laden sigh escaped her lips; a single tear trickled down her face as she pushed herself off the bed.

In the bathroom, she sponged her face, wincing as she touched her sore cheek. She cringed as she caught a glimpse of her reflection. The cheek was not bruised as badly as she had feared, but her face was swollen from crying, and her eyes were puffy and red-rimmed. Her hair was a fright, and her gown was baldly wrinkled from sleeping in it.

Quickly she stripped out of the dress and put on a fresh dressing gown. Removing her opal jewelry, she placed the valuables on her dressing table and sat down to remove the combs from her hair. As she set methodically brushing her hair in long, comforting strokes, her thoughts turned once again to Brandon.

What a terrible fight they'd had! Never had she been quite so angry with him. They'd argued and fought so many times before, but never had he struck her! If not for her throbbing, bruised cheek, she still might not believe it had really happened. It seemed like a bad dream, a nightmare. Had she pushed him that hard tonight! Had she said something particular that had triggered his violence? She could not clearly recall all they had said to one another, yet she seemed to remember Brandon apologizing for striking her. He had said he was sorry, that it had been completely accidental, but she had been too upset to listen at the time. She had sent him away, and now she wondered if she should have listened to him.

Laurel's eyes lit on the gilt mantel clock, and she was shocked to see that it was after four o'clock in the morning. Where was Brandon? She frowned as a memory tapped at her brain. Had she dreamed hearing the door close and someone riding down the drive? Had it been Brandon? How long ago had he gone? Or was he somewhere else in the house? Usually when he wanted to be alone, he secluded himself in his study. Was he there now, perhaps?

As she put down her hairbrush her fingers brushed the jewels. On impulse, she picked them

up and headed for the stairs. She would go downstairs on the pretext of returning her jewelry to
the safe, and see if Brandon was in the study.

Laurel tiptoed stealthily down the stairs, not
wanting to disturb him if he was asleep, and not
wanting to risk provoking him into another
argument if he wasn't. Quietly she opened the
study door and peeked inside. The desklamp
threw a dim light over the room. A quick glance
about told her Brandon was not here.

Laurel stopped in the doorway. Where was he?
In one of the other bedrooms? In the parlor? She
didn't think so. As often as they'd fought, he'd
never slept apart from her before. But surely he
hadn't actually gone out in the middle of the night.
Where would he have been going at that hour? To
a tavern? To a hotel? Her hand flew to her heart at
a dreadful thought occurred to her. Had he gone
to meet Muriel Cook? After all his adamant
denials, had he and Muriel had an assignation
after all? Was that why he had been behaving so
strangely all day? Had she touched off his terrible
temper tonight by hitting too closely to the truth
in her accusations?

Pain lanced through her at the thought, and she
closed her eyes and swallowed hard to ward off a
deep feeling of despair. "Please, God! Don't let it
be that! We have enough problems to contend
with already. I don't think I could bear any more!"

Blinking back her tears determinedly, Laurel
walked to the desk. She would put her jewels in
the safe and then she would search the other
rooms. Surely Brandon must be somewhere in this
vast house. Opening the drawer where the key to
the safe was kept, Laurel reached for it. Just as
her fingers found it, the Siamese kitten leaped
suddenly to the desk top, startling a strangled

scream from Laurel's throat. Before Laurel could
prevent it, Sassy brushed against a flower vase,
sending it toppling. Water flowed everywhere,
drenching everything on the desk, and streaming
into the open drawer like a miniature waterfall.

With a cry of dismay, Laurel looked about for
something with which to mop up the mess, but
found nothing at hand. "Oh, Sassy! Look what
you've done!"

Scurrying down the hall and into the kitchen,
Laurel grabbed a towel and hurried back to repair
the damage. By now, even the floor around the
desk was soaked, and Sassy sat on a nearby chair,
licking at her wet paws. "That's right!" Laurel
grumbled at her. "Be fussy now you've made a
disaster of Brandon's desk! I just hope you haven't
ruined any really important papers, or he'll be
none too thrilled with either of us."

Laurel dried off the desk top and the items on it,
then started on the waterlogged drawer. She drew
out the papers and sighed heavily as she saw the
sopping mess she held. The top sheet was
completely soaked, the ink running every which
way. Inspecting the one beneath it, she saw, to her
relief, that most of it was legible, at least the final
two paragraphs of what appeared to be a letter
from Miguel Corona. Immediately curious that
Brandon had not mentioned this letter to her, she
was even more so as she recognized her name.
Quickly she scanned what remained clear of the
nearly-ruined letter, and her blood ran cold as she
read Miguel's words:

> Marguerita and Inez are very upset,
> especially knowing that Laurel's carrying
> your child. Madre says you must marry
> Laurel as soon as possible or they may never

forgive you.

I am so sorry to have to write this, but such a situation cannot be left uncorrected. Please let us know what happens, as I feel responsible.

                                   Miguel

What could this mean? Was Miguel out of his mind? She and Brandon were already married! Miguel and most of his family had been present at the wedding! What did he mean by such a ridiculous statement—"You must marry Laurel as soon as possible?" And why would Marguerita and Inez be upset? They had been very happy for her; had helped plan the wedding; had rejoiced over Laurel's discovery that she carried Brandon's baby. None of this made any sense at all!

Hands trembling so badly the page rattled, she read the words again and was even more confused. What did Miguel have to be so sorry over, and why did he feel responsible—over what, pray tell? Since the letter was presumably addressed to Brandon, Miguel obviously felt responsible for something he and Brandon had done—but what? For some reason, the Coronas were insisting that Brandon marry her immediately—which could only mean that she and Brandon were not *now* married!

In a daze, Laurel sank weakly into the chair, barely realizing the seat was dripping wet. She stared blankly at the letter in her hand. How could this be? They had been married in the church by a priest. She recalled every detail of the beautiful wedding. They even had a marriage certificate to prove it, and a baby on the way. What in the world was going on? She didn't understand any of it.

Desperately, she fought back a feeling of nausea, and concentrated on the letter in her shaking hands. Turning again to the first page, she tried to make out the ruined writing, but it was impossibly blurred, not a word of it legible. Laurel nearly cried in frustration. This was possibly the most important message of her life, and she could not read a word of it!

Helplessly, she read again what was left. One thing was clear. Miguel was saying she and Brandon were not married; and somehow both Miguel and Brandon were responsible for that fact. How? Why? Wasn't their Mexican marriage valid? A chill raced up her spine. How could Brandon be responsible in any way for that— unless he had arranged a fake wedding. But why? What possible reason could he have for doing such a thing?

The only answer she could divine was an ugly one. Could Brandon have faked a marriage simply to get back at her father? Was that why he was so eager to keep her away from her family and Crystal City? Did he hate her family so much that he would deliberately set out to ruin all their lives and father an illegitimate child in the bargain? How long would he have continued the farce? Was he going to wait until the baby was born, then send her and her child home in disgrace? Surely he was not that cruel! Surely she had not imagined the love they shared! Surely she had not imagined all his loving words, all the tenderness!

She searched her brain for another explanation but none came readily to mind. Even if there was another reason for their marriage to be invalid, why hadn't Brandon told her about it? How long had he known? When had he received this letter from Miguel? How long had he hidden it, and why, if he were innocent of causing the problem, hadn't he taken steps to remedy the situation? If he loved her—if he cared for her and their child at all—why hadn't he arranged for a new marriage?

An even more devastating thought came to her. Perhaps Brandon really didn't love her and never had! Perhaps he had been playing an elaborate, hateful game. Tears raced unchecked down her face as she contemplated their life together. They had fought off and on all along, mostly about her father, with Brandon flatly refusing to take her home. Just last night, he had become so angry he had hit her, and now he was out somewhere, perhaps in the arms of another woman! Now, on top of everything else, it seemed their marriage was not even a reality—but the child growing within her certainly was! Oh, God! What was she to do?

The clock on the mantel struck the half hour, and Laurel automatically glanced up at it. Irrationally, she began to laugh hysterically. It seemed ironic that a scant half an hour ago, she had thought she had problems enough. At least then she'd still had a marriage—or so she had believed! Now she had not even that to comfort her!

As if to recall her attention to its presence, the baby kicked within her. A fierce protective instinct welled up in her and her hands flew to her protruding stomach. Along with this overwhelming need to protect her child, a righteous anger sprang up. Drying her tears with trembling fingers, Laurel made a decision. She would not humble herself and beg Brandon to love her. Neither would she stay and wait for him to reject her. She would leave now while she still had some shred of pride, and be gone before he could return and force her to stay with him.

With a speed born of desperation, she raced back to her room, collecting a few of her things

and throwing them into a travelling case. She took
her jewels and most of the cash from the safe, not
feeling the least twinge of guilt. Brandon owed her
at least this for the pain he was causing her. Most
of her clothing she left behind, out of necessity.
She dismissed the rest with a shrug. They didn't fit
her now anyway.

Afraid Brandon would return before she could
make her escape, she still took time to telephone
the railroad station and check the train schedule.
Luckily, there was a train leaving for Los Angeles
at six o'clock, little more than an hour from now,
and she intended to be on it. As soon as she could
hitch the horses to a buggy, she would be on her
way. But first she had to find Sassy and Tyke.

Tyke was nowhere to be found, and finally she
had to give up searching for him. Laurel hoped
Brandon would look after him properly. Sassy
was upstairs, clawing at the bedroom window in a
strange, agitated manner. When Laurel attempted
to pick her up, the cat went wild, digging her claws
into a small satin pillow on the windowseat. With
time running out, Laurel had no time to try to
discover what was bothering the kitten. She
simply folded the screeching feline into the pillow
and stuffed both pillow and cat into the carrying
cage.

She had a bit of a problem with the horses, too.
They were unusually skittish. Remembering that
animals often sensed human emotions, Laurel
supposed they were simply reacting to her
nervous state. Finally she got them hitched to the
buggy and drove quietly past the house so as not to
awaken the slumbering servants. She had left no
note for Brandon, no explanations for her
desertion. She wanted to be on the train and
headed home before he missed her. No doubt he

would guess immediately where she had gone, but this time she would be home before he could catch her—if he even cared to try.

CHAPTER 20

Laurel had reached the business district south of Market Street, nearly halfway to the railroad station. Luckily the streets were almost deserted at this early hour. It was just a few minutes past five.

Never had she had so much trouble controlling a pair of horses. They were extremely fractious, shying at everything and nothing, and Laurel was afraid they would bolt out of control at any moment. Finally, when they broke stride once too often, each trying to head in opposite directions, Laurel gave up. Securing them outside a store, she grabbed her bag and Sassy's carrier and began to walk south along Second Street. The cable cars would be running soon, and she would catch one heading close to the station. She could still catch her train in plenty of time.

A few minutes later, she paused to rest on a sidewalk bench and wait for a trolley to come. Carrying the bag in one hand and Sassy's cage in the other was awkward. Suddenly the early morning quiet was broken by a mysterious rumbling that grew steadily louder. Then the ground under her feet began to tremble ominously, and the bench to shake beneath her.

Before her startled eyes, a wide crack broke open
in the street, buckling the pavement on either side.
In mute astonishment, she looked up the street. It
actually seemed to be rolling in an eerie wave, as if
it were the ocean and not solid earth at all.

A frightened yelp began in her throat and
emerged as a full-fledged scream as the earth
shook with a violence that seemed to go on and on.
Everything began to happen at once. The air was
filled with the roar of the terrible quaking and the
sound of tumbling masonry and shattering glass.
The earth and all upon it trembled and shook,
creaking and groaning as buildings weaved back
and forth. Bricks, concrete, pieces of metal and
wood flew through the air from taller buildings,
littering the split street. The lamp post nearest
Laurel toppled to the sidewalk; as she watched in
horrified disblief, an entire building not far from
her began to crumble before her eyes, toppling to
earth in a cloud of dust and rubble.

The noise was terrible, the terror even worse!
Unable to move, not sure what she would do if she
could, Laurel sat in abject horror, clutching the
weaving bench. Someone was shrieking. Was it
she? Oh, God! What was happening? Was the
world coming to an end?

Suddenly Laurel was jerked from the bench,
still clutching her bags. Someone forced her back
from the street and into the doorway of the shop
behind her. Vaguely she registered the feel of
strong arms about her, sheltering and protecting
her from the flying debris. From the corner of her
eye, she saw utility poles snap like matchsticks,
sending wires in all directions and sparks sailing
everywhere. With a terrified wail, she buried her
face in the blue shirt front before her and clung to

the safety offered her.

It seemed to go on eternally, the noise and havoc and destruction. Then, just as suddenly as it had begun, it miraculously stopped. The earth ceased to tremble first; and after a few moments of creaking and groaning, a few more bricks thudding down to the broken street, the remaining buildings stopped wobbling and settled in place.

The absolute quiet was unbelievably eerie. Slowly the arms about her eased their hold, and as he took a step from her, Laurel got her first look at her rescuer. Before her stood a big, burly police-man, with a worried look in his bottle-green eyes. "Ma'am, are you all right?"

As he spoke, she thought she detected an Irish lilt. What a thing to notice now! "I—I—I'm fine. Thank you, officer." The events of the past moments were beginning to hit her, and she began to sob again.

"Sergeant Ryan Murphy, ma'am." He handed her a handkerchief and waited while she mopped at her face.

"What happened?" she asked in a wobbly voice, viewing the destruction about them.

"Earthquake." That one, simple word said it all. "It felt like a big one this time," Murphy said half to himself. "Probably caused a lot of damage, if this sight is anything to judge by."

Across the street, a chasm had opened up, swallowing the lower three floors of the building there. The entire structure had settled some thirty feet into the earth, and just sat there as if it had been constructed that way. A few doors down, a broken pipe was shooting a stream of water high into the sky, helping to settle the choking dust of crumbled buildings. The very bench on which

Laurel had sat just minutes before was crushed beneath the weight of a fallen telephone pole.

What little color remained now fled from Laurel's face. Weakness invaded her limbs, and darkness pressed in from the edges of her vision. With a moan, she collapsed against her savior.

Ryan Murphy caught her as she began to fall. "Easy, ma'am. I've got you. Just take a few deep breaths and hold tight."

She did as he instructed, and the feeling of light-headedness eased away. When she could lift her head without feeling faint, she looked up at him. "I could have been killed, if not for you! You saved my life!"

For the first time that morning, a deep chuckle vibrated from Ryan Murphy's barrel-like chest, and a wide grin split his craggy features. "Just part o' my job," he said lightly.

An answering smile wavered on her lips. "All in a day's work? And just how many people do you usually rescue every day, Sergeant?"

His face sobered as he gazed about him at rubble and destruction. "It'll be more today—at least I hope most of them'll be saved. Others will be beyond help. It's going to be one heck of a day!"

Laurel had read about earthquakes and the terrible destruction they wrought, but she'd never expected to encounter one personally. Now, as she listened to Sgt. Murphy, she began to wonder how badly damaged the city really was. How many people lay dead or injured? How many homes and businesses were now in ruins?

Sgt. Murphy broke into her thoughts. "Where were you headed, ma'am?" He eyed her travelling case curiously.

"Oh, dear! I was on my way to catch the six

o'clock train for Los Angeles. I was going to ride a cable car from here."

Murphy shook his head ruefully. "Won't be any cable cars running today, and more than likely, no trains either. The tracks will be torn up—twisted like pretzels. You'd better head home, if you can get there. Where do you live, ma'am?"

Laurel gave him her hand. "Laurel Prescott is my name," she said before she had time to think. A small frown creased her forehead as she mentally corrected that to Burke. How long would it be before she stopped thinking of herself as married to Brandon? "I live on Nob Hill."

"That's quite a walk from here, Mrs. Prescott. I wish I could see you home safely, but I'd best stay down here and see if anyone else needs help."

They heard the clang of a fire truck in the distance. Then, before Laurel knew what was happening, the earth began to shudder beneath them again. Murphy grabbed her again and they huddled together in the doorway.

This second tremor, though frightening, was less severe, lasting only a few seconds before stability was restored. Shaken, Laurel's huge lavender eyes questioned Murphy. "What was *that*?"

"An aftershock. We'll have more yet, I suspect. Trouble is, each tremor will bring more damage to already weakened buildings." His roving green eyes caught the smoke of a fire in the distance. "We'd better go. I'll walk as far as I can with you."

It took nearly half an hour just to reach the next corner. They had to dodge long rifts in the pavement, piles of rubble, snapping electrical lines and streams of water from broken water mains. The smell of gas was strong in the air. They heard more fire engines racing to their destinations.

Murphy's craggy face was creased in deep lines of worry. Fire had been the plague of San Francisco since its earliest beginnings, yet the majority of residents still built wooden structures, crowding one against another in every available space. San Francisco's Fire Department was one of the nation's best, but they'd had plenty of practice to achieve that status.

"They'll be busy today, too," Murphy predicted dourly. "Broken gas mains, unsafe chimneys, overturned lamps and stoves."

Reluctantly, he left her at the corner. 'You take care now, little lady, and get home as soon as you can. There will be looters out after all the merchandise they can steal before shop owners can stop them. If another tremor hits, try to find a stout doorway to stand in. It's safer than standing in the street.'

"I'll remember. Thank you." Laurel hated the thought of going on alone, but she knew she had already kept him too long from his duties. "You take care too, Sergeant Murphy. You're a good man." He actually blushed at her compliment.

"When you get home, run a tub of water and collect all you can in containers. The water mains are busted and you'll be glad for it later, and I sure hope your pantry is stocked."

"Why?"

"It will probably be a while before the stores are open for business, and if the railroad tracks need repair, supplies may be short for a few days."

"Anything else?"

Murphy waited for the noise of another fire truck to pass before answering. ' 'If your chimney is cracked, don't light a fire, even for cooking.

Cook outdoors if you have to. And find your candles before dark."

He scanned the horizon, noting smoke now coming from several areas. "You'd best hurry along, Mrs. Prescott. Good luck to you!"

"And to you, Sergeant Murphy."

She continued up on Second Street, weaving her way around debris and dangers. Often she had to detour past collapsed buildings or rubble blocking her way. Her one thought was to get back to the buggy. Perhaps then she would make better headway, though she wondered how she could drive the buggy down such broken, damaged streets.

Everywhere she saw destruction, but luckily no bodies. If San Francisco had one thing to be thankful for on this Wednesday morning, the eighteenth of April, it was that the earthquake had come before the streets were clogged with traffic and commercial buildings crowded with people. It would have been mass havoc if the quake had come at nine or noon instead of quarter past five in the morning. Thank God it hadn't occurred last evening while Caruso was performing to a packed house!

As Laurel soon discovered to her dismay, she need not have worried about driving the buggy back home. When she reached the place where she had left it, it was gone. Apparently the horses had bolted in panic. Heaven knew where they might be now!

Laurel sat down on the curb to rest, wanting desperately to cry. Why had she chosen this, of all mornings, to find that letter and run away? She should have been home in bed when the quake struck. Then again, so should Brandon! Where

was he now? Was he at home, worried sick about
her? Was the house a shambles and all in it killed,
or had it withstood the tremors? Was Brandon all
right?

Rising once more, she picked up her cases.
Sassy meowed plaintively, but Laurel had no
energy to waste on sympathy for the kitten. She
had to get home and find Brandon. She had to
know that he was well. Thoughts of Crystal City
faded into insignificance against the fear that
Brandon might be hurt.

Laurel trudged on, passing more and more
people as she neared Mission Street. Awakened by
the quake, storeowners were now on their way to
see how their businesses had fared. Others were
merely curious, while still more, as Sgt. Murphy
had predicted, were out to see what they could
steal. Others were fleeing the fires.

When she finally reached Mission Street, Laurel
was ready to collapse. It had been three hours
since the quake had first hit. It had taken her that
long to cover a distance of only several blocks,
advancing and detouring as conditions warranted.

Here the air was thick with smoke. Laurel stood
glancing about, uncertain which direction to take.
Ahead and a little to the right, the sky was black
with billowing clouds of smoke. Between the
buildings Laurel caught a glimpse of red-orange
flames. As she looked back the way she had come,
she saw more dark smoke. A sob of fright choked
her. What was she to do? Which way should she
go? Oh, God! She was so scared! If she stayed
here, she would be caught between the two
advancing fires and would surely die! "I don't
want to die!" she whimpered frantically. "Oh, dear
God, I want to live to hold my child in my arms!"

With familiar landmarks reduced to rubble and

the smoke becoming steadily thicker, it was difficult to get her bearings, but she thought she knew where she was. She started walking in the general direction of the Emporium. It looked to be away from the fire and from there she could find her way home.

She'd taken perhaps half a dozen steps when yet another aftershock hit. Nearly hysterical by now, she still managed to drag herself into a doorway, where she stood quivering and crying long after the tremor had passed. At that moment, she would have given anything to be held in Brandon's strong, warm embrace.

Brandon had problems of his own at that moment. Minutes before the earthquake, he and Judge Henry had been discussing their plot to secure Brandon's marriage plans. Searching his pockets for a cigar, the judge discovered that he had smoked his last one. Excusing himself, the older gentleman headed toward the lobby to obtain more.

Judge Henry had barely left the room when the entire building began to shake. Before Brandon's bleary, astonished eyes, the walls began to crack and break apart. Nearby windows shattered. Tables and chairs jumped about in animated dance, and lamps swayed and pitched to the floor. Over the din of destruction, a deep terrible rumble could be heard.

Hearing a sharper groan and a weird creaking overhead, Brandon looked up to see the entire ceiling about to come down upon him. Leaping from his chair, he dashed for the doorway. The last thing Brandon remembered was the floor coming up to greet him as he dodged a large piece of falling plaster, tripped, and fell against a heavy oak desk.

Brandon groaned and tried to shift his long legs from their cramped position. No good. For some reason they weren't moving. As he came slowly awake, he thought, "Why is it so stuffy in here? Someone ought to open a window. . ."

He licked his dry lips, wondering vaguely why he thought he tasted plaster. His eyelids fluttered open, but only darkness met his gaze—a heavy, unfamiliar darkness. He tried to make out familiar shapes, but nothing was clear in the blackness that surrounded him. Again, he tried to move and this time was rewarded by a sharp pain in his side that caused him to catch his breath.

The pain served to clear his mind, and suddenly Brandon recalled the earthquake. The ceiling had been about to fall, and he had been racing for the doorway. What had happened? Where was he now? Carefully, he tried to feel about him with his hands, though one arm was partially pinned beneath him. He managed to pull it out from under his weight, but the pain in his ribs caused him to cry out.

Later, he would be thankful for the pain that caused someone to hear him.

He lay still for a moment, catching his breath. Over the frantic pounding of his own heart, Brandon heard other voices—voices! Disregarding the discomfort if caused him, he yelled, "Hey! Help! *Help!*" Then he lay back and listened.

Scraping and thumping noises met his ears, the thuds of heavy items being moved about. A muffled voice called out, "Where are you, fella?"

Brandon yelled back. "Over here! Wherever that is!"

"This way, men! Get that timber moved. Careful now! We don't want the whole pile to come down on top of him!"

"No, we certainly don't," Brandon thought prayerfully. He could hear the grunts and groans of the men laboring to free him. He closed his eyes tightly against the plaster and dust falling on his face as they worked. When he opened them once more, he could see a faint shaft of glimmering light. Just knowing he wasn't blind made him weak with relief, for the thought of it had nearly panicked him.

"How you doing in there?" the welcome voice asked.

"I've been better. My legs are caught. I can see light now."

More grunts and groans; a little more light, a thud and a distinct oath from one of the men; creaking. All this came more clearly to Brandon's waiting ears as the men worked to free him.

Suddenly there was a tunnel of light, and he could see the men's legs. "Here! I'm here!" he called loudly.

A dirt-streaked face peered at at him. "So you are!" the man grinned. "Stay put and we'll have you out in a few more minutes."

Brandon grinned with relief. "I'm not going anywhere," he joked despite the pain in his ribs.

After what seemed an eternity, they freed his legs. Though he felt no pain, the circulation had been cut off for so long that he could not move them.

"Easy, boys! We don't know what might be broken!" The man heading the rescue looked down at Brandon. "Are you hurt anywhere?"

"My right side. My ribs, I think. And my head.

My legs are starting to tingle, but I can't move them."

"Don't try yet," he advised. Then he grinned again, teeth flashing white in his filthy face. "Anyone else under that desk with you?"

"Not that I know of."

One man grabbed his legs, another his hips, and they half-pulled, half-lifted him out from under the desk. Brandon caught one quick glimpse of the total destruction of the room before his head began to whirl with pain and darkness claimed him again.

He didn't know when they placed him on the stretcher and carried him out to the makeshift ambulance, a horse-drawn wagon with a mattress in the back. Neither did he see Judge Henry watching worriedly as they loaded his unconscious form onto the wagon bed. Luckily, he didn't feel the jouncing, rough ride over the broken streets as they took him through the city to the Mechanics' Pavillion, now a temporary hospital and morgue since General Hospital had collapsed in the earthquake. He lay blissfully ignorant of all around him, unaware even of the aftershock that rocked San Francisco a full three hours after the first quake.

Earthquakes had struck at San Francisco before, but this one was the worst in decades. It had destroyed much of the business district, bringing buildings tumbling into the streets. Away from the commercial center of the city, there was relatively minor damage, though nearly every chimney in San Francisco had cracked and fallen. Most of the city suffered broken windows, falling plaster, a few cracked walls, and broken bric-a-brac.

After the shock of the initial tremor had passed, people began to assess the damage and count their blessings. They laughed over being caught fleeing their rattling homes in their nightclothes, their feet bare and hair flying. They exchanged tales of their reactions, compared losses, and began to clean up the mess. Many did not realize how badly the downtown area had been hit. Neither did they realize that the worst was yet to come.

When the first few scattered fires began, the Fire Department was not worried. They had plenty of men and equipment. The big surprise came when they hooked up their hoses and got no water from the hydrants. Then they began to realize the magnitude of the damage and become truly alarmed. All the water lines had been ripped apart by the quake.

Reservoir mains from Crystal Springs Lake and San Andreas Lake were twisted and severed. There was no water with which to combat the spreading flames. The city now lay open to an even more frightening peril—fire!

Indeed, before the first paralyzing shudders had stopped, fires had sprung up in several areas. Near the waterfront, an area north of Market Street, firemen worked to contain a blaze. South of Market, more fires now threatened to merge. The army had been called out to help control the looting and robbing. Now they were consulted on the possibility of obtaining dynamite with which to combat the fires in lieu of water. General Funston took charge immediately, helping to coordinate efforts and leading the fight against the new disaster. Soon, dynamite charges were being set off all along a line just ahead of the fires, clearing buildings out of the fire's path to try to stop its relentless rampage. Curious bystanders often found themselves enlisted to clear the rubble and man shovels and picks. Many helped to deliver messages, run errands, haul wagonloads of supplies, and take the injured to makeshift hospitals.

Still the fire raged, consuming everything in its path, leaping boundaries, driving the firemen and military back to yet another line of defense. Now a new area, already called the Ham and Eggs Fire, was blazing north of Market on the far side of town, threatening to join the other fires from yet another direction. Only a miracle would save San Francisco now, and today seemed more a day for doom and disasters than miracles.

CHAPTER 21

In the midst of all this, Laurel was steadily fighting her way toward Market Street from the south. Weak with exhaustion and hunger, she plodded on, fear giving strength to her weary limbs. The streets were crowded with others who were fleeing the ever-encroaching flames. Several fire wagons raced past, and explosions ripped the air regularly. Ashes coated everything, and the thick acrid smoke made breathing difficult and vision poor. Windblown ash, floating in the air, sometimes carried with it live embers that smoldered and threatened to set fire to whatever they landed upon.

Laurel passed homes ruined by the earthquake and now threatened by the fire as well. Some were tilted at odd angles by the ground which had shifted so violently. Others sat askew on their foundations. One house had literally been lifted as the ground had rolled beneath it, and now sat perfectly unharmed in the center of the street! A dazed old woman sat on the steps of one house, and as Laurel looked up, she saw that the steps now led directly to the roof, so low had the house sunk during the quake.

Several apartment buildings and hotels in this area had collapsed, and rescuers were frantically

digging for survivors. The moans and cries of the
injured tore at Laurel's heart. She wished there
was some way she could help, but she was having
enough trouble just staying on her feet and ahead
of the fire. Her mind blanked out the thought that
those who could not be rescued in time would be
roasted alive. It was too horrible even to imagine!

Many houses had already been abandoned. Residents took what they could carry on their backs
and in their hands. The more inventive engineered
ingenious ways to transfer their goods, and Laurel
saw families pushing bureaus along the sidewalks,
or tables loaded to overflowing pushed along with
roller skates strapped to the legs. Baby carriages,
laundry tubs, anything with capacity for goods
and wheels was put to use.

Up and down the steep streets, Laurel saw
refugees lugging their most precious belongings.
One man and woman, who had most likely worked
long and hard to purchase such a luxury, were
trying to push their piano on the top of a hill.
Another family had strapped their belongings to a
long ladder, and were toting it along between
them on their shoulders. Many, like Laurel,
carried pets with them—cats, dogs, birds in cages,
even fishbowls.

Whatever the families managed to take, the
majority of their belongings had to be left behind,
abandoned to Fate and the fire. It seemed
ludicrous, but out of habit, or perhaps as a safe-
guard against looters, many a person took time to
lock his home as he left it. Other doors stood wide
open, a testament to hopelessness.

Like Laurel, most were on foot. Many animals
had been killed or injured in the quake. Others had
gone berserk and injured themselves. Some had
panicked and run off. Horses were in short supply

and those fortunate few who had a wagon or carriage with a horse hitched to it were soon pressed into service by city officials, the hospitals, the military, or the fire department. Those who escaped this involuntary enlistment were demanding outrageous sums to haul families and their goods to safety.

Market Street, when Laurel finally reached it, was a scene of complete and utter chaos. Throngs of people crowded the streets. Stores were being looted in broad daylight despite dire warnings from the police. The military had been issued orders to shoot looters on sight, but many thieves decided the risk was worth it. They knew the majority of the soldiers would be busy trying to fight the fire or guarding more important places such as banks, the Post Office, and the U.S. Mint.

A few looters paid for this gamble with their lives. As Laurel threaded her way through the crowds, she saw a young man dash from a doorway, his arms loaded with stolen goods. A sharp report sounded above the noise of the crowd. In the sudden quiet following the gunfire, stunned onlookers watched in disbelief as the thief pitched face first into the street, still clutching his stolen merchandise. It was an armload of clothes, for which he had paid with his life's blood. Laurel turned and vomited violently in the gutter, leaning heavily on a lamp post as she willed her head to stop spinning.

The dynamiting was nearing Market Street now, as was the ravenous, relentless fire. Lines of policemen and soldiers were pushing the crowds back across the north side of Market Street, which was to be the dynamite crew's next line of defense.

That was fine with Laurel, and she was headed in that dirction anyway. At long last, she was out of direct danger from the fire itself, and the relief she felt was overpowering. For hours she had lived in fear, and now she could relax a little. The air was still heavy with ash and smoke, but the mad dash just steps ahead of the flames, the uncertainty of whether she was going in the right direction or headed into the path of one of the various fires, was over. She was behind the lines of safety now. Surely the men would be able to stop the fire south of Market Street. Surely the efforts of those setting off the dynamite would result in success!

Laurel moved with the crowds down Stockton toward Union Square. At a little grocery store she stopped in amazement and watched as two soldiers oversaw the orderly dispersal of the owner's wares. This certainly was better than the looting she had previously witnessed. Hungry beyond anything she'd ever experienced, Laurel numbly joined the line and waited her turn with the others. She came away with a loaf of bread, a small chunk of cheese, a bottle of oreangeade, and two avocados. She'd paid ten times what she would have yesterday for the same items, but at least she had something to fill her grumbling stomach.

At Union Square she joined the throngs already gathered there. Bone-tired, she sank wearily onto a curb to eat her precious lunch. As she sat munching at her prized fare, she gazed about at the people around her, and suddenly realized what she must look like—tired, bedraggled, and filthy! Her clothes hung limply, sweaty and smelling of smoke. They were streaked with ash and dirt, as she knew her face must be. Her hair was hanging in straggling tendrils. Her hat and most of her hair pins had been lost in her flight. Her gloves, once white, were now grimy.

As she rested, Laurel watched the people come and go. Many were waiting to see if the fire could be contained south of Market Street, hoping against hope that they would miraculously have homes to return to. Others knew better. They merely waited stolidly to see what could be salvaged from the ruins. Still others were fleeing the city altogether, passing through Union Square on a safe route to the Ferry Building and a ride across the bay to Oakland. It was the only reliable means out of San Francisco now, and if Laurel hadn't been so worried about Brandon, she too would have headed in that direction. As it was, she was compelled to assure herself of his safety.

It was ironic that she should be agonizing about Brandon just as Judge Henry literally stumbled upon her at her curbside luncheon. The old gentleman turned to apologize for bumping into her, and upon recognizing Laurel, was struck nearly speechless. "Mrs. Prescott! Is that you?"

Knowing what a sight she must look, Laurel nodded shyly and smiled wearily. "Hello, Judge Henry. Would you like to join me? My lunch isn't fancy, but I'll gladly share with you."

Henry shook his head. "No, thank you. Child, what are you doing here?"

"I'm trying to get home, but I'm making slow headway."

"Then you've been to see Brandon? How is he?"

Laurel stared at him, wondering if her brain and ears were still in working order. She was about to tell him that she was trying to get home when he said, "I can't tell you how worried I was when they loaded his body onto that wagon this morning. I was sure he was dead!"

Laurel's entire body went cold as ice, her eyes as round as saucers in her suddenly colorless face. "Oh, God! Oh, no! Please, no!"

The judge knelt down beside her, realizing he'd made a grave error. "Mrs. Prescott, have you seen Brandon since the quake?" He had to repeat himself before he got a response.

She could not keep her teeth from chattering as she looked up at him. "No," she whispered faintly.

Not knowing what to do, he patted her shoulder. "I may have been hasty. On second thought, Brandon may have merely been unconscious. I wasn't close enough to see much."

"Tell me! Tell me what happened," she implored, her trembling hand clutching at his arm.

"We were together at my club when the quake struck. I had just left the room to get some cigars, when everything began to pitch and shake. I don't recall much of that few minutes, but when it was over, one entire side of the building was demolished, including the room in which I had left your husband. The ceiling had collapsed, and Brandon was trapped somewhere beneath two floors of debris.

"Immediately, several fellows began to try to dig him out. It took quite some time. Afraid the rest of the building might come down, those of us who could not help waited outside. Then they brought him out and loaded him in a wagon and took him to the hospital, along with a couple of other men who'd been hurt."

"Did you see him?" Laurel was frantic for some assurance.

"Yes, I did."

Laurel scrambled to her feet. "Where did they take him? Which hospital?"

"Central Hospital, I'm sure."

Wiping the tears from her dirt-streaked face and smearing it even worse, she asked fearfully, "How do I get to Central Hospital from here?"

"Dear woman!" The judge was on his feet beside her. "You can't meant to go there now? It is much too far for you to walk in your condition, with these crowds and the fire!"

"Of course I'm going, Judge Henry! I have to find him. Surely you understand. *I must!*"

"But it is blocks from here—clear over by Mechanic's Pavillion. You shouldn't be racing about on foot. It would be best if you went home immediately and waited for the hospital to contact you. They'll take excellent care of him, I'm sure."

Laurel gazed at him sorrowfully, tears welling in her eyes and running down her cheeks. "If he's still alive, Judge Henry. He may already be dead, as you have said. I must see for myself. If Brandon is hurt, he will need me. If not . . . I must know." Her voice broke off on a despairing sob.

"Dear child, I'm so sorry." Not for the world would Henry have told her what he and Brandon had been discussing. The poor woman had enough to bear without learning that she and Brandon were not actually wed. He sincerely prayed Brandon was alive. If not, he hoped Laurel never discovered the illegality of their marriage.

All Laurel's concentration and all her energies were bent on getting to the hospital. Brandon was hurt! He needed her! She had to reach him, to hold him, to comfort him—to assure herself that he was alive. But she could not put aside her fear that

Brandon might be dead! "No!" Planting one foot determinedly ahead of the other, she trudged steadily along, desperation lending strength to her weary body. "I refuse to believe that he is dead. Brandon *is* alive! He *has* to be alive!" As she elbowed her way through the crowded streets back toward Market Street, she repeated the refrain like a litany of hope "He's alive. He's alive. He has to be. Please let him be." And her frantic heart cried out, "I'll die if he's not!"

How Laurel ever made it as far down Market Street as she did was amazing, not just to her, but to the soldiers and policemen who finally stopped her. For more than an hour, Market Street had been the line of defense against the demonic fire, a line the weary firemen were desperate to hold and almost doomed to lose. The entire south side of the street was a blazing inferno. Time and again, flaming debris flew over to ignite a blaze on the north side of Market, and time after time the firemen beat it out. They fought valiantly, but the fire was out of control.

To compound their problems, the fire to the east, near the docks, that had earlier been extinguished, now roared to life again north of the Market Street barrier there. To the west, the Ham and Eggs Fire was racing through the Hayes Valley Area and threatening the Mission District. That entire section of Market had been engulfed in flames for some time. It was the same area Laurel was trying so frantically to reach.

She barely noticed when the crowd thinned out. She took no notice that nearly the only persons she saw in those last few blocks were firemen and soldiers. She only knew she must reach the hospital and Brandon, and a constant heartstopping fear of the raging fire mere yards from where she walked.

The heat was suffocating, the brilliant flames nearly blinding. The skin on Laurel's face drew tight with the heat from the fire, and she could almost feel her skin blistering. Perspiration dried almost as soon as it surfaced, leaving her drenched and seared at the same time. Sparks flew all around her, and her clothes were grey with ash. Several times her skirts threatened to catch fire, but she beat them out and went on, ignoring the burns to her fingers. Her tears dried in dirty streaks on her face, and her hair was singed in places. Inside her cage, Sassy was wild with fright, and only compassion kept Laurel from abandoning the kitten, for the cage was getting heavier with every step.

She was almost opposite the Post Office, nearly two-thirds on the way to her destination, when she was finally stopped. The young soldier who spotted her was dumbfounded that she had managed to come so far without being detained. "Lady! Are you crazy?" he shouted. "You're going the wrong way! You're headed right into the fire!" He grabbed her arm and headed her back the way she came.

Though numb with fatigue, Laurel struggled against his grasp. "Let me go! Let go of me!" she screamed. She could not allow herself to be stopped now, not now that she had come so far, was so near her goal. "I must get to the hospital! I must! Please! You've got to help me!" Nearly hysterical with fear, worry, and weariness, she stumbled. The young man caught her, but not before she twisted her ankle, and she cried out at the sharp pain.

The soldier's eyes grew round with apprehension as his gaze fell on her rounded stomach. "Oh God, lady!" he groaned miserably. "Don't do this to me! I've never had to deliver a baby, and I never want to, either. I don't even want kids of my own!"

He helped her hobble to the steps of an apartment building, where he seated her gingerly. "How bad is it?" he asked hesitantly.

Laurel was torn between her own discomfort and laughter at the frightened expression on his young face. "It's not the baby, it's my ankle! I've twisted it, thanks to your unsolicited aid!"

The relief on his face would have been comical under different circumstances. "You said you had to get to the hospital!" he retorted. "What else was I supposed to think?"

"I *do* have to get to the hospital. My husband was injured in the earthquake this morning, and I must reach him." Laurel turned pleading eyes up to his. "Please! Can you help me?"

Her wobbling chin and the tears sparkling in her large lavender eyes made him wish he could. "Was he supposed to be in Central Emergency?" he asked. When she nodded, his expression turned grim. "Central was levelled by the quake this morning, and all the patients transferred to Mechanic's Pavillion."

"Can you help me to get there?"

"Lady, Mechanic's Pavillion burned to the ground an hour ago! It went up like a torch and was completely burned within fifteen minutes."

His blunt announcement hit her like a cudgel. The air rushed from her lungs and her head spun crazily, even as she fought to reject his statement and all it meant. That hope she had nourished on this long, nightmarish trek had just been snuffed out.

"Lady! Lady!" The soldier patted her cheeks and fervently pleaded, "Please don't faint on me, ma'am! If your husband was there, he's been moved to Golden Gate Park with the other patients."

Hope flickered faintly once more. "Did they get everyone out?" she asked weakly.

The fellow nodded vigorously. "All but a few of the dead ones."

His words, meant to encourage, sent a lance of pain and fear through her heart. What if Brandon had not lived? Was his body now a pile of ashes? Would she have not even the small comfort of looking upon his beloved face again? Worse yet, what if they only thought he'd died and he had been burned alive—helpless and weak and unable to escape? Terror clawed at her, making her gasp for breath.

A familiar voice brought her somewhat to her senses, a deep voice with a slight Irish lilt. "Mrs. Prescott! What in the world are *you* doing here? I thought you'd be safe at home by now."

He bent down to speak to her, and without thought, Laurel launched herself into his burly arms. Sobbing hysterically, her explanations made little sense to him. It was the young soldier who explained the situation to Sgt. Murphy.

"Oh, I see. Well, now, Mrs. Prescott, we've got to get you out of here and on your way to Golden Gate Park." One thing was certain, they were all in peril if they stayed here. The entire district was fast being circled by angry flames. Murphy helped Laurel to her feet, surprised when she cried out and collapsed against him in pain.

"It's her ankle, sir," the soldier hastened to explain.

Weary, filthy from head to toe with soot and

ash, Ryan Murphy lifted Laurel into his strong arms and proceeded to carry her. "Grab the cat and her bag, and let's get moving," he told the young man.

To Laurel, whose head lay on his broad chest, he murmured, "It will be all right, lamb. Don't you worry now. Ryan Murphy won't let anything happen to you." Tired as he was, she felt light in his arms, her head resting trustingly over his heart. She resembled a bedraggled waif rather than a lady of means, and his heart went out to her. Who would guess that someone this tiny and fragile would be so strong and determined, would brave earthquake and fire and risk her own safety to find her mate? Like many people on this disastrous day, she'd met adversity and faced it with courage he had to admire. Even now, tired, pregnant, hurt, and nearly beaten in body and spirit, she struggled to go on.

For the first time in hours, Laurel was able to relax and let someone else take charge. They wound their way back along Market, passing harried firemen and soldiers along the way. At last they reached the corner of Powell, where the towering Flood Building stood like a sentinel, untouched as yet by the fire which had already consumed the vast Emporium just across the street. A few blocks north of Market, they stopped.

Sgt. Murphy left her with the soldier and went off down the street. "You stay right here, Mrs. Prescott, and wait for me. I'll be back before you know I'm gone."

It took longer than that—much longer—but Laurel and her young companion waited. How Murphy managed it, she never knew, but he returned with a wagon and several other refugees. Though the poor horse looked ready to drop, and the driver grim and disgruntled, that wagon was the most beautiful sight Laurel had seen all day.

"Your carriage awaits, fair lady," Murphy said with a wide grin. "Ready to take you to Golden Gate Park." With infinite care, he handed her into the wagon.

"Thank you again, Sergeant Murphy," she said, clutching at his huge hand, gratitude beaming from her face.

"You just go to the park, find your husband, and stay there until it is safe to leave," he grumbled good-naturedly. "I've other things to do with my life than rescue fair maidens all day."

For the rest of her life, Laurel would always remember Ryan Murphy standing there waving her off, his blue uniform torn and dirty, his teeth flashing white in his grimy face, his green eyes sparkling with life and laughter on this darkest day in her memory.

CHAPTER 22

Brandon awoke with a splitting headache and throbbing ribs, to find himself lying on a blanket staring at the vaulted ceiling of the Mechanic's Pavillion. What was he doing here, of all places? The last he remembered he was being dislodged from the ruins of Judge Henry's club downtown.

As he gazed about him, he saw doctors and nurses rushing about in organized pandemonium. The Pavillion was packed with patients and earthquake victims lining the floor. Along a far wall, workers were unloading books and merchandise that had been transferred from downtown buildings for safe keeping. To the rear, away from the other patients, a temporary morgue had been set up.

A few minutes of lying still and listening to the talk about him told Brandon that Central Emergency Hospital had been demolished by the quake, and the patients and staff removed across the street to the Pavillion. Damage to the city's business district had been extensive, and now fires raged in various sections of San Francisco. The military had been called out, and dynamite crews set to work trying to halt the fire.

The more he heard, the more anxious Brandon

became. When he had left home last night, leaving Laurel alone, he had never dreamed anything like this would happen! He had to get home to her, to make sure she and the baby were safe.

Brandon attempted to sit up, but the pain that speared through his side sent him flat on his back again, breathless and groaning.

"Hey there, young man! Don't go moving around until I've had a chance to tape up those ribs." Brandon looked up to find a white-coated doctor standing over him.

"I've got to go home—find out how my wife is," Brandon grunted.

Kneeling down, the doctor unrolled a wide strip of bandage. "You'll lie still and do as you are told, or wind up flat on your face in the street somewhere," the physician told him bluntly. "When we have you bandaged, you can see about getting home. Where do you live?"

"Nob Hill. Do you have any word how badly that area was damaged?"

"From what I hear, a few broken windows and fallen chimneys is all there. Downtown and the commercial district were hit the worst."

"And the fire?" Brandon asked anxiously.

"South of Market mostly. Nowhere near Nob or Russian Hills. Your wife is probably in much better condition than you are right now. You're lucky, though. These ribs are bruised and cracked, but they could have broken and punctured a lung. And that lump on your head could have been worse. How is your vision? Blurred?" Finished with taping his ribs, the doctor now probed at the bump on the side of Brandon's head.

Brandon winced. "My vision is fine, but I have a whale of a headache."

"I shouldn't wonder," came the wry reply. "You

might be a bit dizzy for a while. I'd advise you to rest a bit before you start for home, since you'll more than likely have to walk. The streets are pretty badly torn up, from what I hear, and most of the wagons and available vehicles are being commandeered for emergency purposes."

"My wife is home alone, probably frantic by now. I'm worried about her. She's expecting our first child."

The doctor nodded sympathetically but said, "You'll do neither of you any good by rushing around and probably passing out on the street. Take it easy, and you'll more likely get there in one piece."

Knowing the doctor was right, Brandon controlled his impatience with effort. "Thanks, Doc. I appreciate your patching me up."

Barely forty-five minutes later, a new problem had arisen. The Hayes Valley fire had crossed Van Ness, just two blocks west, and was threatening the Pavillion. All the patients had to be evacuated immediately. Every available wagon, cart, and carriage was loaded with patients to be transported to Golden Gate Park. The gravity of the situation spurred everyone beyond their normal capabilities. The less injured patients helped the doctors and nurses move the seriously disabled to vehicles. Ignoring his painful head and ribs, Brandon worked alongside the staff, feverishly trying to load the last of them before the fire reached them.

With fire already licking at the rafters, the final patient was on his way at last. Some of the dead had to be left behind, and all the merchandise, but no more lives were lost.

Anxious to be on his way home, Brandon declined transport to Golden Gate Park, not realizing the extent of the fire now raging along Market Street. Had he accepted the ride, he might have doubled back and reached home safely, though it would have been further to walk. Instead, he ended up in the thick of the firefighting action, his way home much more perilous than he had anticipated.

Brandon fought his way through thick smoke, ash, and sporadic flame, working steadily eastward down Market Street. Behind him, Mechanic's Pavillion collapsed and burned to smoldering debris within a quarter of an hour. He was past the Post Office, in the block between it and the Emporium, when several soldiers and firefighters raced by. Without warning, he found himself drafted into their company as a gruff colonel grabbed him by the arm.

"You there! Come with us!" the officer ordered, shoving Brandon ahead of him.

"Wait just a blasted minute!" Brandon responded angrily.

"No time! The Mint is about to go up in flames!"

"I've got to get home to my wife. You can't order me around!"

The colonel chuckled dryly. "Well, I am, sonny! This is a state of emergency and martial law has been declared. Console yourself with all that lovely gold and money you'll be helping to save for the U.S. government."

Brandon was well and truly caught on the horns of a dilemma. While desperate to reach Laurel, he couldn't risk getting shot for disobeying a direct military order under martial law. He resigned himself to his fate and went along to the U.S. Mint building with the others.

The next several hours were the most hectic he'd ever encountered. Along with the other men,

he worked frantically to save the huge structure.
From basement cisterns, they hauled water to the
rooftop, where they repeatedly wet down the roof
and stamped out innumerable small fires started
by sparks from nearby buildings. All around them
the city was aflame, and Brandon had a bird's eye
view of the true situation in which San Francisco
now found itself. It was truly a frightening and
awesome sight!

For several long and arduous hours, they fought
to beat back the blaze. In addition to wetting down
the roof, they soaked all the windowsills, tearing
the curtains down from the windows. The building
was constructed of cement block, but if the roof or
sills caught fire, the structure would be gutted, its
interior and contents destroyed. As it was, the
intense heat from neighboring burning structures
caused most of the windows to shatter from their
frames. Only their undaunted efforts saved the
U.S. Mint from the same fate as the surrounding
buildings. By the time the fire moved on, the Mint
still stood; scarred and charred, but intact.

Just when Brandon thought he could at last
hope to get home to Laurel, a call for help went up
from the Post Office just two blocks away and the
indomitable colonel ordered his weary makeshift
troops once again to the rescue.

While Brandon was frantically beating out fires
with soaked mail bags inside the Post Office
building, Laurel was being detained not half a
block away by the young soldier. Within shouting
distance of one another, neither knew it, as once
again Fate intervened to keep them apart. Laurel
was soon heading back in the direction she had
come, on her way to Golden Gate Park to try to
find him; Brandon would be hours yet in the Post
Office, helping to hold the fire at bay.

By the time the Post Office, like the Mint, had been saved, night had fallen. The fire had now crossed Market Street and was racing uncontrolled into new territory to the south, and Brandon found himself cut off, unable to reach Nob Hill. With several others, he spent the night at the Post Office, alternately dozing on a pile of mail sacks and watching the progress of the fire with a worried eye. Before the night was out, Chinatown would be in smoldering ashes and the blazing inferno would be racing up Nob Hill.

Golden Gate Park was just one of the spots in the city chosen as places of safe refuge, but it was by far the largest. Already, hundreds of people had fled here from areas south of Market Street, where the fire had driven them from their homes.

At first Laurel was dismayed at the number of people there, until she recalled that Brandon would be among those transferred from the Pavillion. He would be where the other patients were being tended. She asked around until someone directed her to the hospital tents.

The large tent was supplied with dozens upon dozens of cots. Some supplies had been retrieved from the city's wrecked hospitals, others donated by the Army post; more were on the way to San Francisco by ferry.

Laurel left her bags just inside the entrance and, heart thumping wildly in her chest, went in search of Brandon. No doctor or nurse she asked could recall having treated anyone by that name. Of course, they had treated many this day without ever knowing their names. His description meant little. There were many tall, dark men in San Francisco. No, they could not recall one with steel-grey eyes.

At last Laurel found someone who would recognize him on sight. Dr. Davis was helping to tend the injured.

"You are looking for your husband? No, I haven't seen him, but that doesn't mean he is not here."

"He *must* be here! Judge Henry saw them put him in a wagon headed for Central Hospital. Brandon had been injured in the earthquake," she explained.

"How badly was he hurt?"

"I don't know. I wasn't with him then. Judge Henry said Brandon was unconscious. He was afraid he might be . . . be . . . Oh, God! He can't be dead!"

Dr. Davis could see that Laurel was very near hysterical collapse. Gently he led her to an empty cot and sat her down upon it. "Mrs. Prescott, you've got to calm down. Think of your baby."

"I *am* thinking of my baby!" she wailed. "I am thinking of my child without a father. Oh, Dr. Davis! I've got to find him!"

"You will, dear. You will. Just rest for a few minutes. You've been through a lot today. Is anyone here with you?" he asked.

Shaking her head, she answered, "No, I'm alone. I've walked over half of San Francisco today, it seems, always one step ahead of the fire and miles behind Brandon."

"I'm very busy just now, Mrs. Prescott, but I promise you that I will help you look for your husband. In turn, you must promise that you will try to calm down; even rest a bit, for the baby's sake." When she agreed, he said, "You lie back and close your eyes, just for a few minutes, and I will be back soon."

She didn't mean to fall asleep. She meant only to

rest her smoke-irritated eyes for a few minutes. But she was thoroughly exhausted and now her body demanded rest.

When she awoke, Laurel thought she'd slept only a few minutes. In truth, she'd slept for over three hours. What she thought was sunlight outdoors was actually the reflection of the enormous fire still ravaging the city. It created a light so bright that one could literally read a newspaper by it. The cloud of smoke that rose over San Francisco glowed eerily, a huge bright red haze.

Laurel stumbled sleepily to her feet, her ankle throbbing angrily as it took her weight. Slowly she limped from cot to cot, searching smoke-streaked faces for Brandon's. She was halfway down the third row when Dr. Davis found her.

"You are limping."

"I twisted my ankle earlier today."

"Come. Let me look at it. It probably should be wrapped." He led her back to her cot and examined the ankle. "It is swollen. You really should stay off it, but I suppose that is like telling the wind not to blow."

She smiled wanly. "You let me sleep too long. Have you seen Brandon?"

"No." He proceeded to bandage her ankle. "I have looked, and he is not here. Also, I've had others checking throughout the park, to no avail."

Laurel began to panic once more. "He has to be! They told me all the patients from the Pavillion were brought here."

"Yes, but Brandon was not among them, Laurel."

"Did you check them all? Even those who . . ." She could not bear to finish the question, but the doctor understood what she was asking.

"Yes, dear lady. I checked even those who died."

Her bloodless lips trembled violently as her lavender eyes searched his kindly ones. Swallowing hard, she asked hesitantly, "Is it true that all the bodies were not removed from the Pavillion before it burned?"

He debated a moment, then nodded regretfully. "I'm sorry, Laurel. Truly sorry. If Brandon was at Mechanic's Pavillion as you say, he was not among the patients transported here."

"Then . . ." Her heart lodged in her throat, making speech next to impossible. "Then he's dead," she whispered, closing her eyes in agony.

"I don't know. I can only assume so, from what you have told me."

"Oh, God! Oh, dear God!" she screamed. "No! No! No! No!" Great, gulping sobs choked off her pitiful denials, and tears streamed down her already streaked face. Her heartbroken sobs finally made breathing so difficult that she fainted, falling swiftly into a deep, dreamless oblivion.

The sun was rising when Laurel at last awoke once more. She felt a thousand years old, her face swollen from crying even in her sleep. Still in the filthy clothes she'd worn the previous day, she felt drained and dirty, but she could barely muster the spirit to care. Her very reason for living was gone now, gone with Brandon, this time for eternity. There would be no more love, no more sharing. No more laughter to light up his eyes and turn them to silver. No more teasing or arguing or fighting. Now there were only tears and grieving and memories of a marriage that wasn't a marriage at all, of a love that had perhaps been only a dream in her heart all along.

Wearily, her muscles aching only a little less than her heart, Laurel rose, reluctant to face this day, to face the rest of her life without Brandon. She washed with the soap and water the nurse brought to her. She ate the food placed before her, her fork moving from plate to mouth by rote rather than any conscious effort on her part. When a nurse showed her where she could change her clothes, she did so because it was expected of her. Out of compassion for her sole companion in misery, she fed Sassy. Then she sat woodenly on her cot and contemplated her loss.

When Dr. Davis checked on her a little while later, he prodded her into making some very disturbing decisions.

"You've got the welfare of your unborn child to consider, Laurel. Your husband was so proud and happy about the baby. Surely you want to do what is best for your child. It will be a comfort to you in days to come—a lasting tribute to Brandon and the love you shared."

His well-intentioned words almost made her choke. Only she knew the truth about her so-called marriage. Even now she was not sure Brandon had not been using her in a grand plot of revenge. She did not doubt her love for him; only Brandon's love for her. Still, the doctor's words forced her to consider her next move. She would have to go home to Crystal City and tell Hank about Brandon's death. Then she would have to face her father with the truth, no matter how much it hurt to do so.

"What are you going to do now?" Dr. Davis was asking.

"I'll go home."

He gave her a pained look. "I really hate to break this to you, on top of everything else, but you have no home to go to. Nob Hill was completely destroyed by fire this morning."

She confounded him by smiling gently. "I meant I'll go home to Texas, to my aunt and my father, as soon as possible. Do you have any idea how soon that might be?"

"Well, it will be a few days until the train tracks are repaired, and the fire has cut off the roads. However, many people have already left the city, and many more are planning to go. They are taking the ferries across to Oakland and catching trains from there."

This was the first optimistic news Laurel had heard in two days. "How can I get to the Ferry Building from here?" she asked dully.

"Well, I wouldn't suggest any more walking in your condition, especially with that bad ankle. You could take a nasty fall and really harm yourself and the baby. I could try to find you a carriage or wagon, but the drivers are taking advantage of the present crisis. They are charging unheard of prices, and it will probably cost you a good bit."

"I'll pay whatever is necessary, Dr. Davis. Don't worry—I have money in my bag."

The good doctor made the arrangements, and barely an hour later Laurel was on her way to the Ferry Building, determined to leave San Francisco as soon as possible. She desperately needed to go home, now more than ever before. She needed her family and the security they represented. She needed the comfort of Aunt Martha's arms, and a familiar place to hide away and heal, a place to await the birth of her child—a place to cry out her grief.

As Laurel was on her way to the Ferry Building, Brandon was laboriously working his way on foot up Nob Hill. The sight that met his disheartened gaze was devastating. Every building was either

burned to the ground or a gutted skeleton. He
doubted that his home had fared any better. He
could only hope that Laurel had fled to safety, but
where would he even begin looking for her?

As he topped the crest of the hill, he stared in
dismay. Millions of dollars of property lay in
smoldering ruin. Every mansion, every tree, every
stable! Tessie's glorious new hotel was reduced to
a pile of steaming marble; James Flood's famed
bronze fence was a lump of molten metal. The
Stanford Institute, the Hopkins' Art Institute, the
Crocker mansion, the Cook home—all burned.

When he passed through the arch at the end of
his own drive, Brandon was sick at heart. The
lawn was burned black, the row of shade trees
scorched and leafless. From a distance, the house
itself did not look all that bad. The light stone was
blackened, the windows now yawning holes
without glass, but the structure was standing. On
closer inspection, the damage was much worse.
All the chimneys had toppled, as well as one
of the corner turrets. The magnificent stained
glass window had collapsed leaving a gaping hole.

All this Brandon noticed only in passing. What
alarmed him most was that the entire roof had
collapsed, and what he could see through the open
windows was total destruction. The whole interior
had burned; walls, furnishings, everything. And
not a soul was around to tell him of Laurel's
whereabouts.

It was then that Brandon heard a mournful
wailing coming from inside the still smoking
house. The wail became a series of short, sharp
yelps before returning to a long, forlorn howl.
Tyke! It had to be Tyke!

Brandon scrambled through the charred
doorway, picking his way over steaming timbers

and glowing ash toward the sound. All the while, he was wondering, "Why would Laurel leave Tyke behind? The little fox was devoted to her!"

He found the animal huddled in what had once been the pantry. The tiny room was a shambles. A sack of black, smoldering flour sat in one corner near tumbled shelves of burst canned goods. Charred potatoes were barely recognizable next to what had once been Laurel's precious horde of avocados.

Brandon's wandering gaze fixed on the dirty, singed pup. The bedraggled fox was sitting next to a shapeless mass on the floor. "Tyke! Here boy!" Brandon called to him, but the pup did not budge. Tyke merely looked up at him soulfully and began to wail again.

Brandon stepped closer, then stopped abruptly, chills racing up his spine. That smell! That awful, foul smell! It wasn't merely the odor of burnt food and wood. His nose registered the distinct smell of burnt flesh. With a dread that nearly paralyzed him, Brandon looked closely at the charred lump by which Tyke sat. It was a body! His pulse sounded madly in his head, and his stomach flipped over, gagging him.

Walking to his own execution could not have been more difficult for Brandon than approaching that blackened form. The thought that kept resounding in his brain was horrible to contemplate. Was it Laurel? Why else would Tyke be guarding it, mourning it?

The clothing was burned off, leaving what was left of the skin exposed. The flesh had been charred until it fell away from the bones in many places. There was no identifying the body by the hair, for it had been singed completely off the head. By size alone, Brandon knew it was a woman's body, face down on the floor. It was impossible to tell if she had been pregnant, for the front of her was literally melded to the burnt floor beneath her. Even her rings were melted to an unrecognizable lump on her charred fingers. The face, turned to one side, was burnt beyond identification. Was this all that was left of his beloved wife? Had Tyke been faithfully guarding her remains until Brandon returned? It was more than Brandon could bear.

Shocked and sickened, Brandon was stunned into immobility. Then reaction set in. A terrible hoarse cry of agony rent the air, and he stumbled blindly onto the rear veranda where he leaned on the stone rail and retched until his stomach was empty of its contents. Sinking to his knees, he gave vent to his grief, weeping like a child, sobbing as he could never remember doing in all his life. Along with grief came raging anger. *Why?* Why hadn't Laurel escaped the fire? How could God be so cruel as to take his beautiful wife and child from him?

At last, his tears spent, Brandon began to think more clearly, and new hope dawned. Perhaps he was wrong. Maybe it wasn't Laurel's body in there at all. It might be one of the servants. The body was in the pantry, after all. What would Laurel be doing in the pantry?

Then, just as swiftly as hope had sprung up, it dimmed. Brandon knew that Laurel often went into the kitchen or pantry in search of avocados, even in the middle of the night sometimes. And why else would Tyke have stationed himself beside the body and refused to move? The animal worshipped Laurel.

Even as he tried to tell himself that he could not be sure the blackened pile of ashes was Laurel, that it might be someone else, he was devastated with the greatest pain and sense of loss he'd ever felt. It was as if his heart had been ripped from his body, his very soul torn to shreds. He wanted to die as well.

Only by repeatedly telling himself that there was no way to positively identify the body as Laurel's, could he go on. To save his own sanity, he had to assume it was someone else, anyone else but she. He would scour San Francisco in search of her. He would locate friends or servants with whom she might have taken shelter. He would find neighbors who had fled the fire, and perhaps find Laurel with them. It was a thin thread of hope, but it was all he had. He forced himself to center his attention on it. It might take many hours of diligent searching to find her—perhaps days—maybe never. . . .

CHAPTER 23

Brandon went back down Nob Hill by the same route he had come. The fire was still raging down the far slope, edging toward the Western Addition now. He wanted to find Tess and find out if she or any of their other friends had seen Laurel. In order to get to Tessie's house, he had to circle the fire.

The northern tip of San Francisco was as yet untouched by the fire, and by far the safest route. First, however, Brandon had to wind his way through the smoldering ruins of Chinatown. If the streets had been narrow and circuitous before, they were now nearly impassable. It was like walking through a vast black wasteland of ash-covered rubble, devoid of life and silent as a graveyard. Once again his nostrils were assailed by the distinct odor of burnt human flesh, and his nightmarish fears haunted Brandon like a spectre.

It seemed forever before he at last came out onto streets lined with trees and unburned homes. Yet even here a film of ash covered everything, and smoke hung in the air. Now Brandon made better speed. Though there were many people on the streets, headed for the Ferry Building, Brandon found it easier going. When he came to Union, he cut west again, and finally, after two more miles, reached Tess's house.

The lady was busy tending a house full of guests, all refugees from the fire and homeless but for Tess's generosity. She welcomed Brandon readily, setting him down to his first decent meal in nearly two days. While he ate, she listened to his ramblings and answered his questions.

"I'm sorry I'm so little help, Brandon," she told him, "But I was here when the earthquake hit. After staying up so late the evening before, I'd barely gotten to sleep when I was shaken from my bed. Later, I went up to see what damage had been incurred at the hotel, but I didn't see Laurel. When I called at your home to check on you, your butler said you and Laurel were out. I assumed you were together, and hadn't given it another thought until the fire started up the Hill. I thought perhaps you would come here, as several of our friends have."

"She's dead, Tess. I know it! That must have been her body in the pantry." Brandon's voice cracked, and he began to sob brokenly, unashamedly. His broad shoulders shook, and tears streamed down his face as he laid his head on the table and cried.

Moved to tears herself, Tess put her arms about him, rocking and cradling him as she crooned, "No, Brandon. Please! You mustn't give up hope. Perhaps she went to Golden Gate Park, as so many others have. The Cooks and Hadlows are there. Perhaps she is with them."

"How would she get there? She couldn't have walked that far in her condition. She's so big with the baby, and she's so small and delicate otherwise—like the flower for which she was named."

"Laurel grows in the mountains, Brandon, or have you forgotten that?" Tess eyed him sternly, "It's a hardy, strong little blossom despite its fragile appearance, just as your Laurel is. It is entirely possible that she went with the servants in a wagon or your carriage. The damage was much less severe on this side of town; the streets are negotiable for the most part. She's probably somewhere safe, waiting for you."

"Then why did Kramer tell you Laurel was out?"

Tess shook her head. "I don't know. Perhaps she went out looking for you and returned later."

"That still doesn't explain the body in the pantry, or why Tyke was mourning over it. If Laurel left, as you suggest, why didn't she take Tyke with her?"

Tess was stymied on that point. "I can't answer that any better than you can, Brandon. I just know you can't count Laurel dead on the sole basis of an unidentified body. You have to keep searching until you either find Laurel or some kind of answer to your question. Find someone who may have seen her. Better yet, find your servants. They should be able to tell you something."

A weary, ragged sigh tore from his chest. "You're right, Tess. Maybe I am panicking over nothing. I hope so. I pray so."

"I'll pray too," Tess promised solemnly.

Brandon washed up and borrowed clean clothes. Tess also loaned him a horse for his trip to Golden Gate Park. "Don't fret over whether you ever get it back to me, or if it's stolen. It's your wife and child we are concerned with, and much more important than one stupid horse. I'm just sorry none of us knows where she is."

Brandon had questioned their other friends and neighbors, but no one here had seen or heard of her since the party on Tuesday night. He hoped to have better luck elsewhere.

As he rode toward the park, Brandon was thankful for one thing. At least Laurel knew nothing of the problems surrounding their marriage. The study and all within it, including Miguel's letter, had been destroyed. With the exception of the stone fireplace, the safe was the only thing left unburned, and it had been too hot to open. Brandon knew that to do so would set everything within it aflame as soon as the air reached the interior of the safe.

Brandon felt somewhat better knowing Laurel had no idea their marriage was illegal. There had been trouble enough between them the night before the earthquake. If—when—he found her, he would correct the problem as Judge Henry had suggested, and Laurel need be none the wiser. If she was dead, God forbid, he was grateful she had been spared the knowledge.

Before he had left his house, Brandon had found a shovel and dug a shallow grave in the soft earth of the garden. He'd forced himself to bury the remains of the body, saying a short prayer for her soul and a more fervent one that it not be Laurel he was laying to rest. Later, if it truly was Laurel, he would have a minister conduct a proper service. Then, taking Tyke with him, he had left Nob Hill as swiftly as possible.

Brandon reached Golden Gate Park in the late afternoon. Like Laurel, he was amazed and dismayed to discover so many people there. In this confusion, he would be lucky to find anyone he knew, let alone one small pregnant woman. He had but one thing in his favor. He would have no trouble describing her. There couldn't be many petite, obviously pregnant women with her

distinctive coloring. Anyone who had seen her
would surely remember.

Once again, however, Fate was against him. Just
hours before Brandon arrived, the temporary
hospital had been removed to the Army post at the
Presidio. All the patients, doctors, and nurses had
relocated there, including Dr. Davis and everyone
else who might have given Brandon information
about Laurel.

This being the case, Brandon met no one who
had seen her. The more people he asked, the more
disheartening answers he received, the more
depressed he became.

Night had fallen before he finally located
Thomas and Hanna. The two servants were
delighted to see him, and a few moments of joyous
reunion ensued before they began to discuss
Laurel's whereabouts. Immediately they all
sobered.

"But we thought she was with you!" the housekeeper exclaimed in dismay. "When we couldn't
find either of you, we thought you'd gone out
together somewhere, or gone somewhere after the
party instead of coming home."

Thomas added, "Things were pretty hectic
around there for a while. Two of the chimneys
crashed through the roof, and the fallen turret had
torn off the far corner of the house. Everyone was
running about like idiots just after the earthquake, most of us in our nightclothes. Several of
the doors were jammed, and Millie was frantic at
being stuck in her room alone."

"Oh, my, yes!" Hanna avowed. "Poor Wanda
nearly got struck in her bed when the chimney
crashed into her room, and the stableboy had his
foot trampled by a frightened horse. We were all

terribly upset. When things finally settled down a bit, we went about trying to set the house to rights as best we could."

"We were worried about you and Mrs. Prescott as well," Thomas put in. "And rightly so, it seems."

Upon hearing their tale, Brandon was more anxious than ever. "Did no one see Laurel at all that day?" he asked.

"No, sir."

He then told them about the body he had discovered in the pantry. Hanna paled visibly, and Thomas was upset as well. "Have you any idea who was in there? Might it have been Laurel?" Brandon awaited their reply with trepidation.

It was Thomas who answered solemnly and somewhat reluctantly. "That door was one of them that jammed shut during the quake, sir. Kramer and I both tried to open it, but it refused to budge. With so much else to do, and plenty of food in the kitchen, we left it for later. None of us had any idea someone was in there. We heard no noise from the pantry—but those walls and door are so thick, you know. Then, later, when the fire started toward the Hill, we were busy getting ready to leave. The soldiers came about midnight and told us all to come here. Of course, a couple of the others, like Ching and his son, had already left to see to their own families."

Another thought nagged at Brandon.

"Did anyone notice Tyke about?"

Hanna was crying softly, but managed to answer. "Not at first. Later I recall him being underfoot in the kitchen, and I tried to shoo him out. But he just wandered over and lay whining by the pantry door, so I let him be . . ." At the thought of what this implied, the housekeeper began to sob in earnest. "Oh that poor woman! That poor, dear woman!"

A wave of black despair washed over Brandon. The more they talked, the more positive he became that Laurel was indeed dead. With Thomas's help, he found Kramer, and the butler's story was much the same.

"I'm so sorry, sir," the man declared. "How horrible! And all the while we thought the missus was with you!"

Silence reigned for some minutes. Then the butler said with a sigh, "We all thought we were doing you a great service to save some of your belongings, and the most precious of all was left behind."

Even through his pain, Brandon was touched. "You tried to save some of our things?"

Kramer nodded sadly. "You'll find some fresh clothes in a bag in the carriage. We packed some of Mrs. Prescott's, too. We even brought a bit of food. But I wish we'd broken down the door to get into that pantry!"

"Don't blame yourself," Brandon said hoarsely.

Feeling himself close to tears again, and not wanting to break down in front of them, Brandon walked to the nearby carriage. Disregarding his own things, Brandon opened the bag containing Laurel's belongings. His eyes moistened. The clothes still smelled of her sweet scent, that special fragrance she always wore. His fingers brushed something soft and warm—they had even packed her fur coat. Then his gaze caught something much more precious propped up on the seat, and his heart lodged in his throat. It was the portrait of himself and Laurel in their wedding finery. Her lavender eyes smiled out at him, shining in love and laughter. It was a final twist of

the knife in his heart. This was the only reminder
he would have of her, a lasting remembrance of
her glowing beauty. With an anguished cry,
Brandon beat at the floor of the carriage with his
fists, cursing the quake, the fire, and the Fates that
had stolen her from him forever.

While Brandon was spending an anguished
night in Golden Gate Park, Laurel waited for an
interminable time at the Ferry Building. After a
harrowing ride through San Francisco, she had
spent all day with several thousands of other
people outside the station. The lines stretched for
blocks, and inched forward at a depressingly slow
pace.

The majority of people waiting to catch a ferry
to Oakland were, for the most part, well behaved.
The few who began to cause trouble were quickly
set to rights by soldiers sent to keep order. Their
common adversity in the face of the disaster made
friends of the oddest of strangers.

Laurel beheld it all through a heartbroken haze.
The first shock of Brandon's death was wearing
off, and the blessed numbness was fast dissolving.
She sobbed quietly for hours, overcome with pain
and memories.

All she could think of was Brandon. For years,
her entire world had revolved around him. Even
during those two years in Boston when she had
believed him married to Becky, she had at least
known he was alive and that she might see him
again some day. In Mexico, when he had been
bitten by the rattlesnake and lay so near to death,
she had nursed him back to health with fervent
prayers and devotion.

But now there was no way she could pull him
back to her by the force of her love, and it hurt so

badly she thought she would surely die. Each sweet memory was an arrow piercing her heart, making it bleed even more; each bittersweet thought was a torment to her soul.

How deeply she regretted their angry words the night before the earthquake! Laurel would have given anything to erase that night, to recall her sharp words and make things right between them. Given the chance to turn back the clock, she would listen to his explanations and apology, would forgive him for striking her, would believe that the blow was unintentional. If there was some reasonable explanation for Miguel's letter and all it implied, she would hear Brandon out, let him explain his side of it. At least this is what she told herself now.

Yet, still deep inside, she wondered how he had come to be with Judge Henry and why. Unreasonable though it was, she was angry that he had not been home with her, forgetting that she had turned him out of their room in anger.

Tears of rage and sorrow mingled. Her intense sense of loss was making it impossible for her to think clearly. Regardless of everything that had happened, she loved him with all her heart and soul and longed for a miracle to restore him to her. If not for the baby growing within her, Laurel would have gladly joined him in death, so deep was her despair. She wept for Brandon, for their fatherless child, and for herself. Like any widow, she was bereft; yet legally she was *not* Brandon's widow, despite her agony and loss. She had lived with him, loved him, spent glorious nights in his arms, believed herself to belong completely to him. Now she would return to her home, to bear his child in the shadow of shame. Yet deep in her heart, Laurel felt no shame, only grief and love, and a glowing pride that she would bear their child. She would cherish this baby as the only thing she had left of Brandon, and give it all the love she could no longer give to him.

All through the endless afternoon and evening Laurel waited, gradually inching her way toward the interior of the Ferry Building. Every muscle and bone in her body ached from Wednesday's long trek across San Franciso, and her ankle throbbed abominably each time she put her foot down. She spent the day alternately standing on one foot and sitting on her baggage. As the day wore on, her good ankle swelled from the strain of taking all her weight, her back ached, and the baby seemed to be using her stomach for a boxing arena. But she tried to wait patiently, enduring her misery without complaint. She was thankful for the bit of food Dr. Davis had insisted she bring with her.

It was a strange mixture of people crowded together about her. Laurel saw Chinese, Italians, rich, poor, entire families, single refugees, men, women, and children from all walks of life. Varied languages reached her ears, filling the air with a bewildering blend of sound. Some dragged trunks with them, others carried hand baggage. Some had pets; many held small children and babies in their arms.

Some had nothing but the clothes on their backs. There were men and women still wearing tuxedos and gowns from Tuesday night's opera performance, jewels sparkling and furs dragging about tattered, dirty formal wear. A fortunate few had found time to clean up and don more appropriate clothes, while others were grimy, and some were still in nightwear and bare feet. It was an odd gathering, but all were grateful just to be alive.

Just in front of Laurel, a woman juggled two travelling bags and a small infant. Apparently she too was alone. She looked exhausted, and every once in a while a resigned sigh or a weary sob would escape her. The baby cried constantly. Laurel offered to hold the child for a while, and the two young women struck up a conversation.

The woman's tale was every bit as sorrowful as Laurel's own. Her name was Rose Crider, and she and her husband had come to San Francisco three years ago just after their marriage. He was several years older than she, and an only child, His parents and close relations were all deceased. Rose's family had died in a fire when she was seven, and she had been raised in an orphanage in Chicago. Now her husband was dead, killed in the quake, and she was going back to Chicago to seek refuge with friends. She and her child were alone in the world, homeless and penniless, with nothing other than what Rose had been able to salvage from their home before the fire ravaged it.

Laurel sympathized with the woman. At least she had her father and Aunt Martha to go home to in Texas. She gladly shared her meager lunch with the other woman, helping her to tend her baby son as they waited together.

It was dark by the time they finally reached the inside of the Ferry Building, and later still before seats became available to them. Wedging baby Charles between them, they dozed fitfully in the noisy, chaotic station, ever wary lest their few belongings be stolen or their places in line lost.

At one point, a commotion drew their attention. Laurel recognized Enrico Caruso with another man in the midst of a heated discussion. The great tenor was extremely agitated, almost hysterical. He gestured wildly toward the ferry now being loaded. From where she sat, Laurel could not make out their words above the confusion, but it was plain that Caruso was frantic to board the boat. He showed the attendant a large picture of President Teddy Roosevelt, pointing to the photo and then to himself. After another brief exchange, Caruso and his companion were ushered aboard the ferry ahead of others who waited in line, which caused much grumbling among the crowd. But Laurel was too tired and despondent to care.

In the wee hours of Friday morning she and Rose finally boarded the ferry for Oakland. They stood at the rail and watched San Franciso continue to burn brightly behind them. A part of Laurel was being left behind, the major part of her heart and soul, and she gazed in sorrow at the city in which her beloved Brandon's ashes lay. Tears streamed down her face as she bade a last farewell and faced the grim and lonely life ahead of her and her unborn child.

CHAPTER 24

When the ferry docked in Oakland, it was only a little less chaotic than the scene they had left behind in San Francisco. Several registration areas had been set up so that friends and relatives who had been separated by the disaster might possibly be reunited. Refugees were listed, divided into groups and dispersed to refuge centers in the area. Some people were merely biding their time until they could return to San Francisco to rebuild their homes and lives. Others, homeless and bereft, were more than willing to accept free fares on the Southern Pacific and Sante Fe railroad lines to other destinations. All were given shelter and food, and medical attention if necessary.

Because they were both on their way out of Oakland, Laurel and Rose Crider were taken with a few others to a church near the railroad depot where a shelter had been set up for those awaiting trains departing for their ultimate destinations.

Laurel had hoped to catch a train to Texas that very day, but she soon realized that her chances of that were slim.

Laurel and Rose were issued cots. They were also given the opportunity to wash and change clothes and were served a hearty meal of thick soup and bread which neither woman could fully appreciate, so tired were they. Rose was especially grateful when one of the women volunteer workers offered to care for baby Charles so that she could eat and rest without having to worry over the fussing infant. Then she and Laurel collapsed onto their cots in a state of complete exhaustion, free at last to rest their weary bodies, if not their battered hearts.

It was late afternoon before Laurel awoke. Her aching muscles and stiff limbs rebelled at the act of sitting upright, and she was hard pressed to suppress a groan of agony. For long moments she sat in a dejected stupor of pain and heartbreak, a sob catching in her throat as reality returned full force in all its grim details. Running trembling hands through her mass of tangled, silvery hair, she sat with head bowed under the weight of her tremendous loss as she contemplated her bleak future without Brandon. Tears streamed down her pale cheeks and her delicate shoulders shook with silent sobs, overwhelmed once again by deep sorrow.

A hand on her shoulder made her aware of a man's presence, and a deep, melodious voice asked gently, "Young woman, is there anything I can do for you? Shall I pray with you?"

Laurel looked up with pain-glazed violet eyes to see a minister standing at her side. "Why?" she choked out bitterly. "What could I pray for?"

Gentle blue eyes gazed sympathetically down at her. "For the strength to see you through your sorrow," the pastor answered softly.

Laurel shook her head in denial. "How can I ask that of the same God who caused my sorrow to begin with? It was He who took Brandon from me

so cruelly. He who left my unborn child without a
father to love and care for it!"

His eyes lost none of their compassion as he
studied her tearstained face. "Did your husband
die in the disaster?"

Guilt tore at her as she wondered how to answer
his question. Naturally, he would assume
Brandon was her husband. Even now her wedding
ring blazed on her left hand, a hand resting now
over her baby. It was a natural conclusion, one she
herself had felt secure in until a few days ago . . .

Feeling like a fraud and a liar, she gave him the
only possible answer. "Yes, he died in the earthquake Wednesday morning."

A frown of concern lined his forehead. "You
must not burden your soul further by blaming
God for his death, child," he advised kindly.

"Why not?" she blurted in her intense pain and
anger. "Who else can one blame for an earthquake? Only God could create such a monstrous
catastrophe, such monumental destruction!"

With a shake of his head, the minister smiled
wearily. "No, my dear. Such calamities and
disasters are in Satan's realm; they are the forces
of evil at work in the world."

"But God could have stopped it!" she cried. "He
could have prevented the deaths of so many
innocent people! Why didn't He? Oh, why didn't
He?"

"Only He can answer that, and it is not for us to
question His ways and plans for the world." He
patted her shoulder again. "Are you sure you don't
want me to pray with you?"

Laurel shook her head.

"Then I will pray *for* you, that you might not be
overwhelmed by sorrow and misery. Where are

you going from here?"

She interpreted his words literally. "I am going home to Texas; back to my father." She rose from the cot and faced him. "How do I get to the train depot from here? I need to obtain a ticket as soon as possible."

He gave her directions, then said, "If you cannot get a train out today, you are welcome to return here and await your time of departure."

Laurel softened under his continued gentle regard. "Thank you. You have been most kind."

She gave him her hand and he held it for the briefest of seconds, noting how cold it felt within his own. "Bless you, child. I wish you well on your journey, and may God go with you."

She turned away from him, wondering bitterly if she wanted God to go with her, after all she had been dealt at His hand. Immediately she felt guilty at such a blasphemous thought, remorse mixing with her anger.

His concerned voice followed her retreating form. "Do not blame God for your adversities. He is a kind and loving Father and will help you through these trying times if you will only allow Him."

Laurel gave him a final backward glance. "I'll try," she promised sadly.

When Laurel said goodbye to Rose, the two women clung together like old and dear friends. Their mutual problems had brought them closer than sisters in the past hours and they exchanged addresses and promises to write.

"Be sure to let me know when you get settled in Chicago, Rose."

Rose nodded. "Write to me, Laurel, and let me

know when your baby is born. And if you ever come to Chicago, be sure to look me up."

"If you can't find a job, or your friends can't take you in, write to me in Crystal City. Maybe my family can assist you in some way." Even as Laurel made the offer, she was certain Rose would never ask for aid. Rose seemed the type who would stand on her own and make her own way for herself and her son.

At this point, Laurel was less than certain of her own reception at her former home. Depending on her father's reaction and the depth of his anger, she might conceivably find herself in worse straits than Rose—without a home for herself and her unborn child, without means of supporting either herself or her baby. It might be she who would one day need Rose's assistance, rather than the other way round.

Rested and fed, Laurel felt slightly better equipped to cope with her problems as she set out for the train depot, a picnic basket of sandwiches and soup added to her other luggage. Acquiring a ticket on the Southern Pacific headed for Texas was no problem. It was waiting for a seat on a train that wore down Laurel's frayed nerves, but the line gradually diminished, and was nothing compared with the Ferry Building the night before.

Near midnight, she finally boarded the south-bound train and took her seat. The passenger car was crowded and dirty and smelled of sweat and smoke, but Laurel didn't care. She was going home at last. Though she carried with her an anguished heart filled with broken dreams and tarnished love, she also carried cherished memories of the only man she had ever loved, as

she carried their child within her body. As the
train at last began to move, she gazed out of the
grimy window to see the fires still lighting the
western horizon. She was leaving behind a part
of her life she would never forget; a time of love
and disaster she would remember all the rest of
her days, reliving the pain along with the joy again
and again. . . .

As the inferno raged on, threatening to sweep
through the elite homes of the Western Addition,
Brandon gave in to his servants' urgings and
stayed with them in the safety of Golden Gate
Park. He cared little where he stayed or what
became of him. He had lost his reason for living
when he lost Laurel.

Even Tyke was forlorn, a furry four-legged
embodiment of Brandon's grief. The fox lay at
Brandon's feet, for the most part unmoving, only
occasionally letting out a mournful wail that
sounded curiously like a small child lost in the
night. They were a truly pitiful sight, torn with
grief and beyond comfort.

It was in this condition that Muriel Cook discovered Brandon on Friday morning.

"Oh, Brandon! How good to see a familiar face
in this swarm of humanity!" she cried.

"Hello, Muriel," he answered dully, not bothering to rise to greet her.

Not put off in the least, Muriel rattled on, "Why,
I hardly recognized you! You look so morose. Of
course, with our homes and all our lovely
possessions gone, it's no wonder. Thank goodness
Daddy had insurance! Still, it will never replace
everything. That's why I packed my jewels and my
precious furs when they told us we had to
evacuate. I certainly wasn't going to leave those

behind. Poor Daddy is frantic about having to abandon his paintings. So many were terribly valuable!"

While Muriel's chatter was barely penetrating Brandon's grief-stunned brain, it was irritating Kramer greatly. "Miss Cook, in case it has escaped your notice, Mr. Prescott is not up to visiting with you just now," he pointed out bluntly. "Perhaps another time would be more appropriate."

Muriel gave the man an icy stare and said indignantly, "Brandon! Are you going to sit there and allow your servant to speak to me in such a rude manner? I realize that circumstances are somewhat altered just now, but proper respect must be maintained nonetheless!"

"Not now, Muriel," he groaned, his head in his hands. "I can't deal with your petty complaints on top of everything else."

Brought up short, Muriel retorted, "And just where is your darling wife, when she should be at your side to comfort you?"

"Oh, dear!" Hanna exclaimed. "Miss Cook, please don't say anything more. Mr. Prescott lost his wife Wednesday morning!"

"Lost?" Muriel echoed. Then, misinterpreting the woman's words, she said blithely, "Oh, she'll turn up sooner or later. That type always lands on her feet!"

Brandon was on *his* feet and shaking Muriel before he knew what he was doing, his hands viciously gripping her arms. "Shut your vile mouth, you viper! Don't you dare talk about Laurel that way! She was worth ten of you, and now she's gone—she and our child died in the fire!'"

Thomas and Kramer pulled him away from the frightened woman, prying his fingers loose from her bruised arms. "Mr. Prescott! No! Come and sit down again. Please!"

Muriel's face had lost all its color. It was several seconds before his words registered. "Dead? Laurel is—dead?" she murmured.

Brandon was too distraught to see the speculative gleam that lit her eyes, quickly hidden as she knelt beside him. "Oh, Brandon, I'm so sorry. Truly I am! I thought she was only missing temporarily. Please forgive me for my unkind words. It was thoughtless and wicked of me, and I do apologize."

Brandon replied wearily, "Of course, Muriel. You didn't know. I, also, apologize if I hurt you, but I have been so stricken with grief that I barely know what I am doing."

"I quite understand, Brandon. It must be terrible for you. If there is anything I can do, please let me know."

"I just want to be left alone right now, if you don't mind."

"Then I'll go." Muriel rose and dusted the ash from her skirts. "Daddy and I are camped nearby. Please send word if you need anything, Brandon, even if it is only someone to talk to."

He nodded briefly and stared unseeingly as she walked away; his thoughts were turned inward to sweet memories of Laurel.

By Saturday morning, the fire that had devastated San Francisco for the past three days was finally under control. The entire city drew a collective sigh of relief as the last blaze was extinguished. Over two-thirds of the city lay in smoldering ruins, with more than two hundred thousand homeless people taking refuge in Golden Gate Park alone, not to mention those in other areas.

There was no water and no electricity. Gas mains were broken and miles of smoldering rubble needed to be cleared. It would be months before any progress was evident. Everyone was frightened, stricken, and bone-weary—ill prepared to begin cleaning up and rebuilding. Yet, battered as they were, these San Franciscans were not beaten. Time and again, fire had nearly leveled their city but they had always found the courage to rebuild bigger and better than before. They would again.

Brandon hadn't the heart to think of such things yet. His soul was torn apart, his grief too fresh. As soon as the danger was past, he found himself drawn back to the house on Nob Hill, like a moth unable to resist a flickering flame. The mansion was uninhabitable as it stood, and Brandon was unconcerned with restoring it. His beloved wife and child had died here; it was to him almost a shrine to Laurel's memory.

The servants had rigged a tarpaulin over the remains of the rear parlor and kitchen, both of which had stone floors that had survived the fire. The mayor of San Francisco had issued a proclaimation against indoor fires of any kind until all chimneys had been inspected by city officials. Thus, the rear veranda served as a temporary kitchen.

Upon his arrival, Brandon immediately dismissed most of the household staff. However, Thomas, Kramer, and Hanna elected to stay, and since they had resided here longer than he, there was little Brandon could do about it. These three loyal servants took it upon themselves to salvage what they could and create a serviceable shelter for themselves and their employer.

Within hours after the fires had been extin-

guished in San Francisco, rain began to fall from
the fickle skies that had withheld their moisture
when most desperately needed. Through the
dreary downpour, the inhabitants huddled
together beneath their makeshift roof. When the
rain finally ended, they labored through the
sodden, ash-grey mess, determined to clear away
some of the rubble that cluttered the once-elegant
rooms. The entire upper portion of the house was
gone; the remnants of roof, floors, furniture, and
interior walls lay like charred mountains on the
first floor. Starting in the rear parlor and kitchen,
which were least damaged, Brandon's servants
proceeded to remove heaps of burned rubble.
Little they found was usable; only a few cast iron
pots and pans and a few metal utensils. Once
Brandon located the cellar, he was of little help,
for there he found a case of whiskey and several
flasks of wine which were undamaged and
proceeded to drink himself into a morose stupor
in an effort to ease his agony. His three
companions sympathized, and after a few feeble
attempts to stop him, left him alone and went
about their business.

After he had recovered from a monumental
hangover, Brandon recovered the safe from the
study. Though the city banks refused to open their
main vaults for an entire week after the fire for
fear the contents would catch fire if they were
opened before they had cooled sufficiently,
Brandon was certain this small safe would cause
no problem. He was proven right, for everything
within the locked box was intact. Some documents
and papers were slightly charred around the edges
but legible.

As Brandon examined the contents, he frowned
in confusion. He was certain he had stored more

cash in the safe. Of course, he might be mistaken, but it made him uneasy. What really astonished him was to open the boxes which had held Laurel's most precious jewelry, only to discover them empty. There were two possible explanations for this—either a thief had managed to steal the cash and jewels, which was unlikely since the box was locked and apparently untampered with; or Laurel had removed the items herself. But why would she do so? What possible reason would she have for placing all her jewels elsewhere? Brandon was at a loss to understand it.

As the days wore on, and the men hauled pile after pile of burned debris from the house, Hanna sifted carefully through the rubble. Precious few items were identifiable, some as puzzling as the safe. She found Laurel's personal, engraved jewel box she'd kept in her bedroom. It was badly melted and misshapen, but Brandon managed to pry open the lid. It too was empty! It was all beyond his comprehension, and he could only deduct that in the confusion following the earthquake, one of his servants had taken the opportunity to turn thief. It was the only possible explanation, distasteful as it was. When Thomas recalled belatedly that one of the maids was missing, presumably having run off to find her family, Brandon was sure his theory was correct.

Possibly the most ridiculous things to be retrieved were the toilets and tubs. These fixtures had surfaced a bit chipped and charred, but otherwise undamaged. For reasons of health and safety, the mayor had ordered that latrines be dug, thus reducing the risk of disease ravaging the already devastated city. The men installed the tiolet fixtures over the required latrines and draped tiny canvas tents about them. As Hanna stated adamantly, "If I must relieve myself out of doors, I shall do so in as much privacy as possible!"

Every day or so, Thomas drove into town for food, water, and supplies. Without running water or electricity, they were reduced to a simpler way of living. Candles and kerosene lamps served once again for light. Cots, odd chairs, and an old library table were their only furniture. A lean-to housed the horses now in place of the stable.

At one point, Kramer suggested to Brandon that it would be a good idea to consider replacing the roof. Brandon immediately opposed the idea.

"What is there to save in this wreck of a house?" he asked. "I don't ever intend to live here again, and I may sell the property for whatever it will bring as it exists now. I am merely biding my time until I decide what I want to do with it."

"I understand that, sir," Kramer stated quietly, "but the outside structure is basically sound. A roof would help save the foundation and what remains of the flooring; and boarding up the windows and doors would discourage vandals and vagrants from invading the place until you dispose of it."

At length Brandon reluctantly gave in. "Do as you wish, but don't bother me with it. If you must undertake this project, I will pay for it, but you must oversee the work. If it were up to me, the entire place could go to the devil, and I couldn't care less."

One thing *did* nag at the fringes of Brandon's befuddled, drink-fogged mind. "Has anyone seen that blasted cat of Laurel's?" he asked one day.

"Not hide nor hair," Hanna replied, and the others agreed.

"I wonder whatever became of that loathsome creature?" he wondered.

Hanna tried to put his mind at ease as gently as possible, without stirring up morbid memories. "I suppose the kitten became frightened during the earthquake and ran off somewhere. Cats are notoriously fickle animals, sir, unlike dogs. They look out for themselves most of the time."

Brandon sighed into his drink. "I suppose you are right. I just can't help wondering if we hauled its bones out with the rest of the rubble." He turned and stumbled down the veranda steps, toward the garden and the hastily-dug grave. "Still, you might let me know if it shows up again. I rather miss having that spitting ball of fur underfoot." The note of despair sounded clearly in his voice, though his words were slurred from the alcohol he continued to consume so steadily.

Hanna shook her head sadly as she watched him weave through the ruins of the once-lovely garden. The man was slowly drinking himself to death. Already he resembled a ghost of his former self. Lines of weariness and sorrow lined his brow and his downturned mouth, mute testimony of sleepless nights and tormenting thoughts. Not only did he drink to excess and sleep little, but he ate next to nothing. His lean, muscled form was becoming noticably thinner, and he looked continually tired and haggard. The loss of wife and child were weighing heavily on him, and only time would heal his deep sorrow—if he didn't manage to grieve himself to death before then.

Every few days, Tess looked in on Brandon. She, too, worried over his health. With the disaster over, she was trying to salvage her demolished hotel. Her grand dream now lay in a huge mass of tumbled marble and debris. Hiring crews to clear the lot, she intended to start rebuilding immediately. Consequently, she was at the site regularly to oversee the labor and always stopped by to see how Brandon was faring.

Invariably she found him either stumbling drunk, or sleeping off a night of excess. From Hanna she learned that he often disappeared for long hours at a time, presumably making the rounds of the bay taverns and trying to drown his sorrows in a more varied atmosphere. How he always managed to find his way home again without being waylaid by thieves was a wonder to all.

Tess pleaded with him to come and live at her house, where many of their friends were still residing until their homes were habitable. She was aware how his memories haunted him, and how much time he spent lingering forlornly over Laurel's gravesite. "This place is not good for you, Brandon. Besides, it is still such a shambles. You would be much more comfortable at my house. I have plenty of room, and we would respect your privacy, I assure you."

As often as she offered, he refused. "Thanks, Tess, but no. I'll stay here until I decide what to do or where to go next. Eventually, I suppose I'll leave San Francisco, but until then this place will do as well as any."

Finally even the even-tempered Tess lost patience. "When are you going to get off of your duff and stop trying to hide in the bottom of a whiskey bottle?" she railed at him. "Look at yourself! You look worse than a wharf bum! When are you going to shake off your liquor-hazed self-pity and take stock of your life? How long before you make a sober decision and go on with living—or are you truly intent on drinking yourself into an early grave? I know how much you loved her,

Brandon, but she is gone and there isn't a blessed
thing you can do to bring her back. It is time you
picked up your marbles, little boy, and found a
new game and a new life, distasteful as it may
sound! You are alive, like it or not, and it is time
you did something constructive for a change!"

"It's easy for you to criticize my actions, Tess!"
he retorted with a sneer. "You've not lost anyone
dear to you in the disaster. You've not had your
guts torn out, or stood over a charred mess of
flesh and bone that was once the most precious
person in your life! Until you have done that, don't
preach to me of self-pity or excesses."

But Tess stood her ground. "I refuse to
apologize for speaking truth, my friend. While I
am sincerely sorry for your loss, I hate seeing you
destroy yourself because of it. It is not out of spite
that I tell you these things, but out of love and
friendship. I truly cannot believe Laurel would
want to see you this way."

Brandon gave a slight smile. "I suppose you're
right. Someday I will have to pull my head out of
the sand, like a dumb ostrich that finds it impera-
tive to breathe, but not now. I can't bear it just yet,
Tessie."

His smile wavered and disappeared as tears
filled his red-rimmed eyes. "You know, just for a
moment, as you were screaming at me and
heaping coals of fire on my head, you reminded
me of Laurel when she was angry at me . . ."

So Brandon stayed where he was, drinking more
than ever before in an effort to obliterate his
intense pain and remorse. But he still couldn't
forget that his last evening with Laurel had ended
in a disastrous fight. He regretted that most of all.
Again and again he relived that night in his mind,
seeing her stricken, tear-stained face, recalling

their angry words. He wished he could erase that night and replace it with one of ardent loving and tender words. He would have given everything he owned to be able to do that, to have her alive and warm in his arms again.

Days and weeks passed by while Brandon contemplated his loss and tried desperately to hide from reality. He let life and time pass him by, trying only to forget that he lived in a world without Laurel to light it for him.

CHAPTER 25

Travelling from Oakland to Los Angeles, the train made so many stops that Laurel began to wonder if she couldn't make faster progress walking to Texas. Not only did they make regularly scheduled stops at various towns, but also some unexpected halts as well. The earthquake had damaged more than just the city of San Francisco. Areas both north and south had been hard hit. The track between Oakland and Los Angeles passed over some of its path, marked by huge fissures and destruction.

Now, with the rain falling steadily, some of the loosened earth was beginning to shift. In some places very near the railroad track, the land had fallen away, and the train would stop until the engineer could determine if it were safe to go on, or if the track had been dangerously undermined. Other stops were required when muddy landslides had covered sections of rail, and workmen would have to clear the track before they could continue.

The halts, while frustrating, at least allowed Laurel the opportunity to let Sassy make nature calls. She dared not turn the kitten loose for fear she would run off, but the travelling cage was small, and Sassy was becoming increasingly fussy. With a long ribbon belt from one of Laurel's dresses to serve as a leash, the problem was temporarily overcome, and Sassy got a bit of exercise.

Laurel wondered whatever had become of Tyke. Had the little silver fox survived the quake? Was he alone and hungry, or had he found someone to give him shelter? She hoped someone was caring for him, for she deeply regretted having to leave him behind.

After all she had been through the last few days, all the grieving and worrying, hurrying then standing in endless lines, it felt odd to sit and wait until the train eventually reached Texas—as if her life were suddenly suspended in time.

Her sore, exhausted body could find no real relief on the hard train seat. Every bounce set her bruised bones and muscles into fresh agony. There was no comfortable position to be found for her cramped limbs and awkward, aching body. The noise and smells of the crowded car set her head to pounding in time to the clack of the wheels until Laurel thought it would burst.

Yet her physical discomfort was nothing compared with her mental and emotional agony. The long hours gave Laurel much time to think—too much in her present state of mind. Even when exhaustion set her head to nodding and her eyelids drooping, sleep brought poignant dreams of Brandon. Awake or asleep, she could not escape her memories of the time they had spent together. Thoughts of him assailed her relentlessly, beating at her spirit, haunting her battered soul, tearing at her broken heart. There seemed to be no rest for either her body or her heart on this arduous journey home.

She had left Texas as a rebellious girl. She was returning home as a woman, one thoroughly familiar with the joys and heartaches of loving a man—for as many times as they had fought, there had been glorious moments of breathtaking loving. For every cross word, there were a dozen endearments echoing in her mind. Embedded in her very skin was the memory of his fiery caresses, his sweet lips wandering from her head to her toes and all points in between. The taste, the smell, the feel of him were hers to cherish forever in her dreams.

Hot tears stung her eyes. Brandon's untimely death had left her in a precarious situation, but she could not regret the love they had shared. Surely it had been as real for him as it had for her, despite the fact that their marriage, for whatever reason, was illegal. Their love had *not* been a sham! She would not let herself think otherwise. Perhaps if Brandon had lived, he would have explained everything to her.

Now she might never know, but of one thing she was certain. She would never regret having loved Brandon, in spite of the pain it had brought her. Their short time together had been glorious and she would live on the memory of it forever. She would bring their child into the world without shame, and teach it all she could about its father. Surely time would heal this unbearable pain and leave only glowing memories to light the dark days ahead. She was sure she would never again love a man as she had Brandon; never again give her heart so completely. How could she, when she had left part of it behind in San Francisco with his ashes?

At last the train reached Los Angeles, and after a brief stop and a change of locomotives, started east toward Phoenix. From there it went on to Tucson, then south to El Paso. They left the Pacific Coast behind, climbing into mountainous terrain, every turn of the wheels carrying Laurel closer to home.

It was late April, and the snow still capped the highest peaks, the melted run-off making rivers swell and roar as they rushed to the lower plains. Flowers were blossoming on peaks and in deep gorges, where streams ran merrily over rocks and ledges, proclaiming spring in a riot of color and sound. All this made little impression on Laurel, locked in her pain-filled remembrances, her hand gently caressing the swell of her belly where the baby grew and kicked impatiently.

Several days later, stiff and tired from the long journey, Laurel stepped off the train in El Paso. It was good to be on Texas soil again, if not all the way home. From here she would catch the smaller rail line to Crystal City.

Upon checking at the station, Laurel was dismayed to find she had just missed the train. Another was not due for two days, which meant she would have to find accommodations at a hotel for the next two nights. She was none too thrilled at the thought of spending much time in this notoriously rough border town. El Paso was well known for its lawlessness, and brawls regularly broke out even in broad daylight. The rowdy activities at night were even worse. Rarely was there a shoot-out, as in days gone by, but fights and killings were still common occurences. El Paso was no place for a lady to find herself stranded alone.

Briefly, Laurel considered sending a telegram to her father, but decided she would wait until she was ready to board the train to Crystal City. It would spare him two days of anxiety over her arrival. Besides, if the train were delayed for any reason, he would worry. She would send the message before she left El Paso, which would give him ample time to meet her at the depot.

Gaining directions to a nearby hotel, Laurel rented a room. Then, having nothing else to do, she again braved the bustling streets, deciding to spend some time looking through the stores. After buying little more than a newspaper and a few magazines to pass the evening hours, she found a small restaurant in which to eat lunch. After a nap in her room revived her somewhat, she went down to dinner in the hotel dining room. As the town began to come to life for the night, she retired early to toss and turn upon her lumpy bed and eventually to sleep.

The next day was much the same. Laurel waited impatiently for the time to pass. By dinner time, her nerves were frayed from the delay. Only the fact that tomorrow evening would find her at home made the inactivity easier to bear.

As Laurel sat dawdling over her dinner, eating solely for the sake of her baby, she glanced idly about at the other diners. The hotel, being so near the railway station, collected all sorts of people. It was not the most elite of establishments, and had it not been so conveniently located, Laurel would not have chosen to stay here.

At one table, an elderly couple dined quietly. A minister sat nearby. At yet another table a businessman was talking to a prospective client—Laurel could overhear bits and pieces of their conversation. A few travelers whom Laurel recognized from the train were scattered here and there. One man was with a woman Laurel could only assume was a prostitute, from the amount of paint she wore on her face. A couple of cowboys were enjoying a night on the town. At a nearby

table, a trio of ragged looking men were eating and
talking noisily, their loud laughter and crude
manners drawing Laurel's attention.

As Laurel's gaze skimmed quickly over them,
she felt apprehensive. Having lived around men all
her life, she knew instinctively that this group
meant trouble. They wore jeans and shirts and
scuffed boots no different from any other ranch
hand, but something about their belligerent atti-
tudes marked them as agitators. Laurel knew she
was right in her assumption when she saw the gun
tucked into the belt of one of them. A knife
handle protruded from the boot of another. They
might be drifters or even hired killers, but these
men were not ordinary cowboys.

Knowing this made Laurel doubly aware of
being by herself in a strange town. The feeling of
unease grew until she gave up all pretense of
eating her meal, wanting only to return to the
solitude of her room. As she rose to leave, her gaze
inadvertently met that of one of the three men. His
hat, which he had chosen not to remove, was
pushed back on his head, revealing coal black hair
and giving Laurel a clear look at his face and jet
black eyes that bore into hers.

For a moment Laurel was confused by the
direct, challenging look in those dark eyes. Then
her own flew open in surprise and bewilderment,
and she choked back a gasp as recognition hit her.
She knew the man! The last time she had seen him,
he had worn the cassock of a priest and had
married her to Brandon in the little church in
Chihuahua.

The man pushed back his chair and rose with an
air of cool deliberation. His gaze never left hers,
and Laurel could literally feel the evil that

emanated from him. A crooked smile curved his mouth as he observed her frightened face.

Danger! Laurel's mind flashed out a warning, and her body responded to it immediately. The man she knew as "Father Pedro" had taken no more than a single step in her direction before Laurel was fleeing the dining room on feet made nimble by the desperate need to escape. She did not know why he was here or who he really was, but of one thing she was sure—this man was *not* a priest! As she ran through the lobby and up the stairs, heedless of her flying skirts and the curious looks she was receiving, she knew only that she must reach the safety of her room and bolt the door. The man had also recognized her, and unless she missed her guess, he meant to do her harm for some reason.

Breathless sobs of fear choked her as she flung herself into her room, slammed the door shut behind her, and rammed the bolt home. For an instant, she sagged weakly against the door, trembling with fright. Then, as she heard the steady tread of boots coming down the hallway, she whimpered in panic. She had no weapon with which to defend herself, no one to help her, and only a flimsy bolted door between herself and her pursuer. She realized now that she should have stayed in the relative safety of the crowded dining room, where at least someone might have come to her aid. Here she was completely alone, with only her own wits to rely on.

A quick glance about the room for a possible weapon gave her little hope, but as the footsteps stopped outside her door, she grabbed the water pitcher that stood on the dresser. Laurel nearly dropped it, and had to stifle a shriek of terror as a knock sounded on the door. She stood clutching it to her heaving chest as a voice called out, "*Señora*, open the door."

When she did not answer, he said quietly, but clearly enough for her ears. "*Señora*, I know you recognized me. We must talk. Let me in."

Laurel closed her eyes and prayed he would go away. She tried to swallow, and almost gagged at the attempt.

"*Por favor*, do not ignore me, *señora*. It will do you no good. Listen to me and open the door, and I promise you will come to no harm."

When she remained silent, he pounded on the door again, harder this time. "You force me to take desperate measures," he growled. Laurel soon discovered his intention as his boot connected loudly with the door, making the wood groan with the force, and eliciting a squeal of terror she could not suppress.

Quivering with terror, she stood to the side of the door, waiting with upraised pitcher as he kicked the door again. It sprang open on the third attempt, and just as Laurel was about to throw the pitcher at his head, he swung about and captured her wrists in his hands. With one foot, he calmly shoved the door shut, forcing her back against it and holding her there with the weight of his big body as he took the pitcher from her lifeless hands.

He smiled an evil, sneering grin again, his teeth flashing white in his dark face. "*Señora*," he taunted, his face mere inches from hers, "If I had not seen your reflection in the mirror, you would have tried to split my skull open. I would not have appreciated that at all."

"Let me go!" Laurel whimpered, her eyes huge

lavender pools of fear in her white face. "Please!"

"I cannot do that, you know. Perhaps if you had not recognized me tonight, I could have done so—but not now."

Looking about the room, as though searching for something, he asked, "Where is your husband?"

"He has gone out. He'll be back any minute," Laurel lied, desperate to keep him from knowing she was alone.

It was of no avail, for he merely laughed at her. "I see no sign of a man's things in this room. You are a poor liar, *señora*." Then he laughed again and taunted, "Perhaps I should be calling you *señorita* instead, since we both now know that it was not a priest who performed the marriage ceremony. You were a lovely bride, but I am afraid you are not a wife."

"You bastard!" Laurel spit the words at him, her anger and frustration temporarily overcoming her fear.

His leering grin never changed, though his eyes grew harder at her words. "You may curse me all you want, my pretty little bird, but that does nothing to change things."

He leaned away from her, his knowing gaze charting her body. "Your obvious condition changes nothing either. You will be coming with me."

"No!" The word was both exclamation and plea. "No, I can't!"

"Ah, but you will." He released her arms and gave her a shove toward the bed. "Be a good *muchacha* and pack your things. We will walk out of here as man and wife," he chuckled wickedly. "You will come quietly—or unconsciously. It makes no difference to me."

"Please! You can't do this! Please just go away, and I swear I will never say a word to anyone about you! After all, what do I really know? Not even your real name!" Laurel was desperate to convince him, and for a moment she thought she might succeed.

But he dashed her hopes. "No. You know enough to hang me, and that is what counts. One word to your so-called husband, or the law, or your Mexican friends, would be all it would take."

Tears dimmed her eyes as she begged, "Please! On my child's life, I promise not to say anything to anyone!"

A dark brow cocked cynically over one eye. "You will forgive me if I do not believe you, *señorita*. Now either pack your things or leave them behind. I am tired of wasting time." His smooth voice was now as hard as his eyes.

Laurel did as he ordered, biting at her lip to hold back desperate sobs. Her voice quavered as she asked, "Where are you taking me? What are you going to do?"

He merely answered, "You will find out soon enough. Now hurry!"

When she had packed her few things, she reached for Sassy's cage. "leave that," he commanded flatly. "I don't need to be dragging a cat about, as well as a pregnant woman."

"But won't it look strange if I leave her behind?" Laurel spoke without thinking, and immediately realized she had lost a possible opportunity to alert someone to her peril.

A light of appreciation lit his dark eyes for a brief instant. "Smart thinking. So helpful of you to call my attention to the fact, *señorita*." He flashed his taunting smile at her again. "Let's go. You carry the cat, and I'll get your bag. If anyone stops us, say nothing. Let me do the talking. And do not try screaming or running. I am very fast with my gun, and I will not hesitate to kill you. Do you understand?"

She nodded miserably.

"Walk to the side and a little ahead of me," he instructed.

A walk to the gallows could not have been more frightening. As they descended a back staircase leading out into an alley, Laurel feared her shaking legs would give out beneath her. Even the earthquake had held less terror for her than this!

They met no one, and once in the dark alley, she found his two companions awaiting them with their horses.

"Any trouble?" one asked.

"No. Here—you take the cat and I will take the woman." He took Sassy from Laurel and handed the cage to the second man.

"*Por Dios*, Pedro! What am I to do with this?" the man complained.

"For now, Carlos, just take it. Later you can give it to your latest *puta*, or the next woman to take your fancy. Or you can eat it for all I care. Now shut up and do as I tell you."

Pedro took his horse's reins from the third man, handing him Laurel's bag. For just a second, his eyes were off her, and Laurel tried to run. But Pedro was too quick for her, his long arm snaking around her thickened waist. "Whoa, *muchacha*. You go the wrong way." With a nasty laugh, he lifted her into the saddle and mounted behind her, confining her within the span of his arms as he took up the reins.

They rode southeast along the Rio Grande Valley for what seemed a lifetime to Laurel. If there was one bright spot in this horrid nightmare, it was that their chosen direction was taking her closer to home with every mile.

The rest of the journey was pure hell. After walking most of San Francisco, fleeing the fire, losing Brandon, and enduring the long train ride, she was now being bounced about on the back of a horse for hours. It was almost more than her weary body could bear. Even cushioned against Pedro's body and pinioned in the cradle of his hard thighs, she was being jarred terribly. Her back ached abominably, and she was sure she could not endure much of this abuse without dire results.

With only brief stops to rest the horses, they rode until sunset of the next day. By then Laurel was in agony and terribly frightened for her own life as well as that of her child. She sat listlessly as the men set up their camp. Her hands were securely tied before her, though she couldn't have run off if she had the chance. She was just too weary to budge, but she listened carefully as the men talked among themselves.

"Where are we headed, Pedro?"

"There's an abandoned mine I came across several months back. It's not too far from here— about another day and a half's ride."

"Why don't we head back into Mexico?" Jorge asked.

Carlos snorted in disgust at this suggestion. "You are *un estupido!* My horse has more brains than you! We cannot go back to Mexico until the law no longer looks for us in every town and village."

Jorge shrugged. "We are wanted in Texas and New Mexico, too," he pointed out.

"*Si*, but here our faces are not as well known."

Jorge defended himself with a short laugh and a finger pointed at Laurel. "You can say this when the *gringa* recognizes Pedro so readily?"

"That is why we are going to hole up at the mine for a while," Pedro said curtly.

"What about the woman? What is to be done about her?"

Laurel listened apprehensively as Pedro answered. "She goes with us until I decide what is best."

Carlos leered in Laurel's direction. "We will have to kill her sooner or later, but I wouldn't mind a bit of that before we do. She is a sweet piece, even big as she is."

Laurel stiffened and turned her head away, sickened by his words.

All three men laughed, but it was with relief that Laurel heard Pedro say, "Not yet, Carlos. First I have in mind to send a letter of ransom to the *señora's* husband. I wonder how much he will be willing to pay to have her back again?"

Jorge was confused. "You can't let her go, Pedro. She can identify all of us."

"I know that, Jorge, but it still might be worth a lot of money to let her man think we will return her for a big ransom."

"Oh! We get the money, and then we kill her anyway." Jorge understood now, and unfortunately so did Laurel. Unless something miraculous happened, she was going to die.

Carlos was still thinking lustful thoughts. "Can I have her before we kill her, Pedro?" he asked wistfully.

Pedro laughed. "We'll *all* have her before she dies, but not until we reach the safety of the mine. We can't afford to have anything else go wrong now." His hard look told Laurel he meant every word. There would be no mercy for her at his hands.

Laurel sat frozen with fear. She was going to die at the hands of these vile outlaws! At least in San Francisco there had been some hope of survival. Now there was none. She knew for a fact that if she somehow managed to survive multiple rape and certain miscarriage of her child, they would kill her in the end. By the time they did, she would probably welcome death, for she was sure they would abuse her horribly before they let her die.

The prospect of these men taking her by turns was too terrible to imagine. Tears of impotent rage slipped silently down her pale cheeks. She would never live to bear her child, to hold it in her loving arms. Her poor baby would never grow and learn, laugh and love and cry. A hopeless gloom settled over her as Laurel sat and waited helplessly for the last few hours of her life to pass. She had survived the earthquake, only to come to this! It was not fair, but there was nothing she could do about it except wait and pray the end would come quickly.

Chills raced through her, and her blood seemed actually to curdle in her veins at what lay ahead. The more she tried not to think of it, the more morbid her thoughts became. Soon she was shaking so hard that her teeth were chattering uncontrollably. She could not seem to stop trembling! She wished they would kill her now, for the waiting and wondering was worse than anything she had imagined.

At last Laurel slept, her stiff limbs curled into a

tight ball under the thin blanket Pedro had tossed over her. The night was cool and the blanket inadequate, but it was fright that would not let her body rest, that kept her trembling violently. The ache in her lower back grew steadily worse, and she shifted restlessly. Even in her troubled dreams, she prayed for a miracle to save her and her unborn child.

CHAPTER 26

Laurel awoke, not to a miracle, but to an additional nightmare. The sight that met her sleep-bleared gaze was heartstopping, and she hoped fervently that she was still dreaming.

Indians! Indians were attacking their camp, and here she lay, trussed up like a Christmas turkey, helplessly watching the massacre with no way in which to defend herself and no chance for escape.

Before her astounded gaze, she saw Jorge try to run, earning an arrow in the back for his efforts. Carlos lay in his bedroll, blood streaming from his slit throat. Pedro was trying to defend himself from his attacker, fighting hand-to-hand with an Indian brave. A knife gleamed wickedly between them as Pedro tried to disarm his assailant. Three other Indians watched the contest; even if Pedro managed to defeat this one, Laurel knew he stood not a chance of eluding all of them.

As she watched with disbelieving eyes, a part of her was aware that one of the Indians stood very near to her. Her heart thumped madly in her chest as she awaited her turn to be murdered. Small animal-like whimpers escaped her fear-constricted throat, but she could neither prevent them nor scream outright.

The savages did not approach her while the

fighting was taking place. It was not until the Indian's knife slipped soundlessly into Pedro's chest and he collapsed in a heap, that four bronze faces turned her way. Three of them stood watching from a short distance as the fourth walked calmly to her side.

For several seconds the brave looked down at her, his night-black eyes gleaming in the light of the fire. Laurel could not prevent a yelp of pure fear as, without a word, the man reached down and flipped the blanket from her.

A grim look flashed over his stony features as he saw her tied wrists. Again she cried out as the Indian brandished an evil-looking hunting knife.

Panic stricken, Laurel squeezed her eyes tightly shut and waited helplessly for the feel of cold steel entering her flesh, robbing her of her life. Time stood still. She held her breath and prayed as she had never prayed before. Tears squeezed out from beneath clenched eyelids.

At the first touch of the blade against the skin of her wrists, she flinched violently. There was a tug of the ropes binding her hands together, then— nothing! All was silent. Laurel could bear the suspense no more. When she dared to open her eyes, she saw the Indian kneeling over her, his eyes on her face. No! His gaze was on her hair! Oh, dear Lord! He was going to scalp her!

A bronze hand reached out to grasp a shining lock, and Laurel gasped in fright and closed her eyes again. Her teeth grated audibly as she clenched them tightly together in anticipation of the horror and pain to come.

A deep voice in distinct English said. "Open your eyes."

Surprise alone made her obey. As she stared fearfully up into the face so near hers, he said,

"We have met before, Woman with the Winter Hair. You are Brandon Prescott's woman."

She must have made some small involuntary movement that he took as an acknowledgement, for he continued to speak. "I am Red Feather, and these are my fellow warriors."

She remembered him now, though she feared him more than when she had first seen him on the banks of the river the previous fall. "What . . . What are you doing here?" she asked falteringly, her words coming out faintly, as though her throat had frozen shut.

"I was about to ask you the same question," Red Feather countered. "Where is Prescott?"

Afraid of what might happen next if she were to tell him that Brandon was dead, Laurel settled on a half-truth. "He is—in San Francisco." Her voice still sounded as weak and shaky as she felt.

Red Feather's onyx eyes speared hers as he said smoothly, "I have heard there is a terrible shaking of the earth and a great fire there."

His look commanded the truth from her. "Yes," she nodded miserably. "Brandon was killed in the earthquake."

"Why are you here now?"

Wetting her lips, Laural sat up. "I was going home to have my baby when those outlaws kidnapped me in El Paso."

The warrior nodded. "We have been nearby for several hours. We heard their talk of you. They were going to kill you."

"Yes." Laurel swallowed hard and dared to speak. "Are *you* going to kill me?" Her huge lavender eyes searched his face for mercy.

To her utter amazement, Red Feather smiled. "No. We are going to take you home. You will remember that once I asked Prescott if he would sell you to me, and he refused. He said you were his woman."

For just a minute Laurel feared that Red Feather meant to take her to *his* home, wherever that was. His next words set her mind at ease somewhat. "According to our ways, you now belong to Prescott's brother. We will take you to him. Then if he does not wish to keep you, I will bargain for you."

"But you can't!" Laurel protested, earning a frown from the warrior. "I carry Brandon's child."

Red Feather's brow cleared. "Do not worry, woman. If the younger Prescott does not wish to keep his brother's child, you may bring it with you and I will accept it into my family. Our people love children, and he will be raised among us as one of the tribe."

Laurel said no more, but inwardly she cried out in frustration. In the space of a few minutes she had gone from one desperate set of circumstances into another. Could nothing ever be simple? Then she reminded herself that Hank would hardly sell her or her child to an Indian. He would surely find some way to send Red Feather away without injuring his pride. Then she would finally be able to go home to her family at last.

Belatedly, Laurel recalled her narrow escape from death. With sincere gratitude, she said, "Red Feather, I thank you for saving me from those horrible men. You have saved my life this night, and I will never be able to properly repay you."

"We will speak of debts and gratitude later, Woman of the Winter Hair. Now we must prepare to leave this place."

"I have a travelling bag over there. The men were going through my things earlier. I think they put my jewel case and what little money I have left in one of the saddlebags. Also, my kitten is in that carrying case next to my bag."

A frown of disapproval and wonderment creased Red Feather's brow. "Why do you have an animal caged in this way? Do you not know how cruel this is? All creatures are meant to run free."

Laurel was concerned that she had greatly offended him. She hastened to explain, lest he become angry with her and refuse to take her home. "Please do not misunderstand, Red Feather. I adore the kitten, and would do nothing to harm her. She is only caged while we travel, so that she does not run off. Once I am home again, she will be free to wander where she will be safe. She will stay near me of her own will then, for she is very fond of me."

"I have your word that you will release her at that time?"

"I promise it."

Their route took them into the lower regions of the surrounding mountains. Laurel was amazed that the Indians could find their way so confidently in the dark, but their horses were well-trained, and the Indians trusted them to keep their footing on the treacherous trails. Laurel's mount followed the horse before her, plodding along in its wake. The warriors rode ahead and behind her, and where the trail was wide enough, they flanked her on all four sides in a protective manner. She would be well guarded for the rest of her journey home.

The longer they rode, the worse Laurel was feeling. Her back was aching badly again, and now she was experiencing alarming cramps in her stomach. With every step the horse took, she gritted her teeth, feeling weaker and shakier every minute. For as long as she could, she fought to stay on her horse, fighting back the nausea, ignoring the cold beads of perspiration gathering on her brow.

Finally it was too much for her, and she would have fallen from the saddle if not for Red Feather's quick reaction. "What is it?" he asked, noting her pallor and the chills that shook her.

Laurel leaned weakly against him, struggling to focus her gaze on his face. "My baby," she moaned. "I think I am losing my baby!"

Red Feather grunted something unintelligible and pulled her onto his horse with him. "We will find a place to rest," he told her, then issued orders to his companions.

A short time later, they halted in a secluded mountain glade. By this time, Laurel was in too much pain to realize what was going on around her. She drifted in and out of some netherland where pain and reality swelled and faded on waves of mist.

If Laurel had been fully conscious, she would have been mortified by the examination Red Feather conducted to determine the extent of her condition. It was brief and impersonal, and Laurel was soon wrapped in blankets near a warm fire, knowing nothing beyond her swirling world of trembling pain.

As if in a dream, she heard a voice urging her to drink, and like a trusting child, she obeyed. Abruptly, her stomach rebelled, jerking her back to reality as she began to retch. The warrior supported her and held her head as she was violently sick. As he laid her back on her pallet of blankets, a glimpse of his stony features told her that Red Feather considered this beneath his usual status. Still, he was helping her, for whatever reasons of his own.

Again he tipped the cup to her lips. "Drink," he ordered.

The nasty liquid was revolting and Laurel hesitated, trying to push it from her. "What *is* that awful brew?"

"Do not ask foolish questions, woman. If you wish to keep the child in your belly, you will do as I say." His face was stern as he tilted the cup and poured the drink past her quivering lips.

This time, it stayed down. Whether it was the mixture that made her dizzy or her physical discomfort, Laurel did not know. Neither did she care, for soon she succumbed to the lure of a beckoning dark void where all discomfort was far away and not even dreams of Brandon could reach her. She lay unconscious beneath the Indian brave's watchful eye.

Several times more, Laurel was roused from her stupor and made to drink, sinking immediately back into her private dark world. How long she lay there, unconsciously fighting the chills that shook her delicate frame, her will working with that of the warrior to save the life of her child, she knew not.

When she finally woke to full awareness, the sun was high in the sky. As her confusion left her, her hand flew immediately to her belly. Relief flooded through her as she felt the familiar bulge. The pain and chills seemed to be gone. As she shifted tentatively, afraid that any movement would bring a return of the pain, the baby moved within her, giving a mighty kick under the palm of her hand.

A joyous smile lit Laurel's face. Her baby was still alive within her, safe and healthy! Then her gaze met that of the man sitting quietly nearby, watching her. "Thank you," she whispered, her heart overflowing with gratitude, her lavender eyes shining like dew-damp blossoms.

A small smile tugged at the straight line of his lips. "Rest," he commanded in a low tone.

And rest she did, for three days, until Red Feather finally deemed it safe to continue their journey. Even then, Laurel rode cradled in his arms, his hard body absorbing the impact of the rough ride. He held her for hours, guiding his horse with his knees; and when he tired of her weight, another of the braves would carry her. All through the arduous trek across western Texas, they took turns, assuring her safe return home.

Laurel would remember that ride all her life. No one could have been more protective of her or more gentle than these stern warriors. Cradled in strong arms, her head resting on broad bronze chests, she lay trustingly, listening to the heavy heartbeats beneath her ear. Never did they grumble about their fragile burden, though Laurel suspected that this act of tenderness was normally beneath their dignity.

Though she was unaware and unconcerned with the fact, May had supplanted April when they arrived at last on Prescott land. Their small, unusual group drew much attention and curious stares as they rode into the ranch yard. Sam, the Bar P's foreman, approached cautiously as they came to a halt near the house.

"We are here to speak with the younger Prescott," Red Feather announced.

"Hank?" Sam questioned, a look of incredulity puckering his rough old features as he spied Laurel.

At Red Feather's nod, Sam hurried off,

returning several minutes later with Hank. Hank stared up at the Indians and Laurel in bewilderment, wondering what to say or do first. He decided it would be appropriate first to address the man he recognized as Red Feather. "Greetings, Red Feather. What is all this about? What is Laurel doing with you?"

"We are returning your brother's woman to you, if you desire it. She was being held by outlaws who meant to kill her when we found her."

Hank's gaze swung to the face of the woman Red Feather held in his arms. "Laurel, what is going on here? Where is Brandon?"

Before she could answer, Red Feather spoke again. "First tell us if this woman is welcome in your home."

More confused than ever, Hank stammered, "Of course she is welcome! She is my brother's wife."

At this, Red Feather dismounted and set Laurel on her feet. She swayed slightly, and his bronze hand reached out to steady her.

Hank's eyes narrowed slightly at the familiar gesture. "Laurel?" he prompted.

Her small, slender hand reached out to Hank, her face a mask of misery as she said softly, "Oh, Hank! How can I tell you? There is no painless way to say what I must—Brandon is dead! He died in the San Francisco earthquake."

A stunned look of utter disbelief flashed onto Hank's face, mirrored in Sam's. The look quickly changed into one of pain as he read the truth in Laurel's tearful eyes. "Oh, my God! What happened? When? How? We read of it and wondered how you were . . . but this!" He knew he wasn't making much sense, but the shock of her announcement was so great that he felt as if a tree had fallen on him.

Sam recovered first, remembering his manners. "Mrs. Prescott, you must be tired. Would you like to go inside and sit down, ma'am?"

With effort, Hank gathered his wits about him. "Forgive me, Laurel. Sam is right. We can talk more indoors, where you are more comfortable." His gaze took in her obviously bulging figure.

Turning to Red Feather, he said, "Thank you for returning Laurel safely to us. You must allow me to repay you in some way. What would you like in return for this favor?"

Red Feather met his look directly, his face registering no particular emotion as he answered, "According to our custom, your brother's wife now belongs to you. If you do not want her, I would be glad to bargain with you for her."

Surprise registered anew on Hank's face, but he answered evenly, "I must decline your offer, Red Feather. I hope you will not take offense when I say that Laurel is to stay here with me. Is there anything else you would like for saving her life?"

Red Feather accepted Hank's words with a nod. "I will take six steers of my choice in place of the woman."

Laurel could almost hear Hank's sigh of relief and saw Sam visibly relax, as she now did. "They are yours," Hank said. "Would you like to rest yourselves and your horses before you go? You are welcome to the hospitality of my home."

"No, Prescott." Red Feather declined the offer. "We will take our cattle and go." He mounted his horse and prepared to leave. With one final glance at Laurel, he said, "If you change your mind about the woman, I will return in the fall." They rode off without waiting for further comment.

When the Indians had gone, Hank turned to her. "Come, Laurel. Let's get you inside where you can rest. Then you can tell me everything."

"I'm sorry, Hank. So desperately sorry!"

"So am I. It will take some time before I really believe it. Brandon dead! It doesn't seem possible!"

Sam followed them into the house, not waiting for an invitation. He, too, was anxious to hear her news.

When they were seated in the parlor, Hank said quietly, "Brandon wrote that you were expecting a baby. He sounded so thrilled about being a father."

"I know. That is one of the reasons I am so thankful that Red Feather found me when he did. When I nearly lost the baby, he nursed me back to health and brought me here safely. He not only saved my life, but that of my child. Still, in spite of all I owe him, I am glad you found a way to send him away without offending him. I cannot see myself as his squaw."

She proceeded to tell them all about the earthquake and fire, and of Brandon's death. "I am sorry I couldn't bring his body home to you for burial. It hurts to think that we will never see his face again, even in death." A sob caught in her throat, stopping her words for a moment. Then she told them of her flight from San Francisco and her abduction in El Paso, ending with the Indians rescuing her before the outlaws could harm her.

"But why did this Pedro and his men kidnap you? I don't understand? What did you see them do, that they didn't want you to identify them?"

This was the moment Laurel had dreaded. She knew in her heart she would have to confess to Hank, and she regretted it with her whole being.

"There is something else I must tell you, Hank. Before I do, I would like your word that you will say nothing of this to anyone until I can tell my family." Her imploring gaze included Sam in her plea.

"You have my word, Laurel," Hank promised.

"And mine," Sam echoed. "What is it?"

Laurel explained about finding Miguel's letter, and of recognizing Pedro as the "priest" who had married them in Chihuahua. "So you see," she concluded sorrowfully, "Brandon and I were never truly married at all. I am still not sure what part Brandon played in all of this, that he and Miguel should feel responsible. I found only part of the letter on the morning of the earthquake, and I never had a chance to question Brandon about it."

"How can you think Brandon had anything to do with it, Laurel?" Hank readily defended his older brother. "He loved you dearly and was looking forward to the birth of your child."

Sam nodded in agreement. "I can't believe Brandon knew about it at the time. It just doesn't make sense."

"I know," she sighed, "but Brandon kept the letter from me, and I have no way of guessing how long he knew of it and said nothing to me. As much as I don't want to believe he deceived me, I can't help wondering if it was all part of his grand scheme of revenge against my father. He accused him of cattle rustling and Jim Lawson's death, you know. Brandon and I had many arguments over that, for I cannot conceive of my father doing anything that horrible."

"Yet you believe Brandon could have done something just as bad?" Sam huffed in disgust.

Tears filled her eyes as she gazed at the two men before her. Slowly, sadly, she shook her head. "I don't *want* to believe it, but I keep thinking of all the bad blood between our families in the past. I guess I'll never know for sure. All I am positive of now is that I will soon be giving birth to our child, and Brandon and I were never married, despite living as man and wife for months. My child will have no living father to care for it, and not even the benefit of his name to make his birth legitimate."

"Laurel, Sam and I will never tell anyone about this. As far as I am concerned, you and Brandon were married."

"You mean I should continue the deceit?" The two men nodded in agreement. "No," she said. "I couldn't."

"Not even for the sake of your child?"

"I would be living a lie, and I don't know if I could do that, Hank."

Hank drew a deep breath, then blurted, "I'll marry you, Laurel, and your child will carry his rightful surname. Brandon would want it that way, I am sure."

Laurel was both touched and shocked at his sudden proposal. "I appreciate the offer, Hank, but I must refuse. It wouldn't be right, and we would both suffer for it. No, I will go home and face my father and Aunt Martha with the facts. Then I will decide what to do next."

"You'll not give the baby up for adoption, will ya?" Sam asked anxiously.

"Heavens, no!" she exclaimed. "Whether my father approves or not, I intend to raise my child and love it. It is all I have left of Brandon, and nothing on this earth will part me from my baby. I only hope my father is not so angry that he turns me out of my own home."

"If he does, you'll always have a home here, Laurel. I give you my solemn word on that," Hank said serioiusly. "You—and my brother's child."

"And we won't tell a soul, unless you say so," Hank added grimly.

Laurel's meeting with her aunt and father went much as she had anticipated. Prepared as she was, she was still stunned by the extent of Rex's anger.

"So the swine didn't marry you after all! He got you pregnant quickly enough, though! The lousy bastard! If he wasn't already dead, I'd kill him with my bare hands!"

"Now, Rex, perhaps it wasn't Brandon's fault at all," Martha put in. "You heard what Laurel said about that Pedro character. Brr! Just the thought of Laurel in his evil hands makes me shiver!"

"It's the thought of Laurel in Prescott's *bed* that makes me quake—with fury! Mark my words, Brandon planned all this from the start! He probably paid that outlaw to pose as a priest!"

"Brandon did not plan to die, Daddy," Laurel pointed out, wearily. "I'm sure if he were here to defend himself, he could explain."

"Hogwash, daughter! And you are a fool to think so. You were a lovesick idiot to run off to Mexico with him in the first place. God knows, I never thought my own flesh and blood could be so stupid! When the good Lord passed out brains, you must have thought he said trains, and asked for a slow one!"

"All this ranting and raving will getyou nothing but a stroke. It will solve nothing." Martha glared at him. "How can you stand there screaming at your daughter and upsetting her in her delicate condition? You should be ashamed of yourself, Rex Burke!"

"I'm not the one that's done anything to be ashamed of," he countered. "It's this young woman who has dragged our good name through the mud, and over half the country at that! Can you imagine what our friends and neighbors will say when they find out? We won't be able to hold our heads up in this town any longer—all because of Laurel and that rogue she went hot-footing after like a bitch in heat!''

Rex paced back and forth before Laurel, who was seated on the divan, her hands clenched tightly in her lap, her face taut with anxiety. At her request, Hank had dropped her off at the house and left quickly. Now she almost wished she had let him stay as he had wanted to do. "Dad, I'm sorry I brought all this on your doorstep, but Brandon is dead and there is nothing we can do to change any of this problem now. I loved him dearly." At Rex's angry glare, she repeated, "Yes, I loved him. I know you don't like to hear me say it, but it's true. Regardless of what he did or didn't do, I cannot help the way I feel. I will proudly bear his child and raise it, no matter what people say, no matter how they may criticize or ostracize me for it. For my child's sake, I will ignore their snide comments and catty tongues gladly!''

"No, you will not!" Rex roared, his temper long past the cautious stage. "Tomorrow morning I will drive you to San Antonio, before anyone has a chance to see you or know you're home. I will personally see you and your Aunt Martha on a train to New Orleans, and there you will stay until your baby is born. Arrangements will be made for the infant to be adopted, and you can come home when the deed is done."

"*No!*" Laurel sprang from her seat, her face flushed and her eyes huge. "No one will ever take my baby from me! If you no longer want me to live here, I will go elsewhere. If you no longer care to acknowledge me as your daughter, I will try to understand that, but under no circum . . ." Her words trailed off as she sank to the floor in a faint.

When she came to herself, she was in her own bed, in her old room. Aunt Martha was sponging her face with a damp cloth. "I knew all that excitement was going to be too much for you," she said gently upon seeing Laurel's eyelids flutter open. "Especially since you told us you almost lost the babe not long ago."

Laurel's hands flew to her stomach. "My baby! Did I hurt my baby when I fainted?"

Martha shook her head and smiled. "I don't think so. Everything seems to be fine, sugarplum."

"I won't give up my baby, Aunt Martha. No matter what else happens, or how adamant Daddy is."

"Don't you fret, sweet. Your father is upset, and you know how stubborn he can be, but I think he's met his match this time. He'll come around sooner or later, you'll see. Once he has time to think things through and realize all he stands to lose, he'll change his mind."

"It had better be sooner, because this baby is due in August, whether Dad approves or not."

"Things will work out, Laurel, I promise you. If you could have seen how worried he was while you were gone! Then when we read in the papers about the earthquake in San Francisco, it was all I could do to prevent him from dashing off to try to find you. It took all my persuasion to convince him that we should wait to hear from you. When he settles down, he will realize how lucky he is to have you home safely. That is all he talked about while you were gone. When his temper cools, he'll be thankful to have you home. I really don't think he'd risk sending you away again, regardless of what he says now. He loves you too much."

"I love him, too, and you, Aunt Martha. You are all the family I have, until my baby is born, and I need you both. I hope Dad can learn to accept the baby, because without a father, it is going to need all the love and care we can give it."

"Rex will love your baby, Laurel," Martha predicted with a wise smile, "because it is a part of you—no matter who fathered it or how much he despises the Prescotts. You wait and see, honey. He is going to be one proud grandpapa!"

CHAPTER 27

After two days of intense verbal warfare at the Burke ranch, Laurel still would not budge from her decision to keep the baby. On the second day, Hank riled Rex further by daring to stop by to check on Laurel's welfare. The two men had a discussion of their own.

"I came to see how Laurel was doing, and to assure her that Sam and I will never reveal that she and Brandon were never actually married. If she agrees, it would save her and the baby a great deal of unnecessary embarrassment," Hank explained reasonably.

"Do you think I would take the word of a Prescott for one instant and believe he spoke one syllable of truth?" Rex roared.

"That is for Laurel to decide," Hank replied stiffly. "I only came to offer her the option and my help if she needs it. I certainly didn't come out of any concern for *you*, Burke."

"Now that I *do* believe! As for Laurel, she seems to have no sense at all where you Prescotts are involved. The girl is too gullible for her own good."

"I also offered to marry her and make things right for her and my brother's child, but she turned me down. However, if there is anything else she needs, she has only to ask."

"I'll take care of my own daughter, and I'll thank you to keep your nose where it belongs. Refusing you is the first bit of sense Laurel has shown lately. Maybe there's hope for her yet!"

"I wish I could say the same for you," Hank shot back sharply. "Laurel has more genuine feeling in her little finger than you will ever have. She must take after her mother, because it's for sure she didn't inherit her loving nature from you, old man! And another thing—it's time you gave Laurel credit for having good sense and stopped thinking of her as a little girl. She's a grown woman now, with a mind and will of her own."

"And an illegitimate babe in her belly for her comfort!" Rex's face contorted with rage and frustration.

"Like I said, no one will ever learn that from me. I'll do all I can to protect Laurel and my brother's child from scandal. Are you willing to do the same for your own daughter, Burke?" Hank left him with that final thought.

Think about it, Rex did. Finally he approached Laurel with his conclusion. "I have decided you can live here and keep your child as long as you promise not to tell anyone your marriage to Brandon was illegal. As much as it galls me, you will continue to refer to yourself as Laurel Prescott, and your child will bear that name. Those are my conditions."

"But Dad, it's a lie. Besides, I've already told Hank."

"Hank Prescott has sworn never to tell anyone. We will see if he can be trusted to keep his word. Now, I want your promise."

Under her aunt's urging, Laurel reluctantly

agreed. "What harm can it do, Laurel?" Martha insisted. "It is only to protect you and your baby from gossip."

So it was that Laurel resumed her life in Crystal City. She wore her wedding rings, accepted everyone's condolences when they heard of Brandon's death, and called herself Laurel Prescott. Because she had been married such a brief time, and because her condition warranted close association with her only female relative, no one thought it strange that she preferred to live at her father's home instead of the Prescott ranch. Everyone accepted what they saw on the surface and did not think to question the bereaved widow. They readily offered sympathy and friendship, not realizing the guilt Laurel carried about with her at her deception.

Laurel wanted only to hide away at home and lick her wounds. She did not feel like associating with anyone, preferring to sit in solitary despair.

But her friends and aunt had other ideas. Their common consensus was that it was not good for Laurel to lock herself away with her grief and her memories. They were determined to pull Laurel back into the world of the living.

They started stopping by the ranch regularly, ignoring Laurel's silences and gloom, and overlooking her sometimes sharp tongue. Gradually they set out to overcome Laurel's stubborn resistance.

Laurel realized what they were doing, and eventually resigned herself to their continued visits. If she hadn't been so consumed by heartache, she would have enjoyed their company and she truly appreciated their concern. In truth, she was deeply touched and soon found herself anticipating their visits despite herself.

She especially enjoyed Deborah's visits. Because Deb was her best friend and the two girls had been so close for so many years, Deb's visits were easy to endure, for she never pressed Laurel to talk or urged her to be cheerful. She seemed to understand that Laurel needed to come to terms with her loss in her own good time. Instead, they talked of Laurel's baby, what San Francisco had been like before the quake, Deb's life since Laurel had been gone, old times.

It was during one of these conversations that Laurel became aware that Deb had mentioned Hank's name three times in as many sentences. Jerking herself out of her own doldrums, Laurel began to pay closer attention to her friend. She noticed that each time Hank was mentioned, Deb's face became soft and dreamy, glowing as if lit from within. When she spoke his name, it was a sweet sound, making an ordinary name seem suddenly special.

"Deb," Laurel asked after a while, "how long have you been in love with Hank Prescott?"

Deb blushed prettily. "Is it that evident?"

"Now that I have finally taken notice, yes."

"Oh, Laurel! He's so wonderful!"

"This must be rather sudden. You certainly didn't give any indication of it last summer."

"Well, it really didn't start until after you and Brandon left. Then Hank and I just sort of drifted together to exchange news of you, since he was Brandon's brother and I'm your best friend. One thing led to another, and before I knew what hit me, I was head over heels in love with a man I've known all my life and never really knew at all!"

Laurel smiled one of her rare smiles. "Tell me more of the 'one thing led to another' part."

Deb laughed joyously. "It all started very

simply; chance meetings in town, sodas at the ice cream parlor. Then he began sitting with me in church and accepting invitations to Sunday dinner and taking me for buggy rides when the weather was mild. We'd hold hands, or he would put his arm about me, and I thought I'd die of joy."

"Go on." This romance of Deb's suddenly perked Laurel's interest.

"Hank invited me to the Christmas Cotillion at the town hall, and I had the most wonderful night of my life. I tell you, Laurel, I was dancing on clouds! I don't believe my feet touched the ground all evening! He was so charming and handsome, and I felt like a princess in my new gown. It was glorious to be held in his arms like that. And when he took me home, we sat for hours and talked. Mother and Dad let us have the parlor to ourselves. I don't think I've ever been so nervous as when he took me into his arms and kissed me. If I had been half in love with him before, I know I lost my heart to him completely that night.

"Mother and Dad adore him. New Year's Eve, Hank came over and we all played games and music and ate fudge and popcorn until midnight. It was such fun, and Dad didn't even mind losing to Hank at checkers. Can you imagine that?"

Laurel's attention was suddenly diverted. "Fudge," she said, her tongue snaking out to lick at her lips. "Fudge! Oh, Deb, let's go out to the kitchen this minute and see if we have the ingredients to make a batch! You can tell me all about you and Hank while we cook."

Deb frowned slightly, wondering how the conversation had suddenly been side-tracked. "Are you sure you should be eating such things in your condition? Shouldn't you be eating decent meals and lots of milk?"

Laurel was already halfway down the hall, dragging Deb with her. "I've been craving avocados until I think I'll die for lack of one, but suddenly fudge sounds almost as good. I'm going to eat my fill, and I don't care if I burst!"

"Which you just might!" Deb inserted dryly. "I know I'm inexperienced in this area, but aren't you awfully big? You can't see your shoes now, and the baby isn't due until August. Are you sure that doctor knew what he was talking about, Laurel?"

Laurel didn't know whether to take offense or not, but Deb seemed genuinely concerned. "Dr. Davis and I both calculated the baby would arrive in August. And if this is a polite way of asking whether Brandon and I slept together before we left Cyrstal City, the answer is yes. But I was not expecting then."

Deb was hurt and slightly miffed at Laurel's tart reply. "I meant nothing of the sort, and you know it, Laurel! How you can even *think* such a thing is beyond me! I thought we were friends."

"We are, Deb. I'm sorry. I'm just extremely touchy these days."

"I'll accept your apology and forgive you on the grounds that your condition is making you irritable." Deb grinned. "I still think you are showing much more than most women do at this stage. Why, the only person I recall being this big was Helen Ames, and she had *twins!* Mary Lou wasn't this size when she delivered Chad, and neither was Becky Lawson with any of hers. Are you sure there is just one little person growing in there?"

The look on Laurel's face was stunned. "Good Lord, I hope so! What a sobering thought! I'm going to have my hands full raising *one* child by myself. Whatever would I do with two?''

Deb shrugged. "Well, you probably won't have to worry about it anyway. I'm no authority on such things, as you well know."

Their talk drifted back to Deb's romance with Hank, and Laurel temporarily forgot about their conversation about babies. From what Deb said, she and Hank had been seeing each other steadily for some time now.

"Am I correct in assuming that Hank feels the same way about you? Has he asked you to marry him?" In the back of her mind, Laurel was remembering the desperate look on Hank's face when he had suggested he marry her for the baby's sake.

"I'm sure he must care for me a great deal, though he hasn't proposed yet," Deb was saying. "He was at the house continually until just lately, and I know he hasn't been seeing anyone else. Perhaps he just hasn't decided how best to ask me. It is odd that I haven't seen much of him the last couple of weeks, but I suppose he has a lot on his mind just now. I know how bad he feels about losing his brother."

At Deb's crestfallen face, Laurel assured her, "I'm sure he'll come around soon, Deb. The news of Brandon's death hit him hard, and I'm sure he needs time to adjust to it." Privately, Laurel determined to speak with Hank as soon as possible. If he was avoiding Deb with the mistaken idea that Laurel might change her mind and decide to marry him, she would soon set him straight. It was bad enough that her own life was in such a mess. She certainly wasn't going to be responsible for destroying two more lives, and her best friend's happiness.

In the days that followed, Laurel had much to consider. It hardly dawned on her that her thoughts had been diverted from herself and her own sorrows just a little. She still grieved terribly, but now she was thinking of someone else.

In those first few terrible days at home, with so much strife and her father so angry, Laurel's birthday had passed unnoticed. Martha wanted to rectify that oversight, but she knew it was not the right time for a party of any sort. Besides, Rex was still being so surly and Laurel was so very depressed these days. Just when she thought she might have to forget the entire idea, Martha came up with a solution, one that she hoped would pull Laurel further out of her dark mood.

A few days later, Laurel entered the parlor to find her dearest friends assembled there—Deb, Mary Lou, Imogene, Sara, Amy; even Becky Lawson. A pile of gaily wrapped gifts sat on a nearby table, and just as Laurel was about to ask what was going on, Martha entered the room carrying a large cake. She placed it on a stand next to the tea service and turned to Laurel. "Sit down, dear."

"Aunt Martha, what is all this?" Laurel gestured about her in confusion.

"We decided since you have shown no interest in shopping for clothing for your baby, that we would do it for you. It is a celebration in honor of your coming motherhood, and we have all bought gifts for your baby. We can't have the poor thing enter the world without so much as a stitch of cloth to cover his bottom, now can we?"

Laurel sat, too surprised to do otherwise. "You are all so sweet and thoughtful, I could just cry!"

"Don't you dare!" Deb declared, making everyone laugh, Laurel included.

The party was a great success, and Martha was well pleased with herself. There were lovely shawls, dresses, booties and sweaters for the women to coo over; everything from receiving blankets and diapers to lace-trimmed bonnets. Laurel was delighted with each tiny garment, remembering with fleeting sorrow the beautiful baby items burned in the house in San Francisco. If she was slightly confused by unwrapping a few items for herself, Aunt Martha explained that they were belated birthday gifts, included now.

"And later we will drag out all of your old baby furniture stored in the attic and clean it up. We'll fix up the small room next to yours as a nursery." It was one more thing to keep Laurel too busy to mourn.

The first chance she got, Laurel had Martha drive her over to see Hank. He was surprised, and she thought just a bit dismayed at her unannounced visit, but he hid it well and invited the ladies into the house.

"To what do I owe the honor of this call by two of Crystal City's most lovely ladies?" he asked cordially.

Laurel came straight to the point. "Hank, I have to talk to you."

"What about?"

"About you and Deb."

The surprise on his face was nearly comical. "Me and Deb?" he echoed.

"Yes." Laurel speared him with a level look. "I want to know what your intentions are toward my best friend. You had been seeing her regularly until lately, and I want to know the extent of your feelings for her."

Hank was obviously flustered. "Laurel, I don't

know what to say . . ."

"You could start by admitting that you love her.
She's quite in love with *you*, you know."

A deep flush rushed to his neck and suffused his
face. His reaction gave him away even before he
stammered, "Oh, well, I do—uh—I do care for
her."

"Poppycock!" Laurel cut off his words. "You
love her! It's as plain as the nose on your face.
When are you going to put both of you out of your
misery and marry her?"

"But I . . . I . . ." he began.

"You what?"

"I thought perhaps you and I . . ."

"Hank, do you love me?" she asked point-blank.

"Well—no, but . . ."

"But nothing! I loved your brother. I'll never
love another man as I did Brandon. I still love him,
and I am going to bear his child. It's quite enough
that you have allowed me to assume his name, for
my sake and the child's. You need not sacrifice
yourself and your love for my sake. I doubt I
would ever forgive you if you tried. You and I will
never be married, so you may feel perfectly free to
propose to the woman you truly love—as soon as
possible! Do I make myself clear?"

Hank grinned sheepishly. "Perfectly. But
Laurel, are you sure?"

"Absolutely. Now, are you going to ask Deb to
marry you, or not?"

His grin widened until she thought his face
would split in half. "Yes, ma'am, I certainly am!"

She smiled back, and Martha chuckled with
them. "I certainly am glad this is settled," the
older woman said dryly. "Can we go home now so
I can finish the laundry?"

* * *

May eighteenth was a particularly dark day for Laurel, and the rainy weather matched her mood perfectly. This day marked exactly one month since the earthquake and Brandon's death. She sat forlornly in her room, tears flowing down her cheeks as relentlessly as the raindrops hitting her windowpane. Her mood was as bleak as the dreary day, her heart aching unbearably. Even the baby kicking energetically within her could not dispel her gloom.

She refused to eat, ignoring the tempting morsels Martha had brought up on a tray. When she heard a light knock at her door, she thought it was her aunt yet again, so she was surprised when Becky Lawson poked her head in and said, "May I come in? I know you don't want company, but since I've come all this way in the rain . . ."

Laurel could hardly refuse.

Becky joined her at the window. "You know, I used to sit and watch the rain like this after Jim was killed. It seems so much more fitting than sunshine, doesn't it?"

Laurel nodded miserably, brushing away her tears. 'Yes, it does. I sometimes forget that I'm not the only one to have lost someone they love. I suppose that's awfully self-centered of me."

"It's natural," Becky assured her with a gentle smile. "As natural as grieving."

Becky walked to the bed where Sassy lay dozing and stroked the sleeping kitten. "I've never seen a cat like this. What kind is it?"

"She's Siamese. Brandon gave her to me as a Valentine's Day gift. Her name is Sassy." Laurel's face became woeful as she said, "He brought me a silver fox cub too, when we were in Mexico. I remember telling him that we would be overrun with pets if he didn't break the habit soon. He just laughed . . ." Her voice broke on a sob. "I used to love it when he laughed," she whispered.

Becky went to her and put a comforting arm about her shaking shoulders. "I know you won't believe me now, but it does get better, Laurel. Time will heal the terrible ache, and your memories will all become sweet ones, with no sharp edges to pierce your heart to bleeding. I know. I've gone through the same thing you are experiencing now, and it *is* terrible, but you have family and friends to care for you. I don't know what I would have done without my friends to help me through, especially Brandon and your father."

"My father?" Laurel repeated.

Becky smiled. "Yes, he has been wonderful. Not long after you and Brandon left, he started coming by the house. At first it was always on some pretense or other; a calf that needed a mother, a milk cow he didn't know what to do with, a half-dozen steers he didn't have room for, if you can imagine that! His excuses were so lame, it was almost laughable, yet he was so dear and kind, and always found a way to make me accept his gifts or else seem ungrateful!

"Often he would bring groceries and stay to eat with me and the children. He is so patient with them, and they adore him. I came to look forward to his visits, and I still do. In fact, I care very deeply for your father—not in the same way I loved Jim, but just as dearly. I hope you don't mind Rex and me keeping company, Laurel."

Laurel was so amazed at this piece of information that she could hardly speak. "No—of course not, Becky—but . . ."

Becky's face fell. "You *do* object! Oh, Laurel, why? Is the prospect of having me for a step-mother very distasteful to you? I thought we would be more like friends than mother and daughter, since we are both so close in age."

"That's just it, Becky! You are so young! You're young enough to be my sister. I just can't imagine you and my father as man and wife. He's so much older than you!"

"He's not that old, Laurel. It is just that you see him from a daughter's viewpoint and I'm looking at him as a woman does an attractive man. Please don't begrudge me his love. I promise you I'll not turn all motherly on you. Can't you share him with me, Laurel? Rex has been alone for so many years, and he and I both deserve some happiness."

"Becky, I'm not a child jealous of her father's affections for another woman. It is just hard for me to fathom right now. All these years Dad has never shown any inclination to remarry, and now all of a sudden he chooses a woman half his age. This is all new to me, on top of everything else that has happened recently!" Suddenly Laurel began to laugh. "Heavens! Do you realize that in a few short months he will be a *grandfather!* Can you actually imagine my child calling you 'Grandma'?"

Even Becky had to laugh at this. "That never occurred to me. Couldn't we compromise and have him call me Nanna Becky, or something?"

When Becky left, Laurel had a lot to think about. She couldn't help recalling Brandon's accusations against her father and their many fights over them. If—just if—her father had been behind the rustling, if he had anything at all to do with Jim Lawson's death, was this Rex's way of making restitution? Worse yet, could he be covering his tracks and insuring that Becky, once she was his wife, would be in a position where she could never testify against him if she discovered his part in the scheme? Could Laurel's father truly be that devious, or was he actually taken with the young widow?

Before things went any further, Laurel knew she must confront her father, no matter how angry he might become. She had to make certain her father was not about to compound one sin with another.

"What do you mean by asking me if I'm guilty of cattle rustling?" Rex's roar could be heard for miles. "You ungrateful wretch! After all I've done for you—especially lately!"

"Now, Dad, I didn't accuse you. I merely asked. It's not an entirely new thought I've invented out of thin air, either, you know."

"Darned right, I know; and I know who planted the idea in your empty little head, too! It was that blasted lover of yours and his half-baked notions. Is there no end to the trouble he's causing me? It's bad enough that I'm about to be saddled with his illegitimate offspring! God knows it sticks in my craw that you bear *his* child. A Prescott! I'd rather you were having any man's child but his! Now he has the added revenge of turning my daughter completely against me!"

Laurel let him rave until he finally wound down and stopped for breath. "Dad, I've never believed it was true. Brandon and I had so many fights because I would not see it his way. I always insisted you were innocent."

"Then why ask me now? Why the sudden doubt?"

Laurel looked him straight in the eye. "Becky Lawson told me the two of you are getting married. After hearing all Brandon's accusations and reading your letters saying you were making restitution to Becky, I couldn't help wondering about your reasons. In spite of all my faith in you, it struck me that you might be marrying her out of a sense of guilt, or to protect yourself from suspicion. I don't *want* to believe that, Dad, after taking your side against my own husband for so long. I don't want to think I could have been so wrong about you all this time."

"He was *not* your husband, much to your shame," Rex pointed out. "Furthermore, I resent your implication that I could ever be as underhanded as that weasel and his family. I happen to love Becky, and I don't give a hoot how you feel about that! You didn't care how I felt when you went running off to Mexico with that scoundrel, only to come home unwed and pregnant!"

Laurel was on her feet now and screamed back at him, "You'll never forgive me for that, will you? Whether any of it was my fault or not, you'll always resent me and my child!"

"Not you, Laurel. I've loved you since the day you were born, and I will love you always, regardless of what happens."

"But you *do* resent my baby because he was fathered by a Prescott! Well, this child couldn't help who fathered him, or who his mother is, for that matter. He's an innocent babe, completely undeserving of your hatred. He isn't responsible for the actions of his parents and should not be held in contempt by anyone. Can't you see that? Can't you find some love in your heart for your own grandchild?"

Rex shook his head wearily, sadly. "The Prescotts have been a thorn in my side longer than I care to remember, especially Brandon. I don't know if I'll ever be able to look at that child and not see the face of the cursed man who fathered him."

Though tears blurred her vision, Laurel's chin came up defensively. "Then I pity you, Dad. All that hate and distrust must be a heavy load to carry, and it surely must eat at your soul."

Deb and Imogene let it slip one day while visiting, that some of Laurel's old beaus were looking forward to seeing her again. Laurel was incredulous. "How can they think I would be interested in anyone so soon? Good grief, it has only been a month since Brandon died!"

"Don't get all riled, Laurel," Deb soothed. "They know that, and I'm sure they'll wait a respectable length of time before they start pelting you with proposals."

"Yes," Imogene concurred. "We just thought you should be forewarned. Look at it this way—now that you know what to expect when you emerge from your mourning, you can even select ahead of time which men you would prefer and those you will reject outright. Personally, I think every woman should have that privilege."

Deb giggled. "Heavens, Imogene! Next you'll want a variety of suitors paraded past in an arena, like a cattle auction, from which to make your choices."

"Actually, that sounds like a good idea to me. Maybe then I could at least make Amos Turner just the tiniest bit jealous so he wouldn't take me so much for granted, as he does now."

Laurel couldn't help giggling. "And poor Priscilla might even catch a man that way."

"Don't delude yourself, Laurel," Deb said jokingly. "That girl is doomed to spinsterhood unless some halfwit comes along soon to rescue her, and then I pity the poor fellow who will have to endure her homely face and spiteful tongue. Hell would be a holiday compared to a lifetime with Priscilla."

"Back to the problem of prospective beaus," Laurel reminded them. "Why don't you spread the word that it's suspected I might give birth to twins? That should scare off all but the most determined."

"Or the most foolhardy!" Deb laughed.

"You gave me the idea, Deb. I share the credit with you."

"Well, it will certainly separate the men from the boys!" Imogene crowed.

Deb had inadvertently planted the possibility of twins in Laurel's mind, and now Laurel could not seem to rid herself of the thought. Though she tried not to dwell on the awesome idea, she found herself subconsciously preparing for just such an occurrence in case it proved to be true. On a shopping spree with her aunt, she purchased twice the amount of clothing one infant might require. At odd times, she found herself considering names for two little people. Then she would chide herself for being such a silly goose and push the entire concept from her mind. It was too ridiculous even to think about seriously.

CHAPTER 28

It was at this point that Hank received one of the most astonishing messages of his life. Out of the blue, with no forewarning, he received a letter addressed to him and bearing a San Francisco postmark. To his total disbelief, when he opened it, he found a letter from Brandon! If it had not been written in his brother's bold, distinctive script, he would never have believed it.

In the letter, Brandon informed Hank of the earthquake and resulting fire and also—of all incredible things—Laurel's death! Astounded and totally baffled, Hank hurriedly read on:

> I have been wandering about in a drunken stupor for nearly a month, or I would have thought to write sooner.
>
> Life without Laurel is unbearable for me! Her memory lingers on, even in this shell of a house, and I find I cannot bear it any longer. Neither can I come home just yet, for everything there would also remind me of her.
>
> I have decided to go abroad. There is a ship leaving for Australia next week, and I shall be on it. I cannot say how long I will be gone; however long it takes for me to come to terms with the loss of my beloved wife and child.

There is one favor you can do for me, if you will. Rex Burke should be informed of his daughter's death, but I cannot seem to make myself write such terrible news to him. He should be told in person, but I am taking the coward's way out and asking you to do the deed for me. I cannot face the man just yet. I cannot even face myself at this stage.

In case you need to get in touch with me for any reason, I will write and send my new address when I am settled somewhere.

Affectionately,
Your brother, Brandon

Hank stared in joyful bewilderment at the letter in his hands. How had such a thing happened? Brandon was laboring under the misconception that Laurel was dead, and all the while Laurel was alive and mourning Brandon's demise! He knew he must do something quickly to set things straight.

Hank had one foot out the door, with the intention of informing Laurel immediately, when a thought suddenly occurred to him. Brandon had referred to Laurel as his wife, yet Laurel claimed they were not married. What the devil was going on?

After a few minutes of deliberation, Hank decided that he must wire Brandon at once before he set sail for Australia. He would ride to Eagle Pass and send the message, so no one in Crystal City would know of it, and he would wait for Brandon's reply before telling Laurel anything.

As Hank dashed out of the house, he prayed he could reach Brandon in time, and stop this craziness before it was confounded any further.

Brandon tipped the empty whiskey bottle over the rim of his glass and shook it. "Blast! Empty!"

Stumbling to his feet, he headed for the kitchen
and a fresh bottle. The little fox trailed at his
heels. "You been drinkin' my whiskey, Tyke old
pal?" Brandon mumbled.

Upon hearing his name, Tyke yipped. Brandon
chuckled and patted his head. "Yeah, I thought so,
but tha's all right. You deserve a little forgetfulness, too."

Tess stood in the doorway and shook her head.
She could count on her fingers the number of
hours Brandon had been sober in the past month.
He'd lost more weight and his face was gaunt, his
cheekbones jutting out prominently beneath the
dark shadows under his red-rimmed eyes. Usually
so impeccably dressed, his clothes now hung
haphazardly on his big body. Rarely did he walk
straight and tall these days. Rather, he stumbled
along in a drunken haze. Tess thought it remarkably lucky Brandon hadn't fallen and broken
every bone in his body by now—but on second
thought, his body was probably too relaxed with
alcohol for him to break anything.

"God looks after fools, children, and drunks,"
she said softly.

Still, Brandon heard her and swung about
sharply to face her, his lips lifting slightly from
their perpetual droop. "H'lo, Tess."

"Hello yourself. I stopped by to tell you I mailed
your letter to your brother."

"Thanks. C'mon in, you can join me in a drink. If
I can find that other bottle."

"You already drank it. The cupboard is bare,"
Hanna called from the veranda where she was
stirring the soup for lunch.

"The story of my life," Brandon said with a
grimace.

"It has been lately," Tess agreed. "Brandon,

when are you going to snap out of this? You cannot go on like this indefinitely, drowning your torment in alcohol. Sooner or later, you've got to come to grips with yourself and face the world. It might as well be now."

"Oh, quit carping at me, Tess! You're beginning to sound like a shrew. I sobered up long enough to write that blasted letter, like you asked, didn't I? That was quite long enough for me."

"And high time you wrote to your brother, too! He must have been worried sick, and a lot you cared! You are much too busy hiding from your responsibilities in a liquor-induced fog! It is so much easier to exist from bottle to bottle than to pick yourself up by your bootstraps and face the future. You're becoming an alcoholic coward, Brandon Prescott!"

Brandon glared at her with bloodshot eyes. "If you were a man, I'd probably shoot you for saying that."

Tess stared back unflinchingly. "Would that make it any less true?"

"Go home, Tess," Brandon growled. "Get out of here before I forget we're friends and give in to the temptation to strangle you."

"I'll be back tomorrow."

Brandon sighed heavily. "I know you will. You've made it your mission in life to torment me mercilessly."

"No—I've taken on the impossible task of trying to save you from yourself."

He laughed mirthlessly. "Give it up, Tess. I'm not worth it."

Tossing him a smile on her way out, she said, "Probably not, but that won't keep me from trying."

"Shrew!" Brandon muttered. But he had to

admit that Tess was right about one thing. He was becoming a coward. Hadn't he written as much to Hank? Brandon's courage seemed to have deserted him. It was as if his backbone had turned to jelly when Laurel died. He just didn't have the will to face the world without her, and if the truth were told, there wasn't even much false courage to be found in a bottle. The whiskey merely numbed his senses and made the reality of Laurel's death a little less painful.

At times, if he was drunk enough, he could forget she was gone, pretending to himself that she was out shopping or upstairs dressing to go out with him to dinner or the theatre. Any minute now, she would come down the staircase, her hair floating about her delicate face like shimmering moonlight, her eyes like sparkling amethysts. She would laugh up at him, her lips begging to be kissed; her perfume wafting up from her small, warm body, teasing him until he took her into his arms and slaked his desire. She would come to him, hot and willing and totally tantalizing, and he would lose himself in her and carry her with him to the highest realms of ecstasy, delighting in her soft moans of desire and her cries of fulfillment. . .

Then reality would come crashing through his fragile dreams, and the jagged edges of his loss would tear at his bleeding heart. He would never hear her tinkling laughter or soft cries again. He would never hold her in the night or wake to find her head nestled securely on his shoulder. Her eyes would never again light up in wonder as he made love to her. So Brandon would go in search of another bottle of forgetfulness, trying desperately to cling to the wisp of a dream that too often eluded him and only came when he was too drunk to recall that reality was a charred body on a pantry floor.

Laurel had no such relief for her pain. She could not obliterate the agony that assaulted her daily. She had only her friends and her child to ease her way, and dear as they were, it helped so little.

Many a long, endless night was spent tossing and turning fretfully in her solitary bed, her body on fire for him, her mind recalling the warmth of his tender caresses and the hot demand of his lips on hers. On those rare nights when sleep overtook her, she would dream vividly of him. Sometimes she would see him out-of-doors, his brown hair tossed and windblown over his forehead, his smile flashing bright in his sun-darkened face. At others, he would stand before her in all his nude male beauty, and his eyes would glow like quicksilver as he came to her, to claim her as his own. Sweet, muffled words of love would echo in her ears as his hands wandered her body, sensually touching all those places he knew so well, and she would plead with him to take her to the stars with his glorious lovemaking.

But her dreams ended as she reached out to pull his body closer, and she would wake with empty arms outstretched and Brandon's name on her lips. Then she would cry; great choking sobs that shook her body as she hugged her pillow to her and wept. Dawn would be sending its first rays of light over her windowsill before she slept again. And if the gentle summer breeze should drift through her window to play across her flushed cheek, it felt like Brandon's warm breath touching her skin and she would sigh tremulously, loath to wake.

* * *

"Have you seen Hank in the last couple of days?" Deb asked Laurel with a slight frown one day.

"No. Why do you ask?" Laural answered absently, her mind on the rose bush she was trimming.

"He was supposed to come to supper last night, and he never showed up. Then when I stopped by his place before coming here, Sam told me he'd gone to Eagle Pass for a few days."

Laurel shrugged. "He probably had some business to attend to—something to do with the ranch, most likely."

"That's what Sam said, more or less. Still, don't you think he could have taken a few minute to tell me before he dashed off?"

"It takes some men a little time before they realize they have someone other than themselves to account to. I'm sure Hank will learn to be more considerate in future."

"I certainly hope so."

Laurel put down her shears and looked up at her friend. "What is really bothering you, Deb?"

Deb laughed self-consciously. "You know me too well, Laurel." Then, with a sigh, she added, "I suppose I'm just not as secure as I let on. Even now, with our engagement announced, I'm afraid Hank will have second thoughts."

"And you think his sudden disappearance means he has done just that and run off "

Deb nodded. "Am I being silly?"

"Indeed you are!" Laurel assured her. "Hank will come back soon and set your fears at rest. You'll see."

"Well, he had better be back by Saturday for the

engagement party Mary Lou is giving for us, or I
may never forgive him!''

"You'll forgive him the minute he tells you he
loves you and starts spouting all that sweet talk in
your ear. You'll melt the first moment he looks at
you, and you know it," Laurel predicted, reminded
anew of Brandon's courtship of her.

Brandon was having yet another of his whiskey-
sweetened dreams. It felt so real he could actually
feel Laurel's hands upon him, her fingers running
caressingly through the dark pelt of hair on his
chest. He groaned with the delicious feel of her
lips making contact with the flesh of his shoulder,
her teeth lightly nipping as her hands now eased
his shirt from him. "Laurel . . ." he murmured.

"I'll make you forget her, Brandon, I promise.
I'll make it good for you."

Brandon shook his head, unable to understand
what Laurel was talking about. Who would she
make him forget? Why? He was about to ask why
her voice sounded so different, when her lips
covered his in an urgent kiss. He forgot all but the
warmth of her touch, the softness of her lips. Her
tongue pressed past the barrier of his teeth and
delved into his mouth. It seemed odd that Laurel
would be quite so bold, but who was he to
complain? It felt so good to be touched by her, her
slim fingers lacing through his hair to hold his
head close to hers.

"Laurel, honey, you feel so good. It's been so
long!" he moaned softly as her lips left his to
feather kisses along his jawline to his ear. There
her tongue snaked a wet trail and her hot breath
chased gooseflesh over his skin.

"Brandon, open those marvelous eyes of yours

and look at me. See who is making you feel this way. Darling, see me for who I really am!"

Her fingers traced a path down the quivering flesh of his stomach and stopped to loosen his belt buckle. It was then that Brandon finally realized what was wrong—why Laurel's voice seemed so peculiar. His eyelids opened slowly, reluctant to give up his dream of Laurel.

His blurred vision slowly cleared to settle upon a beautiful face framed by red hair. In place of Laurel's lavender eyes, he beheld the brilliant blue of Muriel's. Even before his mind had time to register all this, his large hands were covering hers to stop their movement.

"Muriel," he growled, his voice still thick from sleep and drink. "What the . . . ?"

"Brandon, darling, let me love you. Let me show you how good it can be for us," Muriel purred, her eyes smoky with desire, her pouting lips so persuasively close to his. "I've wanted you for so long, but someone was always around, and I had to bide my time until they were all gone on errands." Her hands moved under his, unerringly finding and caressing him through the cloth of his trousers.

He jumped as if shot, his hands almost crushing her fingers as they closed hard over hers and flung them from him. "Get away from me, you witch! What the hell do you think you are doing?" Brandon was stone-cold sober for the first time in weeks, the shock of Muriel's seduction jerking him instantly alert. His eyes gleamed like the polished steel of twin knife blades.

Muriel was a bit frightened by his violent reaction, yet she was still determined to convince him of her sincerity. "I'm just trying to help you get over your sorrow, Brandon. Laurel wasn't the only woman in the world, you know. I can comfort you, darling, if you will let me."

Brandon laughed harshly. "Muriel, I could get the same comfort from a dockside tart, but with more compassion than you'll ever possess. You want your own selfish desires satisfied, so don't try to dupe me. I'm not that drunk or that much of a fool—yet."

"I'm so glad to hear that." Both Muriel and Brandon swung about to see Tess framed in the doorway. She sauntered into the room. "Well, Muriel," she said smoothly, "that was quite a performance. It was almost worth paying money to witness; and yes, I did see most of it. Personally, I found it quite tawdry on your part, but what can you expect from a born harlot?"

Brandon glared from one woman to the other, his temper flaring. "What gives either of you the right to come and go in my house at will? While I realize it is a bit dilapidated at present, this *is* my home. It may not have a proper door on which to knock, but you could wait to be invited, and not just barge in whenever the mood strikes you!"

Tess calmly settled herself into a chair. "Don't be testy, Brandon. Muriel is leaving, aren't you dear?"

Muriel's blue eyes shot daggers at Tess. "I'll leave when I'm ready! Brandon and I were having a private discussion before you pushed your long nose in here so abruptly."

A sharp laugh broke from between Tess's lips. "Is that what they are calling it these days? I believe Brandon was about to show you the so-called door."

Brandon was beginning to feel like an unnecessary piece of furniture as the two women talked around him. He rose from his cot, grabbed each

woman by an arm and escorted them outside
without a word. Once there, he eyed them both
with an angry gaze. "Tess, go build another hotel
or something and stop mothering me. If I need a
nursemaid, I'll hire one."

To Muriel, he said, "You go find someone else to
sample your shopworn wares. I wouldn't sully
Laurel's memory by touching the likes of you, and
I don't know where you got the impression that I
might. If you were counting on the fact that I'd
been drinking, let me assure you, I could never be
that drunk!" At Muriel's indignant squeal, he said,
"Get out of here and don't come back, or I swear,
you'll rue the day."

"Bravo!" Tess clapped her hands as Muriel
stomped off in a huff.

"Tess, I thought I told you to go home."

She held up her hands defensively and laughed.
"Don't get yourself into a tizzy. I'm going. I'll come
back when you are in a more congenial mood—
and next time I'll remember to knock. I promise."

Brandon shook his head, a reluctant smile
curving his lips. "I swear, Tess," he sighed
defeatedly. "You're like a persistent wart. Every
time I think I've gotten rid of you, you pop up
again."

"True." She grinned delightedly, her eyes
sparkling. "I rather grow on people after a while."
With a final pert wave, she said, "See you soon—
and Brandon, it's good to see you sober. Try to
stay that way."

"Yes, Mother," he sighed.

To the people close to Brandon, it was an
immense relief to see the change in him. Keeping
his word to Tess, he stopped drinking and started
eating again, if only to keep Hanna from nagging

him continually. Though still severely depressed, he started taking charge of his life.

With his sailing just days away, there was much to be done. Once sober, he realized he needed to buy clothes and baggage, and a multitude of other small essentials he had been doing without as he had wandered about in a haze.

His first sight of his own haggard image in a mirror thoroughly shocked him. Was this bearded, bedraggled man really him? Without delay, he hied himself to the nearest barber for a shave and a haircut. Then he took the ferry over to Oakland and purchased some decent clothing. It was amazing how much better a bath and fresh clothes made him feel.

It was during one of his jaunts downtown to settle some business affairs, that he came across Dr. Davis.

"Brandon! Good grief, man! It's like looking at a ghost, but I can't tell you how good it is to see you!"

Brandon would have liked to have said the same, but the sight of Laurel's doctor was like a knife twisting in his gut. It brought bittersweet memories of Laurel and the child he would never see. "Hello, Dr. Davis. How are you?"

"Fine. Busier than usual, what with so many people injured in the quake and the fire. I'm glad to see you came through it all right, though. Last time I saw your wife, she was pretty worried about you."

"Oh? Why was that?" Brandon couldn't fathom why Laurel would have been worried about him on her last visit to the doctor's office.

As for Dr. Davis he was confused that Brandon seemed unaware of Laurel's devastation when she had feared him dead. "Why, surely you realize she thought for sure you . . ."

Their conversation was suddenly cut short as a man came racing down the street, shouting and waving wildly at them. "Doc! Dr. Davis!" Once abreast of them, the man clutched his heaving sides and panted, "Doc, you've got to come quick! Evan Sheller fell off his roof he was fixing, and we're afraid to move him! We think he's broken his back!"

His mind on this newest emergency, the doctor forgot all about Brandon. "I'll need my bag from the office," he told the excited man. "You go back and tell them not to move him until I get there. I'm on my way." Dr. Davis turned and started back the way he had come. "You have Laurel come see me soon, Brandon. I'm a bit concerned about the amount of weight she's been gaining."

Brandon stared after him. "Laurel is dead, Dr. Davis," he called out bluntly.

Some distance away by now, the doctor stopped in stunned disbelief. "My God! I can't believe it! She was doing so well, all things considered, when I last saw her!"

Brandon was equally bewildered at this strange conversation. "When was it you last saw her, Doctor?" he asked after the briskly departing physician.

The doctor's answer was drowned out by the clang of a trolley bell. All Brandon caught of his reply was, "It was the day—the quake—" Then the man was lost in the crowds, and Brandon could only assume he had said "the day before the quake." It was the only thing that made sense.

With few regrets and many sad memories,

Brandon closed up the ruined house on Nob Hill and made arrangements for his loyal staff to be employed elsewhere. He paid his final respects to Laurel, leaving fresh flowers on her grave, then said goodbye to his friends and set off in a hired carriage for the wharf to board his ship for Australia.

He was just walking up the gangplank when he heard a familiar voice frantically calling his name. "Wait! Brandon, wait!"

Breathless, Tess caught up with him, clutching desperately at his arm as she exclaimed, "Thank God I caught you before you sailed!" She waved a telegram at him and wheezed. "It's from your brother. I opened it. I thought it might be important." Still gasping for breath, she blurted, "She's alive! Read it, Brandon! *Laurel is alive!*"

Brandon's face paled, and his knees nearly buckled beneath him. "That's impossible! You've misinterpreted something, Tess. That, or someone is pulling a rotten prank!"

"No! Oh, Brandon, read the telegram! Your brother explains some of it!"

At the top of the boarding plank, a sailor called down, "Hey, mister! You comin' or stayin'? This is the last call."

Tess laughed delightedly and shouted back, "Go on without him! He's definitely staying!" With a strength born of pure stubbornness, she dragged Brandon back onto the wharf.

Brandon's attention was completely absorbed in Hank's message. It read:

BRANDON
   LAUREL ALIVE STOP HERE IN C.C.
WITH BURKE STOP ADVISED YOU WERE

DEAD STOP L. SAYS MARRIAGE FAKE
STOP WHAT IS GOING ON STOP WILL
WAIT IMMED. REPLY IN EAGLE PASS
STOP REPEAT: EAGLE PASS STOP COME
HERE NOW STOP.

                              HANK

After a brief, stunned silence, Brandon let out a
wild whoop of absolute joy. He tossed his hat high
in the air, not caring that it landed in the water,
and lifting Tess off her feet, whirled her about in
dizzying circles. Both were oblivious of the
curious stares they received as they laughed and
cried and clung to one another.

"She's alive! She's really alive!" he shouted over
and over again in delirious happiness.

When they at last calmed down enough to talk
coherently, Tess asked, "Why would Laurel tell
Hank your marriage is a fake? I don't
understand."

"I think I do, though I don't understand much
else at this point. I'll explain it all to you someday,
but right now I have to catch the first train to
Texas." Brandon pulled up short, his mind at last
beginning to function properly. "No—first I have
to telegraph Hank in Eagle Pass and make sure he
doesn't tell anyone anything until I get there, not
even Laurel—especially not Laurel!"

Brandon grabbed Tess's arm and danced her
toward her carriage. "I'm going home, Tess!" he
cried with a wide, shining grin. "I'm going home to
my wife and child as fast as the next train will
carry me! It's a miracle! An honest-to-God
miracle!"

CHAPTER 29

It seemed to Brandon that the train trip to Eagle Pass was the slowest he'd ever endured. Prior to leaving San Francisco, he had talked to Thomas, Kramer, and Hanna, telling them the incredibly good news. They surmissed that the body in the pantry must have been that of the kitchen maid who had disappeared shortly after the earthquake. The men promised to look into the matter further and inform Brandon of their findings. Brandon then sent a telegram to Hank in Eagle Pass, with instructions to meet him there with an extra horse, and a warning not to tell anyone of his impending arrival.

Texas had never looked so good to him before. Even the small, dingy border town of Eagle Pass was a beautiful sight as it came into view.

Hank was there to greet him, and the two brothers exchanged a choked, emotional greeting that brought tears to both their eyes.

"Damn, I never thought your ugly puss would look so good to me!" Hank exclaimed, hugging his brother unabashedly. "We all thought you were dead."

"That's just one of the things I need to talk to you about, but not here. You didn't tell Laurel, did you?"

"No. She's living with her father and I only see her occasionally. But why do you want me to keep it from her? And what is all this about your marriage? I swear I've never seen such a tangle as you and Laurel have made of things!"

"Later, brother," Brandon said. "We'll get it all straightened out very soon. Let's just head for home now. I'm hoping to reach the ranch unnoticed so you and I can talk privately before I see Laurel. How is she? Is everything all right with the baby?"

"She's all right, and so is the baby. Deb sees her almost every day. We tried to get her to come to our engagement party last Saturday, but she said she wasn't up to festivities."

Brandon halted in the act of levering himself into his saddle. "Engagement party? Whose?"

Hank grinned sheepishly, "Mine. I've asked Deborah Werling to marry me."

"Well, I'll be a horned toad!" Brandon exclaimed. "My little brother engaged! Congratulations!"

"If everything wasn't so confused, I'd return the compliment. Brandon, are you, or are you not, married to Laurel?"

They were riding along the road to Crystal City now. "In every way that counts, I am, Hank. But not legally. What did Laurel tell you about it, and who else knows?"

"Just Sam and I, and Laurel's family, as far as I know. For the baby's sake we all agreed to a conspiracy of silence—over Laurel's objection, I might add." Hank told him all he knew of Laurel's experiences in San Francisco, and how she had concluded that Brandon was dead. "But why did you think Laurel had died?" he asked.

When Brandon explained about finding the

body in the pantry, and how no one had seen Laurel since the quake, Hank was stunned. "God, Brandon! How awful for you to think it was Laurel you had found! What agony you must have gone through!" Hank's eyes fell to the small fox trailing their horses. "But why would the fox mourn the kitchen maid like that?"

Brandon shook his head. "The only thing we can figure is that she had befriended him and had been feeding Tyke table scraps. None of us realized what an attachment he had formed toward the girl so naturally when I found him guarding the body, we assumed it was Laurel's. You can't imagine my joy when I received your telegram! It was like being granted a miracle!"

"You don't know quite the extent of the miracle yet!" Hank assured him with a sidelong look.

"Why?" Brandon was instantly alarmed. "Is something wrong? Is there something you haven't told me?"

"No, everything's all right now." Hank went on to tell Brandon of Laurel's abduction and her terrifying experiences at the hands of Pedro and his men. As stormclouds of rage gathered on Brandon's face, accentuated by curt expletives and coldly narrowed steel-grey eyes, Hank hastened to tell of Laurel's rescue by Red Feather and his band, and her safe return to the ranch. "She nearly lost the baby, but Red Feather saved it and Laurel. He also killed that snake, Pedro, so you can stop looking like you want to murder someone. Red Feather already did it for you."

"Looks like I owe him quite a lot," Brandon granted, still thinking of the terror Laurel must have endured in Pedro's hands.

"You're sure those bastards didn't harm her before Red Feather came along?"

"She says not. Red Feather got there too soon. It was the rough ride in her delicate condition that nearly caused her to lose the baby—that and all she had been through so recently." Then Hank added with a grimace, "Red Feather wanted to barter for Laurel as payment, but he settled for six steers when I refused."

Brandon nearly swallowed the cigarillo he had just lit. Coughing and choking, he ground out, "I should hope you wouldn't trade my wife!" When at last he caught his breath, he said, "I'd forgotten how taken Red Feather was with Laurel."

Hank frowned. "He'd met her before? When?"

"Once when Laurel and I were skinny-dipping at the river last fall." Brandon chuckled at the memory. "God, she was embarrassed! Her entire body glowed red, and there wasn't much she could hide in the clear water! She was absolutely mortified—and so darned cute!"

"What are you going to do when we get home?" Hank wanted to know. "Burke isn't exactly going to welcome you with open arms, you know—and I'm not so sure about Laurel, either. As much as she loves you, she wasn't exactly thrilled about your fake marriage. I think she somehow holds you responsible for that."

"What? How?"

"Well, she found part of Miguel's letter to you, and what she read made her believe you and Miguel were to blame somehow. Until she ran into that outlaw in El Paso, she couldn't understand why your marriage wasn't legal. Then, too, she was pretty riled that you didn't tell her about the letter in the first place."

"Thanks for the warning, brother," Brandon said. "In my joy at finding Laurel alive, I keep forgetting she has reason to distrust me, or thinks she has. I'd better be prepared for a less than warm welcome. Guess I've got some explaining to do."

"More than that, Brandon. You've got a wedding to arrange, and soon! Once folks know you're home, they'll wonder why Laurel isn't living with you."

Brandon groaned. "Talking Laurel into a secret ceremony isn't going to be the easiest thing I've ever done."

"I can't decide whether she'll throw herself into your arms, or grab a gun and start shooting," Hank joked.

"Knowing my Laurel, she'll probably do both!" Brandon predicted dourly. "I just hope I can talk and duck fast enough to explain before she kills me! I'd better work on my strategy."

"While you're doing that, here's something else for you to think about. Laurel told Deb that Rex and Becky Lawson are planning to get married soon."

For a second time that afternoon Brandon received a shock. "What? I don't believe it! Burke has more nerve than a raw tooth! Becky can't marry the very man responsible for Jim's death!"

"But she doesn't know that," Hank reminded him.

"Well, it's high time someone told her!"

"You?"

"Why not?"

"You've got no proof, for one thing. For another, if Becky really loves him, she probably won't believe you. Then there is Laurel, for another reason. You have enough going against you now without publicly accusing her father. She'd surely hate you then."

Brandon groaned. "You're right, Hank. What

the hell am I supposed to do?"

"Pick the most important, and let the rest wait," Hank advised.

"Laurel. Laurel is the most important, she and the baby. Nothing else in the world matters to me as much."

Brandon decided his best bet would be to talk to Laurel privately before Rex knew he had returned. Then he had to think of a way to approach her without shocking her senseless.

For lack of a better idea, Brandon decided to use the same strategy that had proved successful months ago when he had persuaded her to run away with him. That very night, after everyone was abed, he crept stealthily into Laurel's bedroom.

She was sleeping uneasily, tossing restlessly about, her hair a tangled silver web on the pillow. By the light of the moon, he drank in the beauty of her delicate features; her lashes forming thick crescents above her cheeks; her full, lush lips slightly parted in sleep. It was a sight he'd never thought he'd see again, except in dreams. She shifted and pushed the thin sheet tangled about her, her hand coming to rest on the mound of her stomach.

He caught his breath sharply and moved closer to the bed, his own hand reaching out to cover hers. What a difference five weeks had wrought! She was swollen now with his child. The baby kicked, and Brandon's face split in a ridiculously pleased grin. His child! His wife and his child, alive and well!

Ever so gently, he bent forward and kissed Laurel's forehead, her cheek, and finally, her irresistible lips. She moaned in her sleep, her lips clinging to his.

With effort, Brandon pulled back. "Laurel, honey," he whispered. "Wake up, my love. Wake up, Moonbeam. It's Brandon. I'm here." She murmured his name and tried to burrow deeper into her pillow.

"Sweetheart, wake up. I'm home!"

Slowly, like a butterfly trying its wings, her lashes fluttered open. As she came slowly awake, her eyes widened. "Oh, Damn! I'm dreaming again," she muttered groggily. "So help me, Brandon, if you disappear before you've made love to me this time, I'll scream, I swear it!"

He chuckled softly and bent to nuzzle her warm neck, inhaling her sweet fragrance. "You have my word, love. I'm here to stay."

"Mmmm," she murmured in delight. "That feels so good . . . you feel so warm and real . . ."

"I am real, Laurel. As real and alive as you and our baby within you." He felt her stiffen as she began to awaken. "Don't be frightened honey. I'm really here. I didn't die in San Francisco."

His lips just managed to stifle her cry of alarm, his hands catching her flailing arms. "Ssh," he warned, his lips touching hers. "Don't wake the others."

"Brandon?" Laurel's lips trembled beneath his. "Oh, Brandon, is it really you?"

"Yes, my love. Are you awake now?"

"I don't know . . . I think so. I hope so," she stammered, her heart hammering in her chest. "Oh, God, Brandon! It *is* you! You *are* alive! Oh, my darling, I've missed you so!"

He cradled her to his chest as she dissolved in

tears. "Hush, baby. Don't cry. It's all right. I'll never leave you again. You can't imagine what hell I've gone through!" He whispered the words near her ear, his lips feathering light wisps of silver-blonde hair. "I thought you were dead, and my life has not been worth living—until now."

Laurel's thoughts were clearing now, her mind beginning to absorb his words. Abruptly her sobs ceased, and she drew away from him with a puzzled frown. "What did you just say?"

"I said I thought you were dead, and it was like a miracle to hear from Hank that you were alive and well. I rushed home as soon as I heard. You don't think I would have stayed away if I had known, surely?"

A look of uncertainty passed over her features. "I don't know what to think anymore, Brandon. So many things I believed have been lies—so many of my dreams trampled under your feet." She was retreating from him with every word, creating a vast distance between them that had nothing to do with physical space. "I read the letter from Miguel."

He met her look squarely. "I know, Laurel. Hank told me. I also know you read only part of it. Darling, you must let me explain. You misinterpreted it terribly."

Laurel pulled completely out of his embrace. "I understood the part about our marriage, Brandon! And running into Pedro confirmed that in a very real and terrifying way." She shivered in remembrance, but when Brandon tried to draw her back into the comfort of his arms, she shrugged him off and glared at him. "You have no right to touch me. You're not my husband! In fact, you are very much a stranger, for I doubt I ever knew you at all."

"Laurel, if you will please just listen to me, I can explain everything."

"Why don't you begin by telling me how long you knew that our marriage was a lie? Did you arrange it that way to get back at my father? Did Miguel help you? Is that why he said he felt as responsible as you?"

"You misunderstood, Laurel," Brandon said patiently. "Miguel and I had nothing to do with it. How could you actually believe that we did?"

"After what I've been through, it's not all that hard to imagine," she retorted. "Then what *did* Miguel mean in his letter?"

Brandon was deeply hurt by her distrust, but he was determined to remain calm. "He simply meant that we should have realized that Father Pedro was not really a priest. Once Miguel found out, it was so easy to see the obvious signs we had missed. We should have questioned Padre Bernardo's absence more thoroughly, and Pedro's obvious lack of familiarity with the wedding ceremony. Instead, we took Pedro's word, and all the while Padre Bernardo's body was outside in the well."

"My God! Pedro killed Padre Bernardo?" Laurel's face went white, her mind flashing back to the fate she would surely have met if Red Feather had not rescued her.

"You didn't read that part of the letter?" Brandon asked quietly.

"No," she admitted, still stunned. "Sassy had overturned a vase on your desk, and the first part of it wasn't legible."

"Damn that cat!" Brandon growled. "So you read only that we were not married and you became instantly angry and suspicious."

"You hid the letter from me, Brandon," she

accused self-righteously. "You never told me about it. Nor did you do anything to correct the illegality of our marriage!"

"That is precisely what I *was* doing the very morning of the earthquake, my love. I had only received Miguel's letter the day before, and I didn't know what to do about it. I didn't want to upset you if I could help it. I was discussing possible solutions with Judge Henry early Wednesday morning at his club."

"I know you were with Judge Henry when the quake hit. He was the one who told me you were injured and rushed off to the hospital. What I do *not* know is where you were prior to that—after our fight. Did you perhaps meet with the beautiful Muriel?" Laurel's tone was venomous and cool.

"Laurel, I love *you*, no matter how angry you make me sometimes—like now, for instance. I wouldn't touch Muriel Cook with a barge pole! You are the only woman I want."

"You certainly have a strange way of showing it," she said scathingly. "You accuse my father of hideous crimes, practically abduct me and drag me off to Mexico for a marriage that isn't a marriage at all, virtually hold me hostage while you blackmail my father, then leave me pregnant, frightened and alone in the middle of an earthquake! Do you have any idea what I went through?" She was practically screaming at him now.

"I went through the same thing, Laurel," he reminded her quietly. "I was worried sick about you, but by the time I left the hospital—or rather, Mechanic's Pavillion—the fire was raging everywhere. I tried to get home to you, but it was impossible. I could only pray you were safe. Then, when I finally got home, I discovered everything burned, and Tyke guarding a charred body that I assumed was yours. I was beside myself with grief, yet still hoped I might be wrong. I searched everywhere for you, darling, until I met up with some of the servants in Golden Gate Park. No one had seen you at all, and their story convinced me that you had indeed died in the house. I fell completely apart. I wanted to die, too—until Hank wired me that you were here and very much alive."

Laurel was confused. "I had told him you were dead. Did he know all along that you were alive? Was this, too, all part of some elaborate hoax you planned against me and my family?" She was becoming more upset and irrational by the minute.

"Laurel, Hank thought I was dead until I finally wrote to him, informing him of *your* death. Only then did he wire me and tell me differently. You're not thinking clearly, or you would realize how absurd your accusations are." Brandon gritted his teeth and strove valiantly to hold onto his rising temper. He'd forgotten how infuriating his adorable wife could be.

"Really?" she snapped. "Do you mean to tell me you *haven't* been using me as a pawn in your scheme of revenge against my father all this time?"

Brandon glared at her, his eyes like shards of gleaming steel, but he said evenly, "Of course not. I love you. I always have. My dislike of your father has nothing to do with what happened between you and me."

"Is that why you never bothered to inform him of my 'death'? That was a shabby thing to do, Brandon. Extremely rotten!"

"I know, but I was in such a stupor of grief that I

could not function properly. When I finally wrote to Hank, I asked him to inform your father for me. As much as I despise him, I could not bring myself to tell him such dreadful news in a letter.''

"A likely story!" she sniffed indignantly, her lavender eyes shooting flames. "Tell me, Brandon, what do you have planned next? Or is that too some grand surprise?''

"Damn it, Laurel! It's been rough on me, too! I want us to get married as soon as possible. I want you to be my wife again.''

"Not likely!''

He stared at her in angry disbelief. "What did you say?''

"You heard me. I said no.''

"Why the hell not?''

"Why should I?''

"Because *I love you*, that's why; and because you love me!" he bellowed. "Then, too, there is our child to consider. I, for one, do not relish the idea of my son or daughter being born on the wrong side of the blanket!''

Laurel laughed, a dry laugh devoid of humor. "That's too bad, Brandon. You'll have to learn to live with it, just as I had to endure so much. It's not easy to forget how hurt I was when I learned that our marriage was all a sham, or to endure days of earthquake and fire alone and terrified, thinking that you had died. Then I had to face coming home to family and friends, unwed and pregnant. Added to that, I literally looked death in the face when Pedro and his fellow outlaws abducted me. If it wasn't for Red Feather, I would be dead now, and so would my child, for I nearly miscarried then. All this I endured alone, believing you were dead, and while I was grieving my heart out, *you* were alive and well in San Francisco! You didn't even have the common decency to come home and face my father."

"I explained all that, Laurel, and I'm sorry for what you went through," said Brandon between clenched teeth.

"You can explain and apologize until you're blue in the face, Brandon, but it will do you no good. I will not marry a man I cannot trust—a man who hates my father and brings me nothing but misery!"

"I brought you a lot of joy too, Laurel. Are you forgetting the passion we shared? The long nights of loving, the sweet kisses and tender caresses, your body so hot and eager for mine?" Brandon had given up trying to persuade her with words. Now was the time for action. Despite her feeble attempt to reject his advances, he held her easily. Pinning her lightly to the bed with only part of his weight, one leg thrown intimately over hers, his hands began stroking her body through the flimsy material of her nightgown. When she turned her head to elude his kiss, his lips found her cheek, then her ear, his teeth nipping lightly at her lobe. When she shivered in involuntary reaction, he laughed triumphantly.

Then she was drowning in desire as his moist mouth travelled the length of her slim neck to tease at the sensitive cord along her shoulder and press lingeringly at the telltale pulse in the hollow of her throat. "You want me, Moonbeam, as much as I want you. You cannot deny it."

"I despise you, Brandon Prescott!" she whispered, then gasped as his mouth claimed the rosy crest of her newly bared breast. His fingers teased at the other nipple, and when his leg parted hers to press against her femininity, she arched into his touch without thought.

"Liar," he growled. "You love what I'm doing, and you love *me*, no matter how you try to deny it. You belong to me, Laurel, body, heart and soul, and you always will."

"No!" she cried out, her voice weak and throaty with rioting passion.

She might have given in to his sweet persuasion and admitted her love to him, but her bedroom door suddenly flew open, startling them both. Framed in the doorway was Rex Burke, the rifle in his hands aimed directly at Brandon. For a split second, no one moved, amazement etched clearly on Rex's face. Then his eyes narrowed dangerously, and he snarled, "Get away from my daughter, Prescott! Stand up and face me! I want to look you straight in the eye when I kill you!"

Brandon eased slowly away from Laurel, rising warily to his feet, never taking his eyes from Rex's enraged face.

"I should have known you were still alive!" Rex sneered. "The news of your death was too good to be true. But no longer! Now you're going to get exactly what you deserve!"

"Dad! *No!*" Laurel's scream split the air. Despite her bulk, she leaped from the bed, throwing herself at her father. Just as Rex's finger tightened on the trigger, Laurel launched herself into him. The gun went off with a deafening blast.

Afraid to look, she forced herself to turn around, and nearly fainted with relief to find Brandon unharmed. The plaster wall behind his head was shattered where the bullet had rammed into it, missing Brandon by barely an inch. He was as white and shaken as she, but he stood still squarely facing her father.

Laurel grabbed for the gun just as Martha raced into the room, wide-eyed with fright. "What in the world—oh, my lands—*Brandon!*" Martha's hands flew to her throat, as though to keep her heart from escaping through her gaping mouth. She stared incredulously, first at Brandon, then Laurel, and finally at Rex.

Laurel wrenched the rifle from her father's grasp, shaking with reaction. "Brandon, you had better leave while you can," she said, more calmly than she felt.

He stared at her for a long moment, then finally nodded and walked past her to the hallway. Rex made a lunge at him, but Laurel and Martha blocked his path.

"No, Dad. Let him go!" Laurel said firmly.

"I'll be back, Laurel," Brandon called quietly from behind her. "I promise you, I'll be back!"

"You'll die trying, Prescott!" Rex bellowed in rage.

Brandon answered as Laurel knew he would. "Your daughter is mine, Burke, and I'll come back to collect her and my child she carries within her. They belong to me, both of them, and I'll never let them go!"

CHAPTER 30

By midafternoon of the following day, the entire town was in an uproar over Brandon's sudden miraculous appearance. Everyone was stunned and curious, and anyone with even the slightest excuse found reason to visit either the Prescott or the Burke ranch.

Martha figured that by half past noon, at least twenty people had "dropped by" to satisfy their undaunted curiosity. She and Laurel were kept busy serving tea and dodging innumerable questions. Rex gladly escaped to the far reaches of the ranch, muttering as he left. "Never in my life have I seen such a bunch of nosy busy bodies!"

For once, Laurel agreed with him. "If I hear just once more how thrilled I must be to have my 'dear husband' safely home, I am going to be sick! Do you know how much of a hypocrite I feel?" she raged.

"I know, dear," Martha commiserated, "but what can we do? Everyone keeps asking why you aren't with him now, and how soon they can call on you at your new home! What am I supposed to say?"

"Tell them what I have been saying—that I want to be near my only female relative at this time. Let them think I'm a coward in my first pregnancy—

446

it's certainly better than anything they'll call me
when they learn the truth!"

Laurel smiled until she thought her face would
crack; and still the visitors came. And then
Brandon arrived. Under the circumstances, they
could not send him away, a fact he was well aware
of.

Martha was at a loss as to what to do, and
sincerely grateful that Rex was not around. She
stood aside and smiled weakly as she showed
Brandon into the parlor. "Laurel, dear, look who's
here!"

Laurel nearly fainted when she turned and saw
Brandon approaching her. The devil-may-care
twinkle in his lightning-bright eyes sent sparks of
apprehension sizzling through her. She knew now
how a poor rabbit must feel when trapped by a
fox. She was fair game for anything Brandon
cared to do, and they both knew it.

His wide smile held just a trace of mockery as
he gathered her into his arms and kissed her full
on the mouth before the half dozen giggling
women who watched in delight. "Oh, it's so
romantic," one woman sighed. "Snatched from
the very jaws of death!"

"My! To be that young again and so in love!"
another added dreamily.

Meanwhile, Laurel was trying to pull away from
Brandon without being obvious about it. Her
hands pushed at his broad chest to no avail. He
took his own sweet time before he finally broke off
the kiss. Even then, he did not release her, but
kept her enclosed in his embrace as he looked
down at her adoringly. "Laurel, honey, I'm sorry
to be so late. With all the people stopping by the
ranch this morning, I couldn't get here any
sooner."

Her eyes shot arrows through him, even as her lips curved in a convincing smile. "Think nothing of it, Brandon, dear. I have been busy this morning myself."

"Not too busy, I hope. I wouldn't want you to overtax yourself, sweetheart." His gaze fell to her protruding stomach and lingered. "We wouldn't want any harm to come to our baby."

"Brandon! It's so wonderful that you are home again," Mrs. Miller simpered.

"Yes, we've been asking Laurel when she will be able to receive us in her new home. No offense, but that house of yours could use a woman's touch to brighten it up."

"Oh?" Brandon cocked an eyebrow at Laurel. "And what did my *wife* have to say to that?"

"Some nonsense about wanting to be near Martha until after the baby is born," Mrs. Werling volunteered.

As Laurel blushed beet-red, Brandon said smoothly, "I don't see why Martha can't move in with us for a while. There is plenty of room, and surely Rex can do without her for a few weeks."

"But . . . but . . ." Laurel stuttered helplessly.

"Yes?" Brandon grinned and his eyes dared her to say more.

"Nothing," Laurel muttered. He had her over a barrel this time.

He rewarded her with a kiss on the forehead. Turning to her guests, he said suddenly, "Ladies, I'm sure you will excuse us if I spirit my wife away from you. After being so long apart under such dreadful conditions, we have a lot to catch up on."

"Oh, of course!"

"We'll just gossip a bit with Martha."

"We understand. You two lovebirds go along."

Under hidden protest, Laurel let herself be led from the room.

Once down the hall, she stopped short. "This is far enough. Say what you've come to say, and then go."

"My! Tough little bird, aren't you?" he chuckled. "You look like an angry, ruffled little dove, all puffed up like that."

"You are a beast!" she hissed, wanting nothing more than to strangle him.

"If you are going to screech and call me names, we'd better go into your father's study so you can curse me without anyone overhearing." Brandon reached behind her to open the door, and gently shoved her over the threshold.

When the door shut behind them, he said, "I've come to discuss our wedding arrangements."

For a long moment, she stared at him. Then she calmly announced, "All right. I'll marry you . . ."

Primed for resistance, Brandon was surprised nearly speechless. Recovering quickly, he smiled and started toward her. "Laurel, love . . ."

She cut him off short with a curt laugh and eyes narrowed into slits. "When cows lay eggs and chickens give milk! And not a moment sooner!"

Brandon sighed and ran his fingers through his dark hair in frustration. "Why are you so damn stubborn, Laurel? You know you'll have to marry me before the baby is born. We can't hope to conceal the situation for long, with you living here and me at my ranch."

"You're wrong, Brand. I don't have to marry you at all. There are other options open to me."

"None that will spare you and our child a lot of shame, and I don't want to see that happen. It is all so unnecessary. You agreed to marry me once.

Why not do it again?"

Laurel shook her head. "Oh, Brandon! If this situation wasn't so sad, it would actually be funny. You, who probably never meant to marry me in the first place, are now practically begging me to do so. What's the matter, darling? Isn't revenge as sweet as you had imagined? Are you having second thoughts now that your child is so near to being born?"

Brandon's nostrils flared in repressed anger, and he had to clench his fists to keep from throttling her. "Your father has done a good job of twisting your thinking to his way of seeing things, hasn't he? You just can't accept on faith that I love you and care what happens to you. Well, think about this, Laurel. We had a wonderful life together once, with a lot of love and laughter. We could have it again."

"I don't *want* to remember how madly in love with you I was." The words were out before she realized the extent of what she was admitting.

He stepped closer, his hands closing about her arms to draw her to him. "You can't help remembering, any more than I can," he said softly, his eyes glowing into hers. "I remember how soft your skin is, how warm your lips beneath mine. I recall how you would cling to me and cry out in ecstasy at the height of our lovemaking. These things and many more are permanently etched into my memory, as they are into yours."

"Stop it!" she cried. "I won't listen to this!" Only his firm grip prevented her from covering her ears with her hands.

"Then I'll tell you without words, in a way you know you can't resist." With that, he brought his lips over hers in a searching, searing kiss that set her senses reeling. She could not prevent her lips from softening and parting beneath his, or her traitorous body from leaning against his. A deep yearning claimed her as lightning sizzled through her blood, causing her heartbeat to echo like a thousand drums in her ears.

"You are going to marry me, Laurel," he whispered.

Though her heart agreed, somehow she found the strength to resist its urgent plea. "No," she heard herself say. "No."

To herself, in rare moments of honesty, Laurel admitted that she would love nothing more than to be Brandon's wife again. Only her stubborn pride and bruised heart kept her from giving in. Brandon had lied to her and deceived her. Only because she loved him so dearly had he been able to hurt her so deeply. Never again would she give him the power to wound her like that, to leave her so heartbroken and bereft. She was determined to forfeit joy and ecstasy in order to avoid the pain that came from loving someone so completely that he could devastate her with a single word. She would make a safe and secure life for herself and her child, with no man to destroy her peace of mind.

While Laurel remained adamant, it took exactly one week for Rex to relent under pressure. Townspeople and friends were beginning to wonder what was going on, and tongues were wagging all over town. Why were Brandon and Laurel still living apart? Why didn't anyone ever see them together? Why was Brandon too busy to came into town and chat with old friends, and why was Laurel often ill or resting when guests visited her? Was there trouble between the two of them already? Something was certainly peculiar!

"I knew I should have sent you off to New Orleans when you first came home," Rex grumbled irritably. "Now look at the mess we're in! In trying to protect your reputation, we've painted ourselves into a corner. Everyone thinks you are married to Prescott, and I can just imagine what will happen if we inform them differently at this late date. It would all have worked out nicely, if only Brandon had not turned up alive."

"Dad! How can you say that? I may not want to marry him again, but I certainly would never wish him dead!"

"Well, you may just *have* to marry him, like it or not, little girl! It may be the only resolution to our problem, so we can still hold our heads up in public."

"I don't believe I'm hearing this!" Laurel exclaimed. "Not a week ago, you were ready to shoot him, and now you are standing there telling me I should marry him just to save face!"

"I didn't say I like the idea," Rex said with a disgusted look. "Besides, I wouldn't be one to point the finger of blame if I were you. You and Brandon created this situation, and if you find the solution not to your liking, that's something you will have to learn to live with. The more I consider it, the more reasonable it seems, since he is the one who created this fiasco and got you with child. The least he can do is assume responsibility for both of you; and the least *you* can do is accept the inevitable."

"Well! You certainly have done a complete turnabout! It seems like you're actually looking forward to having Brandon as a son-in-law!"

"Don't be ridiculous, Laurel! I'd sooner you marry the Devil, but since it is his child you carry, and our family's good name hangs in the balance, I see no other way."

"Dad, I will not marry Brandon, and that is final! I have made up my mind, and there is nothing you can say to change it."

Rex glared at her. "You were willing enough to marry him once, you contrary female. You know the old saying, 'Marry in haste, repent in leisure!' Well, you married him fast enough once, and you can do it again. You can start repenting right after the ceremony!"

"Never!" she declared stubbornly. "I still can't believe, after all that has happened, that you would force me to marry your enemy!"

"I never thought I'd see the day, either," he admitted gruffly, "but we all have to do things we regret sometimes, and this is one of them."

She watched him walk away, anger and betrayal making her eyes glitter with tears. "Men!" she muttered savagely. "The world would be so much better off without them! And they joke about *women* changing their minds!"

Now everyone seemed to be trying to convince her to marry Brandon. Her father, Brandon, Hank, even Aunt Martha banded together against her, and it was almost more than Laurel could take.

"Would it be so terrible, Laurel?" Martha asked. "You were happy with him once, and you were so devastated when you thought he was dead. You love him, dear. You cannot make me believe differently."

"Loving him and wanting to marry him are two different matters," Laurel insisted.

Hank tried to reason with her on his brother's

behalf. "I know he can be a bear to live with some-times, Laurel, but he's a good man and he'll be a good husband and father. He loves you to distraction. Don't you care about the misery you're putting him through?"

"What about the misery he has caused *me!*" she retorted. "He deserves any agony he is feeling, and more!"

In spite of her protests, Rex and Brandon formulated the wedding plans and Martha was delegated to inform Laurel. "We are all to ride over to Eagle Pass next week, where you and Brandon will be secretly married—properly this time—with your father and me there as witnesses. No one from Crystal City need ever know," Martha wheedled.

"I won't go!"

"You *will* go, or your father will drag you along kicking and screaming if need be. He says you can take your choice."

Laurel was well and truly trapped. To her chagrin, Brandon was no longer barred from the Burke residence, but came and went at will. With a common goal to unite them, Brandon and Rex tolerated one another out of necessity. Hating one another as they did, they barely managed to remain civil. Each tried to avoid the other as much as possible, and for the most part succeeded.

To make matters worse, Brandon began courting Laurel all over again. Flowers arrived almost every day—roses, daisies, wild flowers, even a bouquet of laurel Brandon had ordered especially. He dropped by with her favorite ice cream; he gave her a bottle of exquisitely expensive perfume. One day Laurel answered the door to find Mr. Miller delivering an entire crate of avocados. Brandon even brought Tyke along to visit when he came, hoping the little fox might soften her stony heart.

Laurel was at her wits' end to put a stop to it, with no help from her family. Brandon's persistence was harder to resist each day. When he came to see her, if she feigned fatigue, Aunt Martha would only send him up to her room, so there was no avoiding him no matter how she tried. Time and again, she sent him on his way with a firm refusal, but she could feel herself weakening daily. The wedding plans and date had been arranged without her approval or consent, and Brandon was secure in the knowledge that she would soon be his bride again. He was intent on changing her attitude toward him, too; on convincing her that their life together would be a happy one.

"We'll be a family, Laurel. This time you have your father's approval, reluctantly given though it was. We will be living nearby, just as you have always wanted. Your best friend will soon be your sister-in-law. What more could you possibly ask? It will be wonderful, I promise you; even better than before, and I don't need to remind you how glorious it was even at the worst of times. We belong together, Laurel. Deep in your heart, you know that. Don't let your stubborn pride ruin our lives."

Two days before her wedding was to take place, Laurel received a letter from Rose Crider. She had arrived safely in Chicago and her friends had gladly taken her in, helping her to find a small apartment of her own and a job to support herself and baby Charles. Lonely as she was, she was now settling into a life of her own.

This set Laurel to thinking. With all her friends

back East, in Boston, surely there must be one who would be willing to help her. After two years at school there, she knew the city and quite a few people. If she sold her jewels, surely she could support herself until the baby was born, and then she could find employment as Rose had done. The father of one of her former classmates owned a large department store there, and another was the president of a bank. Perhaps they would be willing to hire and train her.

The more Laurel considered the idea, the more convinced she was that she could do it. She could tell her Boston friends that she had married a man her father disapproved of, and that now she found herself alone and widowed with a child on the way. Most of the tale would be true. What she could *not* do was stay here and let herself be coerced into marrying Brandon. As much as she loved him, she was sure it would only bring more misery. Regardless of their current, uneasy truce, Brandon and her father still despised one another. Brandon still believed Rex guilty of cattle rustling; just recently there was another outbreak of it after months of peace. She was sure Brandon was only waiting until after the wedding to accuse Rex again, and their precarious truce would be shattered.

For his own reasons, her father distrusted Brandon as much as ever, and after all Brandon had kept from her, Laurel did too, to some extent. Could she trust him to deal fairly with her in the future? Did he truly love her as much as he claimed, or did he merely want to possess her, as though she were a rare painting or a valuable jewel? That she loved him with all her heart was a painful certainty, but was it worth the risk of heartbreak if she married him again? Surely, if she was destined to be broken-hearted, it was better to endure it now and hope some day to recover, rather than to suffer a lifetime of regret. Far better to leave now, leave behind all the reminders of what she had lost; all she still longed for even as she berated herself for her weakness. Far better to go far away, far enough to make a new life for herself and her child—far enough to forget the only man she would ever love with all her heart.

And so, once again, Laurel packed her bags. There was no need to hide them from her aunt, since she was ostensibly complying with Martha's wishes. Her things were to be ready for transfer to Brandon's house after the wedding.

It was all much simpler than she had antici-pated. Somehow she kept from weeping as she kissed her aunt and bade her father goodnight for the last time. Everyone was sleeping soundly as she tiptoed with her luggage down the front stairs, carefully avoiding the squeaky steps she knew by heart after so many years. No one was about in the barn as she hitched the horse to the buggy.

In the pre-dawn dark, she drove through the sleeping town to the train station, Sassy again in her cage at Laurel's side. Once more, Tyke was left behind, this time safe in Brandon's care.

At the station, she purchased a ticket to Chicago from the sleepy ticket agent, ignoring his curious stare. She counted herself lucky that he did not question her about her trip, and luckier still that the train to St. Louis and points east left at dawn instead of noon. She had counted on that fact, for the schedule varied little from year to year. Once in St. Louis, she would exchange her Chicago ticket for one to Boston, and no one here, even if they questioned the ticket agent, would be able to discover her actual destination. She would wire a friend from St. Louis, and perhaps someone would be there to meet her when she arrived in Boston.

As the train pulled slowly from the station with Laurel aboard, she took a final look at the town where she had grown up and spent most of her life. She was cutting all ties with home and family, leaving all that was dear to her as she faced an uncertain future.

For just a moment, Laurel had a wild impulse to leap off the train and run back to Brandon as fast as her trembling limbs would carry her, to marry him despite her doubts. But the train was moving too fast, and with a resigned sigh, she settled into her seat. Every turn of the wheels was taking her further from him, wrenching her heart to pieces as tears raced down her face.

"Goodbye, my love," she whispered softly, sadly. "Forgive me . . ."

CHAPTER 31

No one noticed Laurel's absence until mid-morning, when Brandon stopped by and Martha went to awaken her. A quick survey revealed that some of her clothes and traveling bags were missing, as well as one of the horses and buggy. Havoc suddenly reigned at the Burke ranch as everyone rushed about trying to find someone who might have seen or heard her leave.

"Blast that girl!" Rex shouted. "I should have known she'd try something like this. She's too damn stubborn for her own good. She needs a keeper, not a husband!"

"If I can find her, I intend to be both." Brandon was mad enough to spit. "Every time I turn around, she's gone again! So help me, I'll chain her to the house when I get her back, with just enough slack to make it from the kitchen to the bedroom!"

"If you two would stop yelling for a minute, maybe you could start looking for her," Martha suggested. "I'm worried. She shouldn't be travelling in her condition."

"I'll stop by my place and get Hank on my way into town. Then we'll start checking with her friends. Maybe one of them is hiding her."

"I hope so," Martha said fretfully. "Surely she

wouldn't risk going far with the baby due so soon."

"Don't count on it," Brandon warned. "The child isn't due for another two and a half months. Laurel could be in China by then!"

"I'll check with Becky and then try the train station," Rex said, grabbing his stetson on the way out the door. "Martha, you stay here in case the twit changes her mind and comes home, or in case one of us finds her right away. Brandon, I'll meet you in town."

"Or back here in an hour, if we miss one another."

Deb had not seen her, nor any of Laurel's friends. Hank and Brandon kept their questions quiet and casual so as not to alarm anyone or cause more raised eyebrows. Rex was doing likewise, though it was difficult while checking with the ticket agent at the depot. One simply did not saunter in and ask if your daughter happened to have bought a train ticket as casually as you asked if she had purchased a hat.

"Yeah," the fellow said. "She was in early this morning and bought a ticket on the 5:45 to Chicago. I thought sure you knew about it, since she left your buggy hitched outside."

"Thanks. I'll be back for the buggy later," said Rex grimly.

He met with Hank and Brandon back at the ranch. "She's bound for Chicago by train," he announced.

Brandon's reply was immediate. "Then I'm going after her."

"You'll never catch her, Brandon. The next train east doesn't leave until tomorrow morning. She'll be a full day ahead of you," Hank said dispiritedly.

"I'll find her if I have to turn the entire city of Chicago inside out!"

Martha wrung her hands in despair. "Oh, I wish there was a faster way to get to Chicago!"

"There isn't—but if memory serves me right, there's sometimes a day's delay on certain trains going to other destinations from St. Louis," Rex said suddenly, a hopeful light entering his worried eyes.

"You're right, Rex! I may be able to take the next train to St. Louis and catch up with her there." Brandon headed for the door. "I'm going home to pack a few things. I'll be ready to leave in the morning. Let me know if you hear anything more."

"I'm going with you," Rex shouted after him.

"Oh, no you're not! Laurel is my responsibility from here on out, Burke. I'll take care of this alone. She's run out on me once too often. It is time she learned a lesson, and I don't need her father along while I'm teaching it to her."

"You will be sensible? I mean, you won't do anything drastic, will you, Brandon?" Martha was suddenly very concerned just how far Brandon's anger would lead him.

"I won't hurt her, if that's what you mean, Martha. But it's time she learns who is the boss, and I can assure you it isn't Laurel. I'll be back soon, with my errant wife in tow."

"She's not your wife, yet," Rex reminded him.

"She will be—and soon! I'm tired of pussy-footing around. Now she'll dance to my tune, like it or not!"

A loud banging on the kitchen door roused Brandon immediately from a light sleep that

night. Sam came bursting into the house to meet
Hank and Brandon as they scrambled down the
stairs. "What is it, Sam? What's all the ruckus?"

"The Lawson ranch has been hit again by those
blamed rustlers! Ed Farley's boy just rode in with
the news that Becky's barn's on fire and there's
been a shoot-out!"

"Anybody hurt?" Brandon asked as he grabbed
his rifle and stuffed extra ammunition in the
pockets of his jacket. With an ease born of daily
usage he strapped his gunbelt about his hips as he
ran for the stable, Hank and Sam keeping pace
with him.

"Don't know. The boy just said there was a lot of
shootin' going on, and to come quick."

"Damn Rex Burke! You'd think he'd have
learned his lesson by now."

"That doesn't make sense, Brandon. Why would
he rustle Becky's cattle when they're about to be
married?" Hank asked. "Besides, a lot of those
steers are from his own stock! Would he steal his
own cattle just for practice? It just plain doesn't
add up!"

Brandon had to agree, when he thought about it.
Who in his right mind would steal his fiancee's
cattle when they would all be his after the
wedding anyway? And why burn the barn?
"Maybe he's just trying to divert suspicion from
himself," he suggested.

"Come on Brandon," Hank scoffed. "Not many
people even know Rex and Becky are planning to
get married. So far, it's been kept pretty quiet. Deb
didn't even suspect Rex was seeing her until
Laurel told her, and Deb's mother knows all the
town gossip almost before it happens!"

Most of the commotion was over by the time the
Prescott men arrived. The barn was beyond

saving, but most of the animals had been rescued, and some of the neighboring ranchers were busy making sure the flames didn't spread.

Brandon rode straight to the house. He found a white-faced Becky in the kitchen, bandaging Rex's wounded shoulder.

"You sure got here in a hurry, Burke," Brandon commented, his eyes narrowed. "What happened to your arm?"

"He's been here all evening, Brandon." Becky didn't try to hide the fact that Rex had been spending the night with her. "One of the rustlers shot him, but it isn't serious, thank God!"

Rex patted her hand and said soothingly, "It's only a flesh wound, Becky. Don't fuss over it." He turned to Brandon. "I got a couple of good shots off at them. One of them is outside, dead. Becky's foreman wounded another, and they have him locked up in the shed until the sheriff gets here. I think I winged another, but he got away with the rest of them."

"How many were there?"

"At least eight—maybe more."

"Did you recognize any of them?" Brandon watched Rex's face closely as he answered.

"The dead one is Bailey, one of my wranglers," Rex admitted. "He's a new fellow I hired last spring. The other man I've never seen before. It was too dark to recognize anyone else at that distance."

The sheriff arrived then to take the wounded bandit to town, and when things calmed down again, Rex told Becky, "You get the children collected. I'm taking you all back to my place for the rest of the night. I don't want you left here alone, just in case those outlaws come back this way."

"We'll ride with you," Brandon suggested. "Sure wouldn't want you coming across that bunch on the way." He was still curious as to Rex's involvement in the evening's activities, and determined to find out all he could.

When they rode into the ranchyard, old Lester came out to meet them. "There's somethin' funny goin' on, boss," the man said to Rex. "I saw Nolan ride in a little while ago, and he sure was actin' sneaky. He put his horse in the barn, but he hasn't unsaddled it. When he left to go to the bunkhouse, I thought I'd nose around a little. There's blood on his saddle."

"Is he still here?" Rex and the others were instantly alerted.

"Yes, still in the bunkhouse as far as I know. His horse is still in the barn."

"Grab a rifle, Lester, and stand guard over the horses. Shoot anyone who tries to leave," Rex ordered. "Becky, you take the children into the house and stay there with Martha. Hank! Brandon! You come with me. I think we're about to catch ourselves a snake-bellied rustler!"

It seemed as if they waited forever in the shadows before Rex's foreman, Nolan, emerged from the bunkhouse. They let him clear the building before making their presence known. "Nolan!" Rex called out. "Stop right there and put your hands up in plain sight. We've got you covered, so don't try anything!"

The foreman dropped his stuffed saddlebags and raised one arm over his head. The other he could only raise halfway, grunting in pain.

"Now turn around. Slowly."

Brandon kept Nolan covered as Hank ran up and searched him, removing his gun from its holster and a knife from a sheath at his belt.

"He's got a habit of tucking a derringer at the small of his back," Rex warned. "I've never said anything to him about it, but I've noticed," Rex added, almost to himself.

Together they escorted Nolan to the barn, where Lester waited. The foreman's wound was not serious, though he had bled plenty. They tied him up and sent for the sheriff once again.

"I should have figured it out," Rex kept saying. "Damn it, I should have guessed, but the man has worked for me for nearly ten years, and I thought I could trust him!"

"Don't feel too badly, Burke," Hank said. "You never know about people. Greed does strange things to a man sometimes."

Rex shook his head, still muttering to himself. "Laurel never did like him. Said she didn't trust him and his snake eyes. I should have listened to her."

"So should I, I guess," Brandon admitted. "I wouldn't believe her when she insisted you had nothing to do with all of this. I was sure you were behind the cattle rustling. All the signs pointed to you. I just couldn't prove it, and now I know why —I had the right ranch, but the wrong man."

Rex accepted the implied apology with gruff humor. "Don't get all upset over it, Prescott. Remember, I never liked you either."

The sheriff arrived and wrung a confession from Nolan, as well as from the other prisoner. Nolan had headed the band of rustlers. He and Bailey were the only ones of Rex's men involved, along with ten others from distant ranches. With seven additional rustlers to track down and arrest now that he knew their identities, the sheriff did not dally. He rode off with his prisoner in tow, eager to gather his deputies and round up the rest of the gang.

Dawn was fast approaching when Brandon left the Burke ranch. "I'm glad it turned out this way, Burke," he said in parting. "I hated to think I had a rustler for a father-in-law. Now maybe Laurel and I can quit fighting about it and have a little peace at last."

"I may not like you much, but I respect your principles." Rex held out his hand, and Brandon shook it. "Who knows—maybe someday we'll actually be friends."

Brandon nodded. "Stranger things have happened, I guess."

"You just find my girl and bring her back."

"Oh, I'll find her if I have to scour every inch of the country. I'll find her, all right! You can bet on it."

St. Louis was humming with activity as Laurel's train pulled into the station two days after her departure from Crystal City. When she exchanged her ticket for one to Boston, she was told that her train would not depart until nearly noon the next day. It immediately reminded her of her delay in El Paso and all that had happened there, and an unreasonable panic threatened to overcome her. Even knowing that Pedro and his cohorts were dead, she felt sick and frightened.

It did not help her unease that she was directed to a nearby hotel that closely resembled the one in which she had stayed in El Paso. She checked in and went straight to her room, where she locked the door behind her and sat stiffly on the bed. Though she told herself she was being foolish, it did nothing to ease her tension. She refused to leave her room even for dinner, and it was far into the lonely night before she eventually slept.

As he stepped off the train in St. Louis, Brandon thanked his lucky stars that Laurel was so easy to describe and so readily noticed. A station attendant remembered securing a ride for her to a nearby hotel. The man behind the ticket counter had not been on duty the previous day, but he was able to inform Brandon that the train to Chicago would not depart until mid-afternoon.

Brandon headed straight for the hotel. The first thing he did was make sure Laurel was still registered there.

"Yes, sir. She went straight upstairs, and she hasn't been down yet this morning. Shall I send a message up that you are waiting for her?"

"No. I have some other matters to tend to, and then I'll return. I just wanted to be sure she hadn't checked out yet."

Brandon had plenty of time to make the necessary arrangements—it was only nine o'clock now. Still, he was anxious to accomplish his urgent errands as soon as possible. Where Laurel was concerned, he never knew what might go wrong.

He dashed around the bustling town, agitated by any and all delays that slowed him down. The judge he had to see was late arriving at his office. Then there was an interminable wait at the courthouse. Everything seemed to be moving at a snail's pace just when he was in a hurry.

At long last, he located a preacher, briefly explaining his mission and enlisting the kindly man's services. Though a bit confused, the preacher agreed to accompany Brandon back to the hotel.

Spying a little flower shop on their way, Brandon impulsively stopped to purchase a bouquet of tea roses for Laurel. It was another in an endless series of delays, but one he hoped Laurel would appreciate.

It was a quarter of twelve when they finally entered the hotel lobby. As he approached the front desk, the clerk said, "Mister, the lady you were asking about has left already. She checked out half an hour ago and hired a hack for the train station."

"What?" Brandon roared. "Are you sure? Her train doesn't leave for another two hours."

"I'm sorry, sir, but the lady was extremely upset at being so late. She was afraid she'd miss the noon train to Boston. I hired the carriage for her myself, and she paid the man extra to get her there on time."

"Boston!" Brandon was off and running, the preacher at his heels. After a few futile attempts to hire a carriage, he finally managed to secure one.

"To the train station, and don't spare the horses! If you get me there in time to catch the noon train to Boston, there is twenty dollars extra for you. If you don't, I'm not sure I'll be able to keep myself from strangling you!"

As the carriage rattled to a jerking halt at the station, the train was just pulling out. With no time to worry about purchasing a ticket, Brandon grabbed the preacher by the arm and started running.

"Wait! I can't go to Boston!" the minister puffed.

"Run, blame you! Faster!" Brandon was in no mood to be stopped now by trivialities. He tightened his grip on the poor man's arm and lengthened his stride.

"We'll never make it!" the preacher shouted breathlessly.

Brandon didn't bother to reply; his goal was in sight. With a mighty lunge, he grabbed the boarding rail of the final car and held on for all he was worth. A few more running strides and he gained the steps, pulling the breathless minister up after him.

For long minutes, the man lay gasping for breath. Finally, Brandon sat up and leaned against the rail. "Sorry, Pastor Eley, but I can't let her get away from me again, not with our child due in a few short weeks."

"Good heavens!" The preacher's eyes widened in amazement at this announcement. "Well, under those cirumstances I can understand your hurry, young man," he said, trying to suck breath into his aching chest. "Indeed, I can!"

Laurel sat wearily in her seat, her eyes closed. She had slept little the night before. Every noise in the hallway outside her door jerked her awake. When she had finally slipped into an exhausted sleep, she had awakened late, with barely enough time to dress and catch her train.

"Pardon me, ma'am. Is that seat taken?" asked a deep, familiar voice.

Slowly, Laurel raised wide eyes upward. Her reluctant gaze travelled past scuffed boots and long trousered legs in the aisle beside her, and on to a broad chest and a darkly scowling face she knew all to well. Brandon was standing there glaring at her, his arms crossed formidably over his heaving chest, his eyes gleaming like polished steel blades.

"Brandon!" she breathed, her hand fluttering to her throat. "How . . . why . . . what are you doing here?"

His nostrils flared in irritation. "That's a foolish question, Laurel. I told you once I'd never let you leave me. You should have remembered that. It would have saved us both a lot of time and effort."

"You've come to drag me home?" she quavered.

"I'm going to marry you first. *Then* I'll drag you home!"

"You're worse than a stubborn old mule, Brandon!" she declared heatedly. "You never listen to me! I told you I am not going to marry you!"

By now, every passenger aboard the car was eavesdropping avidly and openly. "Oh, yes you are, love. I've made sure of it. I've chased you over half the country, and now I have reached the end of my patience. You are most definitely going to marry me—now!"

The woman seated across the aisle could hold her tongue no longer. "Forgive me for saying so, dearie," she said with a pointed glance at Laurel's protruding stomach, "but you don't seem to be in any condition to argue with the man."

"Thank you," Brandon said with a polite nod at the woman.

At the same time, Laurel retorted, "Kindly keep your opinions to yourself, madam."

"Don't be rude, Laurel," Brandon admonished sternly. "These nice people are all going to be witnesses to our wedding."

A cheer rose up from the varied onlookers. Laurel blushed bright scarlet and said angrily, "I refuse to marry a man who holds my father in suspicion and contempt!"

"Aha! There I have you, my sweet! Before I left Crystal City, we found the rustlers, and the sheriff was in the process of arresting them. Your father's foreman was behind it. Rex was completely innocent."

"Just as I've been telling you for months!"

"I apologized to him, Laurel, and now I apologize to you. I was wrong. If it will make you feel any better, I promise to take out a front page in the Crystal City *Gazette* and publicly acknowledged my error."

"We still have other problems," she insisted.

"Nothing we can't work out. I love you, Laurel. I adore you. In fact, I darned near worship the ground you walk on! Now are you finally going to agree to marry me?"

"Come on, lady! Put the poor fella out of his misery!" a man called out in the sudden silence following Brandon's declaration.

"Yeah, time's a-wastin'!"

"If any man said things that sweet to me, I'd marry him in a minute!" one woman declared.

Laurel stared about her in amazement, her gaze finally coming back to lock with Brandon's. "This is ridiculous, Brandon," she said weakly.

"Not as ridiculous as spending our lives apart when we love each other so much. Marry me, sweetheart, and I'll spend my life making you happy."

Laurel swallowed the lump in her throat. She did love him with all her heart. And here was this big, strong man, humbling himself before all these strangers in order to make her his wife.

"You win, Brandon," she whispered. "As soon as we can arrange it, I'll marry you."

A huge grin split his face, and he bent down to kiss her. "When I said we would be married now, I meant *now*, Laurel. I'd like you to meet Pastor Eley." He gestured to the man standing behind him. "Pastor, my adorable bride-to-be."

CHAPTER 32

Laurel would always cherish the memory of her second marriage ceremony. Dressed in a simple travelling costume, with her stomach sticking out so far in front of her that she could not see her own feet, she stood next to Brandon in the narrow train aisle, holding a slightly drooping but dearly treasured bouquet of tea roses. The minister recited the ceremony from memory, as the train lurched and swayed, nearly having to shout to be heard above the clack of the wheels.

Laurel had never removed her wedding ring from the day Brandon had placed it upon her finger, and he saw no need for her to do so now. As he repeated the words "With this ring, I thee wed," he merely held her hand and warmed the metal with his own fingers, his eyes glowing more brightly than the gems. There in the dingy railroad car, with dozens of intrigued strangers acting as witnesses, they were duly and properly wed at last. As Brandon drew his bride into his arms to seal their union with the traditional kiss, the bystanders whistled and cheered. It was the most unusual wedding any of them had ever attended, or probably ever would.

"Are you sure this was all legal?" Laurel dared to ask. "We haven't crossed any state lines or anything, have we? This man is a *real* preacher this time?"

Brandon laughed and hugged her to him. "I knew

472

you would ask that, Laurel. Here, I want to show you something." He pulled out the license from his pocket, showed it to her, then handed it to the minister to sign. "I obtained this special license from a judge in St. Louis this morning, and though I'm sure we haven't crossed any state boundaries yet, it wouldn't matter if we had. All we need is for the minister and two witnesses to sign it, and the two of us as well."

"What about the preacher?" Laurel insisted.

"I can vouch for Pastor Eley," a lady near the front called out. ' 'I've gone to his church for the past seven years."

"And if the lady's testimony is not enough proof for you, I have my legal certificate and diploma right here." The minister produced them for inspection. "Your husband said you might question me, and I see that he was right. Might I ask why?"

Laurel blushed and answered sheepishly, "Last November, Brandon and I were married in Mexico, and just a few short weeks ago, we discovered that the man who married us was not a priest at all, but a bandit on the run from the law. It was quite a shock to learn that our marriage was not legal after all."

The pastor handed Laurel the signed and dated marriage license. "Sign here, below your husband's name, Mrs. Prescott, and you need never have that worry again," he promised with a gentle smile. "What God hath joined together, let no man put asunder."

She affixed her name with a trembling hand and a heartfelt sigh of relief. Then she tucked the precious document safely away in the bodice of her dress. Once again the passengers cheered. It was, indeed, a wedding to remember!

Laurel, Brandon and the minister got off the train at the first stop. They hired a carriage to take them back to St. Louis, where Brandon had left his baggage at the train station in his rush. By late afternoon Laurel and Brandon were installed in a suite in the most elegant hotel St. Louis had to offer, and a private wedding supper was sent up to their room. Their bed was already turned down by an obliging maid, who had also prepared Laurel's bath before she departed silently and swiftly, leaving the newlyweds to their long-awaited privacy.

While Laurel enjoyed the bath and the delicious meal, she was careful not to anticipate more than a few kisses and heated embraces in the evening to come. Six and a half months into her pregnancy, she recalled what Dr. Davis had advised, and she was certain Brandon would, too.

Indeed, Brandon did remember the doctor's advice against intimacy in the last three months of Laurel's term. Though he longed to make love to his wife, he was determined to do nothing that might harm Laurel or their baby.

So it was that they found themselves in bed together, both a bit unsure of just how to handle the situation. For some minutes they lay stiffly apart, neither saying anything. Finally Brandon broke the uncomfortable silence. "Just let me hold you in my arms, Laurel. I've missed that so much."

With a sigh of relief, she snuggled close, her body curled into the warm protection of his. He breathed deeply, inhaling the familiar scent of her. "Oh, honey, you smell so good." His large hand came to rest on her belly.

When the baby kicked, Brandon chuckled softly. "Hey! I think he remembers me!" He kissed her neck while he caressed her stomach.

Before either of them realized it, one kiss led to another, caress following caress, sigh after sigh; until they were clinging breathlessly to one another in eager anticipation.

"We shouldn't be doing this, Laurel," Brandon

gasped.

"I know, but how much difference can two weeks make? Oh, Brandon! I want you so!"

Beads of perspiration dotted his forehead as he strove for his fast-waning control. "Are you sure, honey?"

"Love me, Brandon! Love me, or I'm sure I shall die!"

With the greatest of care and the most tender caresses, they consummated their new marriage and rededicated their hearts to one another. To Laurel, it was like being granted wings of gold and the power to fly over the moon, as Bandon took her with him to the far reaches of the universe and back again. Together they soared through fields of stardust on a rapturous journey of ecstasy that left them breathless and replete.

As they lay contentedly in one another's arms, Laurel sighed blissfully. "Now I truly feel like your wife again—and this time it's real! Oh, Brandon, I'm so happy! I love you, darling, with all my heart."

"There were times when I never thought I'd hear you say those words again, and it hurt unbearably. I'll treasure every day we spend together, like a miser hoarding his gold."

"We'll build new memories together, darling," she promised in a whisper. "We'll color them with our love, and they'll be more beautiful and precious than any work of art ever envisioned, and more lasting."

"Do you realize what today is, Brandon?" Laurel asked as she shoved another spoonful of oatmeal into her baby daughter's mouth.

"Sunday," he grunted, prying a spoon from between his son's shiny white front teeth. "Matt, don't bite the spoon, you little heathen! You're only doing it to show off, and we don't have time for this silliness. You know how irritated your mommy gets when we're late for church."

Laurel wiped Amanda's chin and gave her a drink of milk. "It is exactly one year since the San Francisco earthquake." Grabbing at her daughter's waving hand, she said sternly, "Mandy, don't you dare get cereal in your freshly washed hair!"

"Don't remind me," Brandon answered. "That was the darkest period of my life, one I'd gladly erase from both our memories if possible." Brandon grimaced, both at the recollection and his eight-month-old son. "For heaven's sake, Matt! Stop spitting that cereal back out at me. It's disgusting enough to look at in the first place, let alone the second time around!"

"That's my son you're criticizing," Laurel reminded him, grinning at the picture he made sitting there feeding Matthew.

"I know, but his table manners are atrocious! The little imp would rather wear his food than eat it."

Laurel laughed. "Aren't you glad we didn't have triplets? I still don't see how we managed twins! As far as I know, there have never been twins on my side of the family before."

"Nor on mine, so don't try to shift the blame on me, you sly female!"

"Maybe we've started a new family tradition. What do you think Deb's chances are for twins? She's fairly big for six months along."

"Not nearly as big as you were, love. By that time you waddled like an overstuffed duck." As Laurel threatened to throw a spoon at him, he added hastily, "But you were still the loveliest woman I've ever seen."

"Flatterer!"

"Yes, but will it get me what I really want?" he teased.

"At the risk of puncturing your pride, what *I* really want is some help around the house. With Deb unable to do much anymore, and the twins keeping me so busy, I could really use more servants, or at least a cook."

Brandon considered her request. "I know it is a handful right now, but Hank and Deb's house will be finished soon, and they'll be moving out."

"Yes, but I would still like more time to spend with Matt and Mandy. I never seem to have enough time or energy to really enjoy them, and they are growing so fast! Soon they'll be walking."

"I didn't say you couldn't hire more help, honey. In fact, I think it's a good idea. It's not as if we can't afford it, and it would give you more time for yourself as well. I can't remember the last time we went riding together."

"If it is all right with you, I'll start looking for someone next week. Which do you prefer; Mexican, American, or Chinese?"

"For a housekeeper or nursemaid, I don't care. If you are talking about a cook, you'd better make her American. I shudder to think what a tamale would look like after Matt mangled it!"

Laurel lifted Mandy out of her highchair. "We'd better get going, or we'll be late."

Brandon picked up his son and kissed his golden curls. Both twins had fair hair, like Laurel's, but Matt had his father's distinctive steel grey eyes, while Mandy's were a soft, dreamy lavender. "Are we still going to your father's for dinner?" he asked.

"Yes. I checked with Becky yesterday to be sure. Jason has been giving her fits trying to cut his new teeth, but she assured me she and Aunt Martha have everything under control."

"I still think it's funny," Brandon said with a wry chuckle, "that after all the yelling Rex did about us, his and Becky's son arrived just seven months after their wedding."

"You are a beast, Brandon Prescott—but I love

you terribly! After all these years as an only child, it does seem odd having a baby brother all of a sudden, especially since he's younger than my own children. You have to admit, though, that Jason is the spitting image of my father. Dad is so proud he could burst!"

"And Jason is already displaying that famous Burke stubborn streak, too!" Brandon pointed out.

"It's no worse than yours, Brandon. I have yet to meet anyone as determined and single-minded as you."

"It got me the woman I wanted, didn't it?" Brandon pulled her to him for a quick kiss, the two squirming babies between them.

"I'm not complaining," she murmured.

They rode together side by side, their horses matching strides as they headed for the trees that marked the edge of the stream. The little fox loped along behind them, sunlight gleaming on its silver fur. Brandon sat tall and proud in the saddle of his horse next to his delicate wife on a trim little mare. His eyes strayed often to Laurel's rapt face and the cloud of windblown hair streaming out behind her.

"I adore this mare, Brandon! She's such a beauty, and so easy to handle. You couldn't have chosen a better birthday gift for me."

He smiled that tender smile she loved so much. "I'm glad you like her. I got her at the same auction where your father bought Jason's pony. I still think it's ridiculous for Rex to buy a pony for a baby that young."

Laurel slid him a sidelong glance full of humor. "You didn't think so last Christmas, when I had to talk you out of buying two for the twins!"

He had the grace to look sheepish. "And you convinced me to settle for rocking horses instead," he remembered. "I suppose it's natural for fathers to spoil their children, especially when they love them as much as I do Matt and Mandy."

"They are adorable little rascals," Laurel agreed as Brandon helped her to dismount, "even when they are getting into mischief. I wouldn't trade a ton of gold for either of them."

"Speaking of trading, Red Feather was still eager to bargain for you last fall."

"What did you say to him?" Laurel asked with a giggle.

Brandon's eyes twinkled. "I told him to keep checking back with me, and if you didn't behave, I'd consider the idea."

"Brandon Prescott! For two cents, I'd throw you in the river!"

He dug into his pocket and tossed her two shiny pennies, grinning at her startled expression. "I dare you, Moonbeam!"

The tussle was on. Soon their playful wrestling match turned to heated caresses and hot, demanding kisses, as they tugged eagerly at one another's clothing. Naked at last in his arms, Laurel melted into Brandon's warm embrace.

His lips sipped and teased at the contours of hers, making them tremble for the full weight of his devouring kiss. The points of her breasts hardened under his knowing touch as he lightly grazed them with his calloused fingers.

"You are a handsome, teasing devil," she moaned, half drugged by his caresses.

"And you are certainly no angel, my love, no matter how much you resemble one. You're a sultry seductress, and you've woven your spell about me very well."

"Kiss me, darling. Kiss me until I'm breathless and my head is filled with stars!"

He kissed her until she thought her body would burst into flame, his tongue delving into her mouth. His hands created a fire of their own as they caressed and tantalized every inch of her tingling flesh. She could not get close enough to him to satisfy her urgent desire. She arched and twisted beneath him, pulling him to her, worshiping his muscled form, reveling in his superior strength.

"You drive me crazy," he muttered hoarsely. "I'll never get enough of you. Never!" His mouth lowered to her aching breasts to suckle and tease until she begged, "Now, Brandon! Please, darling! Now!"

He watched her face as he entered her, her eyes a soft, dreamy lavender beneath fluttering lashes. Her teeth caught at her lush, kiss-swollen lips as she stifled a gasp of delight.

As she gazed up at him in rapture, she marvelled at the brilliance of his eyes, shimmering down at her like captured quicksilver. His face was taut with controlled passion, his gaze intense and filled with love for her.

Then they were lost to all but the wonder of the moment and the glory of their lovemaking as the world split open and sucked them into a swirling, shimmering spiral of ecstasy.

When the earth finally stopped spinning, they lay gasping in each other's arms. Brandon brushed back a strand of silver hair from her damp forehead and gazed adoringly into her love-soft eyes. "Never stop loving me, my sweet Laurel. And never, never run away again!"

"I never will, darling," she promised softly. "Only a fool would run from the heaven I've found in your arms."